THE
VIRGINIA WOOLF
READER

THE VIRGINIA WOOLF READER

Edited by

MITCHELL A. LEASKA

A Harvest Book • Harcourt, Inc.

SAN DIEGO   NEW YORK   LONDON

Library of Congress Cataloging-in-Publication Data
Woolf, Virginia, 1882–1941.
The Virginia Woolf reader.
I. Leaska, Mitchell Alexander. II. Title.
PR6045.072A6   1985   823'.912   84-4478
ISBN 0-15-693590-2 (pbk.)

Designed by Margaret M. Wagner
Printed in the United States of America
K M O P N L

Contents

Preface

VIRGINIA WOOLF WAS A WRITER OF EXTRAORDINARY abundance, and the large question in editing this reader was not what to include, but what to leave out. Some readers may be encountering Virginia Woolf for the first time, and others may simply want to reread some of her work in a single volume. There is a wide variety of fiction to consider and an even wider variety of essays. Then there are about four thousand letters to choose from as well as diary entries covering some twenty-six years. Just where does one begin?

With the novels, one cannot do better than to start with the established favorites, those works that today are recognized as undisputed classics. To that end, I have chosen the two best-loved and most widely read: *Mrs. Dalloway* and *To the Lighthouse*. (Their artistic precursors, "The Mark on the Wall" and "Kew Gardens," have been included among the shorter fiction.) From there, *Orlando* stands next in succession—the most daring leap into androgynous fantasy our literary heritage can boast. Finally comes *The Waves*, that solemn and disturbing masterpiece which even today holds its riddle intact. It was Virginia Woolf's most sequestered work. And it remains her most challenging.

In the shorter fiction, "The Legacy," "Lappin and Lapinova," and "The Duchess and the Jeweller," though very different in narrative mode, are all self-contained universes in miniature, each dealing with fundamental ingredients of human motivation: the contest of greed over love, the need for illusion over reality, the surrender to death over life.

The memoir and the diary have also been included in this volume: the memoir because Virginia Woolf tells us the personal story of her early years better than anyone else has to date, and the diary because in its entries—the most private of her writing—we are allowed a glimpse of that broad spectrum of mood and mind, as she contemplated the affairs of daily life, sometimes with sense and reason, sometimes with imaginative freedom. In its pages we occasionally come across the shaded phrasing of uncertainty and indecision; and we move with her into those nether regions of thought where proportions change, and logic is governed by its own subjective laws.

The epistolary Virginia Woolf reveals a woman whose sense of fun was as vibrant as her compassion was deep. In her letters she could amuse and she could console. She could communicate mirth just as she could express grief. In both she was spontaneous, and in both, generous. Some of the wittiest letters are pressed beside some of the saddest, and the emotional stretch from one extreme to the other represents a breadth and depth of feeling that she possessed in life and struck into the statelier permanence of her art.

The essays, as they are grouped here, reveal a considerable range of subject and conviction. The extract from *A Room of One's Own* hardly needs explanation: in the past decade, it has become one of the most widely read of Virginia Woolf's books. "Mr. Bennett and Mrs. Brown," from its first issue, has remained one of her consistently controversial shorter essays, just as "Modern Fiction," as a literary manifesto, has over the years been her most often cited. The remaining essays have been included for their descriptive virtuosity, their brilliance of biographical evocation, and, last but not least, their concern with the "common reader."

A word about the editing. Although the selections from the memoir have been printed consecutively, there have of course been omissions, each of which has been indicated by ellipsis points. The annotations accompanying the text were provided by the original editor, and only occasionally has a note been added by me.

The extracts from the diary entries and from the letters have been reproduced here exactly as they appear in their published form. Idiosyncrasies of spelling and punctuation have been preserved. No alterations in the texts themselves have been made except for omissions within paragraphs, which here too have been marked by ellipsis points. The annotations have been adapted from those written by the original editors, and additional notes have been provided where necessary.

The essays have been grouped in a way that best reflects Virginia Woolf's range of artistic interest and stylistic inflection, and each has been reproduced in its entirety. The short stories too have deliberately not been offered in chronological order. The reason for this is simple: a writer's first works are not always read first to best advantage.

I acknowledge my debt and offer my thanks to the editors of the diary, Anne Olivier Bell; the letters, Nigel Nicolson and Joanne Trautmann; and the memoir, Jeanne Schulkind. Special thanks go to John Ferrone of Harcourt Brace Jovanovich for his generous counsel.

New York University   M.A.L.

F R O M

Moments of
Being

A Sketch of the Past

A Sketch of the Past *is just that—a sketch.* Virginia Woolf *began the memoir at her sister Vanessa Bell's suggestion in April 1939 and turned to it during the intervals of writing Roger Fry's biography and her final novel,* Between the Acts. *The last date recorded in the manuscript was November 1940, nearly five months before her death. In the text that follows, Virginia Woolf, aged fifty-seven and almost at the end of her life, took a backward glance at the earliest years of her past in order to give the world a personal account of the people whose lives and deaths governed her own life and gave shape to her experience of it.*

The Sketch *begins with an absorbing account of how she became a writer. Nowhere in the literary canon does she explore in greater depth the relationship of life to art and art to life. From this emerges a kind of philosophy that behind the "cotton wool," behind the amorphousness of life, there is a clearly defined order—"some real thing behind appearances; and I make it real by putting it into words. It is only by putting it into words that I make it whole; this wholeness means that it has lost its power to hurt me."*

Although the memoir is unfinished and was never finally revised for publication, it is written with the spontaneous ease

*and careless elegance of one who knew intimately all the weights
and accents of the English language. So that in the most beautifully modulated phrasing, we are given a picture of the im-
perious and elusive mother, Julia Stephen, whose death plunged
the thirteen-year-old daughter into her first period of madness;
a portrait of Leslie Stephen, the father who set in motion the
endless fluctuations of love and hate Virginia Woolf would feel
for him throughout her adult life. Then there is a lively sketch
of the St. Ives of early childhood, balanced by a description of
a typical London day at 22 Hyde Park Gate in the first year of
the new century. One scene after another is filled in, each occu-
pying its proper space in that large canvas which extended from
1882 to 1900. The story it tells is both tragic and heroic. It is the
chronicle of a troubled girl whose path to young womanhood
was obstructed by death and madness. It is the story of the
valiant battle from which she emerged triumphant.*

TWO DAYS AGO—SUNDAY 16TH APRIL 1939 TO BE
precise—Nessa said that if I did not start writing my memoirs
I should soon be too old. I should be eighty-five, and should have
forgotten—witness the unhappy case of Lady Strachey.[1] As it
happens that I am sick of writing Roger's life, perhaps I will
spend two or three mornings making a sketch.[2] There are several
difficulties. In the first place, the enormous number of things I
can remember; in the second, the number of different ways in
which memoirs can be written. As a great memoir reader, I know
many different ways. But if I begin to go through them and to
analyse them and their merits and faults, the mornings—I cannot take more than two or three at most—will be gone. So without stopping to choose my way, in the sure and certain knowledge
that it will find itself—or if not it will not matter—I begin: the
first memory.

This was of red and purple flowers on a black ground—my

mother's dress; and she was sitting either in a train or in an omnibus, and I was on her lap. I therefore saw the flowers she was wearing very close; and can still see purple and red and blue, I think, against the black; they must have been anemones, I suppose. Perhaps we were going to St Ives; more probably, for from the light it must have been evening, we were coming back to London. But it is more convenient artistically to suppose that we were going to St Ives, for that will lead to my other memory, which also seems to be my first memory, and in fact it is the most important of all my memories. If life has a base that it stands upon, if it is a bowl that one fills and fills and fills—then my bowl without a doubt stands upon this memory. It is of lying half asleep, half awake, in bed in the nursery at St Ives. It is of hearing the waves breaking, one, two, one, two, and sending a splash of water over the beach; and then breaking, one, two, one, two, behind a yellow blind. It is of hearing the blind draw its little acorn across the floor as the wind blew the blind out. It is of lying and hearing this splash and seeing this light, and feeling, it is almost impossible that I should be here; of feeling the purest ecstasy I can conceive.

I could spend hours trying to write that as it should be written, in order to give the feeling which is even at this moment very strong in me. But I should fail (unless I had some wonderful luck); I dare say I should only succeed in having the luck if I had begun by describing Virginia herself.

Here I come to one of the memoir writer's difficulties—one of the reasons why, though I read so many, so many are failures. They leave out the person to whom things happened. The reason is that it is so difficult to describe any human being. So they say: "This is what happened"; but they do not say what the person was like to whom it happened. And the events mean very little unless we know first to whom they happened. Who was I then? Adeline Virginia Stephen, the second daughter of Leslie and Julia Prinsep Stephen, born on 25th January 1882, descended from a great many people, some famous, others obscure; born into a large connection, born not of rich parents, but of well-to-do parents, born into a very communicative, literate, letter writing, visiting, articulate, late nineteenth century world; so that I could if I liked to take the trouble, write a great deal here not only about my mother and father but about uncles and aunts, cousins and friends. But I do not know how much of this, or what part of this, made me feel what I felt in the nursery at St Ives. I do not know how far I differ from other people. That is another memoir writer's difficulty. Yet to describe oneself truly one must have some standard of comparison; was I clever, stupid, good looking, ugly, passionate, cold—? Owing partly to the fact that I was never at school, never competed in any way with children of my own age, I have never been able to compare my gifts and defects with other people's. But of course there was one external reason for the intensity of this first impression: the impression of the waves and the acorn on the blind; the feeling, as I describe it sometimes to myself, of lying in a grape and seeing through a film of semi-transparent yellow—it was due partly to the many months we spent in London. The change of nursery was a great change. And there was the long train journey; and the excitement. I remember the dark; the lights; the stir of the going up to bed.

But to fix my mind upon the nursery—it had a balcony; there was a partition, but it joined the balcony of my father's and mother's bedroom. My mother would come out onto her balcony in a white dressing gown. There were passion flowers growing on the wall; they were great starry blossoms, with purple streaks, and large green buds, part empty, part full.

If I were a painter I should paint these first impressions in pale yellow, silver, and green. There was the pale yellow blind; the green sea; and the silver of the passion flowers. I should make a picture that was globular; semi-transparent. I should make a picture of curved petals; of shells; of things that were semi-transparent; I should make curved shapes, showing the light through, but not giving a clear outline. Everything would be large and dim; and what was seen would at the same time be heard; sounds would come through this petal or leaf—sounds indistinguishable from sights. Sound and sight seem to make equal parts of these first impressions. When I think of the early morning in bed I also hear the caw of rooks falling from a great height. The sound seems to fall through an elastic, gummy air; which holds it up; which prevents it from being sharp and distinct. The quality of the air above Talland House seemed to suspend sound, to let it sink down slowly, as if it were caught in a blue gummy veil. The rooks cawing is part of the waves breaking—one, two, one, two—and the splash as the wave drew back and then it gathered again, and I lay there half awake, half asleep, drawing in such ecstasy as I cannot describe.

The next memory—all these colour-and-sound memories hang together at St Ives—was much more robust; it was highly sensual. It was later. It still makes me feel warm; as if everything were ripe; humming; sunny; smelling so many smells at once; and all making a whole that even now makes me stop—as I stopped then going down to the beach; I stopped at the top to look down at the gardens. They were sunk beneath the road. The apples were on a level with one's head. The gardens gave off a murmur of bees; the apples were red and gold; there were also pink flowers; and grey and silver leaves. The buzz, the croon, the smell, all seemed to press voluptuously against some membrane; not to burst it; but to hum round one such a complete rapture of pleasure that I stopped, smelt; looked. But again I cannot describe that rapture. It was rapture rather than ecstasy.

The strength of these pictures—but sight was always then so much mixed with sound that picture is not the right word—the strength anyhow of these impressions makes me again digress. Those moments—in the nursery, on the road to the beach—can still be more real than the present moment. This I have just tested. For I got up and crossed the garden. Percy was digging the asparagus bed; Louie was shaking a mat in front of the bedroom door.[3] But I was seeing them through the sight I saw here—the nursery and the road to the beach. At times I can go back to St Ives more completely than I can this morning. I can reach a state where I seem to be watching things happen as if I were there. That is, I suppose, that my memory supplies what I had forgotten, so that it seems as if it were happening independently, though I am really making it happen. In certain favourable moods, memories—what one has forgotten—come to the top. Now if this is so, is it not possible—I often wonder—that things we have felt with great intensity have an existence independent of our minds; are in fact still in existence? And if so, will it not be possible, in time, that some device will be invented by which we can tap them? I see it—the past—as an avenue lying behind; a long ribbon of scenes, emotions. There at the end of the avenue still, are the garden and the nursery. Instead of remembering here a scene and there a sound, I shall fit a plug into the wall; and listen in to the past. I shall turn up August 1890. I feel that strong emotion must leave its trace; and it is only a question of discovering how we can get ourselves again attached to it, so that we shall be able to live our lives through from the start.

But the peculiarity of these two strong memories is that each was very simple. I am hardly aware of myself, but only of the sensation. I am only the container of the feeling of ecstasy, of the feeling of rapture. Perhaps this is characteristic of all childhood memories; perhaps it accounts for their strength. Later we add to feelings much that makes them more complex; and therefore less strong; or if not less strong, less isolated, less complete. But instead of analysing this, here is an instance of what I mean—my feeling about the looking-glass in the hall.

There was a small looking-glass in the hall at Talland House. It had, I remember, a ledge with a brush on it. By standing on tiptoe I could see my face in the glass. When I was six or seven perhaps, I got into the habit of looking at my face in the glass. But I only did this if I was sure that I was alone. I was ashamed of it. A strong feeling of guilt seemed naturally attached to it. But why was this so? One obvious reason occurs to me— Vanessa and I were both what was called tomboys; that is, we played cricket, scrambled over rocks, climbed trees, were said not to care for clothes and so on. Perhaps therefore to have been found looking in the glass would have been against our tomboy code. But I think that my feeling of shame went a great deal deeper. I am almost inclined to drag in my grandfather—Sir James, who once smoked a cigar, liked it, and so threw away his cigar and never smoked another. I am almost inclined to think that I inherited a streak of the puritan, of the Clapham Sect.[4] At any rate, the looking-glass shame has lasted all my life, long after the tomboy phase was over. I cannot now powder my nose in public. Everything to do with dress—to be fitted, to come into a room wearing a new dress—still frightens me; at least makes me shy, self-conscious, uncomfortable. "Oh to be able to run, like Julian Morrell, all over the garden in a new dress", I thought not many years ago at Garsington; when Julian undid a parcel and put on a new dress and scampered round and round like a hare.[5] Yet femininity was very strong in our family. We were famous for our beauty—my mother's beauty, Stella's beauty, gave me as early as I can remember, pride and pleasure. What then gave me this feeling of shame, unless it were that I inherited some opposite instinct? My father was spartan, ascetic, puritanical. He had I think no feeling for pictures; no ear for music; no sense of the sound of words. This leads me to think that my—I would say 'our' if I knew enough about Vanessa, Thoby and Adrian—but how little we know even about brothers and sisters—this leads me to think that my natural love for beauty was checked by some ancestral dread. Yet this did not prevent me from feeling ecstasies and raptures spontaneously and intensely and without any shame or the least sense of guilt, so long as they were disconnected with my own body. I thus detect another element in the shame which I had in being caught looking at myself in the glass in the hall. I must have been ashamed or afraid of my own body. Another memory, also of the hall, may help to explain this. There was a slab outside the dining room door for standing dishes upon. Once when I was very small Gerald Duckworth[6] lifted me onto this, and as I sat there he began to explore my body. I can remember the feel of his hand going under my clothes; going firmly and steadily lower and lower. I remember how I hoped that he would stop; how I stiffened and wriggled as his hand approached my private parts. But it did not stop. His hand explored my private parts too. I remember resenting, disliking it—what is the word for so dumb and mixed a feeling? It must have been strong, since I still recall it. This seems to show that a feeling about certain parts of the body; how they must not be touched; how it is wrong to allow them to be touched; must be instinctive. It proves that Virginia Stephen was not born on the 25th January 1882, but was born many thousands of years ago; and had from the very first to encounter instincts already acquired by thousands of ancestresses in the past.

And this throws light not merely on my own case, but upon the problem that I touched on the first page; why it is so difficult to give any account of the person to whom things happen. The person is evidently immensely complicated. Witness the incident of the looking-glass. Though I have done my best to explain why I was ashamed of looking at my own face I have only been able to discover some possible reasons; there may be others; I do not suppose that I have got at the truth; yet this is a simple incident; and it happened to me personally; and I have no motive for lying about it. In spite of all this, people write what they call 'lives' of other people; that is, they collect a number of events, and leave the person to whom it happened unknown. Let me add a dream; for it may refer to the incident of the looking-glass. I dreamt that I was looking in a glass when a horrible face—the face of an animal—suddenly showed over my shoulder. I cannot be sure if this was a dream, or if it happened. Was I looking in the glass one day when something in the background moved, and seemed to me alive? I cannot be sure. But I have always remembered the other face in the glass, whether it was a dream or a fact, and that it frightened me.

These then are some of my first memories. But of course as an account of my life they are misleading, because the things one does not remember are as important; perhaps they are more important. If I could remember one whole day I should be able to describe, superficially at least, what life was like as a child.

Unfortunately, one only remembers what is exceptional. And there seems to be no reason why one thing is exceptional and another not. Why have I forgotten so many things that must have been, one would have thought, more memorable than what I do remember? Why remember the hum of bees in the garden going down to the beach, and forget completely being thrown naked by father into the sea? (Mrs. Swanwick says she saw that happen.)[7] . . .

As a child then, my days, just as they do now, contained a large proportion of this cotton wool, this non-being. Week after week passed at St Ives and nothing made any dint upon me. Then, for no reason that I know about, there was a sudden violent shock; something happened so violently that I have remembered it all my life. I will give a few instances. The first: I was fighting with Thoby on the lawn. We were pommelling each other with our fists. Just as I raised my fist to hit him, I felt: why hurt another person? I dropped my hand instantly, and stood there, and let him beat me. I remember the feeling. It was a feeling of hopeless sadness. It was as if I became aware of something terrible; and of my own powerlessness. I slunk off alone, feeling horribly depressed. The second instance was also in the garden at St Ives. I was looking at the flower bed by the front door; "That is the whole", I said. I was looking at a plant with a spread of leaves; and it seemed suddenly plain that the flower itself was a part of the earth; that a ring enclosed what was the flower; and that was the real flower; part earth; part flower. It was a thought I put away as being likely to be very useful to me later. The third case was also at St Ives. Some people called Valpy had been staying at St Ives, and had left. We were waiting at dinner one night, when somehow I overheard my father or my mother say that Mr Valpy had killed himself. The next thing I remember is being in the garden at night and walking on the path by the apple tree. It seemed to me that the apple tree was connected with the horror of Mr Valpy's suicide. I could not pass it. I stood there looking at the grey-green creases of the bark—it was a moonlit night—in a trance of horror. I seemed to be dragged down, hopelessly, into some pit of absolute despair from which I could not escape. My body seemed paralysed.

These are three instances of exceptional moments. I often tell them over, or rather they come to the surface unexpectedly. But now that for the first time I have written them down, I realise something that I have never realised before. Two of these moments ended in a state of despair. The other ended, on the contrary, in a state of satisfaction. When I said about the flower "That is the whole," I felt that I had made a discovery. I felt that I had put away in my mind something that I should go back [to], to turn over and explore. It strikes me now that this was a profound difference. It was the difference in the first place between despair and satisfaction. This difference I think arose from the fact that I was quite unable to deal with the pain of discovering that people hurt each other; that a man I had seen had killed himself. The sense of horror held me powerless. But in the case of the flower I found a reason; and was thus able to deal with the sensation. I was not powerless. I was conscious—if only at a distance—that I should in time explain it. I do not know if I was older when I saw the flower than I was when I had the other two experiences. I only know that many of these exceptional moments brought with them a peculiar horror and a physical collapse; they seemed dominant; myself passive. This suggests that as one gets older one has a greater power through reason to provide an explanation; and that this explanation blunts the sledge-hammer force of the blow. I think this is true, because though I still have the peculiarity that I receive these sudden shocks, they are now always welcome; after the first surprise, I always feel instantly that they are particularly valuable. And so I go on to suppose that the shock-receiving capacity is what makes me a writer. I hazard the explanation that a shock is at once in my case followed by the desire to explain it. I feel that I have had a blow; but it is not, as I thought as a child, simply a blow from an enemy hidden behind the cotton wool of daily life; it is or will become a revelation of some order; it is a token of some real thing behind appearances; and I make it real by putting it into words. It is only by putting it into words that I make it whole; this wholeness means that it has lost its power to hurt me; it gives me, perhaps because by doing so I take away the pain, a great delight to put the severed parts together. Perhaps this is the strongest pleasure known to me. It is the rapture I get when in writing I seem to be discovering what belongs to what; making a scene come right; making a character come together. From this I reach what I might call a philosophy; at any rate it is a constant idea of mine; that behind the cotton wool is hidden a pattern; that we—I mean all human beings—are connected with this; that the whole world is a work of art; that we are parts of the work of art. . . .

[May 2, 1939] Many bright colours; many distinct sounds; some human beings, caricatures; comic; several violent moments of being, always including a circle of the scene which they cut out: and all surrounded by a vast space—that is a rough visual description of childhood. This is how I shape it; and how I see myself as a child, roaming about, in that space of time which lasted from 1882 to 1895. A great hall I could liken it to; with windows letting in strange lights; and murmurs and spaces of deep silence. But somehow into that picture must be brought, too, the sense of movement and change. Nothing remained stable long. One must get the feeling of everything approaching and then disappearing, getting large, getting small, passing at different rates of speed past the little creature; one must get the feeling that made her press on, the little creature driven on as she was by growth of her legs and arms, driven without her being able to stop it, or to change it, driven as a plant is driven up out of the earth, up until the stalk grows, the leaf grows, buds swell. That is what is indescribable, that is what makes all images too static, for no sooner has one said this was so, than it was past and altered. How immense must be the force of life which turns a baby, who can just distinguish a great blot of blue and purple on a black background, into the child who thirteen years later can feel all that I felt on May 5th 1895—now almost exactly to a day, forty-four years ago—when my mother died.

This shows that among the innumerable things left out in my

sketch I have left out the most important—those instincts, affections, passions, attachments—there is no single word for them, for they changed month by month—which bound me, I suppose, from the first moment of consciousness to other people. If it were true, as I said above, that the things that ceased in childhood, are easy to describe because they are complete, then it should be easy to say what I felt for my mother, who died when I was thirteen. Thus I should be able to see her completely undisturbed by later impressions, as I saw Mr Gibbs and C. B. Clarke. But the theory, though true of them, breaks down completely with her. It breaks down in a curious way, which I will explain, for perhaps it may help to explain why I find it now so curiously difficult to describe both my feeling for her, and her herself.

Until I was in the forties—I could settle the date by seeing when I wrote *To the Lighthouse*, but am too casual here to bother to do it—the presence of my mother obsessed me.[8] I could hear her voice, see her, imagine what she would do or say as I went about my day's doings. She was one of the invisible presences who after all play so important a part in every life. This influence, by which I mean the consciousness of other groups impinging upon ourselves; public opinion; what other people say and think; all those magnets which attract us this way to be like that, or repel us the other and make us different from that; has never been analysed in any of those Lives which I so much enjoy reading, or very superficially.

Yet it is by such invisible presences that the "subject of this memoir" is tugged this way and that every day of his life; it is they that keep him in position. Consider what immense forces society brings to play upon each of us, how that society changes from decade to decade; and also from class to class; well, if we cannot analyse these invisible presences, we know very little of the subject of the memoir; and again how futile life-writing becomes. I see myself as a fish in a stream; deflected; held in place; but cannot describe the stream.

To return to the particular instance which should be more definite and more capable of description . . . is the influence of my mother. It is perfectly true that she obsessed me, in spite of the fact that she died when I was thirteen, until I was forty-four. Then one day walking round Tavistock Square I made up, as I sometimes make up my books, *To the Lighthouse*; in a great, apparently involuntary, rush.[9] One thing burst into another. Blowing bubbles out of a pipe gives the feeling of the rapid crowd of ideas and scenes which blew out of my mind, so that my lips seemed syllabling of their own accord as I walked. What blew the bubbles? Why then? I have no notion. But I wrote the book very quickly; and when it was written, I ceased to be obsessed by my mother. I no longer hear her voice; I do not see her.

I suppose that I did for myself what psycho-analysts do for their patients. I expressed some very long felt and deeply felt emotion. And in expressing it I explained it and then laid it to rest. But what is the meaning of "explained" it? Why, because I described her and my feeling for her in that book, should my vision of her and my feeling for her become so much dimmer and weaker? Perhaps one of these days I shall hit on the reason; and if so, I will give it, but at the moment I will go on, describing what I can remember, for it may be true that what I remember of her now will weaken still further. (This note is made provisionally, in order to explain in part why it is now so difficult to give any clear description of her.)

Certainly there she was, in the very centre of that great Cathedral space which was childhood; there she was from the very first. My first memory is of her lap; the scratch of some beads on her dress comes back to me as I pressed my cheek against it. Then I see her in her white dressing gown on the balcony; and the passion flower with the purple star on its petals. Her voice is still faintly in my ears—decided, quick; and in particular the little drops with which her laugh ended—three diminishing ahs . . . "Ah—ah—ah . . ." I sometimes end a laugh that way myself. And I see her hands, like Adrian's, with the very individual square-tipped fingers, each finger with a waist to it, and the nail broadening out. (My own are the same size all the way, so that I can slip a ring over my thumb.) She had three rings; a diamond ring, an emerald ring, and an opal ring. My eyes used to fix themselves upon the lights in the opal as it moved across the page of the lesson book when she taught us, and I was glad that she left it to me (I gave it to Leonard). Also I hear the tinkle of her bracelets, made of twisted silver, given her by Mr Lowell, as she went about the house; especially as she came up at night to see if we were asleep, holding a candle shaded; this is a distinct memory, for, like all children, I lay awake sometimes and longed for her to come. Then she told me to think of all the lovely things I could imagine. Rainbows and bells . . . But besides these minute separate details, how did I first become conscious of what was always there—her astonishing beauty? Perhaps I never became conscious of it; I think I accepted her beauty as the natural quality that a mother—she seemed typical, universal, yet our own in particular—had by virtue of being our mother. It was part of her calling. I do not think that I separated her face from that general being; or from her whole body. Certainly I have a vision of her now, as she came up the path by the lawn at St Ives; slight, shapely—she held herself very straight. I was playing. I stopped, about to speak to her. But she half turned from us, and lowered her eyes. From that indescribably sad gesture I knew that Philips, the man who had been crushed on the line and whom she had been visiting, was dead. It's over, she seemed to say. I knew, and was awed by the thought of death. At the same time I felt that her gesture as a whole was lovely. Very early, through nurses or casual visitors, I must have known that she was thought very beautiful. But that pride was snobbish, not a pure and private feeling: it was mixed with pride in other people's admiration. It was related to the more definitely snobbish pride caused in me by the nurses who said one night talking together while we ate our supper: "They're very well connected. . . ."

But apart from her beauty, if the two can be separated, what was she herself like? Very quick; very direct; practical; and amusing, I say at once offhand. She could be sharp, she disliked affectation. "If you put your head on one side like that, you shan't come to the party," I remember she said to me as we drew up in a carriage in front of some house. Severe; with a background of knowledge that made her sad. She had her own sorrow waiting behind her to dip into privately. Once when she had set us to write exercises I looked up from mine and watched her reading—the Bible perhaps; and, struck by the gravity of her face, told myself that her first husband had been a clergyman and that she was thinking, as she read what he had read, of him. This was a fable on my part; but it shows that she looked very sad when she was not talking.

But can I get any closer to her without drawing upon all those descriptions and anecdotes which after she was dead imposed themselves upon my view of her? Very quick; very definite; very upright; and behind the active, the sad, the silent. And of course she was central. I suspect the word "central" gets closest to the general feeling I had of living so completely in her atmosphere that one never got far enough away from her to see her as a person. (That is one reason why I see the Gibbses and the Beadles and the Clarkes so much more distinctly.) She was the whole thing; Talland House was full of her; Hyde Park Gate was full of her. I see now, though the sentence is hasty, feeble and inexpressive, why it was that it was impossible for her to leave a very private and particular impression upon a child. She was keeping what I call in my shorthand the panoply of life—that which we all lived in common—in being. I see now that she was living on such an extended surface that she had not time, nor strength, to concentrate, except for a moment if one were ill or in some child's crisis, upon me, or upon anyone—unless it were Adrian. Him she cherished separately; she called him 'My Joy'. The later view, the understanding that I now have of her position must have its say; and it shows me that a woman of forty with seven children, some of them needing grown-up attention, and four still in the nursery; and an eighth, Laura,[10] an idiot, yet living with us; and a husband fifteen years her elder, difficult, exacting, dependent on her; I see now that a woman who had to keep all this in being and under control must have been a general presence rather than a particular person to a child of seven or eight. Can I remember ever being alone with her for more than a few minutes? Someone was always interrupting. When I think of her spontaneously she is always in a room full of people; Stella, George and Gerald are there; my father, sitting reading with one leg curled round the other, twisting his lock of hair; "Go and take the crumb out of his beard," she whispers to me; and off I trot. There are visitors, young men like Jack Hills who is in love with Stella; many young men, Cambridge friends of George's and Gerald's; old men, sitting round the tea table talking—father's friends, Henry James, Symonds,[11] (I see him peering up at me on the broad staircase at St Ives with his drawn yellow face and a tie made of a yellow cord with two plush balls on it); Stella's friends—the Lushingtons, the Stillmans; I see her at the head of the table underneath the engraving of Beatrice given her by an old governess and painted blue; I hear jokes; laughter; the clatter of voices; I am teased; I say something funny; she laughs; I am pleased; I blush furiously; she observes; someone laughs at Nessa for saying that Ida Milman is her B.F.; Mother says soothingly, tenderly, "Best friend, that means." I see her going to the town with her basket; and Arthur Davies goes with her; I see her knitting on the hall step while we play cricket; I see her stretching her arms out to Mrs Williams when the bailiffs took possession of their house and the Captain stood at the window bawling and shying jugs, basins, chamber pots onto the gravel—"Come to us, Mrs Williams"; "No, Mrs Stephen," sobbed Mrs Williams, "I will not leave my husband."—I see her writing at her table in London and the silver candlesticks, and the high carved chair with the claws and the pink seat; and the three-cornered brass ink pot; I wait in agony peeping surreptitiously behind the blind for her to come down the street, when she has been out late, the lamps are lit and I am sure that she has been run over. (Once my father found me peeping; questioned me; and said rather anxiously but reprovingly, "You shouldn't be so nervous, Jinny.") And there is my last sight of her; she was dying; I came to kiss her and as I crept out of the room she said: "Hold yourself straight, my little Goat." . . . What a jumble of things I can remember, if I let my mind run, about my mother; but they are all of her in company; of her surrounded; of her generalised; dispersed, omnipresent, of her as the creator of that crowded merry world which spun so gaily in the centre of my childhood. It is true that I enclosed that world in another made by my own temperament; it is true that from the beginning I had many adventures outside that world; and often went far from it; and kept much back from it; but there it always was, the common life of the family, very merry, very stirring, crowded with people; and she was the centre; it was herself. This was proved on May 5th 1895. For after that day there was nothing left of it. I leant out of the nursery window the morning she died. It was about six, I suppose. I saw Dr Seton walk away up the street with his head bent and his hands clasped behind his back. I saw the pigeons floating and settling. I got a feeling of calm, sadness, and finality. It was a beautiful blue spring morning, and very still. That brings back the feeling that everything had come to an end. . . .

May 28th 1939. Led by George with towels wrapped round us and given each a drop of brandy in warm milk to drink, we were taken into the bedroom. I think candles were burning; and I think the sun was coming in. At any rate I remember the long looking-glass; with the drawers on either side; and the washstand; and the great bed on which my mother lay. I remember very clearly how even as I was taken to the bedside I noticed that one nurse was sobbing, and a desire to laugh came over me, and I said to myself as I have often done at moments of crisis since, "I feel nothing whatever". Then I stooped and kissed my mother's face. It was still warm. She [had] only died a moment before. Then we went upstairs into the day nursery.

Perhaps it was the next evening that Stella took me into the bedroom to kiss mother for the last time. She had been lying on her side before. Now she was lying straight in the middle of her pillows. Her face looked immeasurably distant, hollow and stern. When I kissed her, it was like kissing cold iron. Whenever I touch cold iron the feeling comes back to me—the feeling of my mother's face, iron cold, and granulated. I started back. Then Stella stroked her cheek, and undid a button on her nightgown. "She always liked to have it like that," she said. When she came up to the nursery later she said to me, "Forgive me. I saw you were afraid." She had noticed that I had started. When Stella asked me to forgive her for having given me that shock, I cried— we had been crying off and on all day—and said, "When I see mother, I see a man sitting with her." Stella looked at me as if I had frightened her. Did I say that in order to attract attention to myself? Or was it true? I cannot be sure, for certainly I had a great wish to draw attention to myself. But certainly it was true that when she said: "Forgive me," and thus made me visualize my mother, I seemed to see a man sitting bent on the edge of the bed.

"It's nice that she shouldn't be alone", Stella said after a moment's pause.

. . . The shrouded, cautious, dulled life took the place of all the chatter and laughter of the summer. There were no more parties; no more young men and women laughing. No more flashing visions of white summer dresses and hansoms dashing off to private views and dinner parties, none of that natural life and gaiety which my mother had created. The grown-up world into which I would dash for a moment and pick off some joke or little scene and dash back again upstairs to the nursery was ended. There were none of those snatched moments that were so amusing and for some reason so soothing and yet exciting when one ran downstairs to dinner arm in arm with mother; or chose the jewels she was to wear. There was none of that pride when one said something that amused her, or that she thought very remarkable. How excited I used to be when the 'Hyde Park Gate News' was laid on her plate on Monday morning, and she liked something I had written![12] Never shall I forget my extremity of pleasure—it was like being a violin and being played upon—

when I found that she had sent a story of mine to Madge Symonds; it was so imaginative, she said; it was about souls flying
round and choosing bodies to be born into.

The tragedy of her death was not that it made one, now and
then and very intensely, unhappy. It was that it made her unreal;
and us solemn, and self-conscious. We were made to act parts
that we did not feel; to fumble for words that we did not know.
It obscured, it dulled. It made one hypocritical and immeshed in
the conventions of sorrow. Many foolish and sentimental ideas
came into being. Yet there was a struggle, for soon we revived,
and there was a conflict between what we ought to be and what
we were. Thoby put this into words. One day before he went
back to school, he said: "It's silly going on like this . . .",
sobbing, sitting shrouded, he meant. I was shocked at his heart-
lessness; yet he was right, I know; and yet how could we escape?

It was Stella who lifted the canopy again. A little light crept
in.

June 20th 1939 . . . I think of her less disconnectedly and more
truly than anyone now living, save for Vanessa and Adrian; and
perhaps old Sophie Farrell.[13] Of her childhood I know practically
nothing. She was the only daughter of the handsome barrister
Herbert Duckworth, but as he died when she was three or four,
she did not remember him, or those years when her mother was as
happy as anyone can be. I think, from stray anecdotes and from
what I noticed myself, that when she came to consciousness as a
child the unhappy years were at their height. That would account
for some qualities in Stella. Her first memories were of a very sad
widowed mother, who "went about doing good"—Stella wished
to have that on the tombstone—visiting the slums, visiting too
the Cancer Hospital in the Brompton Road. Our Quaker Aunt
told me that this was her habit; for she said how one case there
had "shocked her". Thus Stella as a child lived in the shade of
that widowhood; saw that beautiful crape-veiled figure daily; and
perhaps took then the ply that was so marked—that attitude of

devotion, almost canine in its touching adoration, to her mother; that passive, suffering affection; and also that complete unquestioning dependence.

They were sun and moon to each other; my mother the positive and definite; Stella the reflecting and satellite. My mother was stern to her. All her devotion was given to George who was like his father; and her care was for Gerald, born posthumously and very delicate. Stella she treated severely; so much so that before their marriage my father ventured a protest. She replied that it might be true; she was hard on Stella because she felt Stella "part of myself". A pale silent child I imagine her; sensitive; modest; uncomplaining; adoring her mother, thinking only how she could help her, and without any ambition or even character of her own. And yet she had character. Very gentle, very honest, and in some way individual—so she made her own impression on people. Friends, like Kitty Maxse, the brilliant, the sparkling, loved her with a real laughing tenderness for her own sake. Her charm was great; it came partly from this modesty, from this honesty, from this perfectly simple unostentatious unselfishness; it came too from her lack of pose, her lack of snobbery; and from the genuineness, from something that was— could I put my finger on it—perfectly herself, individual. This unnamed quality—the sensitiveness to real things—was queer in the sister of George and Gerald, who were so opaque and conventional; who had so innate a respect for the conventions and respectabilities. By some odd fling in her birth, she had escaped all taint of Duckworth philistinism; she had none of their shrewd middle-class complacency. Instead of their little brown eyes that were so greedy and twinkling, hers were very large and rather a pale blue. They were dreamy, candid eyes. She was without their instinctive worldliness. She was lovely too, in a far vaguer, less perfect way than my mother.

19th July 1939 . . . Jim[14] was one of her lovers. The other—that is, the most important—was Jack Hills. It was at St Ives that she refused him; late one night we heard her sobbing through the

attic wall. He had gone at once. A refusal in those days was cata-
strophic. It meant a complete breach. Human relations, at least between the sexes, were carried on as relations between countries are
now—with ambassadors, and treaties. The parties concerned met
on the great occasion of the proposal. If this were refused, a state
of war was declared. That explains why she cried so bitterly. For
she had done something of great practical as well as emotional
importance. He went off at once—to Norway to fish; later perhaps they met in a completely formal way at parties. Negotia-
tions were kept faintly alive through my mother; an interpreter
was necessary. All this procedure gave love its solemnity. Feelings were banked up; silence interposed; there was in every
family a code, a religious code, that penetrated, somehow or
other, to the children. It was secret; but we guessed.

Thus, when my mother died, Stella was left without any ne-
gotiator, for my father did not fill the part. He must have come
back—it proves how deep the feeling was to admit such a return
—the night before my mother died.

June 8th 1940 . . . We were in the back drawing room, and there
was the tea tray, for we had a curious habit of drinking tea about
nine o'clock. The silver hot water jug which I still possess—but it
has a hole in it—had a handle that grew hot. Aunt Mary, summoned from Brighton, picked it up and put it down quickly.[15]
"Only Mrs Stephen and Stella can manage that", said Jack Hills
with the queer sad little smile that went with the little joke. And
I remember that he said 'Stella'. And since he was there, that last
night, the affair must have been in being—sufficiently so to make
it possible for him to be with us in intimacy. That was the 4th
May, 1895.

The next thing I remember is the night at Hindhead (August
22nd 1896)—the black and silver night of mysterious voices,
the night when father packed us off to bed early; and we heard
voices in the garden; and saw Stella and Jack passing; and disappearing; and the tramp came; and Thoby countered him; and
Nessa and I sat up in our bedroom waiting; and Stella never

came; and at last in the early morning she came and told us that she was engaged; and I whispered, "Did mother know?" and she murmured, "Yes"....

But to return to Jack—when Stella accepted him, we approved, in our republic, which, though rapidly losing shape, was still in being after mother's death. The marriage would have been, I think, a very happy marriage. It should have borne many children. And still she might have been alive. Certainly he was passionately in love; she at first passively. And it was through that engagement that I had my first vision—so intense, so exciting, so rapturous was it that the word vision applies—my first vision then of love between man and woman. It was to me like a ruby; the love I detected that winter of their engagement, glowing, red, clear, intense. It gave me a conception of love; a standard of love; a sense that nothing in the whole world is so lyrical, so musical, as a young man and a young woman in their first love for each other. I connect it with respectable engagements; unofficial love never gives me the same feeling. "My Love's like a red, red rose, that's newly sprung in June"—that was the feeling they gave; the feeling that has always come back, when I hear of 'an engagement'; not when I hear of 'an affair'. It derives from Stella and Jack. It springs from the ecstasy I felt, in my covert, behind the folding doors of the Hyde Park Gate drawing room. I sat there, shielded, being half insane with shyness and nervousness; reading Fanny Burney's diary; and feeling come over me intermittent waves of very strong emotion—rage sometimes; how often I was enraged by father then!—love, or the reflection of love, too. It was bodiless; a light; an ecstasy. But also extraordinarily enduring. Once I came on a letter from him which she had slipped between the blotting paper—a sign of the lack of privacy in which we lived—and read it. "There is nothing sweeter in the whole world than our love", he wrote. I put the page down, not so much guiltily, at having pried; but in a quiver of ecstasy at the revelation. Still I cannot read words that give me that quiver twice over. If I get a letter that pleases me intensely, I never read it again. Why I wonder? For fear lest it shall dwindle? This colour, this incandescence, was in Stella's whole body. Her pallor became lit up, her eyes bluer. She had something of moonlight about her that winter, as she went about the house. "There's never been anything like it in the world", I said—or something like it—when she found me awake one night. And she laughed, tenderly, very gently, and kissed me and said, "Oh lots of people are in love as we are. You and Nessa will be one day", she said. Once she told me, "You must expect people to look at you both".

"Nessa", she said, "is much more beautiful than I ever was" —at twenty-six she spoke of her beauty as a thing of the past. . . .

For some reason Stella and Jack's engagement lasted all the months from July till April. It was a clumsy, cruel, unnecessary trial for them both. Looking back, it seems everything was done without care or consideration, clumsily, wantonly. I conceive that as the months of that long waiting time passed she slowly roused herself out of the numb, frozen state in which mother's death had left her. At first she found in Jack rest and support; a refuge from all the worries and responsibilities of 'the family', relief too from those glooms which father never controlled, and spent on her. Slowly she became more positive, less passive; and asserted Jack's rights; her desire too for her own house; her own husband; a life, a home of their own. At last the promise, apparently exacted by father, and tacitly accepted, that they were to live on with us after their marriage, an arrangement now incredible but then accepted, became intolerable; and she went up to father one night in his study; and told him so; and there was 'an explosion'.

As the engagement went on, father became indeed increasingly tyrannical. He didn't like the name 'Jack', I remember his saying; it sounded like the smack of a whip. He was jealous clearly. But in those days nothing was clear. He had his traditional pose; he was the lonely; the deserted; the old unhappy man. In fact he was possessive; hurt; a man jealous of the young man. There was every excuse, he would have said, had he been asked, for his explosions. And as by this time he had entrenched himself away from all truth, in a world which it is almost impossible to describe, for I know no one now who could inhabit such a world—the engagement was incredibly involved, frustrated, and impeded. At last in April 1897 the marriage took place—conventionally, ceremoniously, with bells ringing, and company collected, and silver engraved wedding invitations, at St Mary Abbots. Nessa and I handed flowers to the guests; father marched up the aisle with Stella on his arm.

"He took it for granted that he was to give her away", George and Gerald grumbled. He ignored the fact that they had any claim. No one would have dared to take that privilege from him. It was somehow typical—his assumption; and his enjoyment of the attitude. They went to Italy; we to Brighton. One fortnight was the length of their honeymoon. And directly she came back she was taken ill. It was appendicitis; she was going to have a baby. And that was mismanaged too; and so, after three months of intermittent illness, she died—at 24 Hyde Park Gate, on July 27th, 1897.

22nd September 1940 . . . Father, I think, was on one of his walking tours, in 1881 it must have been, when he discovered St Ives. He must have seen Talland House, which belonged to the G.W.R.;[16] and have found it to let. He must have seen the town, almost as it had been in the sixteenth century; and the bay as it had been since time began. It was the first year, I think I have heard, that the line from St Erth to St Ives was open. Until then St Ives was about eight miles from any railway. And I suppose, munching his sandwich perhaps up at Tregenna, he had thought this might do for a summer place for us—and worked out, with [his] usual caution, ways and means. I was about to be born; and though they wished to limit their family, my conception (birth 1882) showed that they were not going to succeed. Adrian was to follow (1883)—also against their intention. It proves the ease and amplitude of those days that a man to whom money was an obscene nightmare, yet thought it feasible to take a house on the very toenail, as he said, of England—so that every summer he would be faced with the expense of moving family, nurses, servants, from one end of England to the other. Yet he did it. The distance was a drawback; for it meant that we could only go to St Ives in the summer. Our country was canalised into two or two months and a half. Yet that made the country more intense. And, in retrospect, probably nothing that we had as children was quite so important to us as our summer in Cornwall. To go away to the end of England; to have our own house, our own garden— to have that bay, that sea, and the mount: Clodgy and Halestown bog; Carbis Bay; Lelant; Zennor, Trevail, the Gurnard's Head; to hear the waves breaking that first night behind the yellow blind; to sail in the lugger; to dig in the sands; to scramble over the rocks and see the anemones flourishing their antennae in the pools; now and then to find a small fish flapping there; to look up over the lesson book in the dining room and see the lights changing on the waves; to go down to the town and buy penny boxes of tintacks or whatever it might be at Lanham's: Mrs Lanham wore false curls all round her face: the servants said Mr Lanham had married her 'from an advertisement'; to smell all the fishy smells in the steep little streets; and see the innumerable cats; and the women on the raised steps outside the houses pouring pails of dirty water down the gutters; every day to have a great dish of Cornish cream, skinned with a yellow skin, handed round with plenty of brown sugar . . . I could fill pages remembering one thing after another that made the summer at St Ives the best beginning to a life conceivable. When they took Talland House, my father and mother gave me, at any rate, something I think invaluable. . . .

Our house, Talland House, was outside the town; on the hill. [When it was built, for] whom it was built by the G.W.R., I do not know; some time in the forties [or] fifties I suppose; a square house, like a child's drawing of a house; remarkable only for its flat roof, and the railing with crossed bars of wood that ran round the roof. It had, when we came there, a perfect view— right across the Bay to Godrevy Lighthouse. It had, running down the hill, little lawns, surrounded by thick escallonia bushes, whose leaves one picked and pressed and smelt: it had so many corners and lawns that each was named: the coffee garden; the fountain; the cricket ground; the love corner, under the greenhouse; jackmanii grew there; on the seat under the jackmanii, Leo Maxse became engaged to Kitty Lushington (I thought I heard Paddy talking to his son, Thoby announced); the strawberry bed; the kitchen garden; the pond; and the big tree. All different places were crowded together in that one garden; for it was a large garden—two or three acres at most, I suppose. You entered Talland House by a large wooden gate, the sound of whose latch clicking comes back: you went up the carriage drive, with its steep wall scattered with mesembryanthemums; and then came to the Lookout place on the right. This was a mound, grassy, unplanted, that jutted out over the garden wall. There one stood to look if the signal was down. If it were down, it was time to start for the station to meet the train from St Erth—the train that brought Mr Lowell, Mr Gibbs, the Stillmans, the Symondses, the Lushingtons. But that was entirely a grown-up affair—receiving friends. We never had friends to stay with us. Did we want them? I think 'us four' were completely self-sufficing. When once a girl called Elsie was brought over by Mrs Westlake from Zennor I "broomed her round the garden", the grown ups laughing and approving. They liked us to be independent. . . .

The kitchen, Sophie's kitchen, was directly beneath our night nursery. We would let down a basket on a string and dangle it over the kitchen window, at night while dinner was going on. If she were in a good temper, the basket would be drawn in and laden with something left from the grown-ups' dinner; but if she were in a bad temper, the basket would be jerked in and the string cut. I can remember the different sensations: drawing up the heavy basket; and feeling the jerk; and the lightness of the string.

Every afternoon we went for a walk. Later these walks became a penance—father must have one of us to walk with him—mother, too much obsessed with his health, his pleasure, was too willing, I think now, to offer us up for sacrifice on that altar, leaving thus a legacy of dependence on his side which became a terrible imposition after her death. In spite of that, St Ives was the country. How much better it would have been for him and for us if she had left him to walk alone; to overwork if he chose. His health was her fetish; she died of overwork easily at forty-nine: he found it very difficult to die of cancer at seventy-two. . . .

I recover then today (October 12th 1940: a milky[17] autumn day; London is being battered nightly) from these rapid notes only one actual picture of Thoby: steering us in round the point without letting the sail flap. I recover the picture of a schoolboy whose jacket was rather tight; whose arms were too long for their sleeves; whose eyes became bluer when he was thus on his mettle; his face flushed a little. He was feeling, rather earlier than most boys, the responsibility laid on him by father's pride in him; the burden, the glory of being a man. Why do I shirk the task, not so very hard to a professional like myself, of wafting this boy from the boat into my bed sitting room at Hyde Park Gate? Because I want to think of St Ives; because I have left out many other pictures of him there; because always round him like the dew that collects on a rough coat in autumn hangs the country; butterflies; birds; mud; horses; and finally, because I do not want to go into my room at Hyde Park Gate again. I shrink from the years 1897–1904—the seven unhappy years. So many lives were free from our burden. Why should our lives have been so tortured and fretted? by two unnecessary blunders—the lash of a random unheeding flail that pointlessly and brutally killed the two people who should, normally and naturally, have made those years, not perhaps happy but normal and natural. Mother's death: Stella's death. I am not thinking of them. I am thinking of the stupid damage that their deaths inflicted. That is why I do not wish to bring Thoby out of the boat into my room.

Without their deaths, to hark back to an earlier train of thought, he would not have been so dumbly, yet genuinely, bound to us. If there is any good (I doubt it) in this mutilation

[of] natural feelings, it is that it sensitizes—if to be aware of the insecurity of life; [to] remember something gone; to feel, now and then, as I felt for father when he made no claim, an odd fumbling fellowship—if it is a good thing to be at fifteen or sixteen or seventeen aware of this; to feel, by fits and starts, this sort of profound feeling, this unchildish feeling—if, if, if—. But was it good? Would it not have been better (if there is any sense in using good and better when there is no possible judge) to go on feeling at St Ives the rush and tumble of things? to go on exploring and adventuring privately, while all the while the family as a whole continued its solid rumbling progress, from year to year? To be so surrounded would have given one perhaps a greater scope, more variety. But at fifteen to have that protection removed, to be tumbled out of the family shelter, to see cracks and gashes in that fabric, to be cut by them, to see beyond them—was that good? Did it give one an experience that even if it was painful, yet meant that the gods (as I used to phrase it) were taking one seriously . . . ? I had my visual way of putting it. I would see (after Thoby's death) two great grindstones . . . and myself between them. I would typify a contest between myself and "them"—some invisible giant. I would reason, or fancy, that if life were thus made to rear and kick, it was at any rate, the real thing. Nobody could say I had been fobbed off with an unmeaning slip of the precious matter. So I came to think of life as something of extreme reality. And this, of course, increased my feeling of my own importance. Not in relation to human beings: in relation to the force which had respected me sufficiently to make me feel what was real.[18]

It seems to me therefore that our relation (mine and Thoby's) was more serious than it would have been without those deaths. The unspoken thought—something like what I have visualized—was there, in him, in me; when he came into my back room at Hyde Park Gate. It was behind our arguments. We were of course naturally attracted to each other. Besides his brother's feeling, he had, I think, an amused, surprised, questioning attitude towards me. I was a year and a half younger than he. I was a girl. And he found me reading Greek, writing an essay—the first, the only essay I ever showed father, upon the Elizabethan voyagers—when he was writing one for a prize at Trinity. A shell-less little creature, I think he thought me; so sequestered, in the room at Hyde Park Gate, compared with himself; a very simple, eager recipient of his school stories; without any experience of my own with which to cap his; but all the same, not passive; rather, on the contrary, bubbling, inquisitive, restless, carrying on my own contradicting, at any rate questioning. . . . But I am going too far ahead of myself in Hyde Park Gate. I will return to the year Stella died—1897.

I could sum it all up in one scene. I always see when I think of the month after her death the certain leafless bush; a skeleton tree in the dark of a summer night. This tree stands outside a garden house. Inside I am sitting with Jack Hills. He grips my hand in his. He groans. "It tears one asunder" he groaned. He was in agony. He gripped my hand to make his agony endurable; as if he were in physical torture. "But you can't understand" he broke off. "Yes, I can", I murmured. Subconsciously I knew that he meant that his sexual desire tore him asunder, together with his anguish at her loss. Both were torturing him. And the tree, outside in the dark garden, was to me the emblem, the symbol, of the skeleton agony to which her death had reduced him; and us; everything. Either Vanessa or I would go off alone with Jack after dinner. He would come down every week-end—it was to Painswick. Every day one or other of us had a letter. "Poor boy, he looks very bad", father once muttered audibly. And Jack, overhearing, stammered some awkward sentence to prevent him from saying more. The leafless tree and Jack's agony—I always see them as if they were one and the same, when I think of that summer.

The leafless tree was a very painful element in our life. Trees don't remain leafless. They begin to have little red chill buds. By that image I would convey the discomfort and misery and the quarrels, the suppressed irritations, the sharp words, the insinuations—which as soon as family life started again in Hyde

Park Gate began to cover over the fact that Stella's death had left us all to take up new relationships. . . .

(November 17th.) . . . Very soon after Stella's death we saw life as a struggle to get some kind of standing place for ourselves. . . . We were always battling for that which was always being interfered with, muffled up, snatched away. The most imminent obstacle and burden was of course father. How could we, to take a concrete case, arrange that he should be out when perhaps Kitty Maxse, perhaps Katie Thynne, came to tea?[19] How could we escape Mr Bryce?[20] Must I spend the afternoon walking round Kensington Gardens? Could we possibly arrange to take our friends straight up to the Studio (the day nursery)? Then, what could one talk about at luncheon? Could we avoid Brighton at Easter? Must we be in because Aunt Mary was coming?

Over the whole week of these evasions and propitiations brooded the horror of Wednesday. On that day the weekly books were shown him. If they were over eleven pounds, that lunch was a torture. The books were presented. Silence. He was putting on his glasses. He had read the figures. Down came his fist on the account book. There was a roar. His vein filled. His face flushed. Then he shouted "I am ruined." Then he beat his breast. He went through an extraordinary dramatization of self-pity, anger and despair. He was ruined—dying . . . tortured by the wanton extravagance of Vanessa and Sophie. "And you stand there like a block of stone. Don't you pity me? Haven't you a word to say to me?" and so on. Vanessa stood by his side absolutely dumb. He flung at her all the phrases—about shooting Niagara and so on—that came handy. She remained static. Another attitude was adopted. With a deep groan he picked up his pen and with ostentatiously trembling fingers wrote out the cheque. This was wearily tossed to Vanessa. Slowly and with many groans the pen, the account book were put away. Then he sank into his chair and sat with his head on his breast. And then at last, after glancing at a book, he would look up and say half plaintively, "And what are you doing this afternoon, Ginny?"

Never have I felt such rage and such frustration. For not a word of my feeling could be expressed.

This, as far as I can describe it, is an unexaggerated account of a bad Wednesday. Even now I can find nothing to say of his behaviour save that it was brutal. If, instead of words, he had used a whip the brutality would have been no greater. How can one explain it? He had been indulged of course ever since he broke the flower pot and threw the fragments at his mother (whatever the truth of that story, it ran something like that). Delicacy excused that. Then as he grew older there was the genius legend to which I have already referred.[21] Men of genius are very ill to live with . . . But there are certain qualifications to be noted. These scenes were never indulged in before men. Fred Maitland[22] for example resolutely refused to believe in them when Caroline Emelia (the Quaker sister) tried to insinuate that Leslie had a temper. If Thoby had presented those books or George, the explosion would have been suppressed. Why had he no shame in front of women? Partly of course because the woman was his slave—being the most typical of Victorians. But that does not explain the self-dramatization, the attitudinizing, the histrionic element, the breast beating, the groaning, which played so large a part, so disgusting a part in these scenes. His dependence upon women perhaps explains that. He needed always a woman to sympathize, to flatter, to console. Why? Because he was conscious of his failure as a philosopher, as a writer. But his creed made him ashamed to confess this need of sympathy to men. The attitude that his intellect made him adopt with men, made him the most modest, the most reasonable of men.[23] [illegible] Vanessa, on Wednesdays, was the recipient of much discontent that he had suppressed; and her refusal to accept her role, part slave, part angel of sympathy, exacerbated him so that he was probably unconscious of his own barbarous violence: and would have been horrified had anyone said straight out "You are a blackguard to treat a girl like that." I cannot conceive how he would have taken an honest expression of opinion. . . .

Here of course, from my distance of time, I perceive what one could not then see—the difference of age. Two different ages confronted each other in the drawing room at Hyde Park Gate: the Victorian age; and the Edwardian age. We were not his children, but his grandchildren. When we both felt that he was not only terrifying but also ridiculous we were looking at him with eyes that saw ahead of us something—something so easily seen now by every boy and girl of sixteen and eighteen that the sight is perfectly familiar. The cruel thing was that while we could see the future, we were completely in the power of the past. That bred a violent struggle. By nature, both Vanessa and I were explorers, revolutionists, reformers. But our surroundings were at least fifty years behind the times. Father himself was a typical Victorian: George and Gerald were unspeakably[24] conventional. So that while we fought against them as individuals we also fought against them in their public capacity. We were living say in 1910: they were living in 1860.

In 22 Hyde Park Gate round about 1900 there was to be found a complete model of Victorian society. If I had the power to lift out a month of life as we lived it about 1900 I could extract a section of Victorian life, like one of those cases with glass covers in which one is shown ants or bees going about their affairs. Our day would begin with family breakfast at 8.30. Adrian bolted his; and whichever of us, Vanessa or myself, was down, would see him off. Standing at the front door we would wave a hand till he disappeared round the Martins' bulging wall. This was a relic left us by Stella—a flutter of the dead hand which lay beneath the surface of family life. Father would eat his breakfast sighing and snorting. If no letters, "Everyone has forgotten me", he would groan. A long envelope from Barkers would mean of course a sudden roar. George and Gerald came down. Vanessa disappeared behind the curtain. Dinner ordered, she would dash for the red bus to take her to the Academy. If Gerald coincided, he would give her a lift in his daily hansom— the same hansom, generally; the cabman in summer wore a carnation. George having breakfasted more deliberately—sometimes he would persuade me to sit on, on the three-cornered chair, and tell me gossip from last night's party—he too would button on his frock coat and give his top hat a promise with the velvet glove and disappear—smart and debonair, in his ribbed socks and very small well polished shoes, to the Treasury. Left alone in the great house, with Father shut in his study at the top, the housemaid polishing brass rods, Shag asleep on his mat, and some maid doing bedrooms while Sophie I suppose took in joints and milk from tradespeople at the back door, I mounted to my room and spread my Liddell and Scott upon my table and sat down to make out Euripides or Sophocles for my bi-weekly lesson with Janet Case.[25]

From ten to one we escaped the pressure of Victorian society. Vanessa, I suppose, under the eye of Val Prinsep[26] or Ouless[27] or occasionally Sargent, painted from the life—she would bring home now and then very careful pencil drawings of Hermes perhaps, and spray them with fixative; or an oil head of a very histrionic looking male nude. And for the same three hours I would be reading perhaps Plato's *Republic*, or spelling out a Greek chorus. Our minds would escape to the world which on this November morning of 1940 she inhabits at Charleston and I in my garden room at Monks House. Our clothes would not be much different. She wore a blue painting smock; I perhaps a blouse and skirt. If our skirts were longer, that would be the only difference. Forty years ago she was rather tidier, rather better dressed than I. The change would come in the afternoon. About 4.30 Victorian society exerted its pressure. Then we must be 'in'. For at 5 father must be given his tea. And we must be better dressed and tidier, for Mrs Green was coming; Mrs H. Ward was coming; or Florence Bishop; or C. B. Clarke; or . . . We would have to sit at that table, either she or I, decently dressed, having nothing better to do, ready to talk.

. . . But in the evening society had it all its own way. At 7.30 we went upstairs to dress. However cold or foggy it might be, we slipped off our day clothes and stood shivering in front of washing basins. Neck and arms had to be scrubbed, for we had to come into the drawing room at 8 o'clock in evening dress: arms and neck bare. Dress and hair-doing became far more important than pictures and Greek. I would stand in front of George's Chippendale glass trying to make myself not only tidy but presentable. On an allowance of fifty pounds it was difficult, even for the skilful, to be well dressed of an evening. For though a house dress could be made by Jane Bride, at a cost of a pound or two, a party dress cost perhaps fifteen guineas if made by Mrs Young. The house dress therefore might be, as on this particular night, made of a green stuff bought erratically at a furniture shop—Story's—because it was cheaper than dress stuff; also more adventurous. Down I came: in my green evening dress; all the lights were up in the drawing room; and there was George, in his black tie and evening jacket, in the chair by the fire. He fixed on me that extraordinary observant [illegible] gaze with which he always inspected clothes. He looked me up and down as if [I] were a horse turned into the ring. Then the sullen look came over him; a look in which one traced not merely aesthetic disapproval; but something that went deeper; morally, socially, he scented some kind of insurrection; of defiance of social standards. I was condemned from many more points of view than I can analyse as I stood there, conscious of those criticisms; and conscious too of fear, of shame and of despair—"Go and tear it up", he said at last, in that curiously rasping and peevish voice which expressed his serious displeasure at this infringement of a code that meant more to him than he would admit. . . .

Now society exerted its full pressure, about 11 o'clock say, on a June night in 1900. I remember the dazed, elated, frozen feeling: as the lights beat on me, going upstairs; the unreality; the excitement; the paralysis. Can I recover anything further? At the Savoy I remember a dinner before the opera. It was *The Ring* and we were dining in full daylight. George had placed Mrs J. Chamberlain opposite the window, a failure in tact for which he reproached himself afterwards. For she had just passed her prime. I sat next a youth whom I now identify as Eddie Marsh. On that occasion I thought he was Richard Marsh; I vaguely connected him with novel writing. I recover only: "What is your father writing now?" he asked, and then I floundered, struck out wildly this way and that like a beginner on the ice.

At Mrs. Chamberlain's[28] I sat next a chubby official youth. We discussed oratory. "Our host", he said, "is generally supposed to be a good speaker." And then I see myself floundering again—stressing a theory that the crime of merrymaking is worse than theft. Silence falls. I felt myself struggling like a fly in glue. I felt that if one said things one thought, anything beyond the usual patter, glue stuck to one's feet. On the threshold of a ballroom, I remember Geoffrey Young primly telling me: "It is very good of you to come." Had I asserted that I hated dancing? He left me. At Trinity Ball, I remember galloping round the room with—I have forgotten the name. At Lady Sligo's I remember pressing some youth to tell me facts about the Garter. Meanwhile George was proposing to Flora Russell.[29] At the Lyulph Stanleys I remember failing to secure a partner. Elena Rathbone[30] introduced me to a girl. I remember the humiliation of standing, unasked, against a wall. I remember of these parties humiliation—I could not dance; frustration—I could not get young men to talk; and also, for happily that good friend has never deserted me—the scene as a spectacle to be described later. And some moments of elation: some moments of lyrical ecstasy. But the pressure of society in 1900 almost forbade any natural feeling. Perhaps I was too young. Perhaps I was wrongly adjusted. At any rate I never met a man or a woman with whom I struck up any real relationship. All the same there was the excitement of clothes, of lights, of society, in short; and the queerness, the strangeness of being alone, on my own, for a moment, with some complete stranger: he in white waistcoat and gloves, I in white satin and gloves. A more unreal relationship cannot be imagined; but there was a thrill in the unreality. For when I was once more in my own room I would see it small and untidy: I would ride the waves of the party still: I would lie in bed, tossing up and down on the things I had said, heard and done. And next morning I would still be thinking, as I read my Sophocles, of the party.

If that had been all, these parties would have slid off us easily enough. But there was George. To him a party was a very serious matter. We were not merely enjoying ourselves. We were made to feel that every party was an examination, a test: a matter of the greatest importance; it led to success; it led to failure. What did success lead to? The only success he valued— social success. Failure led to the only failure—dowdiness, eccentricity. He held these beliefs implicitly. But he held them confusedly. You could never challenge him directly. "But if I hate parties why should I go to them?" He would wrinkle all those lines piteously. "You're too young to have an opinion. Besides, I love you. I hate going alone. I must have you with me." Here he would snatch Vanessa in his arms. Duty and emotion were indistinguishably mixed. And the ghosts of Stella and Mother presided over these scenes.

Hence these parties became wrangles, became efforts, became often humiliations. Vaguely, he felt that we criticised the whole conception. This angered him. In his anger he upbraided us with selfishness, with narrowness. He complained to his circle of enamoured dowagers. He invoked their help. He lavished clothes, jewels. He acted, in public, the role of the good brother. He acted with success. How could we resist his wishes—how could we cherish other desires? Society in those days was a very competent machine. It was convinced that girls must be changed into married women. It had no doubts, no mercy; no understanding of any other wish; of any other gift. Nothing was taken seriously. . . . How strange it was to think that somewhere, there was a world where people did not go to parties—where they perhaps discussed pictures—books—philosophy— But it was not our world.

The division in our life was curious. Downstairs there was pure convention: upstairs pure intellect. But there was no connection between them. Father's deafness had cut off any ties that he would have had, naturally, with the younger generation of writers. Yet he kept his own attitude perfectly distinct. No one cared less for convention. No one respected intellect more. Thus I would go from the drawing room and George's gossip—"Mrs

William Grenfell asked me to stay . . . And I said, on the whole I thought I couldn't. She was taken by surprise"—to father's study to fetch a [new book]. There I would find him, swinging in his rocking chair, pipe in mouth. Slowly he would realise my presence. Rising, he would go to the shelves, put the book back and very kindly ask me what had I made of it? Perhaps I was reading Johnson. For some time we would talk and then, feeling soothed, stimulated, full of love for this unworldly, very distinguished, lonely man, I would go down to the drawing room again and hear George's patter. There was no connection. . . .

N O T E S

1. Lady Strachey, mother of Lytton, died at the age of eighty-nine, in 1928. In old age she wrote "Some Recollections of a Long Life," which were very short—less than a dozen pages in *Nation and Athenaeum*. This may indicate, as Michael Holroyd has suggested, that by the early 1920s she had forgotten more than she remembered.

2. VW was at work on *Roger Fry: A Biography* (The Hogarth Press, London, 1940).

3. The gardener and daily help, respectively, at Monks House, the country home of the Woolfs in Rodmell, Sussex, from 1919.

4. In marrying Jane Catherine Venn, James Stephen had allied himself with the very heart of the Clapham Sect.

5. Julian Morrell was the daughter of Ottoline and Philip Morrell; Garsington Manor was their house in Oxfordshire.

6. Gerald Duckworth was Virginia's half-brother, twelve years her senior; George and Stella were the two other children of Julia's marriage to Herbert Duckworth.

7. Mrs Swanwick was the only daughter of Oswald and Eleanor Sickert. In her autobiography, *I Have Been Young* (London, 1935), she recalls having known Leslie Stephen at St Ives: "We watched with delight his naked babies running about the beach or being towed into the sea between his legs, and their beautiful mother."

8. *To the Lighthouse* was begun in 1925 and published in 1927 when VW was forty-five.

9. 52 Tavistock Square was the London home of the Woolfs from 1924 to 1939.

10. Laura was the daughter of Leslie Stephen's first marriage, to Harriet Marian Thackeray.

11. John Addington Symonds, man of letters, was the father of Katherine,

who married the artist Charles Furse, and Margaret (Madge), who married William Wyamar Vaughan.

12. The "Hyde Park Gate News" appeared weekly, as far as is known, from 9 February 1891 until April 1895. The paper was at first the joint venture of Virginia and Thoby but gradually it became almost entirely Virginia's responsibility. See Quentin Bell, *Virginia Woolf: A Biography* (The Hogarth Press; London, 1972), I, pp. 28–32.

13. Sophie Farrell was the Stephens' cook at 22 Hyde Park Gate and at 46 Gordon Square, Bloomsbury. After Vanessa's marriage she went with Virginia and Adrian to 29 Fitzroy Square and later to George Duckworth.

14. James Kenneth Stephen, second son of James Fitzjames Stephen, brother of Leslie.

15. Aunt Mary (née Jackson), Julia's elder sister, who married Herbert Fisher and had seven sons and four daughters.

16. Great Western Railway.

17. Doubtful reading.

18. The marginal note in the ms reads: "to make me wince; ground between grindstones".

19. Lady Katherine Thynne, who married Lord Cromer.

20. "Bryce", a doubtful reading.

21. There is no such reference in the Monks House Papers.

22. Frederic William Maitland wrote the authorized "Life" of Leslie Stephen. He married Florence Fisher, one of Aunt Mary's daughters.

23. "Thus to Fred Maitland or to Herbert Fisher he was entirely without vanity, without conceit" was deleted by VW.

24. Doubtful reading.

25. In the margin is written "Clara Pater", the sister of Walter Pater, who taught Virginia Greek and Latin before Miss Case. Miss Case, in addition to being a severe and thorough teacher, became a lifelong friend of Virginia's.

26. Julia Stephen's cousin, son of Sarah and Thoby Prinsep.

27. Walter William Ouless, R.A. (1848–1933).

28. VW has written "Mrs C^n".

29. Flora Russell was a niece of the Duke of Bedford. The engagement was brief. She died unmarried.

30. Elena Rathbone, who later married Bruce Richmond, editor of the *Times Literary Supplement*.

Novels

F R O M

Mrs. Dalloway

Although Virginia Woolf's first two novels, The Voyage Out
(1915) and Night and Day *(1919), contain some of the poetic
techniques she would later come to rely upon, they are in themselves conventional works. Her third book,* Jacob's Room, *was
her first full-length experimental novel, the seeds of which can
be found in the technical strategies she developed in her early
stories "The Mark on the Wall" and "Kew Gardens."*

Mrs. Dalloway, *Virginia Woolf's fourth novel, was published
in 1925, when she was in her forty-third year. In form and style,
the novel represents a radical advance in the art of storytelling.
Fictional events are no longer given in the traditional manner
of cause and effect. The focus now is on the internal atmosphere
of her characters, whose lives are dramatized for the reader
through a series of interior monologues of their remembered
past; and the novel moves forward through successive moments
of condensed experience. The mechanical ticking of the clock
no longer measures external events in these pages: here it is
mental time, psychological time, that governs the story's fictional
progress. So that the entire novel covers, simultaneously, the waking hours of one day in the life of Clarissa Dalloway as well as
the last day in the life of her insane "double," Septimus Warren
Smith.*

Two separate worlds are evoked in the novel: one of them is Clarissa Dalloway's glittering domain. Part of this world is occupied by a Doris Kilman, tutor to Clarissa's daughter, Elizabeth. Kilman, the religious fanatic, is bitter, frustrated, desperately in need of Elizabeth's affection; and the portrait we are given of this pathetic woman is a cruel one.

The other world belongs to Septimus Warren Smith. In this grim republic of insanity and suicide, Virginia Woolf paints the sinister character of Sir William Bradshaw, one of London's leading Harley Street psychiatrists. The portrayal of this so-called authority on diseases of the mind is a powerful indictment of that small population of specialists who were themselves too deficient in sympathy to deal with the suffering of those who sought their help.

LOVE BETWEEN MAN AND WOMAN WAS REPULSIVE TO Shakespeare. The business of copulation was filth to him before the end. But, Rezia said, she must have children. They had been married five years.

They went to the Tower together; to the Victoria and Albert Museum; stood in the crowd to see the King open Parliament. And there were the shops—hat shops, dress shops, shops with leather bags in the window, where she would stand staring. But she must have a boy.

She must have a son like Septimus, she said. But nobody could be like Septimus; so gentle; so serious; so clever. Could she not read Shakespeare too? Was Shakespeare a difficult author? she asked.

One cannot bring children into a world like this. One cannot perpetuate suffering, or increase the breed of these lustful animals, who have no lasting emotions, but only whims and vanities, eddying them now this way, now that.

He watched her snip, shape, as one watches a bird hop, flit in the grass, without daring to move a finger. For the truth is (let her ignore it) that human beings have neither kindness, nor faith, nor charity beyond what serves to increase the pleasure of the moment. They hunt in packs. Their packs scour the desert and vanish screaming into the wilderness. They desert the fallen. They are plastered over with grimaces. There was Brewer at the office, with his waxed moustache, coral tie-pin, white slip, and pleasurable emotions—all coldness and clamminess within,—his geraniums ruined in the War—his cook's nerves destroyed; or Amelia What'shername, handing round cups of tea punctually at five—a leering, sneering obscene little harpy; and the Toms and Berties in their starched shirt fronts oozing thick drops of vice. They never saw him drawing pictures of them naked at their antics in his notebook. In the street, vans roared past him; brutality blared out on placards; men were trapped in mines; women burnt alive; and once a maimed file of lunatics being exercised or displayed for the diversion of the populace (who laughed aloud), ambled and nodded and grinned past him, in the Tottenham Court Road, each half apologetically, yet triumphantly, inflicting his hopeless woe. And would *he* go mad?

At tea Rezia told him that Mrs. Filmer's daughter was expecting a baby. *She* could not grow old and have no children! She was very lonely, she was very unhappy! She cried for the first time since they were married. Far away he heard her sobbing; he heard it accurately, he noticed it distinctly; he compared it to a piston thumping. But he felt nothing.

His wife was crying, and he felt nothing; only each time she sobbed in this profound, this silent, this hopeless way, he descended another step into the pit.

At last, with a melodramatic gesture which he assumed mechanically and with complete consciousness of its insincerity, he dropped his head on his hands. Now he had surrendered; now other people must help him. People must be sent for. He gave in.

Nothing could rouse him. Rezia put him to bed. She sent for a doctor—Mrs. Filmer's Dr. Holmes. Dr. Holmes examined him. There was nothing whatever the matter, said Dr. Holmes. Oh, what a relief! What a kind man, what a good man! thought

Rezia. When he felt like that he went to the Music Hall, said Dr. Holmes. He took a day off with his wife and played golf. Why not try two tabloids of bromide dissolved in a glass of water at bedtime? These old Bloomsbury houses, said Dr. Holmes, tapping the wall, are often full of very fine panelling, which the landlords have the folly to paper over. Only the other day, visiting a patient, Sir Somebody Something in Bedford Square—

So there was no excuse; nothing whatever the matter, except the sin for which human nature had condemned him to death; that he did not feel. He had not cared when Evans was killed; that was worst; but all the other crimes raised their heads and shook their fingers and jeered and sneered over the rail of the bed in the early hours of the morning at the prostrate body which lay realising its degradation; how he had married his wife without loving her; had lied to her; seduced her; outraged Miss Isabel Pole, and was so pocked and marked with vice that women shuddered when they saw him in the street. The verdict of human nature on such a wretch was death.

Dr. Holmes came again. Large, fresh coloured, handsome, flicking his boots, looking in the glass, he brushed it all aside— headaches, sleeplessness, fears, dreams—nerve symptoms and nothing more, he said. If Dr. Holmes found himself even half a pound below eleven stone six, he asked his wife for another plate of porridge at breakfast. (Rezia would learn to cook porridge.) But, he continued, health is largely a matter in our own control. Throw yourself into outside interests; take up some hobby. He opened Shakespeare—*Antony and Cleopatra*; pushed Shakespeare aside. Some hobby, said Dr. Holmes, for did he not owe his own excellent health (and he worked as hard as any man in London) to the fact that he could always switch off from his patients on to old furniture? And what a very pretty comb, if he might say so, Mrs. Warren Smith was wearing!

When the damned fool came again, Septimus refused to see him. Did he indeed? said Dr. Holmes, smiling agreeably. Really he had to give that charming little lady, Mrs. Smith, a friendly push before he could get past her into her husband's bedroom.

"So you're in a funk," he said agreeably, sitting down by his patient's side. He had actually talked of killing himself to his wife, quite a girl, a foreigner, wasn't she? Didn't that give her a very odd idea of English husbands? Didn't one owe perhaps a duty to one's wife? Wouldn't it be better to do something instead of lying in bed? For he had had forty years' experience behind him; and Septimus could take Dr. Holmes's word for it—there was nothing whatever the matter with him. And next time Dr. Holmes came he hoped to find Smith out of bed and not making that charming little lady his wife anxious about him.

Human nature, in short, was on him—the repulsive brute, with the blood-red nostrils. Holmes was on him. Dr. Holmes came quite regularly every day. Once you stumble, Septimus wrote on the back of a postcard, human nature is on you. Holmes is on you. Their only chance was to escape, without letting Holmes know; to Italy—anywhere, anywhere, away from Dr. Holmes.

But Rezia could not understand him. Dr. Holmes was such a kind man. He was so interested in Septimus. He only wanted to help them, he said. He had four little children and he had asked her to tea, she told Septimus.

So he was deserted. The whole world was clamouring: Kill yourself, kill yourself, for our sakes. But why should he kill himself for their sakes? Food was pleasant; the sun hot; and this killing oneself, how does one set about it, with a table knife, uglily, with floods of blood,—by sucking a gaspipe? He was too weak; he could scarcely raise his hand. Besides, now that he was quite alone, condemned, deserted, as those who are about to die are alone, there was a luxury in it, an isolation full of sublimity; a freedom which the attached can never know. Holmes had won of course; the brute with the red nostrils had won. But even Holmes himself could not touch this last relic straying on the edge of the world, this outcast, who gazed back at the inhabited regions, who lay, like a drowned sailor, on the shore of the world. . . .

It was precisely twelve o'clock; twelve by Big Ben; whose stroke was wafted over the northern part of London; blent with that of other clocks, mixed in a thin ethereal way with the clouds and wisps of smoke, and died up there among the seagulls—twelve o'clock struck as Clarissa Dalloway laid her green dress on her bed, and the Warren Smiths walked down Harley Street. Twelve was the hour of their appointment. Probably, Rezia thought, that was Sir William Bradshaw's house with the grey motor car in front of it. The leaden circles dissolved in the air.

Indeed it was—Sir William Bradshaw's motor car; low, powerful, grey with plain initials interlocked on the panel, as if the pomps of heraldry were incongruous, this man being the ghostly helper, the priest of science; and, as the motor car was grey, so to match its sober suavity, grey furs, silver grey rugs were heaped in it, to keep her ladyship warm while she waited. For often Sir William would travel sixty miles or more down into the country to visit the rich, the afflicted, who could afford the very large fee which Sir William very properly charged for his advice. Her ladyship waited with the rugs about her knees an hour or more, leaning back, thinking sometimes of the patient, sometimes, excusably, of the wall of gold, mounting minute by minute while she waited; the wall of gold that was mounting between them and all shifts and anxieties (she had borne them bravely; they had had their struggles) until she felt wedged on a calm ocean, where only spice winds blow; respected, admired, envied, with scarcely anything left to wish for, though she regretted her stoutness; large dinner-parties every Thursday night to the profession; an occasional bazaar to be opened; Royalty greeted; too little time, alas, with her husband, whose work grew and grew; a boy doing well at Eton; she would have liked a daughter too; interests she had, however, in plenty; child welfare; the after-care of the epileptic, and photography, so that if there was a church building, or a church decaying, she bribed the sexton, got the key and took photographs, which were scarcely to be distinguished from the work of professionals, while she waited.

Sir William himself was no longer young. He had worked very hard; he had won his position by sheer ability (being the son of a shopkeeper); loved his profession; made a fine figurehead at ceremonies and spoke well—all of which had by the time he was knighted given him a heavy look, a weary look (the stream of patients being so incessant, the responsibilities and privileges of his profession so onerous), which weariness, together with his grey hairs, increased the extraordinary distinction of his presence and gave him the reputation (of the utmost importance in dealing with nerve cases) not merely of lightning skill, and almost infallible accuracy in diagnosis but of sympathy; tact; understanding of the human soul. He could see the first moment they came into the room (the Warren Smiths they were called); he was certain directly he saw the man; it was a case of extreme gravity. It was a case of complete breakdown—complete physical and nervous breakdown, with every symptom in an advanced stage, he ascertained in two or three minutes (writing answers to questions, murmured discreetly, on a pink card).

How long had Dr. Holmes been attending him?

Six weeks.

Prescribed a little bromide? Said there was nothing the matter? Ah yes (those general practitioners! thought Sir William. It took half his time to undo their blunders. Some were irreparable).

"You served with great distinction in the War?"

The patient repeated the word "war" interrogatively.

He was attaching meanings to words of a symbolical kind. A serious symptom, to be noted on the card.

"The War?" the patient asked. The European War—that little shindy of schoolboys with gunpowder? Had he served with distinction? He really forgot. In the War itself he had failed.

"Yes, he served with the greatest distinction," Rezia assured the doctor; "he was promoted."

"And they have the very highest opinion of you at your office?" Sir William murmured, glancing at Mr. Brewer's very generously worded letter. "So that you have nothing to worry you, no financial anxiety, nothing?"

He had committed an appalling crime and been condemned to death by human nature.

"I have—I have," he began, "committed a crime—"

"He has done nothing wrong whatever," Rezia assured the doctor. If Mr. Smith would wait, said Sir William, he would speak to Mrs. Smith in the next room. Her husband was very seriously ill, Sir William said. Did he threaten to kill himself?

Oh, he did, she cried. But he did not mean it, she said. Of course not. It was merely a question of rest, said Sir William; of rest, rest, rest; a long rest in bed. There was a delightful home down in the country where her husband would be perfectly looked after. Away from her? she asked. Unfortunately, yes; the people we care for most are not good for us when we are ill. But he was not mad, was he? Sir William said he never spoke of "madness"; he called it not having a sense of proportion. But her husband did not like doctors. He would refuse to go there. Shortly and kindly Sir William explained to her the state of the case. He had threatened to kill himself. There was no alternative. It was a question of law. He would lie in bed in a beautiful house in the country. The nurses were admirable. Sir William would visit him once a week. If Mrs. Warren Smith was quite sure she had no more questions to ask—he never hurried his patients— they would return to her husband. She had nothing more to ask—not of Sir William.

So they returned to the most exalted of mankind; the criminal who faced his judges; the victim exposed on the heights; the fugitive; the drowned sailor; the poet of the immortal ode; the Lord who had gone from life to death; to Septimus Warren Smith, who sat in the arm-chair under the skylight staring at a photograph of Lady Bradshaw in Court dress, muttering messages about beauty.

"We have had our little talk," said Sir William.

"He says you are very, very ill," Rezia cried.

"We have been arranging that you should go into a home," said Sir William.

"One of Holmes's homes?" sneered Septimus.

The fellow made a distasteful impression. For there was in Sir William, whose father had been a tradesman, a natural respect for breeding and clothing, which shabbiness nettled; again, more profoundly, there was in Sir William, who had never had time for reading, a grudge, deeply buried, against cultivated people who came into his room and intimated that doctors, whose profession is a constant strain upon all the highest faculties, are not educated men.

"One of *my* homes, Mr. Warren Smith," he said, "where we will teach you to rest."

And there was just one thing more.

He was quite certain that when Mr. Warren Smith was well he was the last man in the world to frighten his wife. But he had talked of killing himself.

"We all have our moments of depression," said Sir William.

Once you fall, Septimus repeated to himself, human nature is on you. Holmes and Bradshaw are on you. They scour the desert. They fly screaming into the wilderness. The rack and the thumbscrew are applied. Human nature is remorseless.

"Impulses came upon him sometimes?" Sir William asked, with his pencil on a pink card.

That was his own affair, said Septimus.

"Nobody lives for himself alone," said Sir William, glancing at the photograph of his wife in Court dress.

"And you have a brilliant career before you," said Sir William. There was Mr. Brewer's letter on the table. "An exceptionally brilliant career."

But if he confessed? If he communicated? Would they let him off then, his torturers?

"I—I—" he stammered.

But what was his crime? He could not remember it.

"Yes?" Sir William encouraged him. (But it was growing late.)

Love, trees, there is no crime—what was his message? He could not remember it.

"I—I—" Septimus stammered.

"Try to think as little about yourself as possible," said Sir William kindly. Really, he was not fit to be about.

Was there anything else they wished to ask him? Sir William

would make all arrangements (he murmured to Rezia) and he would let her know between five and six that evening he murmured.

"Trust everything to me," he said, and dismissed them.

Never, never had Rezia felt such agony in her life! She had asked for help and been deserted! He had failed them! Sir William Bradshaw was not a nice man.

The upkeep of that motor car alone must cost him quite a lot, said Septimus, when they got out into the street.

She clung to his arm. They had been deserted.

But what more did she want?

To his patients he gave three-quarters of an hour; and if in this exacting science which has to do with what, after all, we know nothing about—the nervous system, the human brain—a doctor loses his sense of proportion, as a doctor he fails. Health we must have; and health is proportion; so that when a man comes into your room and says he is Christ (a common delusion), and has a message, as they mostly have, and threatens, as they often do, to kill himself, you invoke proportion; order rest in bed; rest in solitude; silence and rest; rest without friends, without books, without messages; six months' rest; until a man who went in weighing seven stone six comes out weighing twelve.

Proportion, divine proportion, Sir William's goddess, was acquired by Sir William walking hospitals, catching salmon, begetting one son in Harley Street by Lady Bradshaw, who caught salmon herself and took photographs scarcely to be distinguished from the work of professionals. Worshipping proportion, Sir William not only prospered himself but made England prosper, secluded her lunatics, forbade childbirth, penalised despair, made it impossible for the unfit to propagate their views until they, too, shared his sense of proportion—his, if they were men, Lady Bradshaw's if they were women (she embroidered, knitted, spent four nights out of seven at home with her son), so that not only did his colleagues respect him, his subordinates fear him, but the friends and relations of his patients felt for him the keenest gratitude for insisting that these prophetic Christs and

Christesses, who prophesied the end of the world, or the advent of God, should drink milk in bed, as Sir William ordered; Sir William with his thirty years' experience of these kinds of cases, and his infallible instinct, this is madness, this sense; in fact, his sense of proportion.

But Proportion has a sister, less smiling, more formidable, a Goddess even now engaged—in the heat and sands of India, the mud and swamp of Africa, the purlieus of London, wherever in short the climate or the devil tempts men to fall from the true belief which is her own—is even now engaged in dashing down shrines, smashing idols, and setting up in their place her own stern countenance. Conversion is her name and she feasts on the wills of the weakly, loving to impress, to impose, adoring her own features stamped on the face of the populace. At Hyde Park Corner on a tub she stands preaching; shrouds herself in white and walks penitentially disguised as brotherly love through factories and parliaments; offers help, but desires power; smites out of her way roughly the dissentient, or dissatisfied; bestows her blessing on those who, looking upward, catch submissively from her eyes the light of their own. This lady too (Rezia Warren Smith divined it) had her dwelling in Sir William's heart, though concealed, as she mostly is, under some plausible disguise; some venerable name; love, duty, self sacrifice. How he would work— how toil to raise funds, propagate reforms, initiate institutions! But conversion, fastidious Goddess, loves blood better than brick, and feasts most subtly on the human will. For example, Lady Bradshaw. Fifteen years ago she had gone under. It was nothing you could put your finger on; there had been no scene, no snap; only the slow sinking, water-logged, of her will into his. Sweet was her smile, swift her submission; dinner in Harley Street, numbering eight or nine courses, feeding ten or fifteen guests of the professional classes, was smooth and urbane. Only as the evening wore on a very slight dulness, or uneasiness perhaps, a nervous twitch, fumble, stumble and confusion indicated, what it was really painful to believe—that the poor lady lied. Once, long ago, she had caught salmon freely: now, quick to minister to the craving which lit her husband's eye so oilily for dominion, for power, she cramped, squeezed, pared, pruned, drew back, peeped through; so that without knowing precisely what made the evening disagreeable, and caused this pressure on the top of the head (which might well be imputed to the professional conversation, or the fatigue of a great doctor whose life, Lady Bradshaw said, "is not his own but his patients'") disagreeable it was: so that guests, when the clock struck ten, breathed in the air of Harley Street even with rapture; which relief, however, was denied to his patients.

There in the grey room, with the pictures on the wall, and the valuable furniture, under the ground glass skylight, they learnt the extent of their transgressions; huddled up in arm-chairs, they watched him go through, for their benefit, a curious exercise with the arms, which he shot out, brought sharply back to his hip, to prove (if the patient was obstinate) that Sir William was master of his own actions, which the patient was not. There some weakly broke down; sobbed, submitted; others, inspired by Heaven knows what intemperate madness, called Sir William to his face a damnable humbug; questioned, even more impiously, life itself. Why live? they demanded. Sir William replied that life was good. Certainly Lady Bradshaw in ostrich feathers hung over the mantelpiece, and as for his income it was quite twelve thousand a year. But to us, they protested, life has given no such bounty. He acquiesced. They lacked a sense of proportion. And perhaps, after all, there is no God? He shrugged his shoulders. In short, this living or not living is an affair of our own? But there they were mistaken. Sir William had a friend in Surrey where they taught, what Sir William frankly admitted was a difficult art—a sense of proportion. There were, moreover, family affection; honour; courage; and a brilliant career. All of these had in Sir William a resolute champion. If they failed him, he had to support police and the good of society, which, he remarked very quietly, would take care, down in Surrey, that these unsocial impulses, bred more than anything by the lack of good blood, were held in control. And then stole out from her hiding-place and mounted her throne that Goddess whose lust is to override opposition, to stamp indelibly in the sanctuaries of others the image of herself. Naked, defenceless, the exhausted, the friendless received the impress of Sir William's will. He swooped; he devoured. He shut people up. It was this combination of decision and humanity that endeared Sir William so greatly to the relations of his victims.

But Rezia Warren Smith cried, walking down Harley Street, that she did not like that man. . . .

She stood quite still and looked at her mother; but the door was ajar, and outside the door was Miss Kilman, as Clarissa knew; Miss Kilman in her mackintosh, listening to whatever they said.

Yes, Miss Kilman stood on the landing, and wore a mackintosh; but had her reasons. First, it was cheap; second, she was over forty; and did not, after all, dress to please. She was poor, moreover; degradingly poor. Otherwise she would not be taking jobs from people like the Dalloways; from rich people, who liked to be kind, Mr. Dalloway, to do him justice, had been kind. But Mrs. Dalloway had not. She had been merely condescending. She came from the most worthless of all classes—the rich, with a smattering of culture. They had expensive things everywhere; pictures, carpets, lots of servants. She considered that she had a perfect right to anything that the Dalloways did for her.

She had been cheated. Yes, the word was no exaggeration, for surely a girl has a right to some kind of happiness? And she had never been happy, what with being so clumsy and so poor. And then, just as she might have had a chance at Miss Dolby's school, the war came; and she had never been able to tell lies. Miss Dolby thought she would be happier with people who shared her views about the Germans. She had had to go. It was true that the family was of German origin; spelt the name Kiehlman in the eighteenth century; but her brother had been killed. They turned her out because she would not pretend that the Germans were all villains—when she had German friends, when the only happy days of her life had been spent in Germany! And after all, she could read history. She had had to take whatever she could get. Mr. Dalloway had come across her working for the Friends. He had allowed her (and that was really generous of him) to teach his daughter history. Also she did a little Extension lecturing and so on. Then Our Lord had come to her (and here she always bowed her head). She had seen the light two years and three months ago. Now she did not envy women like Clarissa Dalloway; she pitied them.

She pitied and despised them from the bottom of her heart, as she stood on the soft carpet, looking at the old engraving of a little girl with a muff. With all this luxury going on, what hope was there for a better state of things? Instead of lying on a sofa—"My mother is resting," Elizabeth had said—she should have been in a factory; behind a counter; Mrs. Dalloway and all the other fine ladies!

Bitter and burning, Miss Kilman had turned into a church two years three months ago. She had heard the Rev. Edward Whittaker preach; the boys sing; had seen the solemn lights descend, and whether it was the music, or the voices (she herself when alone in the evening found comfort in a violin; but the sound was excruciating; she had no ear), the hot and turbulent feelings which boiled and surged in her had been assuaged as she sat there, and she had wept copiously, and gone to call on Mr. Whittaker at his private house in Kensington. It was the hand of God, he said. The Lord had shown her the way. So now, whenever the hot and painful feelings boiled within her, this hatred of Mrs. Dalloway, this grudge against the world, she thought of God. She thought of Mr. Whittaker. Rage was succeeded by calm. A sweet savour filled her veins, her lips parted, and, standing formidable upon the landing in her mackintosh, she looked with steady and sinister serenity at Mrs. Dalloway, who came out with her daughter.

Elizabeth said she had forgotten her gloves. That was because Miss Kilman and her mother hated each other. She could not bear to see them together. She ran upstairs to find her gloves.

But Miss Kilman did not hate Mrs. Dalloway. Turning her

large gooseberry-coloured eyes upon Clarissa, observing her small pink face, her delicate body, her air of freshness and fashion, Miss Kilman felt, Fool! Simpleton! You who have known neither sorrow nor pleasure; who have trifled your life away! And there rose in her an overmastering desire to overcome her; to unmask her. If she could have felled her it would have eased her. But it was not the body; it was the soul and its mockery that she wished to subdue; make feel her mastery. If only she could make her weep; could ruin her; humiliate her; bring her to her knees crying, You are right! But this was God's will, not Miss Kilman's. It was to be a religious victory. So she glared; so she glowered.

Clarissa was really shocked. This a Christian—this woman! This woman had taken her daughter from her! She in touch with invisible presences! Heavy, ugly, commonplace, without kindness or grace, she know the meaning of life!

"You are taking Elizabeth to the Stores?" Mrs. Dalloway said.

Miss Kilman said she was. They stood there. Miss Kilman was not going to make herself agreeable. She had always earned her living. Her knowledge of modern history was thorough in the extreme. She did out of her meagre income set aside so much for causes she believed in; whereas this woman did nothing, believed nothing; brought up her daughter—but here was Elizabeth, rather out of breath, the beautiful girl.

So they were going to the Stores. Odd it was, as Miss Kilman stood there (and stand she did, with the power and taciturnity of some prehistoric monster armoured for primeval warfare), how, second by second, the idea of her diminished, how hatred (which was for ideas, not people) crumbled, how she lost her malignity, her size, became second by second merely Miss Kilman, in a mackintosh, whom Heaven knows Clarissa would have liked to help.

At this dwindling of the monster, Clarissa laughed. Saying good-bye, she laughed.

Off they went together, Miss Kilman and Elizabeth, downstairs.

With a sudden impulse, with a violent anguish, for this woman was taking her daughter from her, Clarissa leant over the bannisters and cried out, "Remember the party! Remember our party tonight!"

But Elizabeth had already opened the front door; there was a van passing; she did not answer.

Love and religion! thought Clarissa, going back into the drawing-room, tingling all over. How detestable, how detestable they are! For now that the body of Miss Kilman was not before her, it overwhelmed her—the idea. The cruelest things in the world, she thought, seeing them clumsy, hot, domineering, hypocritical, eavesdropping, jealous, infinitely cruel and unscrupulous, dressed in a mackintosh coat, on the landing; love and religion. . . .

Volubly, troublously, the late clock sounded, coming in on the wake of Big Ben, with its lap full of trifles. Beaten up, broken up by the assault of carriages, the brutality of vans, the eager advance of myriads of angular men, of flaunting women, the domes and spires of offices and hospitals, the last relics of this lap full of odds and ends seemed to break, like the spray of an exhausted wave, upon the body of Miss Kilman standing still in the street for a moment to mutter "It is the flesh."

It was the flesh that she must control. Clarissa Dalloway had insulted her. That she expected. But she had not triumphed; she had not mastered the flesh. Ugly, clumsy, Clarissa Dalloway had laughed at her for being that; and had revived the fleshly desires, for she minded looking as she did beside Clarissa. Nor could she talk as she did. But why wish to resemble her? Why? She despised Mrs. Dalloway from the bottom of her heart. She was not serious. She was not good. Her life was a tissue of vanity and deceit. Yet Doris Kilman had been overcome. She had, as a matter of fact, very nearly burst into tears when Clarissa Dalloway laughed at her. "It is the flesh, it is the flesh," she muttered (it being her habit to talk aloud) trying to subdue this turbulent and painful feeling as she walked down Victoria Street. She prayed to God. She could not help being ugly; she could not afford to buy pretty clothes. Clarissa Dalloway had laughed—but she would concentrate her mind upon something else until she had reached the pillar-box. At any rate she had got Elizabeth. But she would think of something else; she would think of Russia; until she reached the pillar-box.

How nice it must be, she said, in the country, struggling, as Mr. Whittaker had told her, with that violent grudge against the world which had scorned her, sneered at her, cast her off, beginning with this indignity—the infliction of her unlovable body which people could not bear to see. Do her hair as she might, her forehead remained like an egg, bald, white. No clothes suited her. She might buy anything. And for a woman, of course, that meant never meeting the opposite sex. Never would she come first with any one. Sometimes lately it had seemed to her that, except for Elizabeth, her food was all that she lived for; her comforts; her dinner, her tea; her hot-water bottle at night. But one must fight; vanquish; have faith in God. Mr. Whittaker had said she was there for a purpose. But no one knew the agony! He said, pointing to the crucifix, that God knew. But why should she have to suffer when other women, like Clarissa Dalloway, escaped? Knowledge comes through suffering, said Mr. Whittaker.

She had passed the pillar-box, and Elizabeth had turned into the cool brown tobacco department of the Army and Navy Stores while she was still muttering to herself what Mr. Whittaker had said about knowledge coming through suffering and the flesh. "The flesh," she muttered.

What department did she want? Elizabeth interrupted her.

"Petticoats," she said abruptly, and stalked straight on to the lift.

Up they went. Elizabeth guided her this way and that; guided her in her abstraction as if she had been a great child, an unwieldy battleship. There were the petticoats, brown, decorous, striped, frivolous, solid, flimsy; and she chose, in her abstraction, portentously, and the girl serving thought her mad.

Elizabeth rather wondered, as they did up the parcel, what

Miss Kilman was thinking. They must have their tea, said Miss Kilman, rousing, collecting herself. They had their tea.

Elizabeth rather wondered whether Miss Kilman could be hungry. It was her way of eating, eating with intensity, then looking, again and again, at a plate of sugared cakes on the table next them; then, when a lady and a child sat down and the child took the cake, could Miss Kilman really mind it? Yes, Miss Kilman did mind it. She had wanted that cake—the pink one. The pleasure of eating was almost the only pure pleasure left her, and then to be baffled even in that!

When people are happy, they have a reserve, she had told Elizabeth, upon which to draw, whereas she was like a wheel without a tyre (she was fond of such metaphors), jolted by every pebble, so she would say staying on after the lesson standing by the fire-place with her bag of books, her "satchel," she called it, on a Tuesday morning, after the lesson was over. And she talked too about the war. After all, there were people who did not think the English invariably right. There were books. There were meetings. There were other points of view. Would Elizabeth like to come with her to listen to So-and-so (a most extraordinary looking old man)? Then Miss Kilman took her to some church in Kensington and they had tea with a clergyman. She had lent her books. Law, medicine, politics, all professions are open to women of your generation, said Miss Kilman. But for herself, her career was absolutely ruined and was it her fault? Good gracious, said Elizabeth, no.

And her mother would come calling to say that a hamper had come from Bourton and would Miss Kilman like some flowers? To Miss Kilman she was always very, very nice, but Miss Kilman squashed the flowers all in a bunch, and hadn't any small talk, and what interested Miss Kilman bored her mother, and Miss Kilman and she were terrible together; and Miss Kilman swelled and looked very plain. But then Miss Kilman was frightfully clever. Elizabeth had never thought about the poor. They lived with everything they wanted,—her mother had breakfast in bed every day; Lucy carried it up; and she liked old women because they were Duchesses, and being descended from some Lord. But Miss Kilman said (one of those Tuesday mornings when the lesson was over), "My grandfather kept an oil and colour shop in Kensington." Miss Kilman made one feel so small.

Miss Kilman took another cup of tea. Elizabeth, with her oriental bearing, her inscrutable mystery, sat perfectly upright; no, she did not want anything more. She looked for her gloves— her white gloves. They were under the table. Ah, but she must not go! Miss Kilman could not let her go! this youth, that was so beautiful, this girl, whom she genuinely loved! Her large hand opened and shut on the table.

But perhaps it was a little flat somehow, Elizabeth felt. And really she would like to go.

But said Miss Kilman, "I've not quite finished yet."

Of course, then, Elizabeth would wait. But it was rather stuffy in here.

"Are you going to the party to-night?" Miss Kilman said. Elizabeth supposed she was going; her mother wanted her to go. She must not let parties absorb her, Miss Kilman said, fingering the last two inches of a chocolate éclair.

She did not much like parties, Elizabeth said. Miss Kilman opened her mouth, slightly projected her chin, and swallowed down the last inches of the chocolate éclair, then wiped her fingers, and washed the tea round in her cup.

She was about to split asunder, she felt. The agony was so terrific. If she could grasp her, if she could clasp her, if she could make her hers absolutely and forever and then die; that was all she wanted. But to sit here, unable to think of anything to say; to see Elizabeth turning against her; to be felt repulsive even by her—it was too much; she could not stand it. The thick fingers curled inwards.

"I never go to parties," said Miss Kilman. . . .

To the Lighthouse

TIME PASSES

To the Lighthouse, Virginia Woolf *said in her diary in May
1925, "is going to be fairly short: to have father's character done
complete in it: & mothers; & St Ives; & childhood; & all the
usual things I try to put in—life, death &c. But the centre is
father's character. . . ." This consciously autobiographical novel,
published in May 1927, gave its author the full play of her creative powers, and is considered by many critics today to be her
crowning achievement as a novelist. The fictional version of the
story centers on the Ramsay family on summer holiday in the
Hebrides. Although many artistic liberties have been taken with
historical detail and with the characters' life models, we know
that factually the novel's setting was St. Ives in Cornwall and that
Mr. and Mrs. Ramsay were drawn from Leslie and Julia Stephen.*

*The first and longest section of the novel, "The Window,"
describes the day on which James, aged six, is promised a trip
to the lighthouse—a promise that remains unfulfilled until the
family, or what remains of it, return after an absence of ten
years, in the third and final section, called "The Lighthouse,"
when James is sixteen years old. These two sections are separated by the lyrical interlude called "Time Passes."*

*Virginia Woolf has also taken some liberty with the novel's
time scheme. The first section, historically, took place on a sum-*

mer's day in 1894 or earlier—that is, prior to Julia Stephen's death on May 5, 1895; and the last section, in fact, occurred in August of 1905, when the four Stephens returned to the Cornwall and St. Ives of their childhood. In reality, Stella Duckworth (the Stephen children's half-sister) died in July 1897, Leslie Stephen in February 1904, and Thoby in November 1906. In the fictional version of "Time Passes," we are given the death of Mrs. Ramsay (Julia Stephen), Prue (Stella Duckworth), and Andrew (Thoby Stephen). Virginia Woolf has kept her father, Leslie Stephen (Mr. Ramsay), alive for the novel's third section, "The Lighthouse."

The "Time Passes" interlude printed here serves to bridge the fading hours of the first section to the early-morning hours of the third. Aesthetically, Virginia Woolf posed a very difficult problem for herself in attempting—and succeeding—to translate into highly poetic language the passage of time, with all its wanton destructiveness and harsh indifference. No chapter in English or American prose fiction has yet surpassed this middle section in lyrical force or resonance.

I

"WELL, WE MUST WAIT FOR THE FUTURE TO SHOW," said Mr. Bankes, coming in from the terrace.

"It's almost too dark to see," said Andrew, coming up from the beach.

"One can hardly tell which is the sea and which is the land," said Prue.

"Do we leave that light burning?" said Lily as they took their coats off indoors.

"No," said Prue, "not if every one's in."

"Andrew," she called back, "just put out the light in the hall."

One by one the lamps were all extinguished, except that Mr.

Carmichael, who liked to lie awake a little reading Virgil, kept his candle burning rather longer than the rest.

I I

So with the lamps all put out, the moon sunk, and a thin rain drumming on the roof a downpouring of immense darkness began. Nothing, it seemed, could survive the flood, the profusion of darkness which, creeping in at keyholes and crevices, stole round window blinds, came into bedrooms, swallowed up here a jug and basin, there a bowl of red and yellow dahlias, there the sharp edges and firm bulk of a chest of drawers. Not only was furniture confounded; there was scarcely anything left of body or mind by which one could say, "This is he" or "This is she." Sometimes a hand was raised as if to clutch something or ward off something, or somebody groaned, or somebody laughed aloud as if sharing a joke with nothingness.

Nothing stirred in the drawing-room or in the dining-room or on the staircase. Only through the rusty hinges and swollen sea-moistened woodwork certain airs, detached from the body of the wind (the house was ramshackle after all) crept round corners and ventured indoors. Almost one might imagine them, as they entered the drawing-room questioning and wondering, toying with the flap of hanging wall-paper, asking, would it hang much longer, when would it fall? Then smoothly brushing the walls, they passed on musingly as if asking the red and yellow roses on the wall-paper whether they would fade, and questioning (gently, for there was time at their disposal) the torn letters in the waste-paper basket, the flowers, the books, all of which were now open to them and asking, Were they allies? Were they enemies? How long would they endure?

So some random light directing them with its pale footfall upon stair and mat, from some uncovered star, or wandering ship, or the Lighthouse even, the little airs mounted the staircase and nosed round bedroom doors. But here surely, they must cease. Whatever else may perish and disappear, what lies here is steadfast. Here one might say to those sliding lights, those fumbling airs that breathe and bend over the bed itself, here you can neither touch nor destroy. Upon which, wearily, ghostlily, as if they had feather-light fingers and the light persistency of feathers, they would look, once, on the shut eyes, and the loosely clasping fingers, and fold their garments wearily and disappear. And so, nosing, rubbing, they went to the window on the staircase, to the servants' bedrooms, to the boxes in the attics; descending, blanched the apples on the dining-room table, fumbled the petals of roses, tried the picture on the easel, brushed the mat and blew a little sand along the floor. At length, desisting, all ceased together, gathered together, all sighed together; all together gave off an aimless gust of lamentation to which some door in the kitchen replied; swung wide; admitted nothing; and slammed to.

[Here Mr. Carmichael, who was reading Virgil, blew out his candle. It was midnight.]

I I I

But what after all is one night? A short space, especially when the darkness dims so soon, and so soon a bird sings, a cock crows, or a faint green quickens, like a turning leaf, in the hollow of the wave. Night, however, succeeds to night. The winter holds a pack of them in store and deals them equally, evenly, with indefatigable fingers. They lengthen; they darken. Some of them hold aloft clear planets, plates of brightness. The autumn trees, ravaged as they are, take on the flash of tattered flags kindling in the gloom of cool cathedral caves where gold letters on marble pages describe death in battle and how bones bleach and burn far away in Indian sands. The autumn trees gleam in the yellow moonlight, in the light of harvest moons, the light which mellows the energy of labour, and smooths the stubble, and brings the wave lapping blue to the shore.

It seemed now as if, touched by human penitence and all its toil, divine goodness had parted the curtain and displayed behind it, single, distinct, the hare erect; the wave falling; the boat rocking, which, did we deserve them, should be ours always. But alas, divine goodness, twitching the cord, draws the curtain; it does not please him; he covers his treasures in a drench of hail, and so breaks them, so confuses them that it seems impossible that their calm should ever return or that we should ever compose from their fragments a perfect whole or read in the littered pieces the clear words of truth. For our penitence deserves a glimpse only; our toil respite only.

The nights now are full of wind and destruction; the trees plunge and bend and their leaves fly helter skelter until the lawn is plastered with them and they lie packed in gutters and choke rain pipes and scatter damp paths. Also the sea tosses itself and breaks itself, and should any sleeper fancying that he might find on the beach an answer to his doubts, a sharer of his solitude, throw off his bedclothes and go down by himself to walk on the sand, no image with semblance of serving and divine promptitude comes readily to hand bringing the night to order and making the world reflect the compass of the soul. The hand dwindles in his hand; the voice bellows in his ear. Almost it would appear that it is useless in such confusion to ask the night those questions as to what, and why, and wherefore, which tempt the sleeper from his bed to seek an answer.

[Mr. Ramsay, stumbling along a passage one dark morning, stretched his arms out, but Mrs. Ramsay having died rather suddenly the night before, his arms, though stretched out, remained empty.]

I V

So with the house empty and the doors locked and the mattresses rolled round, those stray airs, advance guards of great armies, blustered in, brushed bare boards, nibbled and fanned, met nothing in bedroom or drawing-room that wholly resisted them but only hangings that flapped, wood that creaked, the bare legs of tables, saucepans and china already furred, tarnished, cracked. What people had shed and left—a pair of shoes, a shooting cap, some faded skirts and coats in wardrobes—those alone kept the human shape and in the emptiness indicated how once they were filled and animated; how once hands were busy with hooks and buttons; how once the looking-glass had held a face; had held a world hollowed out in which a figure turned, a hand flashed, the door opened, in came children rushing and tumbling; and went out again. Now, day after day, light turned, like a flower re-flected in water, its sharp image on the wall opposite. Only the shadows of the trees, flourishing in the wind, made obeisance on the wall, and for a moment darkened the pool in which light reflected itself; or birds, flying, made a soft spot flutter slowly across the bedroom floor.

So loveliness reigned and stillness, and together made the shape of loveliness itself, a form from which life had parted; solitary like a pool at evening, far distant, seen from a train window, vanishing so quickly that the pool, pale in the evening, is scarcely robbed of its solitude, though once seen. Loveliness and stillness clasped hands in the bedroom, and among the shrouded jugs and sheeted chairs even the prying of the wind, and the soft nose of the clammy sea airs, rubbing, snuffling, iterating, and reiterating their questions—"Will you fade? Will you perish?"—scarcely disturbed the peace, the indifference, the air of pure integrity, as if the question they asked scarcely needed that they should answer: we remain.

Nothing it seemed could break that image, corrupt that inno-cence, or disturb the swaying mantle of silence which, week after week, in the empty room, wove into itself the falling cries of birds, ships hooting, the drone and hum of the fields, a dog's bark, a man's shout, and folded them round the house in silence. Once only a board sprang on the landing; once in the middle of the night with a roar, with a rupture, as after centuries of quiescence, a rock rends itself from the mountain and hurtles crashing into the valley, one fold of the shawl loosened and swung to and fro. Then again peace descended; and the shadow wavered; light bent to its own image in adoration on the bedroom wall; and Mrs. McNab, tearing the veil of silence with hands that had stood in the wash-tub, grinding it with boots that had crunched the shingle, came as directed to open all windows, and dust the bedrooms.

V

As she lurched (for she rolled like a ship at sea) and leered (for her eyes fell on nothing directly, but with a sidelong glance that deprecated the scorn and anger of the world—she was witless, she knew it), as she clutched the banisters and hauled herself upstairs and rolled from room to room, she sang. Rubbing the glass of the long looking-glass and leering sideways at her swinging figure a sound issued from her lips—something that had been gay twenty years before on the stage perhaps, had been hummed and danced to, but now, coming from the toothless, bonneted, care-taking woman, was robbed of meaning, was like the voice of witlessness, humour, persistency itself, trodden down but springing up again, so that as she lurched, dusting, wiping, she seemed to say how it was one long sorrow and trouble, how it was getting up and going to bed again, and bringing things out and putting them away again. It was not easy or snug this world she had known for close on seventy years. Bowed down she was with weariness. How long, she asked, creaking and groaning on her knees under the bed, dusting the boards, how long shall it endure? but hobbled to her feet again, pulled herself up, and again with her sidelong leer which slipped and turned aside even from her own face, and her own sorrows, stood and gaped in the glass, aimlessly smiling, and began again the old amble and hobble, taking up mats, putting down china, looking sideways in the glass, as if, after all, she had her consolations, as if indeed there twined about her dirge some incorrigible hope. Visions of joy there must have been at the wash-tub, say with her children (yet two had been base-born and one had deserted her), at the public-house, drinking; turning over scraps in her drawers. Some cleavage of the dark there must have been, some channel in the depths of obscurity through which light enough issued to twist her face grinning in the glass and make her, turning to her job again, mumble out the old music hall song. The mystic, the visionary, walking the beach on a fine night, stirring a puddle, looking at a stone, asking themselves "What am I," "What is this?" had suddenly an answer vouchsafed them: (they could not say what it was) so that they were warm in the frost and had comfort in the desert. But Mrs. McNab continued to drink and gossip as before.

V I

The spring without a leaf to toss, bare and bright like a virgin fierce in her chastity, scornful in her purity, was laid out on fields wide-eyed and watchful and entirely careless of what was done or thought by the beholders. [Prue Ramsay, leaning on her father's arm, was given in marriage. What, people said, could have been more fitting? And, they added, how beautiful she looked!]

As summer neared, as the evenings lengthened, there came to the wakeful, the hopeful, walking the beach, stirring the pool, imaginations of the strangest kind—of flesh turned to atoms which drove before the wind, of stars flashing in their hearts, of cliff, sea, cloud, and sky brought purposely together to assemble outwardly the scattered parts of the vision within. In those mirrors, the minds of men, in those pools of uneasy water, in which clouds for ever turn and shadows form, dreams persisted, and it was impossible to resist the strange intimation which every gull, flower, tree, man and woman, and the white earth itself seemed to declare (but if questioned at once to withdraw) that good triumphs, happiness prevails, order rules; or to resist the extraordinary stimulus to range hither and thither in search of some absolute good, some crystal of intensity, remote from the known pleasures and familiar virtues, something alien to the processes of domestic life, single, hard, bright, like a diamond in the sand, which would render the possessor secure. Moreover, softened and acquiescent, the spring with her bees humming and gnats dancing threw her cloak about her, veiled her eyes, averted her head, and among passing shadows and flights of small rain seemed to have taken upon her a knowledge of the sorrows of mankind.

[Prue Ramsay died that summer in some illness connected with childbirth, which was indeed a tragedy, people said, everything, they said, had promised so well.]

And now in the heat of summer the wind sent its spies about the house again. Flies wove a web in the sunny rooms; weeds that had grown close to the glass in the night tapped methodically at the window pane. When darkness fell, the stroke of the Lighthouse, which had laid itself with such authority upon the carpet in the darkness, tracing its pattern, came now in the softer light of spring mixed with moonlight gliding gently as if it laid its caress and lingered stealthily and looked and came lovingly again. But in the very lull of this loving caress, as the long stroke leant upon the bed, the rock was rent asunder; another fold of the shawl loosened; there it hung, and swayed. Through the short summer nights and the long summer days, when the empty rooms seemed to murmur with the echoes of the fields and the hum of flies, the long streamer waved gently, swayed aimlessly; while the sun so striped and barred the rooms and filled them with yellow haze that Mrs. McNab, when she broke in and lurched about, dusting, sweeping, looked like a tropical fish oaring its way through sun-lanced waters.

But slumber and sleep though it might there came later in the summer ominous sounds like the measured blows of hammers dulled on felt, which, with their repeated shocks still further loosened the shawl and cracked the tea-cups. Now and again some glass tinkled in the cupboard as if a giant voice had shrieked so loud in its agony that tumblers stood inside a cupboard vibrated too. Then again silence fell; and then, night after night, and sometimes in plain mid-day when the roses were bright and light turned on the wall its shape clearly there seemed to drop into this silence, this indifference, this integrity, the thud of something falling.

[A shell exploded. Twenty or thirty young men were blown up in France, among them Andrew Ramsay, whose death, mercifully, was instantaneous.]

At that season those who had gone down to pace the beach and ask of the sea and sky· what message they reported or what vision they affirmed had to consider among the usual tokens of divine bounty—the sunset on the sea, the pallor of dawn, the moon rising, fishing-boats against the moon, and children making mud pies or pelting each other with handfuls of grass—something out of harmony with this jocundity and this serenity. There was the silent apparition of an ashen-coloured ship for instance, come, gone; there was a purplish stain upon the bland surface of the sea as if something had boiled and bled, invisibly, beneath. This intrusion into a scene calculated to stir the most sublime reflections and lead to the most comfortable conclusions stayed their pacing. It was difficult blandly to overlook them; to abolish their significance in the landscape; to continue, as one walked by the sea, to marvel how beauty outside mirrored beauty within.

Did Nature supplement what man advanced? Did she complete what he began? With equal complacence she saw his misery, his meanness, and his torture. That dream, of sharing, completing, of finding in solitude on the beach an answer, was then but a reflection in a mirror, and the mirror itself was but the surface glassiness which forms in quiescence when the nobler powers sleep beneath? Impatient, despairing yet loth to go (for beauty offers her lures, has her consolations), to pace the beach was impossible; contemplation was unendurable; the mirror was broken.

[Mr. Carmichael brought out a volume of poems that spring, which had an unexpected success. The war, people said, had revived their interest in poetry.]

V I I

Night after night, summer and winter, the torment of storms, the arrow-like stillness of fine weather, held their court without interference. Listening (had there been any one to listen) from the upper rooms of the empty house only gigantic chaos streaked with lightning could have been heard tumbling and tossing, as the winds and waves disported themselves like the amorphous bulks of leviathans whose brows are pierced by no light of reason, and mounted one on top of another, and lunged and plunged in the darkness or the daylight (for night and day, month and year ran shapelessly together) in idiot games, until it seemed as if the universe were battling and tumbling, in brute confusion and wanton lust aimlessly by itself.

In spring the garden urns, casually filled with wind-blown plants, were gay as ever. Violets came and daffodils. But the stillness and the brightness of the day were as strange as the chaos and tumult of night, with the trees standing there, and the flowers standing there, looking before them, looking up, yet beholding nothing, eyeless, and so terrible.

V I I I

Thinking no harm, for the family would not come, never again, some said, and the house would be sold at Michaelmas perhaps, Mrs. McNab stooped and picked a bunch of flowers to take home with her. She laid them on the table while she dusted. She was fond of flowers. It was a pity to let them waste. Suppose the house were sold (she stood arms akimbo in front of the looking-glass) it would want seeing to—it would. There it had stood all these years without a soul in it. The books and things were mouldy, for, what with the war and help being hard to get, the house had not been cleaned as she could have wished. It was beyond one person's strength to get it straight now. She was too old. Her legs pained her. All those books needed to be laid out on the grass in the sun; there was plaster fallen in the hall; the rain-pipe had blocked over the study window and let the water in; the carpet was ruined quite. But people should come them-selves; they should have sent somebody down to see. For there were clothes in the cupboards; they had left clothes in all the bedrooms. What was she to do with them? They had the moth in them—Mrs. Ramsay's things. Poor lady! She would never want *them* again. She was dead, they said; years ago, in London. There was the old grey cloak she wore gardening (Mrs. McNab fingered it). She could see her, as she came up the drive with the washing, stooping over her flowers (the garden was a pitiful sight now, all run to riot, and rabbits scuttling at you out of the beds)—she could see her with one of the children by her in that grey cloak. There were boots and shoes; and a brush and comb left on the dressing-table, for all the world as if she expected to come back tomorrow. (She had died very sudden at the end, they said.) And once they had been coming, but had put off coming, what with the war, and travel being so difficult these days; they had never come all these years; just sent her money; but never wrote, never came, and expected to find things as they had left them, ah, dear! Why the dressing table drawers were full of things (she pulled them open), handkerchiefs, bits of ribbon. Yes, she could see Mrs. Ramsay as she came up the drive with the washing.

"Good-evening, Mrs. McNab," she would say.

She had a pleasant way with her. The girls all liked her. But, dear, many things had changed since then (she shut the drawer); many families had lost their dearest. So she was dead; and Mr. Andrew killed; and Miss Prue dead too, they said, with her first baby; but every one had lost some one these years. Prices had gone up shamefully, and didn't come down again neither. She could well remember her in her grey cloak.

"Good-evening, Mrs. McNab," she said, and told cook to keep a plate of milk soup for her—quite thought she wanted it, carrying that heavy basket all the way up from town. She could see her now, stooping over her flowers; and faint and flickering, like a yellow beam or the circle at the end of a telescope, a lady in a grey cloak, stooping over her flowers, went wandering over the bedroom wall, up the dressing-table, across the wash-stand, as Mrs. McNab hobbled and ambled, dusting, straightening. And cook's name now? Mildred? Marian?—some name like that. Ah, she had forgotten—she did forget things. Fiery, like all red-haired women. Many a laugh they had had. She was always welcome in the kitchen. She made them laugh, she did. Things were better then than now.

She sighed; there was too much work for one woman. She wagged her head this side and that. This had been the nursery. Why, it was all damp in here; the plaster was falling. Whatever did they want to hang a beast's skull there? gone mouldy too. And rats in all the attics. The rain came in. But they never sent; never came. Some of the locks had gone, so the doors banged. She didn't like to be up here at dusk alone neither. It was too much for one woman, too much, too much. She creaked, she moaned. She banged the door. She turned the key in the lock, and left the house alone, shut up, locked.

I X

The house was left; the house was deserted. It was left like a shell on a sandhill to fill with dry salt grains now that life had left it. The long night seemed to have set in; the trifling airs, nibbling, the clammy breaths, fumbling, seemed to have triumphed. The saucepan had rusted and the mat decayed. Toads had nosed their way in. Idly, aimlessly, the swaying shawl swung to and fro. A thistle thrust itself between the tiles in the larder. The swallows nested in the drawing-room; the floor was strewn with straw; the plaster fell in shovelfuls; rafters were laid bare; rats carried off this and that to gnaw behind the wainscots. Tortoise-shell butter-flies burst from the chrysalis and pattered their life out on the window-pane. Poppies sowed themselves among the dahlias; the lawn waved with long grass; giant artichokes towered among roses; a fringed carnation flowered among the cabbages; while the gentle tapping of a weed at the window had become, on winters' nights, a drumming from sturdy trees and thorned briars which made the whole room green in summer.

What power could now prevent the fertility, the insensibility of nature? Mrs. McNab's dream of a lady, of a child, of a plate of milk soup? It had wavered over the walls like a spot of sunlight and vanished. She had locked the door; she had gone. It was beyond the strength of one woman, she said. They never sent. They never wrote. There were things up there rotting in the drawers—it was a shame to leave them so, she said. The place was gone to rack and ruin. Only the Lighthouse beam entered the rooms for a moment, sent its sudden stare over bed and wall in the darkness of winter, looked with equanimity at the thistle and the swallow, the rat and the straw. Nothing now withstood them; nothing said no to them. Let the wind blow; let the poppy seed itself and the carnation mate with the cabbage. Let the swallow build in the drawing-room, and the thistle thrust aside the tiles, and the butterfly sun itself on the faded chintz of the arm-chairs. Let the broken glass and the china lie out on the lawn and be tangled over with grass and wild berries.

For now had come that moment, that hesitation when dawn trembles and night pauses, when if a feather alight in the scale it will be weighed down. One feather, and the house, sinking, falling, would have turned and pitched downwards to the depths of darkness. In the ruined room, picnickers would have lit their kettles; lovers sought shelter there, lying on the bare boards; and the shepherd stored his dinner on the bricks, and the tramp slept with his coat round him to ward off the cold. Then the roof would have fallen; briars and hemlocks would have blotted out path, step, and window; would have grown, unequally but lustily over the mound, until some trespasser, losing his way, could have told only by a red-hot poker among the nettles, or a scrap of china in the hemlock that here once some one had lived; there had been a house.

If the feather had fallen, if it had tipped the scale downwards, the whole house would have plunged to the depths to lie upon the sands of oblivion. But there was a force working; something not highly conscious; something that leered, something that lurched; something not inspired to go about its work with dignified ritual or solemn chanting. Mrs. McNab groaned; Mrs. Bast creaked. They were old; they were stiff; their legs ached. They came with their brooms and pails at last; they got to work. All of a sudden, would Mrs. McNab see that the house was ready, one of the young ladies wrote: would she get this done; would she get that done; all in a hurry. They might be coming for the summer; had left everything to the last; expected to find things as they had left them. Slowly and painfully, with broom and pail, mopping, scouring, Mrs. McNab, Mrs. Bast, stayed the corruption and the rot; rescued from the pool of Time that was fast closing over them now a basin, now a cupboard; fetched up from oblivion all the Waverley novels and a tea-set one morning; in the afternoon restored to sun and air a brass fender and a set of steel fire-irons. George, Mrs. Bast's son, caught the rats, and cut the grass. They had the builders. Attended with the creaking of hinges and the screeching of bolts, the slamming and banging of damp-swollen woodwork some rusty laborious birth seemed to be taking place, as the women, stooping, rising, groaning, singing, slapped and slammed, upstairs now, now down in the cellars. Oh, they said, the work!

They drank their tea in the bedroom sometimes, or in the study; breaking off work at mid-day with the smudge on their faces, and their old hands clasped and cramped with the broom handles. Flopped on chairs, they contemplated now the magnificent conquest over taps and bath; now the more arduous, more partial triumph over long rows of books, black as ravens once, now white-stained, breeding pale mushrooms and secreting furtive spiders. Once more, as she felt the tea warm in her, the telescope fitted itself to Mrs. McNab's eyes, and in a ring of light she saw the old gentleman, lean as a rake, wagging his head, as she came up with the washing, talking to himself, she supposed, on the lawn. He never noticed her. Some said he was dead; some said she was dead. Which was it? Mrs. Bast didn't know for certain either. The young gentleman was dead. That she was sure. She had read his name in the papers.

There was the cook now, Mildred, Marian, some such name as that—a red-headed woman, quick-tempered like all her sort, but kind, too, if you knew the way with her. Many a laugh they had had together. She saved a plate of soup for Maggie; a bite of ham, sometimes; whatever was over. They lived well in those days. They had everything they wanted (glibly, jovially, with the tea hot in her, she unwound her ball of memories, sitting in the wicker arm-chair by the nursery fender). There was always plenty doing, people in the house, twenty staying sometimes, and washing up till long past midnight.

Mrs. Bast (she had never known them; had lived in Glasgow at that time) wondered, putting her cup down, whatever they hung that beast's skull there for? Shot in foreign parts no doubt.

It might well be, said Mrs. McNab, wantoning on with her memories; they had friends in eastern countries; gentlemen staying there, ladies in evening dress; she had seen them once through the dining-room door all sitting at dinner. Twenty she dared say all in their jewellery, and she asked to stay help wash up, might be till after midnight.

Ah, said Mrs. Bast, they'd find it changed. She leant out of the window. She watched her son George scything the grass. They might well ask, what had been done to it? seeing how old Kennedy was supposed to have charge of it, and then his leg got so bad after he fell from the cart; and perhaps then no one for a year, or the better part of one; and then Davie Macdonald, and seeds might be sent, but who should say if they were ever planted? They'd find it changed.

She watched her son scything. He was a great one for work—one of those quiet ones. Well they must be getting along with the cupboards, she supposed. They hauled themselves up.

At last, after days of labour within, of cutting and digging without, dusters were flicked from the windows, the windows were shut to, keys were turned all over the house; the front door was banged; it was finished.

And now as if the cleaning and the scrubbing and the scything and the mowing had drowned it there rose that half-heard melody, that intermittent music which the ear half catches but lets fall; a bark, a bleat; irregular, intermittent, yet somehow related; the hum of an insect, the tremor of cut grass, dissevered yet somehow belonging; the jar of a dorbeetle, the squeak of a wheel, loud, low, but mysteriously related; which the ear strains to bring together and is always on the verge of harmonising, but they are never quite heard, never fully harmonised, and at last, in the evening, one after another the sounds die out, and the harmony falters, and silence falls. With the sunset sharpness was lost, and like mist rising, quiet rose, quiet spread, the wind settled; loosely the world shook itself down to sleep, darkly here without a light to it, save what came green suffused through leaves, or pale on the white flowers in the bed by the window.

(Lily Briscoe had her bag carried up to the house late one evening in September.)

X

Then indeed peace had come. Messages of peace breathed from the sea to the shore. Never to break its sleep any more, to lull it rather more deeply to rest, and whatever the dreamers dreamt holily, dreamt wisely, to confirm—what else was it murmuring—as Lily Briscoe laid her head on the pillow in the clean still room and heard the sea. Through the open window the voice of the beauty of the world came murmuring, too softly to hear exactly what it said—but what mattered if the meaning were plain? entreating the sleepers (the house was full again; Mrs. Beckwith was staying there, also Mr. Carmichael), if they would not actually come down to the beach itself at least to lift the blind and look out. They would see then night flowing down in purple; his head crowned; his sceptre jewelled; and how in his eyes a child might look. And if they still faltered (Lily was tired out with travelling and slept almost at once; but Mr. Carmichael read a book by candlelight), if they still said no, that it was vapour, this splendour of his, and the dew had more power than he, and they preferred sleeping; gently then without complaint, or argument, the voice would sing its song. Gently the waves would break (Lily heard them in her sleep); tenderly the light fell (it seemed to come through her eyelids). And it all looked, Mr. Carmichael thought, shutting his book, falling asleep, much as it used to look.

Indeed the voice might resume, as the curtains of dark wrapped themselves over the house, over Mrs. Beckwith, Mr. Carmichael, and Lily Briscoe so that they lay with several folds of blackness on their eyes, why not accept this, be content with this, acquiesce and resign? The sigh of all the seas breaking in measure round the isles soothed them; the night wrapped them; nothing broke their sleep, until, the birds beginning and the dawn weaving their thin voices in to its whiteness, a cart grinding, a dog somewhere barking, the sun lifted the curtains, broke the veil on their eyes, and Lily Briscoe stirring in her sleep. She clutched at her blankets as a faller clutches at the turf on the edge of a cliff. Her eyes opened wide. Here she was again, she thought, sitting bolt upright in bed. Awake.

F R O M

Orlando

When Orlando *was published in the autumn of 1928, book-
sellers were at a loss as to where to display it. Was it biography?
Or was it fiction? "I doubt therefore," wrote Virginia Woolf in
her diary, "that we shall do more than cover expenses—a high
price to pay for the fun of calling it a biography." She need not
have worried, however, for the book has become one of the
great fictional biographies of our time. It is in reality as much
a biography as Sterne's* Tristram Shandy *or Defoe's* Moll Flan-
ders.

*Orlando has all the conventional features of an authentic
biography: a preface, acknowledgments, even an index; but in
tone and spirit, it is a fantasy: a fantastic tale based on the life
and personal history of Vita Sackville-West, who in married
life was Mrs. Harold Nicolson. Nigel Nicolson called* Orlando
*"the longest and most charming love-letter in literature." That
love-letter, let it be added, executes the most daring of literary
stunts in mocking historical fact in the interest of imaginative
truth.* Orlando *begins in the reign of Queen Elizabeth, with
its titular hero a full-blooded youth. It ends on the chiming of
midnight, October 11, 1928, with Orlando now a woman—the
hero has turned heroine. The book is filled with audacity and
irreverence. Time and space become mere abstractions in a*

profusion of detail, and the concept of androgyny is acted out with playful pedantry. No one and nothing escape notice. Critics and poets are satirized. Conventions are ridiculed. And biographers are told how to write biography. Nothing is holy in these pages. No one is immune.

The Great Frost scene printed below is a brilliant picture of the frozen Thames, where great ice carnivals were ordered during the reign of King James. During the festivities, Orlando meets the Russian Princess, Sasha (modeled after Violet Trefusis, with whom Vita Sackville-West had once had a turbulent love affair). And Orlando is under Sasha's spell almost at once. But the Princess is unsteady, capricious, inconstant; and in the end Orlando is jilted—left to seek his consolation in the pursuit of literature.

The book was an immediate sensation, and it was soon the talk of the town. One of the London daily newspapers said of Orlando: "The book in Bloomsbury is a joke, in Mayfair a necessity, and in America a classic."

THE GREAT FROST WAS, HISTORIANS TELL US, THE most severe that has ever visited these islands. Birds froze in midair and fell like stones to the ground. At Norwich a young countrywoman started to cross the road in her usual robust health and was seen by the onlookers to turn visibly to powder and be blown in a puff of dust over the roofs as the icy blast struck her at the street corner. The mortality among sheep and cattle was enormous. Corpses froze and could not be drawn from the sheets. It was no uncommon sight to come upon a whole herd of swine frozen immovable upon the road. The fields were full of shepherds, ploughmen, teams of horses, and little bird-scaring boys all struck stark in the act of the moment, one with his hand to his nose, another with the bottle to his lips, a third with a stone raised to throw at the raven who sat, as if stuffed, upon the hedge within a yard of him. The severity of the frost was so extraordinary that a kind of petrifaction sometimes ensued; and it was commonly supposed that the great increase of rocks in some parts of Derbyshire was due to no eruption, for there was none, but to the solidification of unfortunate wayfarers who had been turned literally to stone where they stood. The Church could give little help in the matter, and though some landowners had these relics blessed, the most part preferred to use them either as landmarks, scratching posts for sheep, or, when the form of the stone allowed, drinking troughs for cattle, which purposes they serve, admirably for the most part, to this day.

But while the country people suffered the extremity of want, and the trade of the country was at a standstill, London enjoyed a carnival of the utmost brilliancy. The Court was at Greenwich, and the new King seized the opportunity that his coronation gave him to curry favour with the citizens. He directed that the river, which was frozen to a depth of twenty feet and more for six or seven miles on either side, should be swept, decorated and given all the semblance of a park or pleasure ground, with arbours, mazes, alleys, drinking booths, etc., at his expense. For himself and the courtiers, he reserved a certain space immediately opposite the Palace gates; which, railed off from the public only by a silken rope, became at once the centre of the most brilliant society in England. Great statesmen, in their beards and ruffs, despatched affairs of state under the crimson awning of the Royal Pagoda. Soldiers planned the conquest of the Moor and the downfall of the Turk in striped arbours surmounted by plumes of ostrich feathers. Admirals strode up and down the narrow pathways, glass in hand, sweeping the horizon and telling stories of the north-west passage and the Spanish Armada. Lovers dallied upon divans spread with sables. Frozen roses fell in showers when the Queen and her ladies walked abroad. Coloured balloons hovered motionless in the air. Here and there burnt vast bonfires of cedar and oak wood, lavishly salted, so that the flames were of green, orange, and purple fire. But however fiercely they burnt, the heat was not enough to melt the ice which, though of singular transparency, was yet of the hardness of steel. So clear indeed was it that there could be seen, congealed at a depth of several feet, here a porpoise, there a flounder. Shoals of eels lay motionless in a trance, but whether their state was one of death or merely of suspended animation which the warmth would revive puzzled the philosophers. Near London Bridge, where the river had frozen to a depth of some twenty fathoms, a wrecked wherry boat was plainly visible, lying on the bed of the river where it had sunk last autumn, overladen with apples. The old bumboat woman, who was carrying her fruit to market on the Surrey side, sat there in her plaids and farthingales with her lap full of apples, for all the world as if she were about to serve a customer, though a certain blueness about the lips hinted the truth. 'Twas a sight King James specially liked to look upon, and he would bring a troupe of courtiers to gaze with him. In short, nothing could exceed the brilliancy and gaiety of the scene by day. But it was at night that the carnival was at its merriest. For the frost continued unbroken, the nights were of perfect stillness; the moon and stars blazed with the hard fixity of diamonds, and to the fine music of flute and trumpet the courtiers danced.

Orlando, it is true, was none of those who tread lightly the coranto and lavolta; he was clumsy; and a little absent-minded. He much preferred the plain dances of his own country, which he had danced as a child to these fantastic foreign measures. He had indeed just brought his feet together about six in the evening of the seventh of January at the finish of some such quadrille or minuet when he beheld, coming from the pavilion of the Muscovite Embassy, a figure, which, whether boy's or woman's, for the loose tunic and trousers of the Russian fashion served to disguise the sex, filled him with the highest curiosity. The person, whatever the name or sex, was about middle height, very slenderly fashioned, and dressed entirely in oyster-coloured velvet, trimmed with some unfamiliar greenish-coloured fur. But these details were obscured by the extraordinary seductiveness which issued from the whole person. Images, metaphors of the most extreme and extravagant twined and twisted in his mind. He called her a melon, a pineapple, an olive tree, an emerald, and a fox in the snow all in the space of three seconds; he did not know whether he had heard her, tasted her, seen her, or all three together. (For though we must pause not a moment in the narrative we may here hastily note that all his images at this time were simple in the extreme to match his senses and were mostly taken from things he had liked the taste of as a boy. But if his senses were simple they were at the same time extremely strong. To pause therefore and seek the reasons of things is out of the question.) . . . A melon, an emerald, a fox in the snow—so he raved, so he called her. When the boy, for alas, a boy it must be—no woman could skate with such speed and vigour—swept almost on tiptoe past him, Orlando was ready to tear his hair with vexation that the person was of his own sex, and thus all embraces were out of the question. But the skater came closer. Legs, hands, carriage, were a boy's, but no boy ever had a mouth like that; no boy had those breasts; no boy had those eyes which looked as if they had been fished from the bottom of the sea. Finally, coming to a stop and sweeping a curtsey with the utmost grace to the King, who was shuffling past on the arm of some Lord-in-waiting, the unknown skater came to a standstill. She was not a handsbreadth off. She was a woman. Orlando stared; trembled; turned hot; turned cold; longed to hurl himself through the summer air; to crush acorns beneath his feet; to toss his arms with the beech trees and the oaks. As it was, he drew his lips up over his small white teeth; opened them perhaps half an inch as if to bite and shut them as if he had bitten. The Lady Euphrosyne hung upon his arm.

The stranger's name, he found, was the Princess Marousha Stanilovska Dagmar Natasha Iliana Romanovitch, and she had come in the train of the Muscovite Ambassador, who was her uncle perhaps, or perhaps her father, to attend the coronation. Very little was known of the Muscovites. In their great beards and furred hats they sat almost silent; drinking some black liquid which they spat out now and then upon the ice. None spoke English, and French with which some at least were familiar was then little spoken at the English Court.

It was through this accident that Orlando and the Princess became acquainted. They were seated opposite each other at the great table spread under a huge awning for the entertainment of the notables. The Princess was placed between two young Lords, one Lord Francis Vere and the other the young Earl of Moray. It was laughable to see the predicament she soon had them in, for though both were fine lads in their way, the babe unborn had as much knowledge of the French tongue as they had. When at the beginning of dinner the Princess turned to the Earl and said, with a grace which ravished his heart, "Je crois avoir fait la connaissance d'un gentilhomme qui vous était apparenté en Pologne l'été dernier," or "La beauté des dames de la cour d'Angleterre me met dans le ravissement. On ne peut voir une dame plus gracieuse que votre reine, ni une coiffure plus belle que la sienne," both Lord Francis and the Earl showed the highest embarrassment. The one helped her largely to horse-radish sauce, the other whistled to his dog and made him beg for a marrow bone. At this the Princess could no longer contain her laughter, and Orlando, catching her eyes across the boars' heads and stuffed peacocks, laughed too. He laughed, but the laugh on his lips froze in wonder. Whom had he loved, what had he loved, he asked himself in a tumult of emotion, until now? An old woman, he answered, all skin and bone. Red cheeked trulls too many to mention. A puling nun. A hard-bitten cruel-mouthed adventuress. A nodding mass of lace and ceremony. Love had meant to him nothing but sawdust and cinders. The joys he had had of it tasted insipid in the extreme. He marvelled how he could have gone through with it without yawning. For as he looked the thickness of his blood melted; the ice turned to wine in his veins; he heard the waters flowing and the birds singing; spring broke over the hard wintry landscape; his manhood woke; he grasped a sword in his hand; he charged a more daring foe than Pole or Moor; he dived in deep water; he saw the flower of danger growing in a crevice; he stretched his hand—in fact he was rattling off one of his most impassioned sonnets when the Princess addressed him, "Would you have the goodness to pass the salt?"

He blushed deeply.

"With all the pleasure in the world, Madame," he replied, speaking French with a perfect accent. For, heaven be praised, he spoke the tongue as his own; his mother's maid had taught him. Yet perhaps it would have been better for him had he never learnt that tongue; never answered that voice; never followed the light of those eyes. . . .

The Princess continued. Who were those bumpkins she asked him, who sat beside her with the manners of stablemen? What was the nauseating mixture they had poured on her plate? Did the dogs eat at the same table with the men in England? Was that figure of fun at the end of the table with her hair rigged up like a Maypole (une grande perche mal fagotée) really the Queen? And did the King always slobber like that? And which of those popinjays was George Villiers? Though these questions rather discomposed Orlando at first, they were put with such archness and drollery that he could not help but laugh; and as he saw from the blank faces of the company that nobody understood a word, he answered her as freely as she asked him, speaking, as she did, in perfect French.

Thus began an intimacy between the two which soon became the scandal of the Court.

Soon it was observed Orlando paid the Muscovite far more attention than mere civility demanded. He was seldom far from her side, and their conversation, though unintelligible to the rest, was carried on with such animation, provoked such blushes and laughter, that the dullest could guess the subject. Moreover, the change in Orlando himself was extraordinary. Nobody had ever seen him so animated. In one night he had thrown off his boyish clumsiness; he was changed from a sulky stripling, who could not enter a ladies' room without sweeping half the ornaments from the table, to a nobleman, full of grace and manly courtesy. To

see him hand the Muscovite (as she was called) to her sledge, or
offer her his hand for the dance, or catch the spotted kerchief
which she had let drop, or discharge any other of those manifold
duties which the supreme lady exacts and the lover hastens to
anticipate was a sight to kindle the dull eyes of age, and to make
the quick pulse of youth beat faster. Yet over it all hung a cloud.
The old men shrugged their shoulders. The young tittered between their fingers. All knew that Orlando was betrothed to'
another. The Lady Margaret O'Brien O'Dare O'Reilly Tyrconnel
(for that was the proper name of Euphrosyne of the Sonnets)
wore Orlando's splendid sapphire on the second finger of her left
hand. It was she who had the supreme right to his attentions. Yet
she might drop all the handkerchiefs in her wardrobe (of which
she had many scores) upon the ice and Orlando never stooped to
pick them up. She might wait twenty minutes for him to hand her
to her sledge, and in the end have to be content with the services
of her Blackamoor. When she skated, which she did rather
clumsily, no one was at her elbow to encourage her, and, if she
fell, which she did rather heavily, no one raised her to her feet
and dusted the snow from her petticoats. Although she was naturally phlegmatic, slow to take offence, and more reluctant than
most people to believe that a mere foreigner could oust her from
Orlando's affections, still even the Lady Margaret herself was
brought at last to suspect that something was brewing against her
peace of mind.

Indeed, as the days passed, Orlando took less and less care to
hide his feelings. Making some excuse or other, he would leave
the company as soon as they had dined, or steal away from the
skaters, who were forming sets for a quadrille. Next moment it
would be seen that the Muscovite was missing too. But what
most outraged the Court, and stung it in its tenderest part, which
is its vanity, was that the couple was often seen to slip under the
silken rope, which railed off the Royal enclosure from the public
part of the river and to disappear among the crowd of common
people. For suddenly the Princess would stamp her foot and cry,
"Take me away. I detest your English mob," by which she meant

the English Court itself. She could stand it no longer. It was full of prying old women, she said, who stared in one's face, and of bumptious young men who trod on one's toes. They smelt bad. Their dogs ran between her legs. It was like being in a cage. In Russia they had rivers ten miles broad on which one could gallop six horses abreast all day long without meeting a soul. Besides, she wanted to see the Tower, the Beefeaters, the Heads on Temple Bar, and the jewellers' shops in the city. Thus, it came about that Orlando took her to the city, showed her the Beefeaters and the rebels' heads, and bought her whatever took her fancy in the Royal Exchange. But this was not enough. Each increasingly desired the other's company in privacy all day long where there were none to marvel or to stare. Instead of taking the road to London, therefore, they turned the other way about and were soon beyond the crowd among the frozen reaches of the Thames where, save for sea birds and some old country woman hacking at the ice in a vain attempt to draw a pail full of water or gathering what sticks or dead leaves she could find for firing, not a living soul ever came their way. The poor kept closely to their cottages, and the better sort, who could afford it, crowded for warmth and merriment to the city.

Hence, Orlando and Sasha, as he called her for short, and because it was the name of a white Russian fox he had had as a boy—a creature soft as snow, but with teeth of steel, which bit him so savagely that his father had it killed—hence they had the river to themselves. Hot with skating and with love they would throw themselves down in some solitary reach, where the yellow osiers fringed the bank, and wrapped in a great fur cloak Orlando would take her in his arms, and know, for the first time, he murmured, the delights of love. Then, when the ecstasy was over and they lay lulled in a swoon on the ice, he would tell her of his other loves, and how, compared with her, they had been of wood, of sackcloth, and of cinders. And laughing at his vehemence, she would turn once more in his arms and give him, for love's sake, one more embrace. And then they would marvel that the ice did not melt with their heat, and pity the poor old woman who had no such natural means of thawing it, but must hack at it with a chopper of cold steel. And then, wrapped in their sables, they would talk of everything under the sun; of sights and travels; of Moor and Pagan; of this man's beard and that woman's skin; of a rat that fed from her hand at table; of the arras that moved always in the hall at home; of a face; of a feather. Nothing was too small for such converse, nothing was too great.

Then, suddenly Orlando would fall into one of his moods of melancholy; the sight of the old woman hobbling over the ice might be the cause of it, or nothing; and would fling himself face downwards on the ice and look into the frozen waters and think of death. For the philosopher is right who says that nothing thicker than a knife's blade separates happiness from melancholy; and he goes on to opine that one is twin fellow to the other; and draws from this the conclusion that all extremes of feeling are allied to madness; and so bids us take refuge in the true Church (in his view the Anabaptist) which is the only harbour, port, anchorage, etc., he said, for those tossed on this sea.

"All ends in death," Orlando would say, sitting upright, his face clouded with gloom. (For that was the way his mind worked now, in violent see-saws from life to death stopping at nothing in between, so that the biographer must not stop either, but must fly as fast as he can and so keep pace with the unthinking passionate foolish actions and sudden extravagant words in which, it is impossible to deny, Orlando at this time of his life indulged.)

"All ends in death," Orlando would say, sitting upright on the ice. But Sasha who after all had no English blood in her but was from Russia where the sunsets are longer, the dawns less sudden, and sentences often left unfinished from doubt as to how best to end them—Sasha stared at him, perhaps sneered at him, for he must have seemed a child to her, and said nothing. But at length the ice grew cold beneath them, which she disliked, so pulling him to his feet again, she talked so enchantingly, so wittily, so wisely (but unfortunately always in French, which notoriously loses its flavour in translation) that he forgot the frozen waters or night coming or the old woman or whatever it was, and would try to tell her—plunging and splashing among a thousand images which had gone as stale as the women who inspired them—what she was like. Snow, cream, marble, cherries, alabaster, golden wire? None of these. She was like a fox, or an olive tree; like the waves of the sea when you look down upon them from a height; like an emerald; like the sun on a green hill which is yet clouded —like nothing he had seen or known in England. Ransack the language as he might, words failed him. He wanted another land-scape, and another tongue. English was too frank, too candid, too honeyed a speech for Sasha. For in all she said, however open she seemed and voluptuous, there was something hidden; in all she did, however daring, there was something concealed. So the green flame seems hidden in the emerald, or the sun prisoned in a hill. The clearness was only outward; within was a wander-ing flame. It came; it went; she never shone with the steady beam of an Englishwoman—here, however, remembering the Lady Margaret and her petticoats, Orlando ran wild in his transports and swept her over the ice, faster, faster, vowing that he would chase the flame, dive for the gem, and so on and so on, the words coming on the pants of his breath with the passion of a poet whose poetry is half pressed out of him by pain.

But Sasha was silent. When Orlando had done telling her that she was a fox, an olive tree, or a green hill-top, and had given her the whole history of his family; how their house was one of the most ancient in Britain; how they had come from Rome with the Caesars and had the right to walk down the Corso (which is the chief street in Rome) under a tasselled palanquin, which he said is a privilege reserved only for those of imperial blood (for there was an orgulous credulity about him which was pleasant enough) he would pause and ask her, Where was her own house? What was her father? Had she brothers? Why was she here alone with her uncle? Then, somehow, though she answered readily enough, an awkwardness would come between them. He sus-pected at first that her rank was not as high as she would like; or that she was ashamed of the savage ways of her people, for he had heard that the women in Muscovy wear beards and the men are covered with fur from the waist down; that both sexes are smeared with tallow to keep the cold out, tear meat with their fingers and live in huts where an English noble would scruple to keep his cattle; so that he forebore to press her. But on reflection, he concluded that her silence could not be for that reason; she herself was entirely free from hair on the chin; she dressed in velvet and pearls, and her manners were certainly not those of a woman bred in a cattle shed.

What, then, did she hide from him? The doubt underlying the tremendous force of his feelings was like a quicksand beneath a monument which shifts suddenly and makes the whole pile shake. The agony would seize him suddenly. Then he would blaze out in such wrath that she did not know how to quiet him. Perhaps she did not want to quiet him; perhaps his rages pleased her and she provoked them purposely—such is the curious obliquity of the Muscovitish temperament.

To continue the story—skating farther than their wont that day they reached that part of the river where the ships had anchored and been frozen in midstream. Among them was the ship of the Muscovite Embassy flying its double-headed black eagle from the main mast, which was hung with many-coloured icicles several yards in length. Sasha had left some of her clothing on board, and supposing the ship to be empty they climbed on deck and went in search of it. Remembering certain passages in his own past, Orlando would not have marvelled had some good citizens sought this refuge before them; and so it turned out. They had not ventured far, when a fine young man started up from some business of his own behind a coil of rope and saying, apparently, for he spoke Russian, that he was one of the crew and would help the Princess to find what she wanted, lit a lump of candle and disappeared with her into the lower parts of the ship.

Time went by, and Orlando, wrapped in his own dreams, thought only of the pleasures of life; of his jewel; of her rarity; of means for making her irrevocably and indissolubly his own.

Obstacles there were and hardships to be overcome. She was determined to live in Russia, where there were frozen rivers and wild horses and men, she said, who gashed each other's throats open. It is true that a landscape of pine and snow, habits of lust and slaughter, did not entice him. Nor was he anxious to cease his pleasant country ways of sport and tree planting; relinquish his office; ruin his career; shoot the reindeer instead of the rabbit; drink vodka instead of canary, and slip a knife up his sleeve —for what purpose, he knew not. Still, all this and more than all this he would do for her sake. As for his marriage with the Lady Margaret, fixed though it was for this day sennight, the thing was so palpably absurd that he scarcely gave it a thought. Her kinsmen would abuse him for deserting a great lady; his friends would deride him for ruining the finest career in the world for a Cossack woman and a waste of snow—it weighed not a straw in the balance compared with Sasha herself. On the first dark night they would fly north; thence to Russia. So he pondered; so he plotted as he walked up and down the deck.

He was recalled, turning westward, by the sight of the sun, slung like an orange on the cross of St. Paul's. It was blood red and sinking rapidly. It must be almost evening. Sasha had been gone this hour and more. Seized instantly with those dark forebodings which shadowed even his most confident thoughts of her, he plunged the way he had seen them go into the hold of the ship; and, after stumbling among chests and barrels in the darkness, was made aware by a faint glimmer in a corner that they were seated there. For one second, he had a vision of them; saw Sasha seated on the sailor's knee; saw her bend towards him; saw them embrace before the light was blotted out in a red cloud by his rage. He blazed into such a howl of anguish that the whole ship echoed. Sasha threw herself between them, or the sailor would have been stifled before he could draw his cutlass. Then a deadly sickness came over Orlando, and they had to lay him on the floor and give him brandy to drink before he revived. And then, when he had recovered and was sat upon a heap of sacking on deck, Sasha hung over him, passing before his dizzied eyes softly, sinuously, like the fox that had bit him, now cajoling, now denouncing, so that he came to doubt what he had seen. Had not the candle guttered; had not the shadows moved? The box was heavy, she said; the man was helping her to move it. Orlando believed her one moment—for who can be sure that his rage has not painted what he most dreads to find?—the next was the more violent with anger at her deceit. Then Sasha herself turned white; stamped her foot on deck; said she would go that night, and called upon her Gods to destroy her, if she, a Romanovitch, had lain in the arms of a common seaman. Indeed, looking at them together (which he could hardly bring himself to do) Orlando was outraged by the foulness of his imagination that could have painted so frail a creature in the paws of that hairy sea brute. The man was huge; stood six feet four in his stockings; wore common wire rings in his ears; and looked like a dray horse upon which some wren or robin has perched in its flight. So he yielded; believed her; and asked her pardon. Yet, when they were going down the ship's side, lovingly again, Sasha paused with her hand on the ladder and called back to this tawny wide-cheeked monster a volley of Russian greetings, jests, or endearments, not a word of which Orlando could understand. But there was something in her tone (it might be the fault of the Russian consonants) that reminded Orlando of a scene some nights since, when he had come upon her in secret gnawing a candle end in a corner, which she had picked from the floor. True, it was pink; it was gilt; and it was from the King's table; but it was tallow, and she gnawed it. Was there not, he thought, handing her on to the ice, something rank in her, something coarse flavoured, something peasant-born? And he fancied her at forty grown unwieldy though she was now slim as a reed, and lethargic though she was now blithe as a lark. But again as they skated towards London such suspicions melted in his breast, and he felt as if he had been hooked by a great fish through the nose and rushed through the waters unwillingly, yet with his own consent.

It was an evening of astonishing beauty. As the sun sank, all the domes, spires, turrets, and pinnacles of London rose in inky blackness against the furious red sunset clouds. Here was the fretted cross at Charing; there the dome of St. Paul's; there the massy square of the Tower buildings; there like a grove of trees stripped of all leaves save a knob at the end were the heads on the pikes at Temple Bar. Now the Abbey windows were lit up and burnt like a heavenly, many-coloured shield (in Orlando's fancy); now all the west seemed a golden window with troops of angels (in Orlando's fancy again) passing up and down the heavenly stairs perpetually. All the time they seemed to be skating on fathomless depths of air, so blue the ice had become; and so glassy smooth was it that they sped quicker and quicker to the city with the white gulls circling about them, and cutting in the air with their wings the very same sweeps that they cut on the ice with their skates.

Sasha, as if to reassure him, was tenderer than usual and even more delightful. Seldom would she talk about her past life, but now she told him how, in winter in Russia, she would listen to the wolves howling across the steppes, and thrice, to show him, she barked like a wolf. Upon which he told her of the stags in the snow at home, and how they would stray into the great hall for warmth and be fed by an old man with porridge from a bucket. And then she praised him; for his love of beasts; for his gallantry; for his legs. Ravished with her praises and shamed to think how he had maligned her by fancying her on the knees of a common sailor and grown fat and lethargic at forty, he told her that he could find no words to praise her; yet instantly bethought him how she was like the spring and green grass and rushing waters, and seizing her more tightly than ever, he swung her with him half across the river so that the gulls and the cormorants swung too. And halting at length, out of breath, she said, panting slightly, that he was like a million-candled Christmas tree (such as they have in Russia) hung with yellow globes; incandescent; enough to light a whole street by; (so one might translate it) for what with his glowing cheeks, his dark curls, his black and crimson cloak, he looked as if he were burning with his own radiance, from a lamp lit within.

All the colour, save the red of Orlando's cheeks, soon faded. Night came on. As the orange light of sunset vanished and was succeeded by an astonishing white glare from the torches, bonfires, flaming cressets, and other devices by which the river was lit up the strangest transformation took place. Various churches and noblemen's palaces, whose fronts were of white stone showed in streaks and patches as if floating on the air. Of St. Paul's, in particular, nothing was left but a gilt cross. The Abbey appeared like the grey skeleton of a leaf. Everything suffered emaciation and transformation. The sounds too seemed closed and concentrated. As they approached the carnival, they heard a deep note like that struck on a tuning-fork which boomed louder and louder until it became an uproar. Every now and then a great shout followed a rocket up into the air. Gradually they could discern little figures breaking off from the vast crowd and spinning hither and thither like gnats on the surface of a river. Above and around this brilliant circle like a bowl of darkness pressed the deep black of a winter's night. And then into this darkness there began to rise with pauses, which kept the expectation alert and the mouth open, flowering rockets; crescents; serpents; a crown. At one moment the woods and distant hills showed green as on a summer's day; the next all was winter and blackness again.

By this time Orlando and the Princess were close to the Royal enclosure and found their way barred by a great crowd of the common people, who were pressing as near to the silken rope as they dared. Loth to end their privacy and encounter the sharp eyes that were on the watch for them, the couple lingered there, shouldered by apprentices; tailors; fishwives; horse dealers; cony catchers; starving scholars; maid-servants in their whimples; orange girls; ostlers; sober citizens; bawdy tapsters; and a crowd of little ragamuffins such as always haunt the outskirts of a crowd, screaming and scrambling among people's feet—all the riff-raff of the London streets indeed was there, jesting and jostling, here casting dice, telling fortunes, shoving, tickling, pinching; here uproarious, there glum; some of them with mouths gaping a yard wide; others as little reverent as daws on a house-top; all as variously rigged out as their purse or stations allowed; here in fur and broadcloth; there in tatters with their feet kept from the ice only by a dish-clout bound about them. The main press of people, it appeared, stood opposite a booth or stage something like our Punch and Judy show upon which some kind of theatrical performance was going forward. A black man was waving his arms and vociferating. There was a woman in white laid upon a bed. Rough though the staging was, the actors running up and down a pair of steps and sometimes tripping, and the crowd stamping their feet and whistling, or when they were bored, tossing a piece of orange peel at the actors which a dog would scramble for, still the astonishing, sinuous melody of the words stirred Orlando like music. Spoken with extreme speed and a daring agility of tongue which reminded him of the sailors singing in the beer gardens at Wapping, the words even without meaning were as wine to him. But now and again a single phrase would come to him over the ice which was as if torn from the depths of his heart. The frenzy of the Moor seemed to him his own frenzy, and when the Moor suffocated the woman in her bed it was Sasha he killed with his own hands.

At last the play was ended. All had grown dark. The tears streamed down his face. Looking up into the sky there was nothing but blackness there too. Ruin and death, he thought, cover all. The life of man ends in the grave. Worms devour us.

> Methinks it should be now a huge eclipse
> Of sun and moon, and that the affrighted globe
> Should yawn—

Even as he said this a star of some pallor rose in his memory. The night was dark; it was pitch dark; but it was such a night as this that they had waited for; it was on such a night as this that they had planned to fly. He remembered everything. The time had come. With a burst of passion he snatched Sasha to him, and hissed in her ear, "Jour de ma vie!" It was their signal. At midnight they would meet at an inn near Blackfriars. Horses waited there. Everything was in readiness for their flight. So they parted, she to her tent, he to his. It still wanted an hour of the time.

Long before midnight Orlando was in waiting. The night was of so inky a blackness that a man was on you before he could be seen, which was all to the good, but it was also of the most solemn stillness so that a horse's hoof, or a child's cry, could be heard at a distance of half a mile. Many a time did Orlando, pacing the little courtyard, hold his heart at the sound of some nag's steady footfall on the cobbles, or at the rustle of a woman's dress. But the traveller was only some merchant, making home belated; or some woman of the quarter whose errand was nothing so innocent. They passed, and the street was quieter than before. Then those lights which burnt downstairs in the small, huddled quarters where the poor of the city lived moved up to the sleeping-rooms, and then, one by one were extinguished. The street lanterns in this purlieus were few at most; and the negligence of the night watchman often suffered them to expire long before dawn. The darkness then became even deeper than before. Orlando looked to the wicks of his lantern, saw to the saddle girths; primed his pistols; examined his holsters; and did all these things a dozen times at least till he could find nothing more needing his attention. Though it still lacked some twenty minutes to midnight, he could not bring himself to go indoors to the inn parlour, where the hostess was still serving sack and the cheaper sort of canary wine to a few seafaring men, who would sit there trolling their ditties, and telling their stories of Drake, Hawkins, and Grenville, till they toppled off the benches and rolled asleep on the sanded floor. The darkness was more compassionate to his swollen and violent heart. He listened to every footfall; speculated on every sound. Each drunken shout and each wail from some poor wretch laid in the straw or in other distress cut his heart to the quick, as if it boded ill omen to his venture. Yet, he had no fear for Sasha. Her courage made nothing of the adventure. She would come alone, in her cloak and trousers, booted like a man. Light as her footfall was, it would hardly be heard, even in this silence.

So he waited in the darkness. Suddenly he was struck in the face by a blow, soft, yet heavy, on the side of his cheek. So strung with expectation was he, that he started and put his hand to his sword. The blow was repeated a dozen times on forehead and cheek. The dry frost had lasted so long that it took him a minute to realise that these were raindrops falling; the blows were the blows of the rain. At first, they fell slowly, deliberately, one by one. But soon the six drops became sixty; then six hundred; then ran themselves together in a steady spout of water. It was as if the hard and consolidated sky poured itself forth in one profuse fountain. In the space of five minutes Orlando was soaked to the skin.

Hastily putting the horses under cover, he sought shelter beneath the lintel of the door whence he could still observe the courtyard. The air was thicker now than ever, and such a steaming and droning rose from the downpour that no footfall of man or beast could be heard above it. The roads, pitted as they were with great holes, would be under water and perhaps impassable. But of what effect this would have upon their flight he scarcely thought. All his senses were bent upon gazing along the cobbled pathway—gleaming in the light of the lantern—for Sasha's coming. Sometimes, in the darkness, he seemed to see her wrapped about with rain strokes. But the phantom vanished. Suddenly, with an awful and ominous voice, a voice full of horror and alarm which raised every hair of anguish in Orlando's soul, St. Paul's struck the first stroke of midnight. Four times more it struck remorselessly. With the superstition of a lover, Orlando had made out that it was on the sixth stroke that she would come. But the sixth stroke echoed away, and the seventh came and the eighth, and to his apprehensive mind they seemed notes first heralding and then proclaiming death and disaster. When the twelfth struck he knew that his doom was sealed. It was useless for the rational part of him to reason; she might be late; she might be prevented; she might have missed her way. The passionate and feeling heart of Orlando knew the truth. Other clocks struck, jangling one after another. The whole world seemed to ring with the news of her deceit and his derision. The old suspicions subterraneously at work in him rushed forth from concealment openly. He was bitten by a swarm of snakes, each more poisonous than the last. He stood in the doorway in the tremendous rain without moving. As the minutes passed, he sagged a little at the knees. The downpour rushed on. In the thick of it, great guns seemed to boom. Huge noises as of the tearing and rending of oak trees could be heard. There were also wild cries and terrible inhuman groanings. But Orlando stood there immovable till Paul's clock struck two, and then, crying aloud with an awful irony, and all his teeth showing, "Jour de ma vie!" he dashed the lantern to the ground, mounted his horse and galloped he knew not where.

Some blind instinct, for he was past reasoning, must have driven him to take the river bank in the direction of the sea. For when the dawn broke, which it did with unusual suddenness, the sky turning a pale yellow and the rain almost ceasing, he found himself on the banks of the Thames off Wapping. Now a sight of the most extraordinary nature met his eyes. Where, for three months and more, there had been solid ice of such thickness that it seemed permanent as stone, and a whole gay city had stood on its pavement was now a race of turbulent yellow waters. The river had gained its freedom in the night. It was as if a sulphur spring (to which view many philosophers inclined) had risen from the volcanic regions beneath and burst the ice asunder with such vehemence that it swept the huge and many fragments furiously apart. The mere look of the water was enough to turn one giddy. All was riot and confusion. The river was strewn with icebergs. Some of these were as broad as a bowling green and as high as a house; others no bigger than a man's hat, but most fantastically twisted. Now would come down a whole convoy of ice blocks sinking everything that stood in their way. Now, eddying and swirling like a tortured serpent, the river would seem to be hurtling itself between the fragments and tossing them from bank to bank, so that they could be heard smashing against the piers and pillars. But what was the most awful and inspiring of terror was the sight of the human creatures who had been trapped in the night and now paced their twisting and precarious islands in the utmost agony of spirit. Whether they jumped into the flood or stayed on the ice their doom was certain. Sometimes quite a cluster of these poor creatures would come down together, some on their knees, others suckling their babies. One old man seemed to be reading aloud from a holy book. At other times, and his fate perhaps was the most dreadful, a solitary wretch would stride his narrow tenement alone. As they swept out to sea, some could be heard crying vainly for help, making wild promises to amend their ways, confessing their sins and vowing altars and wealth if God would hear their prayers. Others were so dazed with terror that they sat immovable and silent looking steadfastly before them. One crew of young watermen or post-boys, to judge by their liveries, roared and shouted the lewdest tavern songs, as if in bravado, and were dashed to death and sunk with blasphemies on their lips. An old nobleman—for such his furred gown and golden chain proclaimed him—went down not far from where Orlando stood, calling vengenace upon the Irish rebels, who, he cried with his last breath, had plotted this devilry. Many perished clasping some silver pot or other treasure to their breasts; and at least a score of poor wretches were drowned by their own cupidity, hurling themselves from the bank into the flood rather than let a gold goblet escape them, or see before their eyes the disappearance of some furred gown. For furniture, valuables, possessions of all sorts were carried away on the icebergs. Among other strange sights was to be seen a cat suckling its young; a table laid sumptuously for a supper of twenty; a couple in bed; together with an extraordinary number of cooking utensils.

Dazed and astounded, Orlando could do nothing for some time but watch the appalling race of waters as it hurled itself past him. At last, seeming to recollect himself, he clapped spurs to his horse and galloped hard along the river bank in the direction of the sea. Rounding a bend of the river, he came opposite that reach where, not two days ago, the ships of the Ambassadors had seemed immovably frozen. Hastily, he made count of them all; the French; the Spanish; the Austrian; the Turk. All still floated, though the French had broken loose from her moorings, and the Turkish vessel had taken a great rent in her side and was fast filling with water. But the Russian ship was nowhere to be seen. For one moment Orlando thought it must have foundered; but, raising himself in his stirrups and shading his eyes, which had the sight of a hawk's, he could just make out the shape of a ship on the horizon. The black eagles were flying from the mast head. The ship of the Muscovite Embassy was standing out to sea.

Flinging himself from his horse, he made, in his rage, as if he would breast the flood. Standing knee deep in water he hurled at the faithless woman all the insults that have ever been the lot of her sex. Faithless, mutable, fickle, he called her; devil, adulteress, deceiver; and the swirling waters took his words, and tossed at his feet a broken pot and a little straw.

FROM

The Waves

When The Waves, *her seventh novel, was published in 1931,*
Virginia Woolf *was puzzled by the* Times Literary Supplement
review: "Odd, that they (The Times) shd. *praise my characters*
when I meant to have none," she confided to her diary. Al-
though the novel is perhaps her most distinguished, it remains
to this day her most enigmatic. It consists of nine chapters,
each of which describes a stage in the lives of six people—three
female, three male—from childhood to old age. On the female
side are Rhoda, the emotionally and mentally unbalanced;
Jinny, the tireless sensualist; Susan, the rapacious maternalist.
On the male side: Louis, the insecure builder of commercial
empires; Neville, the love-starved homosexual poet; Bernard, the
potential novelist and maker of phrases. Each of the six, in pro-
fessing certain values and making life choices, communicates
to the reader and to each other his or her own private history
through the medium of soliloquy. We become witnesses of their
loves, their hates, their fears, and their hopes—all set on the
shore of time and orchestrated to the rhythmic breaking of the
waves. We find ourselves often reading the emotions lurking
just below the lustrous veneer of words; and it is this quality
in the language that gives the novel its large vitality and high
personal tone.

The four extracts printed here come from Bernard's solilo-
quies during four different stages in his life. Of the six voices
in the novel, Bernard, the novelist manqué, *comes closest to*
being Virginia Woolf's artistic deputy. In the first extract (from
Chapter III), Bernard, in young manhood, questions his identity
and discovers that he is "not one and simple, but complex and
many." In the second (from Chapter IV), his meditations
deepen, and he begins to realize that in order to "be myself . . .
I need the illumination of other people's eyes, and therefore
cannot be entirely sure what is my self." The third (from
Chapter VII) finds Bernard now in his middle years. Maturity
has brought with it the recognition that life, from which all art
is distilled, has its own inevitable sequence and determines its
own ultimate design. In the last extract (from Chapter IX), he
sees, however, that life's unending illumination "floods the
room and drives shadow beyond shadow where they hang in
folds inscrutable. What does the central shadow hold? Some-
thing? Nothing? I do not know."
   It is impossible to describe more precisely this strange, rich
fabric of thought and feeling. No novel like The Waves *had*
ever before been written, and none has been written since. It is
hard to think who other than Virginia Woolf could have con-
ceived and composed a work of such fluidity, depth, and per-
manence.

─────────────────────

"THE COMPLEXITY OF THINGS BECOMES MORE
close," said Bernard, "here at college, where the stir and pressure
of life are so extreme, where the excitement of mere living becomes daily more urgent. Every hour something new is unburied
in the great bran pie. What am I? I ask. This? No, I am that.
Especially now, when I have left a room, and people talking, and
the stone flags ring out with my solitary footsteps, and I behold
the moon rising, sublimely, indifferently, over the ancient chapel

—then it becomes clear that I am not one and simple, but complex and many. Bernard in public, bubbles; in private, is secretive. That is what they do not understand, for they are now undoubtedly discussing me, saying I escape them, am evasive. They do not understand that I have to effect different transitions; have to cover the entrances and exits of several different men who alternately act their parts as Bernard. I am abnormally aware of circumstances. I can never read a book in a railway carriage without asking, Is he a builder? Is she unhappy? I was aware today acutely that poor Simes, with his pimple was feeling, how bitterly, that his chance of making a good impression upon Billy Jackson was remote. Feeling this painfully I invited him to dinner with ardour. This he will attribute to an admiration which is not mine. That is true. But 'joined to the sensibility of a woman' (I am here quoting my own biographer) 'Bernard possessed the logical sobriety of a man.' Now people who make a single impression, and that, in the main, a good one (for there seems to be a virtue in simplicity) are those who keep their equilibrium in mid-stream. (I instantly see fish with their noses one way, the stream rushing past another.) Canon, Lycett, Peters, Hawkins, Larpent, Neville—all fish in mid-stream. But *you* understand, *you*, my self, who always comes at a call (that would be a harrowing experience to call and for no one to come; that would make the midnight hollow, and explains the expression of old men in clubs—they have given up calling for a self who does not come) you understand that I am only superficially represented by what I was saying tonight. Underneath, and, at the moment when I am most disparate, I am also integrated. I sympathise effusively; I also sit like a toad in a hole, receiving with perfect coldness whatever comes. Very few of you who are now discussing me have the double capacity to feel, to reason. Lycett, you see, believes in running after hares; Hawkins has spent a most industrious afternoon in the library. Peters has his young lady at the circulating library. You are all engaged, involved, drawn in, and absolutely energised to the top of your bent—all save Neville, whose mind is far too complex to be roused by any single activity. I also am too complex. In my case something remains floating, unattached.

"Now, as a proof of my susceptibility to atmosphere, here, as I come into my room, and turn on the light, and see the sheet of paper, the table, my gown lying negligently over the back of the chair, I feel that I am that dashing yet reflective man, that bold and deleterious figure, who, lightly throwing off his cloak, seizes his pen and at once flings off the following letter to the girl with whom he is passionately in love.

"Yes, all is propitious. I am now in the mood. I can write the letter straight off which I have begun ever so many times. I have just come in; I have flung down my hat and my stick; I am writing the first thing that comes into my head without troubling to put the paper straight. It is going to be a brilliant sketch which, she must think, was written without a pause, without an erasure. Look how unformed the letters are—there is a careless blot. All must be sacrificed to speed and carelessness. I will write a quick, running, small hand, exaggerating the down stroke of the 'y' and crossing the 't' thus—with a dash. The date shall be only Tuesday, the 17th, and then a question mark. But also I must give her the impression that though he—for this is not myself—is writing in such an off-hand, such a slap-dash way, there is some subtle suggestion of intimacy and respect. I must allude to talks we have had together—bring back some remembered scene. But I must seem to her (this is very important) to be passing from thing to thing with the greatest ease in the world. I shall pass from the service for the man who was drowned (I have a phrase for that) to Mrs. Moffat and her sayings (I have a note of them) and so to some reflections apparently casual but full of profundity (profound criticism is often written casually) about some book I have been reading, some out-of-the-way book. I want her to say as she brushes her hair or puts out the candle, 'Where did I read that? Oh, in Bernard's letter.' It is the speed, the hot, molten effect, the lava flow of sentence into sentence that I need. Who am I thinking of? Byron of course. I am, in some ways, like Byron. Perhaps a sip of Byron will help to put me in the vein. Let me read a page. No; this is dull; this is scrappy. This is rather too formal. Now I am getting the hang of it. Now I am getting his beat into my brain (the rhythm is the main thing in writing). Now, without pausing I will begin, on the very lilt of the stroke— . . .

". . . For myself, I have no aim. I have no ambition. I will let myself be carried on by the general impulse. The surface of my mind slips along like a pale-grey stream reflecting what passes. I cannot remember my past, my nose, or the colour of my eyes, or what my general opinion of myself is. Only in moments of emergency, at a crossing, at a kerb, the wish to preserve my body springs out and seizes me and stops me, here, before this omnibus. We insist, it seems, on living. Then again, indifference descends. The roar of the traffic, the passage of undifferentiated faces, this way and that way, drugs me into dreams; rubs the features from faces. People might walk through me. And, what is this moment of time, this particular day in which I have found myself caught? The growl of traffic might be any uproar—forest trees or the roar of wild beasts. Time has whizzed back an inch or two on its reel; our short progress has been cancelled. I think also that our bodies are in truth naked. We are only lightly covered with buttoned cloth; and beneath these pavements are shells, bones and silence.

"It is, however, true that my dreaming, my tentative advance like one carried beneath the surface of a stream, is interrupted, torn, pricked and plucked at by sensations, spontaneous and irrelevant, of curiosity, greed, desire, irresponsible as in sleep. (I covet that bag—etc.) No, but I wish to go under; to visit the profound depths; once in a while to exercise my prerogative not always to act, but to explore; to hear vague, ancestral sounds of boughs creaking, of mammoths, to indulge impossible desires to embrace the whole world with the arms of understanding, impossible to those who act. Am I not, as I walk, trembling with strange oscillations and vibrations of sympathy, which, unmoored as I am from a private being, bid me embrace these engrossed flocks; these starers and trippers; these errand-boys and furtive and fugitive girls who, ignoring their doom, look in at shop-windows? But I am aware of our ephemeral passage.

"It is, however, true that I cannot deny a sense that life for me is now mysteriously prolonged. Is it that I may have children, may cast a fling of seed wider, beyond this generation, this doom-encircled population, shuffling each other in endless competition along the street? My daughters shall come here, in other summers; my sons shall turn new fields. Hence we are not raindrops, soon dried by the wind; we make gardens blow and forests roar; we come up differently, for ever and ever. This then serves to explain my confidence, my central stability, otherwise so monstrously absurd as I breast the stream of this crowded thoroughfare, making always a passage for myself between people's bodies, taking advantage of safe moments to cross. It is not vanity; for I am emptied of ambition; I do not remember my special gifts, or idiosyncrasy, or the marks I bear on my person, eyes, nose or mouth. I am not, at this moment, myself.

"Yet behold, it returns. One cannot extinguish that persistent smell. It steals in through some crack in the structure—one's identity. I am not part of the street—no, I observe the street. One splits off, therefore. For instance, up that back street a girl stands waiting; for whom? A romantic story. On the wall of that shop is fixed a small crane, and for what reason, I ask, was that crane fixed there? and invent a purple lady swelling, circumambient, hauled from a barouche landau by a perspiring husband sometime in the sixties. A grotesque story. That is, I am a natural coiner of words, a blower of bubbles through one thing and another. And striking off these observations spontaneously I elaborate myself; differentiate myself and listening to the voice that says as I stroll past, 'Look! Take note of that!' I conceive myself called upon to provide, some winter's night, a meaning for all my observations—a line that runs from one to another, a summing up that completes. But soliloquies in back streets soon pall. I need an audience. That is my downfall. That always ruffles the edge of the final statement and prevents it from forming. I cannot seat myself in some sordid eating-house and order the same glass day after day and imbue myself entirely in one fluid—this life. I make my phrase and run off with it to some furnished room where it will be lit by dozens of candles. I need eyes on me to draw out these frills and furbelows. To be myself (I note) I need the illumination of other people's eyes, and therefore cannot be entirely sure what is my self. . . .

". . . I have made up thousands of stories; I have filled innumerable notebooks with phrases to be used when I have found the true story, the one story to which all these phrases refer. But I have never yet found that story. And I begin to ask, Are there stories?

"Look now from this terrace at the swarming population beneath. Look at the general activity and clamour. That man is in difficulties with his mule. Half a dozen good-natured loafers offer their services. Others pass by without looking. They have as many interests as there are threads in a skein. Look at the sweep of the sky, bowled over by round white clouds. Imagine the leagues of level land and the aqueducts and the broken Roman pavement and the tombstones in the Campagna, and beyond the Campagna, the sea, then again more land, then the sea. I could break off any detail in all that prospect—say the mule-cart—and describe it with the greatest ease. But why describe a man in trouble with his mule? Again, I could invent stories about that girl coming up the steps. 'She met him under the dark archway. . . . "It is over," he said, turning from the cage where the china parrot hangs.' Or simply, 'That was all.' But why impose my arbitrary design? Why stress this and shape that and twist up little figures like the toys men sell in trays in the street? Why select this, out of all that,—one detail?

"Here am I shedding one of my life-skins, and all they will say is, 'Bernard is spending ten days in Rome.' Here am I marching up and down this terrace alone, unoriented. But observe how dots and dashes are beginning, as I walk, to run themselves into continuous lines, how things are losing the bald, the separate identity that they had as I walked up those steps. The great red pot is now a reddish streak in a wave of yellowish green. The world is beginning to move past me like the banks of a hedge when the train starts, like the waves of the sea when a steamer moves. I am moving too, am becoming involved in the general sequence when one thing follows another and it seems inevitable that the tree should come, then the telegraph-pole, then the break in the hedge. And as I move, surrounded, included and taking part, the usual phrases begin to bubble up, and I wish to free these bubbles from the trap-door in my head, and direct my steps therefore towards that man, the back of whose head is half familiar to me. We were together at school. We shall undoubtedly meet. We shall certainly lunch together. We shall talk. But wait, one moment wait.

"These moments of escape are not to be despised. They come too seldom. Tahiti becomes possible. Leaning over this parapet I see far out a waste of water. A fin turns. This bare visual impression is unattached to any line of reason, it springs up as one might see the fin of a porpoise on the horizon. Visual impressions often communicate thus briefly statements that we shall in time to come uncover and coax into words. I note under F., therefore, 'Fin in a waste of waters.' I, who am perpetually making notes in the margin of my mind for some final statement, make this mark, waiting for some winter's evening.

"Now I shall go and lunch somewhere, I shall hold my glass up, I shall look through the wine, I shall observe with more than my usual detachment, and when a pretty woman enters the restaurant and comes down the room between the tables I shall say to myself, Look where she comes against a waste of waters. A meaningless observation, but to me, solemn, slate-coloured, with a fatal sound of ruining worlds and waters falling to destruction. . . ."

"So into the street again, swinging my stick, looking at wire trays in stationers' shop-windows, at baskets of fruit grown in the colonies, murmuring Pillicock sat on Pillicock's hill, or Hark,

hark, the dogs do bark, or The World's great age begins anew, or Come away, come away, death—mingling nonsense and poetry, floating in the stream. Something always has to be done next. Tuesday follows Monday; Wednesday, Tuesday. Each spreads the same ripple. The being grows rings, like a tree. Like a tree, leaves fall.

"For one day as I leant over a gate that led into a field, the rhythm stopped: the rhymes and the hummings, the nonsense and the poetry. A space was cleared in my mind. I saw through the thick leaves of habit. Leaning over the gate I regretted so much litter, so much unaccomplishment and separation, for one cannot cross London to see a friend, life being so full of engagements; nor take ship to India and see a naked man spearing fish in blue water. I said life had been imperfect, an unfinished phrase. It had been impossible for me, taking snuff as I do from any bagman met in a train, to keep coherency—that sense of the generations, of women carrying red pitchers to the Nile, of the nightingale who sings among conquests and migrations. It had been too vast an undertaking, I said, and how can I go on lifting my foot perpetually to climb the stair? I addressed myself as one would speak to a companion with whom one is voyaging to the North Pole.

"I spoke to that self who has been with me in many tremendous adventures; the faithful man who sits over the fire when everybody has gone to bed, stirring the cinders with a poker; the man who has been so mysteriously and with sudden accretions of being built up, in a beech wood, sitting by a willow tree on a bank, leaning over a parapet at Hampton Court; the man who has collected himself in moments of emergency and banged his spoon on the table, saying, 'I will not consent.'

"This self now as I leant over the gate looking down over fields rolling in waves of colour beneath me made no answer. He threw up no opposition. He attempted no phrase. His fist did not form. I waited. I listened. Nothing came, nothing. I cried then with a sudden conviction of complete desertion, Now there is nothing. No fin breaks the waste of this immeasurable sea. Life has destroyed me. No echo comes when I speak, no varied words. This is more truly death than the death of friends, than the death of youth. I am the swathed figure in the hairdresser's shop taking up only so much space.

"The scene beneath me withered. It was like the eclipse when the sun went out and left the earth, flourishing in full summer foliage, withered, brittle, false. Also I saw on a winding road in a dust dance the groups we had made, how they came together, how they ate together, how they met in this room or that. I saw my own indefatigable busyness—how I had rushed from one to the other, fetched and carried, travelled and returned, joined this group and that, here kissed, here withdrawn; always kept hard at it by some extraordinary purpose with my nose to the ground like a dog on the scent; with an occasional toss of the head, an occasional cry of amazement, despair and then back again with my nose to the scent. What a litter—what a confusion; with here birth, here death; succulence and sweetness; effort and anguish; and myself always running hither and thither. Now it was done with. I had no more appetites to glut; no more stings in me with which to poison people; no more sharp teeth and clutching hands or desire to feel the pear and the grape and the sun beating down from the orchard wall.

"The woods had vanished; the earth was a waste of shadow. No sound broke the silence of the wintry landscape. No cock crowed; no smoke rose; no train moved. A man without a self, I said. A heavy body leaning on a gate. A dead man. With dispassionate despair, with entire disillusionment I surveyed the dust dance; my life, my friends' lives, and those fabulous presences, men with brooms, women writing, the willow tree by the river—clouds and phantoms made of dust too, of dust that changed, as clouds lose and gain and take gold or red and lose their summits and billow this way and that, mutable, vain. I, carrying a notebook, making phrases, had recorded merely changes; a shadow, I had been sedulous to take note of shadows. How can I proceed now, I said, without a self, weightless and visionless, through a world weightless, without illusion?

"The heaviness of my despondency thrust open the gate I leant on and pushed me, an elderly man, a heavy man with grey hair, through the colourless field, the empty field. No more to hear echoes, no more to see phantoms, to conjure up no opposition, but to walk always unshadowed making no impress upon the dead earth. If even there had been sheep munching, pushing one foot after another, or a bird, or a man driving a spade into the earth, had there been a bramble to trip me, or a ditch, damp with soaked leaves, into which to fall—but no, the melancholy path led along the level, to more wintriness, and pallor and the equal and uninteresting view of the same landscape.

"How then does light return to the world after the eclipse of the sun? Miraculously. Frailly. In thin stripes. It hangs like a glass cage. It is a hoop to be fractured by a tiny jar. There is a spark there. Next moment a flush of dun. Then a vapour as if earth were breathing in and out, once, twice, for the first time. Then under the dullness some one walks with a green light. Then off twists a white wraith. The woods throb blue and green, and gradually the fields drink in red, gold, brown. Suddenly a river snatches a blue light. The earth absorbs colour like a sponge, slowly drinking water. It puts on weight; rounds itself; hangs pendent; settles and swings beneath our feet.

"So the landscape returned to me; so I saw fields rolling in waves of colour beneath me, but now with this difference; I saw but was not seen. I walked unshadowed; I came unheralded. From me had dropped the old cloak, the old response; the hollowed hand that beats back sounds. Thin, as a ghost, leaving no trace where I trod, perceiving merely, I walked alone in a new world, never trodden; brushing new flowers, unable to speak save in a child's words of one syllable; without shelter from phrases— I who have made so many; unattended, I who have always gone with my kind; solitary I who have always had some one to share the empty grate, or the cupboard with its hanging loop of gold.

"But how describe the world seen without a self? There are no words. Blue, red—even they distract, even they hide with thickness instead of letting the light through. How describe or say anything in articulate words again?—save that it fades, save that it undergoes a gradual transformation, becomes, even in the course of one short walk, habitual—this scene also. Blindness returns as one moves and one leaf repeats another. Loveliness returns as one looks with all its train of phantom phrases. One breathes in and out substantial breath; down in the valley the train draws across the fields lop-eared with smoke.

"But for a moment I had sat on the turf somewhere high above the flow of the sea and the sounds of the woods, had seen the house, the garden, and the waves breaking. The old nurse who turns the pages of the picture-book had stopped and had said, 'Look. This is the truth.'

"So I was thinking as I came along Shaftesbury Avenue tonight. I was thinking of that picture in the picture-book. And when I met you in the place where one goes to hang up one's coat I said to myself, 'It does not matter whom I meet. All this little affair of "being" is over. Who this is I do not know; nor care; we will dine together.' So I hung up my coat, tapped you on the shoulder, and said, 'Sit with me.'

"Now the meal is finished; we are surrounded by peelings and bread-crumbs. I have tried to break off this bunch and hand it you; but whether there is substance or truth in it I do not know. Nor do I know exactly where we are. What city does that stretch of sky look down upon? Is it Paris, is it London where we sit or some southern city of pink-washed houses lying under cypresses, under high mountains, where eagles soar? I do not at this moment feel certain.

"I begin now to forget; I begin to doubt the fixity of tables, the reality of here and now, to tap my knuckles smartly upon the edges of apparently solid objects and say, 'Are you hard?' I have seen so many different things, have made so many different sentences. I have lost in the process of eating and drinking and rubbing my eyes along surfaces that thin, hard shell which cases the soul, which, in youth, shuts one in—hence the fierceness, and the tap, tap, tap of the remorseless beaks of the young. And now I ask, 'Who am I?' I have been talking of Bernard, Neville, Jinny, Susan, Rhoda and Louis. Am I all of them? Am I one and distinct? I do not know. We sat here together. But now Percival is dead, and Rhoda is dead; we are divided; we are not here. Yet I cannot find any obstacle separating us. There is no division between me and them. As I talked I felt, 'I am you.' This difference we make so much of, this identity we so feverishly cherish, was overcome. Yes, ever since old Mrs. Constable lifted her sponge and pouring warm water over me covered me with flesh I have been sensitive, percipient. Here on my brow is the blow I got when Percival fell. Here on the nape of my neck is the kiss Jinny gave Louis. My eyes fill with Susan's tears. I see far away, quivering like a gold thread, the pillar Rhoda saw, and feel the rush of the wind of her flight when she leapt.

"Thus when I come to shape here at this table between my hands the story of my life and set it before you as a complete thing, I have to recall things gone far, gone deep, sunk into this life or that and become part of it; dreams, too, things surrounding me, and the inmates, those old half-articulate ghosts who keep up their hauntings by day and night; who turn over in their sleep, who utter their confused cries, who put out their phantom fingers and clutch at me as I try to escape—shadows of people one might have been; unborn selves. There is the old brute, too, the savage, the hairy man who dabbles his fingers in ropes of entrails; and gobbles and belches; whose speech is guttural, visceral—well, he is here. He squats in me. Tonight he has been feasted on quails, salad, and sweetbread. He now holds a glass of fine old brandy in his paw. He brindles, purrs and shoots warm thrills all down my spine as I sip. It is true, he washes his hands before dinner, but they are still hairy. He buttons on trousers and waistcoats, but they contain the same organs. He jibs if I keep him waiting for dinner. He mops and mows perpetually pointing with his half-idiot gestures of greed and covetousness at what he desires. I assure you, I have great difficulty sometimes in controlling him. That man, the hairy, the ape-like, has contributed his part to my life. He has given a greener glow to green things, has held his torch with its red flames, its thick and smarting smoke, behind every leaf. He has lit up the cool garden even. He has brandished his torch in murky by-streets where girls suddenly seem to shine with a red and intoxicating translucency. Oh, he has tossed his torch high! He has led me wild dances!

"But no more. Now tonight, my body rises tier upon tier like some cool temple whose floor is strewn with carpets and murmurs rise and the altars stand smoking; but up above, here in my serene head, come only fine gusts of melody, waves of incense, while the lost dove wails, and the banners tremble above tombs, and the dark airs of midnight shake trees outside the open windows. When I look down from this transcendency, how beautiful are even the crumbled relics of bread! What shapely spirals the peelings of pears make—how thin, and mottled like some sea-bird's egg. Even the forks laid straight side by side appear lucid, logical, exact; and the horns of the rolls which we have left are glazed, yellow-plated, hard. I could worship my hand even, with its fan of bones laced by blue mysterious veins and its astonishing look of aptness, suppleness and ability to curl softly or suddenly crush—its infinite sensibility.

"Immeasurably receptive, holding everything, trembling with fullness, yet clear, contained—so my being seems, now that desire urges it no more out and away; now that curiosity no longer dyes it a thousand colours. It lies deep, tideless, immune, now that he is dead, the man I called 'Bernard,' the man who kept a book in his pocket in which he made notes—phrases for the moon, notes of features; how people looked, turned, dropped their cigarette ends; under B, butterfly powder, under D, ways of naming death. But now let the door open, the glass door that is for ever turning on its hinges. Let a woman come, let a young man in evening-dress with a moustache sit down; is there anything that they can tell me? No! I know all that, too. And if she suddenly gets up and goes, 'My dear,' I say, 'you no longer make me look after you.' The shock of the falling wave which has sounded all my life, which woke me so that I saw the gold loop on the cupboard, no longer makes quiver what I hold.

"So now, taking upon me the mystery of things, I could go like a spy without leaving this place, without stirring from my chair. I can visit the remote verges of the desert lands where the savage sits by the campfire. Day rises; the girl lifts the watery fire-hearted jewels to her brow; the sun levels his beams straight at the sleeping house; the waves deepen their bars; they fling themselves on shore; back blows the spray; sweeping their waters they surround the boat and the sea-holly. The birds sing in chorus; deep tunnels run between the stalks of flowers; the house is whitened; the sleeper stretches; gradually all is astir. Light floods the room and drives shadow beyond shadow to where they hang in folds inscrutable. What does the central shadow hold? Something? Nothing? I do not know.

"Oh, but there is your face. I catch your eye. I, who had been thinking myself so vast, a temple, a church, a whole universe, unconfined and capable of being everywhere on the verge of things and here too, am now nothing but what you see—an elderly man, rather heavy, grey above the ears, who (I see myself in the glass) leans one elbow on the table, and holds in his left hand a glass of old brandy. That is the blow you have dealt me. I have walked bang into the pillar-box. I reel from side to side. I put my hands to my head. My hat is off—I have dropped my stick. I have made an awful ass of myself and am justly laughed at by any passer-by.

"Lord, how unutterably disgusting life is! What dirty tricks it plays us, one moment free; the next, this. Here we are among the breadcrumbs and the stained napkins again. That knife is already congealing with grease. Disorder, sordidity and corruption surround us. We have been taking into our mouths the bodies of dead birds. It is with these greasy crumbs, slobbered over napkins, and little corpses that we have to build. Always it begins again; always there is the enemy; eyes meeting ours; fingers twitching ours; the effort waiting. Call the waiter. Pay the bill. We must pull ourselves up out of our chairs. We must find our coats. We must go. Must, must, must—detestable word. Once more, I who had thought myself immune, who had said, 'Now I am rid of all that,' find that the wave has tumbled me over, head over heels, scattering my possessions, leaving me to collect, to assemble, to heap together, summon my forces, rise and confront the enemy.

"It is strange that we who are capable of so much suffering, should inflict so much suffering. Strange that the face of a person, whom I scarcely know save that I think we met once on the gangway of a ship bound for Africa—a mere adumbration of eyes, cheeks, nostrils—should have power to inflict this insult. You look, eat, smile, are bored, pleased, annoyed—that is all I know. Yet this shadow which has sat by me for an hour or two, this mask from which peep two eyes, has power to drive me back, to pinion me down among all those other faces, to shut me in a hot room; to send me dashing like a moth from candle to candle.

"But wait. While they add up the bill behind the screen wait one moment. Now that I have reviled you for the blow that sent me staggering among peelings and crumblings and old scraps of meat, I will record in words of one syllable how also under your gaze with that compulsion on me I begin to perceive this, that and the other. The clock ticks; the woman sneezes; the waiter comes—there is a gradual coming together, running into one, acceleration and unification. Listen: a whistle sounds, wheels rush, the door creaks on its hinges. I regain the sense of the complexity and the reality and the struggle, for which I thank you. And with some pity, some envy and much good will, take your hand and bid you good night.

"Heaven be praised for solitude! I am alone now. That almost unknown person has gone, to catch some train, to take some cab, to go to some place or person whom I do not know. The face looking at me has gone. The pressure is removed. Here are empty coffee-cups. Here are chairs turned but nobody sits on them. Here are empty tables and nobody any more coming to dine at them tonight.

"Let me now raise my song of glory. Heaven be praised for solitude. Let me be alone. Let me cast and throw away this veil of being, this cloud that changes with the least breath, night and day, and all night and all day. While I sat here I have been changing. I have watched the sky change. I have seen clouds cover the stars, then free the stars, then cover the stars again. Now I look at their changing no more. Now no one sees me and I change no more. Heaven be praised for solitude that has removed the pressure of the eye, the solicitation of the body, and all need of lies and phrases.

"My book, stuffed with phrases, has dropped to the floor. It lies under the table to be swept up by the charwoman when she comes wearily at dawn looking for scraps of paper, old tram tickets, and here and there a note screwed into a ball and left with the litter to be swept up. What is the phrase for the moon? And the phrase for love? By what name are we to call death? I do not know. I need a little language such as lovers use, words of one syllable such as children speak when they come into the room and find their mother sewing and pick up some scrap of bright wool, a feather, or a shred of chintz. I need a howl; a cry. When the storm crosses the marsh and sweeps over me where I lie in the ditch unregarded I need no words. Nothing neat. Nothing that comes down with all its feet on the floor. None of those resonances and lovely echoes that break and chime from nerve to nerve in our breasts making wild music, false phrases. I have done with phrases.

"How much better is silence; the coffee-cup, the table. How much better to sit by myself like the solitary sea-bird that opens its wings on the stake. Let me sit here for ever with bare things, this coffee-cup, this knife, this fork, things in themselves, myself being myself. Do not come and worry me with your hints that it is time to shut the shop and be gone. I would willingly give all my money that you should not disturb me but let me sit on and on, silent, alone.

"But now the head waiter, who has finished his own meal, appears and frowns; he takes his muffler from his pocket and ostentatiously makes ready to go. They must go; must put up the shutters, must fold the tablecloths, and give one brush with a wet mop under the tables.

"Curse you then. However beat and done with it all I am, I must haul myself up, and find the particular coat that belongs to me; must push my arms into the sleeves; must muffle myself up against the night air and be off. I, I, I, tired as I am, spent as I am, and almost worn out with all this rubbing of my nose along the surfaces of things, even I, an elderly man who is getting rather heavy and dislikes exertion must take myself off and catch some last train.

"Again I see before me the usual street. The canopy of civilisation is burnt out. The sky is dark as polished whale-bone. But there is a kindling in the sky whether of lamplight or of dawn. There is a stir of some sort—sparrows on plane trees somewhere chirping. There is a sense of the break of day. I will not call it dawn. What is dawn in the city to an elderly man standing in the street looking up rather dizzily at the sky? Dawn is some sort of whitening of the sky; some sort of renewal. Another day; another Friday; another twentieth of March, January, or September. Another general awakening. The stars draw back and are extinguished. The bars deepen themselves between the waves. The film of mist thickens on the fields. A redness gathers on the roses, even on the pale rose that hangs by the bedroom window. A bird chirps. Cottagers light their early candles. Yes, this is the eternal renewal, the incessant rise and fall and fall and rise again.

"And in me too the wave rises. It swells; it arches its back. I am aware once more of a new desire, something rising beneath me like the proud horse whose rider first spurs and then pulls him back. What enemy do we now perceive advancing against us, you whom I ride now, as we stand pawing this stretch of pavement? It is death. Death is the enemy. It is death against whom I ride with my spear couched and my hair flying back like a young man's, like Percival's, when he galloped in India. I strike spurs into my horse. Against you I will fling myself, unvanquished and unyielding, O Death!"

The waves broke on the shore.

Short Stories

Virginia Woolf published only one book of short stories during her lifetime, Monday or Tuesday, in 1921. At the time of her death in 1941, she was planning a volume of collected stories in which the five gathered here would have appeared. Leonard Woolf carried out her plan in a collection entitled A Haunted House and Other Short Stories, published posthumously in 1944. "All through her life, Virginia Woolf used at intervals to write short stories," wrote Leonard Woolf in his Foreword to A Haunted House. "It was her custom, whenever an idea for one occurred to her, to sketch it out in a very rough form and then to put it away in a drawer. Later, if an editor asked her for a short story, and she felt in the mood to write one (which was not frequent), she would take a sketch out of her drawer and rewrite it, sometimes a great many times."

Because of the brevity of the stories, the reader will see more readily in them than in the longer fiction that nothing on a page written by Virginia Woolf is ever there by chance. Everything, always, is there by very deliberate choice, in a carefully pre-meditated design. Everything is functional—every stray thought and random gesture. Even the most seemingly irrelevant details are put to some precise service: whether to stress a contrast, deepen an atmosphere, or explore some hidden corner of human character. Part of the enduring quality of Virginia Woolf's writing comes from the extraordinary ease with which these endless irrelevancies coalesce in the reader to create emotional evocations, long before the reader is able to articulate the feelings evoked.

The stories that follow are small literary performances sustained at their finest, most human pitch.

The Legacy

Although "The Legacy" was revised in the autumn of 1940 and submitted for publication in Harper's Bazaar, it did not appear in print during Virginia Woolf's lifetime. It is probably the last story she ever wrote, and it is a masterpiece in miniature.

Relying largely upon diary entries as the narrative point of view, she succeeds in just a few pages in sketching out the principal contours that define the married lives of Angela and Gilbert Clandon. In carefully sequenced fragments from her diary—Angela's "legacy" to her husband—and in Gilbert's self-centered reactions to those entry fragments, we are given access to the shadowy precincts of Angela's private life. More than that, we are confronted with the harsh conceits of a vain and overbearing husband. Yet nowhere does the author herself pass judgment overtly on her characters. The whole story is quietly dramatized by the ironic device of giving the right book to the wrong reader—that is, Angela's diary put into Gilbert's hands. Together they produce a vivid tableau of conflict in which Angela emerges exonerated and her husband justifiably condemned.

"FOR SISSY MILLER." GILBERT CLANDON, TAKING up the pearl brooch that lay among a litter of rings and brooches on a little table in his wife's drawing-room, read the inscription: "For Sissy Miller, with my love."

It was like Angela to have remembered even Sissy Miller, her secretary. Yet how strange it was, Gilbert Clandon thought once more, that she had left everything in such order—a little gift of some sort for every one of her friends. It was as if she had foreseen her death. Yet she had been in perfect health when she left the house that morning, six weeks ago; when she stepped off the kerb in Piccadilly and the car had killed her.

He was waiting for Sissy Miller. He had asked her to come; he owed her, he felt, after all the years she had been with them, this token of consideration. Yes, he went on, as he sat there waiting, it was strange that Angela had left everything in such order. Every friend had been left some little token of her affection. Every ring, every necklace, every little Chinese box—she had a passion for little boxes—had a name on it. And each had some memory for him. This he had given her; this—the enamel dolphin with the ruby eyes—she had pounced upon one day in a back street in Venice. He could remember her little cry of delight. To him, of course, she had left nothing in particular, unless it were her diary. Fifteen little volumes, bound in green leather, stood behind him on her writing table. Ever since they were married, she had kept a diary. Some of their very few—he could not call them quarrels, say tiffs—had been about that diary. When he came in and found her writing, she always shut it or put her hand over it. "No, no, no," he could hear her say. "After I'm dead—perhaps." So she had left it him, as her legacy. It was the only thing they had not shared when she was alive. But he had always taken it for granted that she would outlive him. If only she had stopped one moment, and had thought what she was doing, she would be alive now. But she had stepped straight off the kerb, the driver of the car had said at the inquest. She had given him no chance to pull up. . . . Here the sound of voices in the hall interrupted him.

"Miss Miller, Sir," said the maid.

She came in. He had never seen her alone in his life, nor, of course, in tears. She was terribly distressed, and no wonder. Angela had been much more to her than an employer. She had been a friend. To himself, he thought, as he pushed a chair for her and asked her to sit down, she was scarcely distinguishable from any other woman of her kind. There were thousands of Sissy Millers—drab little women in black carrying attaché cases. But Angela, with her genius for sympathy, had discovered all sorts of qualities in Sissy Miller. She was the soul of discretion; so silent; so trustworthy, one could tell her anything, and so on.

Miss Miller could not speak at first. She sat there dabbing her eyes with her pocket handkerchief. Then she made an effort.

"Pardon me, Mr. Clandon," she said.

He murmured. Of course he understood. It was only natural. He could guess what his wife had meant to her.

"I've been so happy here," she said, looking round. Her eyes rested on the writing table behind him. It was here they had worked—she and Angela. For Angela had her share of the duties that fall to the lot of a prominent politician's wife. She had been the greatest help to him in his career. He had often seen her and Sissy sitting at that table—Sissy at the typewriter, taking down letters from her dictation. No doubt Miss Miller was thinking of that, too. Now all he had to do was to give her the brooch his wife had left her. A rather incongruous gift it seemed. It might have been better to have left her a sum of money, or even the typewriter. But there it was—"For Sissy Miller, with my love." And, taking the brooch, he gave it her with the little speech that he had prepared. He knew, he said, that she would value it. His wife had often worn it. . . . And she replied, as she took it almost as if she too had prepared a speech, that it would always be a treasured possession. . . . She had, he supposed, other clothes upon which a pearl brooch would not look quite so incongruous. She was wearing the little black coat and skirt that seemed the uniform of her profession. Then he remembered—she was in mourning, of course. She, too, had had her tragedy—a brother, to whom she was devoted, had died only a week or two before Angela. In some accident was it? He could not remember—only Angela telling him. Angela, with her genius for sympathy, had been terribly upset. Meanwhile Sissy Miller had risen. She was putting on her gloves. Evidently she felt that she ought not to intrude. But he could not let her go without saying something about her future. What were her plans? Was there any way in which he could help her?

She was gazing at the table, where she had sat at her typewriter, where the diary lay. And, lost in her memories of Angela, she did not at once answer his suggestion that he should help her. She seemed for a moment not to understand. So he repeated:

"What are your plans, Miss Miller?"

"My plans? Oh, that's all right, Mr. Clandon," she exclaimed. "Please don't bother yourself about me."

He took her to mean that she was in no need of financial assistance. It would be better, he realized, to make any suggestion of that kind in a letter. All he could do now was to say as he pressed her hand, "Remember, Miss Miller, if there's any way in which I can help you, it will be a pleasure. . . ." Then he opened the door. For a moment, on the threshold, as if a sudden thought had struck her, she stopped.

"Mr. Clandon," she said, looking straight at him for the first time, and for the first time he was struck by the expression, sympathetic yet searching, in her eyes. "If at any time," she continued, "there's anything I can do to help you, remember, I shall feel it, for your wife's sake, a pleasure. . . ."

With that she was gone. Her words and the look that went with them were unexpected. It was almost as if she believed, or hoped, that he would need her. A curious, perhaps a fantastic idea occurred to him as he returned to his chair. Could it be, that during all those years when he had scarcely noticed her, she, as the novelists say, had entertained a passion for him? He caught his own reflection in the glass as he passed. He was over fifty; but he could not help admitting that he was still, as the looking-glass showed him, a very distinguished-looking man.

"Poor Sissy Miller!" he said, half laughing. How he would

have liked to share that joke with his wife! He turned instinctively to her diary. "Gilbert," he read, opening it at random, "looked so wonderful. . . ." It was as if she had answered his question. Of course, she seemed to say, you're very attractive to women. Of course Sissy Miller felt that too. He read on. "How proud I am to be his wife!" And he had always been very proud to be her husband. How often, when they dined out somewhere, he had looked at her across the table and said to himself, "She is the loveliest woman here!" He read on. That first year he had been standing for Parliament. They had toured his constituency. "When Gilbert sat down the applause was terrific. The whole audience rose and sang: 'For he's a jolly good fellow.' I was quite overcome." He remembered that, too. She had been sitting on the platform beside him. He could still see the glance she cast at him, and how she had tears in her eyes. And then? He turned the pages. They had gone to Venice. He recalled that happy holiday after the election. "We had ices at Florians." He smiled —she was still such a child; she loved ices. "Gilbert gave me a most interesting account of the history of Venice. He told me that the Doges . . ." she had written it all out in her schoolgirl hand. One of the delights of travelling with Angela had been that she was so eager to learn. She was so terribly ignorant, she used to say, as if that were not one of her charms. And then—he opened the next volume—they had come back to London. "I was so anxious to make a good impression. I wore my wedding dress." He could see her now sitting next old Sir Edward; and making a conquest of that formidable old man, his chief. He read on rapidly, filling in scene after scene from her scrappy fragments. "Dined at the House of Commons. . . . To an evening party at the Lovegroves'. Did I realize my responsibility, Lady L. asked me, as Gilbert's wife?" Then, as the years passed—he took another volume from the writing table—he had become more and more absorbed in his work. And she, of course, was more often home. . . . It had been a great grief to her, apparently, that they had had no children. "How I wish," one entry read, "that Gilbert had a son!" Oddly enough he had never much regretted that himself. Life had been so full, so rich as it was. That year he had been given a minor post in the government. A minor post only, but her comment was: "I am quite certain now that he will be Prime Minister!" Well, if things had gone differently, it might have been so. He paused here to speculate upon what might have been. Politics was a gamble, he reflected; but the game wasn't over yet. Not at fifty. He cast his eyes rapidly over more pages, full of the little trifles, the insignificant, happy, daily trifles that had made up her life.

He took up another volume and opened it at random. "What a coward I am! I let the chance slip again. But it seemed selfish to bother him with my own affairs, when he had so much to think about. And we so seldom have an evening alone." What was the meaning of that? Oh, here was the explanation—it referred to her work in the East End. "I plucked up courage and talked to Gilbert at last. He was so kind, so good. He made no objection." He remembered that conversation. She had told him that she felt so idle, so useless. She wished to have some work of her own. She wanted to do something—she had blushed so prettily, he remembered, as she said it, sitting in that very chair—to help others. He had bantered her a little. Hadn't she enough to do looking after him, after her home? Still, if it amused her, of course he had no objection. What was it? Some district? Some committee? Only she must promise not to make herself ill. So it seemed that every Wednesday she went to Whitechapel. He remembered how he hated the clothes she wore on those occasions. But she had taken it very seriously, it seemed. The diary was full of references like this: "Saw Mrs. Jones. . . . She has ten children. . . . Husband lost his arm in an accident. . . . Did my best to find a job for Lily." He skipped on. His own name occurred less frequently. His interest slackened. Some of the entries conveyed nothing to him. For example: "Had a heated argument about socialism with B. M." Who was B. M.? He could not fill in the initials; some woman, he supposed, that she had met on one of her committees. "B. M. made a violent attack upon the upper classes. . . . I walked back after the meeting with B. M. and tried to convince him. But he is so narrow-minded." So B. M. was a man—no doubt one of those "intellectuals," as they call themselves, who are so violent, as Angela said, and so narrow-minded. She had invited him to come and see her apparently. "B. M. came to dinner. He shook hands with Minnie!" That note of exclamation gave another twist to his mental picture. B. M., it seemed, wasn't used to parlourmaids; he had shaken hands with Minnie. Presumably he was one of those tame working men who air their views in ladies' drawing-rooms. Gilbert knew the type, and had no liking for this particular specimen, whoever B. M. might be. Here he was again. "Went with B. M. to the Tower of London. . . . He said revolution is bound to come. . . . He said we live in a Fool's Paradise." That was just the kind of thing B. M. would say—Gilbert could hear him. He could also see him quite distinctly—a stubby little man, with a rough beard, red tie, dressed as they always did in tweeds, who had never done an honest day's work in his life. Surely Angela had the sense to see through him? He read on. "B. M. said some very disagreeable things about ———." The name was carefully scratched out. "I told him I would not listen to any more abuse of ———" Again the name was obliterated. Could it have been his own name? Was that why Angela covered the page so quickly when he came in? The thought added to his growing dislike of B. M. He had had the impertinence to discuss him in this very room. Why had Angela never told him? It was very unlike her to conceal anything; she had been the soul of candour. He turned the pages, picking out every reference to B. M. "B. M. told me the story of his childhood. His mother went out charring. . . . When I think of it, I can hardly bear to go on living in such luxury. . . . Three guineas for one hat!" If only she had discussed the matter with him, instead of puzzling her poor little head about questions that were much too difficult for her to understand! He had lent her books. *Karl Marx, The Coming Revolution*. The initials B. M., B. M., B. M., recurred repeatedly. But why never the full name? There was an informality, an intimacy in the use of initials that was very unlike Angela. Had she called him B. M. to his face?

He read on. "B. M. came unexpectedly after dinner. Luckily, I was alone." That was only a year ago. "Luckily"—why luckily? —"I was alone." Where had he been that night? He checked the date in his engagement book. It had been the night of the Mansion House dinner. And B. M. and Angela had spent the evening alone! He tried to recall that evening. Was she waiting up for him when he came back? Had the room looked just as usual? Were there glasses on the table? Were the chairs drawn close together? He could remember nothing—nothing whatever, nothing except his own speech at the Mansion House dinner. It became more and more inexplicable to him—the whole situation: his wife receiving an unknown man alone. Perhaps the next volume would explain. Hastily he reached for the last of the diaries—the one she had left unfinished when she died. There, on the very first page, was that cursed fellow again. "Dined alone with B. M. . . . He became very agitated. He said it was time we understood each other. . . . I tried to make him listen. But he would not. He threatened that if I did not . . ." the rest of the page was scored over. She had written "Egypt. Egypt. Egypt," over the whole page. He could not make out a single word; but there could be only one interpretation: the scoundrel had asked her to become his mistress. Alone in his room! The blood rushed to Gilbert Clandon's face. He turned the pages rapidly. What had been her answer? Initials had ceased. It was simply "he" now. "He came again. I told him I could not come to any decision. . . . I implored him to leave me." He had forced himself upon her in this very house. But why hadn't she told him? How could she have hesitated for an instant? Then: "I wrote him a letter." Then pages were left blank. Then there was this: "No answer to my letter." Then more blank pages; and then this: "He has done what he threatened." After that—what came after that? He turned page after page. All were blank. But there, on the very day before her death, was this entry: "Have I the courage to do it too?" That was the end.

Gilbert Clandon let the book slide to the floor. He could see her in front of him. She was standing on the kerb in Piccadilly.

Her eyes stared; her fists were clenched. Here came the car. . . .

He could not bear it. He must know the truth. He strode to the telephone.

"Miss Miller!" There was silence. Then he heard someone moving in the room.

"Sissy Miller speaking"—her voice at last answered him.

"Who," he thundered, "is B. M.?"

He could hear the cheap clock ticking on her mantelpiece; then a long drawn sigh. Then at last she said:

"He was my brother."

He *was* her brother; her brother who had killed himself. "Is there," he heard Sissy Miller asking, "anything that I can explain?"

"Nothing!" he cried. "Nothing!"

He had received his legacy. She had told him the truth. She had stepped off the kerb to rejoin her lover. She had stepped off the kerb to escape from him.

Lappin and
Lapinova

"*Lappin and Lapinova*" *was first published in April 1939. It is a fragile little tale spun in the manner of most traditional love stories—a newly wedded couple, a new home in which to begin their life together, a private language of endearments. With all of this we are familiar. What is not familiar, however, becomes apparent when we discover that husband and wife live on entirely different planes of experience. Ernest Thorburn, the young groom, is conventional, earth-bound, and exacting. His bride, Rosalind, is his exact opposite. She is at ease only in the airy spaces of fantasy. Neither partner, in consequence, is temperamentally suited to the other. The dissolution of this increasingly unhappy alliance can be postponed only by the wife's imagining her husband a rabbit (King Lappin) and herself a white hare (Queen Lapinova). When the illusion fails, the marriage fails with it. Whether we see this story as comic or tragic depends ultimately upon the extent to which each of us depends upon illusion to maintain the smooth operation of our daily lives.*

THEY WERE MARRIED. THE WEDDING MARCH PEALED out. The pigeons fluttered. Small boys in Eton jackets threw rice; a fox terrier sauntered across the path; and Ernest Thorburn led his bride to the car through that small inquisitive crowd of complete strangers which always collects in London to enjoy other people's happiness or unhappiness. Certainly he looked handsome and she looked shy. More rice was thrown, and the car moved off.

That was on Tuesday. Now it was Saturday. Rosalind had still to get used to the fact that she was Mrs. Ernest Thorburn. Perhaps she never would get used to the fact that she was Mrs. Ernest Anybody, she thought, as she sat in the bow window of the hotel looking over the lake to the mountains, and waited for her husband to come down to breakfast. Ernest was a difficult name to get used to. It was not the name she would have chosen. She would have preferred Timothy, Antony, or Peter. He did not look like Ernest either. The name suggested the Albert Memorial, mahogany sideboards, steel engravings of the Prince Consort with his family—her mother-in-law's dining-room in Porchester Terrace in short.

But here he was. Thank goodness he did not look like Ernest— no. But what did he look like? She glanced at him sideways. Well, when he was eating toast he looked like a rabbit. Not that anyone else would have seen a likeness to a creature so diminutive and timid in this spruce, muscular young man with the straight nose, the blue eyes, and the very firm mouth. But that made it all the more amusing. His nose twitched very slightly when he ate. So did her pet rabbit's. She kept watching his nose twitch; and then she had to explain, when he caught her looking at him, why she laughed.

"It's because you're like a rabbit, Ernest," she said. "Like a wild rabbit," she added, looking at him. "A hunting rabbit; a King Rabbit; a rabbit that makes laws for all the other rabbits."

Ernest had no objection to being that kind of rabbit, and since it amused her to see him twitch his nose—he had never known that his nose twitched—he twitched it on purpose. And she laughed and laughed; and he laughed too, so that the maiden ladies and the fishing man and the Swiss waiter in his greasy black jacket all guessed right; they were very happy. But how long does such happiness last? they asked themselves; and each answered according to his own circumstances.

At lunch time, seated on a clump of heather beside the lake, "Lettuce, rabbit?" said Rosalind, holding out the lettuce that had been provided to eat with the hard-boiled eggs. "Come and take it out of my hand," she added, and he stretched out and nibbled the lettuce and twitched his nose.

"Good rabbit, nice rabbit," she said, patting him, as she used to pat her tame rabbit at home. But that was absurd. He was not a tame rabbit, whatever he was. She turned it into French. "Lapin," she called him. But whatever he was, he was not a French rabbit. He was simply and solely English—born at Porchester Terrace, educated at Rugby; now a clerk in His Majesty's Civil Service. So she tried "Bunny" next; but that was worse. "Bunny" was someone plump and soft and comic; he was thin and hard and serious. Still, his nose twitched. "Lappin," she exclaimed suddenly; and gave a little cry as if she had found the very word she looked for.

"Lappin, Lappin, King Lappin," she repeated. It seemed to suit him exactly; he was not Ernest, he was King Lappin. Why? She did not know.

When there was nothing new to talk about on their long solitary walks—and it rained, as everyone had warned them that it would rain; or when they were sitting over the fire in the evening, for it was cold, and the maiden ladies had gone and the fishing man, and the waiter only came if you rang the bell for him, she let her fancy play with the story of the Lappin tribe. Under her hands—she was sewing; he was reading—they became very real, very vivid, very amusing. Ernest put down the paper and helped her. There were the black rabbits and the red; there were the enemy rabbits and the friendly. There were the wood in which they lived and the outlying prairies and the swamp. Above all

there was King Lappin, who, far from having only the one trick
—that he twitched his nose—became as the days passed an
animal of the greatest character; Rosalind was always finding
new qualities in him. But above all he was a great hunter.

"And what," said Rosalind, on the last day of the honeymoon,
"did the King do today?"

In fact they had been climbing all day; and she had worn a
blister on her heel; but she did not mean that.

"Today," said Ernest, twitching his nose as he bit the end off
his cigar, "he chased a hare." He paused; struck a match, and
twitched again.

"A woman hare," he added.

"A white hare!" Rosalind exclaimed, as if she had been expecting this. "Rather a small hare; silver grey; with big bright
eyes?"

"Yes," said Ernest, looking at her as she had looked at him,
"a smallish animal; with eyes popping out of her head, and two
little front paws dangling." It was exactly how she sat, with her
sewing dangling in her hands; and her eyes, that were so big and
bright, were certainly a little prominent.

"Ah, Lapinova," Rosalind murmured.

"Is that what she's called?" said Ernest—"the real Rosalind?"
He looked at her. He felt very much in love with her.

"Yes; that's what she's called," said Rosalind. "Lapinova."
And before they went to bed that night it was all settled. He was
King Lappin; she was Queen Lapinova. They were the opposite
of each other; he was bold and determined; she wary and unde-
pendable. He ruled over the busy world of rabbits; her world was
a desolate, mysterious place, which she ranged mostly by moonlight. All the same, their territories touched; they were King and
Queen.

Thus when they came back from their honeymoon they possessed a private world, inhabited, save for the one white hare,
entirely by rabbits. No one guessed that there was such a place,
and that of course made it all the more amusing. It made them
feel, more even than most young married couples, in league to-

gether against the rest of the world. Often they looked slyly at each other when people talked about rabbits and woods and traps and shooting. Or they winked furtively across the table when Aunt Mary said that she could never bear to see a hare in a dish—it looked so like a baby: or when John, Ernest's sporting brother, told them what price rabbits were fetching that autumn in Wiltshire, skins and all. Sometimes when they wanted a game-keeper, or a poacher or a Lord of the Manor, they amused themselves by distributing the parts among their friends. Ernest's mother, Mrs. Reginald Thorburn, for example, fitted the part of the Squire to perfection. But it was all secret— that was the point of it; nobody save themselves knew that such a world existed.

Without that world, how, Rosalind wondered, that winter could she have lived at all? For instance, there was the golden-wedding party, when all the Thorburns assembled at Porchester Terrace to celebrate the fiftieth anniversary of that union which had been so blessed—had it not produced Ernest Thorburn?— and so fruitful— had it not produced nine other sons and daughters into the bargain, many themselves married and also fruitful? She dreaded that party. But it was inevitable. As she walked upstairs she felt bitterly that she was an only child and an orphan at that; a mere drop among all those Thorburns assembled in the great drawing-room with the shiny satin wallpaper and the lustrous family portraits. The living Thorburns much resembled the painted; save that instead of painted lips they had real lips; out of which came jokes; jokes about schoolrooms, and how they had pulled the chair from under the governess; jokes about frogs and how they had put them between the virgin sheets of maiden ladies. As for herself, she had never even made an apple-pie bed. Holding her present in her hand she advanced toward her mother-in-law sumptuous in yellow satin; and toward her father-in-law decorated with a rich yellow carnation. All round them on tables and chairs there were golden tributes, some nestling in cotton wool; others branching resplendent—candlesticks; cigar boxes; chains; each stamped with the goldsmith's proof that it was solid gold, hall-marked, authentic. But her present was only a little pinchbeck box pierced with holes; an old sand caster, an eighteenth-century relic, once used to sprinkle sand over wet ink. Rather a senseless present she felt—in an age of blotting paper; and as she proffered it, she saw in front of her the stubby black handwriting in which her mother-in-law when they were engaged had expressed the hope that "My son will make you happy." No, she was not happy. Not at all happy. She looked at Ernest, straight as a ramrod with a nose like all the noses in the family portraits; a nose that never twitched at all.

Then they went down to dinner. She was half hidden by the great chrysanthemums that curled their red and gold petals into large tight balls. Everything was gold. A gold-edged card with gold initials intertwined recited the list of all the dishes that would be set one after another before them. She dipped her spoon in a plate of clear golden fluid. The raw white fog outside had been turned by the lamps into a golden mesh that blurred the edges of the plates and gave the pineapples a rough golden skin. Only she herself in her white wedding dress peering ahead of her with her prominent eyes seemed insoluble as an icicle.

As the dinner wore on, however, the room grew steamy with heat. Beads of perspiration stood out on the men's foreheads. She felt that her icicle was being turned to water. She was being melted; dispersed; dissolved into nothingness; and would soon faint. Then through the surge in her head and the din in her ears she heard a woman's voice exclaim, "But they breed so!"

The Thorburns—yes; they breed so, she echoed; looking at all the round red faces that seemed doubled in the giddiness that overcame her; and magnified in the gold mist that enhaloed them. "They breed so." Then John bawled:

"Little devils! . . . Shoot 'em! Jump on 'em with big boots! That's the only way to deal with 'em . . . rabbits!"

At that word, that magic word, she revived. Peeping between the chrysanthemums she saw Ernest's nose twitch. It rippled, it ran with successive twitches. And at that a mysterious catastrophe befell the Thorburns. The golden table became a moor with the gorse in full bloom; the din of voices turned to one peal of lark's laughter ringing down from the sky. It was a blue sky—clouds passed slowly. And they had all been changed—the Thorburns. She looked at her father-in-law, a furtive little man with dyed moustaches. His foible was collecting things—seals, enamel boxes, trifles from eighteenth-century dressing tables which he hid in the drawers of his study from his wife. Now she saw him as he was—a poacher, stealing off with his coat bulging with pheasants and partridges to drop them stealthily into a three-legged pot in his smoky little cottage. That was her real father-in-law—a poacher. And Celia, the unmarried daughter, who always nosed out other people's secrets, the little things they wished to hide—she was a white ferret with pink eyes, and a nose clotted with earth from her horrid underground nosings and pokings. Slung round men's shoulders, in a net, and thrust down a hole—it was a pitiable life—Celia's; it was none of her fault. So she saw Celia. And then she looked at her mother-in-law—whom they dubbed The Squire. Flushed, coarse, a bully—she was all that, as she stood returning thanks, but now that Rosalind—that is Lapinova saw her, she saw behind her the decayed family mansion, the plaster peeling off the walls, and heard her, with a sob in her voice, giving thanks to her children (who hated her) for a world that had ceased to exist. There was a sudden silence. They all stood with their glasses raised; they all drank; then it was over.

"Oh, King Lappin!" she cried as they went home together in the fog, "if your nose hadn't twitched just at that moment, I should have been trapped!"

"But you're safe," said King Lappin, pressing her paw.

"Quite safe," she answered.

And they drove back through the Park, King and Queen of the marsh, of the mist, and of the gorse-scented moor.

Thus time passed; one year; two years of time. And on a winter's night, which happened by a coincidence to be the anniversary of the golden-wedding party—but Mrs. Reginald Thorburn was dead; the house was to let; and there was only a caretaker in residence—Ernest came home from the office. They had a nice little home; half a house above a saddler's shop in South Kensington, not far from the Tube station. It was cold, with fog in the air, and Rosalind was sitting over the fire, sewing.

"What d'you think happened to me today?" she began as soon as he had settled himself down with his legs stretched to the blaze. "I was crossing the stream when—"

"What stream?" Ernest interrupted her.

"The stream at the bottom, where our wood meets the black wood," she explained.

Ernest looked completely blank for a moment.

"What the deuce are you talking about?" he asked.

"My dear Ernest!" she cried in dismay. "King Lappin," she added, dangling her little front paws in the firelight. But his nose did not twitch. Her hands—they turned to hands—clutched the stuff she was holding; her eyes popped half out of her head. It took him five minutes at least to change from Ernest Thorburn to King Lappin; and while she waited she felt a load on the back of her neck, as if somebody were about to wring it. At last he changed to King Lappin; his nose twitched; and they spent the evening roaming the woods much as usual.

But she slept badly. In the middle of the night she woke, feeling as if something strange had happened to her. She was stiff and cold. At last she turned on the light and looked at Ernest lying beside her. He was sound asleep. He snored. But even though he snored, his nose remained perfectly still. It looked as if it had never twitched at all. Was it possible that he was really Ernest; and that she was really married to Ernest? A vision of her mother-in-law's dining-room came before her; and there they sat, she and Ernest, grown old, under the engravings, in front of the sideboard. . . . It was their golden-wedding day. She could not bear it.

"Lappin, King Lappin!" she whispered, and for a moment his nose seemed to twitch of its own accord. But he still slept. "Wake up, Lappin, wake up!" she cried.

Ernest woke; and seeing her sitting bolt upright beside him he asked:

"What's the matter?"

"I thought my rabbit was dead!" she whimpered. Ernest was angry.

"Don't talk such rubbish, Rosalind," he said. "Lie down and go to sleep."

He turned over. In another moment he was sound asleep and snoring.

But she could not sleep. She lay curled up on her side of the bed, like a hare in its form. She had turned out the light, but the street lamp lit the ceiling faintly, and the trees outside made a lacy network over it as if there were a shadowy grove on the ceiling in which she wandered, turning, twisting, in and out, round and round, hunting, being hunted, hearing the bay of hounds and horns; flying, escaping . . . until the maid drew the blinds and brought their early tea.

Next day she could settle to nothing. She seemed to have lost something. She felt as if her body had shrunk; it had grown small, and black and hard. Her joints seemed stiff too, and when she looked in the glass, which she did several times as she wandered about the flat, her eyes seemed to burst out of her head, like currants in a bun. The rooms also seemed to have shrunk. Large pieces of furniture jutted out at odd angles and she found herself knocking against them. At last she put on her hat and went out. She walked along the Cromwell Road; and every room she passed and peered into seemed to be a dining-room where people sat eating under steel engravings, with thick yellow lace curtains, and mahogany sideboards. At last she reached the Natural History Museum; she used to like it when she was a child. But the first thing she saw when she went in was a stuffed hare standing on sham snow with pink glass eyes. Somehow it made her shiver all over. Perhaps it would be better when dusk fell. She went home and sat over the fire, without a light, and tried to imagine that she was out alone on a moor; and there was a stream rushing; and beyond the stream a dark wood. But she could get no further than the stream. At last she squatted down on the bank on the wet grass, and sat crouched in her chair, with her hands dangling empty, and her eyes glazed, like glass eyes, in the firelight. Then there was the crack of a gun. . . . She started as if she had been shot. It was only Ernest, turning his key in the door. She waited, trembling. He came in and switched on the light. There he stood tall, handsome, rubbing his hands that were red with cold.

"Sitting in the dark?" he said.

"Oh, Ernest, Ernest!" she cried, starting up in her chair.

"Well, what's up, now?" he asked briskly, warming his hands at the fire.

"It's Lapinova . . ." she faltered, glancing wildly at him out of her great startled eyes. "She's gone, Ernest. I've lost her!"

Ernest frowned. He pressed his lips tight together. "Oh, that's what's up, is it?" he said, smiling rather grimly at his wife. For ten seconds he stood there, silent; and she waited, feeling hands tightening at the back of her neck.

"Yes," he said at length. "Poor Lapinova . . ." He straightened his tie at the looking-glass over the mantelpiece.

"Caught in a trap," he said, "killed," and sat down and read the newspaper.

So that was the end of that marriage.

The Duchess and
the Jeweller

In August 1937, Virginia Woolf received a cable from America requesting some fiction, something short. "I've made up a short story about a jeweller and a duchess, and cabled the plot," she wrote to her sister Vanessa Bell, "—how he buys her pearls, £10,000 [£20,000] knowing them to be false. . . ." "The Duchess and the Jeweller" was published in April 1938. The story is conventional enough in form. Even its "plot" of transacted dishonesty seems a little commonplace. But the minute we begin to look for motives, all convention slips away. Does the jeweller seem the kind of man who can be easily hoodwinked? Certainly not. And does the duchess really believe she has deceived him? Of course not. The story goes far deeper than its apparent resolution. Its significance can be discovered in the extraordinary means by which Virginia Woolf, with a few quick lines, has defined the personal history of the jeweller—his shabby origins, his ambitions, his success, his hunger for love. He has now the money with which to buy temporary happiness, and the duchess has a daughter for barter. Each, in other words, has the means. The duchess wants his money; the jeweller wants her daughter. Bring these two characters together at precisely the right moment, and we see acted out before us the phenomenon of "opportunity seized." Seen in this light,

*the story becomes a superb dramatization of a crisis in values.
Who wins? Who loses? That is for each reader to decide.*

OLIVER BACON LIVED AT THE TOP OF A HOUSE OVER-
looking the Green Park. He had a flat; chairs jutted out at
the right angles—chairs covered in hide. Sofas filled the bays of
the windows—sofas covered in tapestry. The windows, the three
long windows, had the proper allowance of discreet net and fig-
ured satin. The mahogany sideboard bulged discreetly with the
right brandies, whiskeys, and liqueurs. And from the middle
window he looked down upon the glossy roofs of fashionable
cars packed in the narrow straits of Piccadilly. A more central
position could not be imagined. And at eight in the morning he
would have his breakfast brought in on a tray by a man-servant:
the man-servant would unfold his crimson dressing-gown; he
would rip his letters open with his long pointed nails and would
extract thick white cards of invitation upon which the engraving
stood up roughly from duchesses, countesses, viscountesses, and
Honourable Ladies. Then he would wash; then he would eat his
toast; then he would read his paper by the bright burning fire of
electric coals.

"Behold Oliver," he would say, addressing himself. "You who
began life in a filthy little alley, you who . . ." and he would
look down at his legs, so shapely in their perfect trousers; at his
boots; at his spats. They were all shapely, shining; cut from the
best cloth by the best scissors in Savile Row. But he dismantled
himself often and became again a little boy in a dark alley. He
had once thought that the height of his ambition—selling stolen
dogs to fashionable women in Whitechapel. And once he had
been done. "Oh, Oliver," his mother had wailed. "Oh, Oliver!
When will you have sense, my son?" . . . Then he had gone
behind a counter; had sold cheap watches; then he had taken a
wallet to Amsterdam. . . . At that memory he would chuckle—
the old Oliver remembering the young. Yes, he had done well

with the three diamonds; also there was the commission on the emerald. After that he went into the private room behind the shop in Hatton Garden; the room with the scales, the safe, the thick magnifying glasses. And then . . . and then . . . He chuckled. When he passed through the knots of jewellers in the hot evening who were discussing prices, gold mines, diamonds, reports from South Africa, one of them would lay a finger to the side of his nose and murmur, "Hum–m–m," as he passed. It was no more than a murmur; no more than a nudge on the shoulder, a finger on the nose, a buzz that ran through the cluster of jewellers in Hatton Garden on a hot afternoon—oh, many years ago now! But still Oliver felt it purring down his spine, the nudge, the murmur that meant, "Look at him—young Oliver, the young jeweller—there he goes." Young he was then. And he dressed better and better; and had, first a hansom cab; then a car; and first he went up to the dress circle, then down into the stalls. And he had a villa at Richmond, overlooking the river, with trellises of red roses; and Mademoiselle used to pick one every morning and stick it in his buttonhole.

"So," said Oliver Bacon, rising and stretching his legs. "So . . ."

And he stood beneath the picture of an old lady on the mantelpiece and raised his hands. "I have kept my word," he said, laying his hands together, palm to palm, as if he were doing homage to her. "I have won my bet." That was so; he was the richest jeweller in England; but his nose, which was long and flexible, like an elephant's trunk, seemed to say by its curious quiver at the nostrils (but it seemed as if the whole nose quivered, not only the nostrils) that he was not satisfied yet; still smelt something under the ground a little further off. Imagine a giant hog in a pasture rich with truffles; after unearthing this truffle and that, still it smells a bigger, a blacker truffle under the ground further off. So Oliver snuffed always in the rich earth of Mayfair another truffle, a blacker, a bigger further off.

Now then he straightened the pearl in his tie, cased himself in his smart blue overcoat; took his yellow gloves and his cane; and swayed as he descended the stairs and half snuffed, half sighed through his long sharp nose as he passed out into Piccadilly. For was he not still a sad man, a dissatisfied man, a man who seeks something that is hidden, though he had won his bet?

He swayed slightly as he walked, as the camel at the zoo sways from side to side when it walks along the asphalt paths laden with grocers and their wives eating from paper bags and throwing little bits of silver paper crumpled up on to the path. The camel despises the grocers; the camel is dissatisfied with its lot; the camel sees the blue lake and the fringe of palm trees in front of it. So the great jeweller, the greatest jeweller in the whole world, swung down Piccadilly, perfectly dressed, with his gloves, with his cane; but dissatisfied still, till he reached the dark little shop, that was famous in France, in Germany, in Austria, in Italy, and all over America—the dark little shop in the street off Bond Street.

As usual, he strode through the shop without speaking, though the four men, the two old men, Marshall and Spencer, and the two young men, Hammond and Wicks, stood straight and looked at him, envying him. It was only with one finger of the amber-coloured glove, waggling, that he acknowledged their presence. And he went in and shut the door of his private room behind him.

Then he unlocked the grating that barred the window. The cries of Bond Street came in; the purr of the distant traffic. The light from reflectors at the back of the shop struck upwards. One tree waved six green leaves, for it was June. But Mademoiselle had married Mr. Pedder of the local brewery—no one stuck roses in his buttonhole now.

"So," he half sighed, half snorted, "so—"

Then he touched a spring in the wall and slowly the panelling slid open, and behind it were the steel safes, five, no, six of them, all of burnished steel. He twisted a key; unlocked one; then another. Each was lined with a pad of deep crimson velvet; in each lay jewels—bracelets, necklaces, rings, tiaras, ducal coronets; loose stones in glass shells; rubies, emeralds, pearls, diamonds. All safe, shining, cool, yet burning, eternally, with their own compressed light.

"Tears!" said Oliver, looking at the pearls.

"Heart's blood!" he said, looking at the rubies.

"Gunpowder!" he continued, rattling the diamonds so that they flashed and blazed.

"Gunpowder enough to blow Mayfair—sky high, high, high!" He threw his head back and made a sound like a horse neighing as he said it.

The telephone buzzed obsequiously in a low muted voice on his table. He shut the safe.

"In ten minutes," he said. "Not before." And he sat down at his desk and looked at the heads of the Roman emperors that were graved on his sleeve links. And again he dismantled himself and became once more the little boy playing marbles in the alley where they sell stolen dogs on Sunday. He became that wily astute little boy, with lips like wet cherries. He dabbled his fingers in ropes of tripe; he dipped them in pans of frying fish; he dodged in and out among the crowds. He was slim, lissome, with eyes like licked stones. And now —now—the hands of the clock ticked on, one, two, three, four. . . . The Duchess of Lambourne waited his pleasure; the Duchess of Lambourne, daughter of a hundred Earls. She would wait for ten minutes on a chair at the counter. She would wait his pleasure. She would wait till he was ready to see her. He watched the clock in its shagreen case. The hand moved on. With each tick the clock handed him—so it seemed—pâté de foie gras, a glass of champagne, another of fine brandy, a cigar costing one guinea. The clock laid them on the table beside him as the ten minutes passed. Then he heard soft slow footsteps approaching; a rustle in the corridor. The door opened. Mr. Hammond flattened himself against the wall.

"Her Grace!" he announced.

And he waited there, flattened against the wall.

And Oliver, rising, could hear the rustle of the dress of the Duchess as she came down the passage. Then she loomed up, filling the door, filling the room with the aroma, the prestige, the arrogance, the pomp, the pride of all the Dukes and Duchesses swollen in one wave. And as a wave breaks, she broke, as she sat down, spreading and splashing and falling over Oliver Bacon, the great jeweller, covering him with sparkling bright colours, green, rose, violet; and odours; and iridescences; and rays shooting from fingers, nodding from plumes, flashing from silk; for she was very large, very fat, tightly girt in pink taffeta, and past her prime. As a parasol with many flounces, as a peacock with many feathers, shuts its flounces, folds its feathers, so she subsided and shut herself as she sank down in the leather armchair.

"Good morning, Mr. Bacon," said the Duchess. And she held out her hand which came through the slit of her white glove. And Oliver bent low as he shook it. And as their hands touched the link was forged between them once more. They were friends, yet enemies; he was master, she was mistress; each cheated the other, each needed the other, each feared the other, each felt this and knew this every time they touched hands thus in the little back room with the white light outside, and the tree with its six leaves, and the sound of the street in the distance and behind them the safes.

"And today, Duchess—what can I do for you today?" said Oliver, very softly.

The Duchess opened her heart, her private heart, gaped wide. And with a sigh but no words she took from her bag a long washleather pouch—it looked like a lean yellow ferret. And from a slit in the ferret's belly she dropped pearls—ten pearls. They rolled from the slit in the ferret's belly—one, two, three, four—like the eggs of some heavenly bird.

"All that's left me, dear Mr. Bacon," she moaned. Five, six, seven—down they rolled, down the slopes of the vast mountain sides that fell between her knees into one narrow valley—the eighth, the ninth, and the tenth. There they lay in the glow of the peach-blossom taffeta. Ten pearls.

"From the Appleby cincture," she mourned. "The last . . . the last of them all."

Oliver stretched out and took one of the pearls between finger and thumb. It was round, it was lustrous. But real was it, or false? Was she lying again? Did she dare?

She laid her plump padded finger across her lips. "If the Duke knew . . ." she whispered. "Dear Mr. Bacon, a bit of bad luck . . ."

Been gambling again, had she?

"That villain! That sharper!" she hissed.

The man with the chipped cheek bone? A bad 'un. And the Duke was straight as a poker; with side whiskers; would cut her off, shut her up down there if he knew—what I know, thought Oliver, and glanced at the safe.

"Araminta, Daphne, Diana," she moaned. "It's for *them*."

The ladies Araminta, Daphne, Diana—her daughters. He knew them; adored them. But it was Diana he loved.

"You have all my secrets," she leered. Tears slid; tears fell; tears, like diamonds, collecting powder in the ruts of her cherry blossom cheeks.

"Old friend," she murmured, "old friend."

"Old friend," he repeated, "old friend," as if he licked the words.

"How much?" he queried.

She covered the pearls with her hand.

"Twenty thousand," she whispered.

But was it real or false, the one he held in his hand? The Appleby cincture—hadn't she sold it already? He would ring for Spencer or Hammond. "Take it and test it," he would say. He stretched to the bell.

"You will come down tomorrow?" she urged, she interrupted. "The Prime Minister—His Royal Highness . . ." She stopped. "And Diana . . ." she added.

Oliver took his hand off the bell.

He looked past her, at the backs of the houses in Bond Street. But he saw, not the houses in Bond Street, but a dimpling river; and trout rising and salmon; and the Prime Minister; and himself too, in white waistcoat; and then, Diana. He looked down at the pearl in his hand. But how could he test it, in the light of the river, in the light of the eyes of Diana? But the eyes of the Duchess were on him.

"Twenty thousand," she moaned. "My honour!"

The honour of the mother of Diana! He drew his cheque book towards him; he took out his pen.

"Twenty—" he wrote. Then he stopped writing. The eyes of the old woman in the picture were on him—of the old woman his mother.

"Oliver!" she warned him. "Have sense! Don't be a fool!"

"Oliver!" the Duchess entreated—it was "Oliver" now, not "Mr. Bacon." "You'll come for a long week-end?"

Alone in the woods with Diana! Riding alone in the woods with Diana!

"Thousand," he wrote, and signed it.

"Here you are," he said.

And there opened all the flounces of the parasol, all the plumes of the peacock, the radiance of the wave, the swords and spears of Agincourt, as she rose from her chair. And the two old men and the two young men, Spencer and Marshall, Wicks and Hammond, flattened themselves behind the counter envying him as he led her through the shop to the door. And he waggled his yellow glove in their faces, and she held her honour—a cheque for twenty thousand pounds with his signature—quite firmly in her hands.

"Are they false or are they real?" asked Oliver, shutting his private door. There they were, ten pearls on the blotting-paper on the table. He took them to the window. He held them under his lens to the light. . . . This, then, was the truffle he had routed out of the earth! Rotten at the centre—rotten at the core!

"Forgive me, oh, my mother!" he sighed, raising his hand as if he asked pardon of the old woman in the picture. And again he was a little boy in the alley where they sold dogs on Sunday.

"For," he murmured, laying the palms of his hands together, "it is to be a long week-end."

The Mark on the Wall

In the spring of 1917, Leonard and Virginia Woolf bought their own printing apparatus and began what today has become the prestigious Hogarth Press. Their first venture, set and printed entirely by themselves, was Two Stories, one by each of them, and published in July 1917. Virginia Woolf's story was called "The Mark on the Wall." In 1919 it was issued by itself in an edition of 1,000 copies. For its author, it was aesthetically important because it documented the beginning of a mode of perception that would become the basis of a new kind of fiction.

The narrator of the piece sees a spot on the wall and begins to guess what it might be. Each guess triggers off what appears to be a random (but in actuality is a highly controlled) series of mental associations. That the mark on the wall is finally identified is by itself entirely irrelevant. What matters is the way in which Virginia Woolf fills the piece with so astonishing an array of thoughts and emotions, all of them stimulated by the indefiniteness of the mark under observation.

In the annals of literary history, this story is one of the first to attach importance to the way in which each human being perceives the world and gives it its singularly personal coloration and emotional weight.

PERHAPS IT WAS THE MIDDLE OF JANUARY IN THE
present year that I first looked up and saw the mark on the wall.
In order to fix a date it is necessary to remember what one saw.
So now I think of the fire; the steady film of yellow light upon the
page of my book; the three chrysanthemums in the round glass
bowl on the mantelpiece. Yes, it must have been the winter time,
and we had just finished our tea, for I remember that I was
smoking a cigarette when I looked up and saw the mark on the
wall for the first time. I looked up through the smoke of my
cigarette and my eye lodged for a moment upon the burning
coals, and that old fancy of the crimson flag flapping from the
castle tower came into my mind, and I thought of the cavalcade
of red knights riding up the side of the black rock. Rather to
my relief the sight of the mark interrupted the fancy, for it is an
old fancy, an automatic fancy, made as a child perhaps. The
mark was a small round mark, black upon the white wall, about
six or seven inches above the mantelpiece.

How readily our thoughts swarm upon a new object, lifting it
a little way, as ants carry a blade of straw so feverishly, and then
leave it. . . . If that mark was made by a nail, it can't have been
for a picture, it must have been for a miniature—the miniature
of a lady with white powdered curls, powder-dusted cheeks, and
lips like red carnations. A fraud of course, for the people who
had this house before us would have chosen pictures in that
way—an old picture for an old room. That is the sort of people
they were—very interesting people, and I think of them so often,
in such queer places, because one will never see them again,
never know what happened next. They wanted to leave this
house because they wanted to change their style of furniture, so
he said, and he was in process of saying that in his opinion art
should have ideas behind it when we were torn asunder, as one is
torn from the old lady about to pour out tea and the young
man about to hit the tennis ball in the back garden of the suburban villa as one rushes past in the train.

But for that mark, I'm not sure about it; I don't believe it
was made by a nail after all; it's too big, too round, for that. I

might get up, but if I got up and looked at it, ten to one I shouldn't be able to say for certain; because once a thing's done, no one ever knows how it happened. Oh! dear me, the mystery of life; the inaccuracy of thought! The ignorance of humanity! To show how very little control of our possessions we have—what an accidental affair this living is after all our civilization—let me just count over a few of the things lost in one lifetime, beginning, for that seems always the most mysterious of losses—what cat would gnaw, what rat would nibble—three pale blue canisters of book-binding tools? Then there were the bird cages, the iron hoops, the steel skates, the Queen Anne coal-scuttle, the bagatelle board, the hand organ—all gone, and jewels, too. Opals and emeralds, they lie about the roots of turnips. What a scraping paring affair it is to be sure! The wonder is that I've any clothes on my back, that I sit surrounded by solid furniture at this moment. Why, if one wants to compare life to anything, one must liken it to being blown through the Tube at fifty miles an hour—landing at the other end without a single hairpin in one's hair! Shot out at the feet of God entirely naked! Tumbling head over heels in the asphodel meadows like brown paper parcels pitched down a shoot in the post office! With one's hair flying back like the tail of a race-horse. Yes, that seems to express the rapidity of life, the perpetual waste and repair; all so casual, all so haphazard....

But after life. The slow pulling down of thick green stalks so that the cup of the flower, as it turns over, deluges one with purple and red light. Why, after all, should one not be born there as one is born here, helpless, speechless, unable to focus one's eyesight, groping at the roots of the grass, at the toes of the Giants? As for saying which are trees, and which are men and women, or whether there are such things, that one won't be in a condition to do for fifty years or so. There will be nothing but spaces of light and dark, intersected by thick stalks, and rather higher up perhaps, rose-shaped blots of an indistinct colour— dim pinks and blues—which will, as time goes on, become more definite, become—I don't know what....

And yet that mark on the wall is not a hole at all. It may even be caused by some round black substance, such as a small rose leaf, left over from the summer, and I, not being a very vigilant housekeeper—look at the dust on the mantelpiece, for example, the dust which, so they say, buried Troy three times over, only fragments of pots utterly refusing annihilation, as one can believe.

The tree outside the window taps very gently on the pane. . . . I want to think quietly, calmly, spaciously, never to be interrupted, never to have to rise from my chair, to slip easily from one thing to another, without any sense of hostility, or obstacle. I want to sink deeper and deeper, away from the surface, with its hard separate facts. To steady myself, let me catch hold of the first idea that passes . . . Shakespeare. . . . Well, he will do as well as another. A man who sat himself solidly in an arm-chair, and looked into the fire, so— A shower of ideas fell perpetually from some very high Heaven down through his mind. He leant his forehead on his hand, and people, looking in through the open door—for this scene is supposed to take place on a summer's evening— But how dull this is, this historical fiction! It doesn't interest me at all. I wish I could hit upon a pleasant track of thought, a track indirectly reflecting credit upon myself, for those are the pleasantest thoughts, and very frequent even in the minds of modest mouse-coloured people, who believe genuinely that they dislike to hear their own praises. They are not thoughts directly praising oneself; that is the beauty of them; they are thoughts like this:

"And then I came into the room. They were discussing botany. I said how I'd seen a flower growing on a dust heap on the site of an old house in Kingsway. The seed, I said, must have been sown in the reign of Charles the First. What flowers grew in the reign of Charles the First?" I asked— (But I don't remember the answer.) Tall flowers with purple tassels to them perhaps. And so it goes on. All the time I'm dressing up the figure of myself in my own mind, lovingly, stealthily, not openly adoring it, for if I did that, I should catch myself out, and stretch my hand at once for a book in self-protection. Indeed, it is curious how instinctively one protects the image of oneself from idolatry or any other handling that could make it ridiculous, or too unlike the original to be believed in any longer. Or is it not so very curious after all? It is a matter of great importance. Suppose the looking-glass smashes, the image disappears, and the romantic figure with the green of forest depths all about it is there no longer, but only that shell of a person which is seen by other people—what an airless, shallow, bald, prominent world it becomes! A world not to be lived in. As we face each other in omnibuses and underground railways we are looking into the mirror; that accounts for the vagueness, the gleam of glassiness, in our eyes. And the novelists in future will realize more and more the importance of these reflections, for of course there is not one reflection but an almost infinite number; those are the depths they will explore, those the phantoms they will pursue, leaving the description of reality more and more out of their stories, taking a knowledge of it for granted, as the Greeks did and Shakespeare perhaps—but these generalizations are very worthless. The military sound of the word is enough. It recalls leading articles, cabinet ministers—a whole class of things indeed which, as a child, one thought the thing itself, the standard thing, the real thing, from which one could not depart save at the risk of nameless damnation. Generalizations bring back somehow Sunday in London, Sunday afternoon walks, Sunday luncheons, and also ways of speaking of the dead, clothes, and habits —like the habit of sitting all together in one room until a certain hour, although nobody liked it. There was a rule for everything. The rule for tablecloths at that particular period was that they should be made of tapestry with little yellow compartments marked upon them, such as you may see in photographs of the carpets in the corridors of the royal palaces. Tablecloths of a different kind were not real tablecloths. How shocking, and yet how wonderful it was to discover that these real things, Sunday luncheons, Sunday walks, country houses, and tablecloths were not entirely real, were indeed half phantoms, and the damnation which visited the disbeliever in them was only a sense of illegitimate freedom. What now takes the place of those things I

wonder, those real standard things? Men perhaps, should you be
a woman; the masculine point of view which governs our lives,
which sets the standard, which establishes Whitaker's Table of
Precedency, which has become, I suppose, since the war, half a
phantom to many men and women, which soon, one may hope,
will be laughed into the dustbin where the phantoms go, the
mahogany sideboards and the Landseer prints, Gods and Devils,
Hell and so forth, leaving us all with an intoxicating sense of
illegitimate freedom—if freedom exists. . . .

In certain lights that mark on the wall seems actually to
project from the wall. Nor is it entirely circular. I cannot be sure,
but it seems to cast a perceptible shadow, suggesting that if I ran
my finger down that strip of the wall it would, at a certain point,
mount and descend a small tumulus, a smooth tumulus like those
barrows on the South Downs which are, they say, either tombs
or camps. Of the two I should prefer them to be tombs, desiring
melancholy like most English people, and finding it natural at
the end of a walk to think of the bones stretched beneath the
turf. . . . There must be some book about it. Some antiquary
must have dug up those bones and given them a name. . . . What
sort of a man is an antiquary, I wonder? Retired Colonels for the
most part, I daresay, leading parties of aged labourers to the top
here, examining clods of earth and stone, and getting into correspondence with the neighbouring clergy, which, being opened
at breakfast time, gives them a feeling of importance, and the
comparison of arrow-heads necessitates cross-country journeys
to the county towns, an agreeable necessity both to them and to
their elderly wives, who wish to make plum jam or to clean out
the study, and have every reason for keeping that great question
of the camp or the tomb in perpetual suspension, while the
Colonel himself feels agreeably philosophic in accumulating
evidence on both sides of the question. It is true that he does
finally incline to believe in the camp; and, being opposed, indites
a pamphlet which he is about to read at the quarterly meeting of
the local society when a stroke lays him low, and his last conscious thoughts are not of wife or child, but of the camp and that

arrow-head there, which is now in the case at the local museum, together with the foot of a Chinese murderess, a handful of Elizabethan nails, a great many Tudor clay pipes, a piece of Roman pottery, and the wineglass that Nelson drank out of— proving I really don't know what.

No, no, nothing is proved, nothing is known. And if I were to get up at this very moment and ascertain that the mark on the wall is really—what shall we say?—the head of a gigantic old nail, driven in two hundred years ago, which has now, owing to the patient attrition of many generations of housemaids, revealed its head above the coat of paint, and is taking its first view of modern life in the sight of a white-walled fire-lit room, what should I gain?— Knowledge? Matter for further speculation? I can think sitting still as well as standing up. And what is knowledge? What are our learned men save the descendants of witches and hermits who crouched in caves and in woods brewing herbs, interrogating shrew-mice and writing down the language of the stars? And the less we honour them as our superstitions dwindle and our respect for beauty and health of mind increases. . . . Yes, one could imagine a very pleasant world. A quiet, spacious world, with the flowers so red and blue in the open fields. A world without professors or specialists or house-keepers with the profiles of policemen, a world which one could slice with one's thought as a fish slices the water with his fin, grazing the stems of the water-lilies, hanging suspended over nests of white sea eggs. . . . How peaceful it is down here, rooted in the centre of the world and gazing up through the grey waters, with their sudden gleams of light, and their reflections—If it were not for Whitaker's Almanack—if it were not for the Table of Precedency!

I must jump up and see for myself what that mark on the wall really is—a nail, a rose-leaf, a crack in the wood?

Here is nature once more at her old game of self-preservation. This train of thought, she perceives, is threatening mere waste of energy, even some collision with reality, for who will ever be able to lift a finger against Whitaker's Table of Precedency? The Archbishop of Canterbury is followed by the Lord High Chancellor; the Lord High Chancellor is followed by the Archbishop of York. Everybody follows somebody, such is the philosophy of Whitaker; and the great thing is to know who follows whom. Whitaker knows, and let that, so Nature counsels, comfort you, instead of enraging you; and if you can't be comforted, if you must shatter this hour of peace, think of the mark on the wall.

I understand Nature's game—her prompting to take action as a way of ending any thought that threatens to excite or to pain. Hence, I suppose, comes our slight contempt for men of action —men, we assume, who don't think. Still, there's no harm in putting a full stop to one's disagreeable thoughts by looking at a mark on the wall.

Indeed, now that I have fixed my eyes upon it, I feel that I have grasped a plank in the sea; I feel a satisfying sense of reality which at once turns the two Archbishops and the Lord High Chancellor to the shadows of shades. Here is something definite, something real. Thus, waking from a midnight dream of horror, one hastily turns on the light and lies quiescent, worshipping the chest of drawers, worshipping solidity, worshipping reality, worshipping the impersonal world which is a proof of some existence other than ours. That is what one wants to be sure of. . . . Wood is a pleasant thing to think about. It comes from a tree; and trees grow, and we don't know how they grow. For years and years they grow, without paying any attention to us, in meadows, in forests, and by the side of rivers—all things one likes to think about. The cows swish their tails beneath them on hot afternoons; they paint rivers so green that when a moorhen dives one expects to see its feathers all green when it comes up again. I like to think of the fish balanced against the stream like flags blown out; and of water-beetles slowly raising domes of mud upon the bed of the river. I like to think of the tree itself: first of the close dry sensation of being wood; then the grinding of the storm; then the slow, delicious ooze of sap; I like to think of it, too, on winter's nights standing in the empty field with all leaves close-furled, nothing tender exposed to the iron bullets of the moon, a naked mast upon an earth that goes tumbling, tumbling, all night long. The song of birds must sound very loud and strange in June; and how cold the feet of insects must feel upon it, as they make laborious progresses up the creases of the bark, or sun themselves upon the thin green awning of the leaves, and look straight in front of them with diamond-cut red eyes. . . . One by one the fibres snap beneath the immense cold pressure of the earth, then the last storm comes and, falling, the highest branches drive deep into the ground again. Even so, life isn't done with; there are a million patient, watchful lives still for a tree, all over the world, in bedrooms, in ships, on the pavement, lining rooms, where men and women sit after tea, smoking cigarettes. It is full of peaceful thoughts, happy thoughts, this tree. I should like to take each one separately—but something is getting in the way. . . . Where was I? What has it all been about? A tree? A river? The Downs? Whitaker's Almanack? The fields of asphodel? I can't remember a thing. Everything's moving, falling, slipping, vanishing. . . . There is a vast upheaval of matter. Someone is standing over me and saying:

"I'm going out to buy a newspaper."

"Yes?"

"Though it's no good buying newspapers. . . . Nothing ever happens. Curse this war; God damn this war! . . . All the same, I don't see why we should have a snail on our wall."

Ah, the mark on the wall! It was a snail.

Kew Gardens

Virginia Woolf took her snail from "The Mark on the Wall" and used him as her principal angle of vision in "Kew Gardens," published in 1919. In this story an unspecified narrator is used to convey to the reader the thoughts and speeches of the passers-by. But most of the physical details of the flower bed and the people walking past—a pair of feet walking "about six inches in front of the woman"—are filtered to us primarily from the restricted snail's-eye view. The same restriction is placed on the seemingly offhand speeches of the four groups of people who pass the oval flower bed of the resident mollusk. We read only those snatches of their conversation that the snail "hears" as they pass; and these are conveyed to us through the peripheral narrator.

This was an entirely new way of storytelling. Time and space appear fragmented and scrambled. Speech and thought seem fractured and random. This is mere simulation, however. Time and space and speech and thought are under the strictest intellectual control, with the aim of creating a natural, unedited impression of a hot July afternoon in a public garden.

From these literary experiments—"The Mark on the Wall" and "Kew Gardens"—Jacob's Room emerged, Virginia Woolf's

*first full-length novel, whose innovative method she would bring
to perfection in* Mrs. Dalloway *and* To the Lighthouse.

―――――――――――――――

FROM THE OVAL-SHAPED FLOWER-BED THERE ROSE
perhaps a hundred stalks spreading into heart-shaped or tongue-
shaped leaves half-way up and unfurling at the tip red or blue or
yellow petals marked with spots of colour raised upon the surface; and from the red, blue or yellow gloom of the throat
emerged a straight bar, rough with gold dust and slightly clubbed
at the end. The petals were voluminous enough to be stirred by
the summer breeze, and when they moved, the red, blue and
yellow lights passed one over the other, staining an inch of the
brown earth beneath with a spot of the most intricate colour.
The light fell either upon the smooth, grey back of a pebble, or,
the shell of a snail with its brown, circular veins, or falling into a
raindrop, it expanded with such intensity of red, blue and yellow
the thin walls of water that one expected them to burst and
disappear. Instead, the drop was left in a second silver grey once
more, and the light now settled upon the flesh of a leaf, revealing
the branching thread of fibre beneath the surface, and again it
moved on and spread its illumination in the vast green spaces
beneath the dome of the heart-shaped and tongue-shaped leaves.
Then the breeze stirred rather more briskly overhead and the
colour was flashed into the air above, into the eyes of the men
and women who walk in Kew Gardens in July.

The figures of these men and women straggled past the flower-
bed with a curiously irregular movement not unlike that of the
white and blue butterflies who crossed the turf in zig-zag flights
from bed to bed. The man was about six inches in front of the
woman, strolling carelessly, while she bore on with greater purpose, only turning her head now and then to see that the children
were not too far behind. The man kept this distance in front of

the woman purposely, though perhaps unconsciously, for he wished to go on with his thoughts.

"Fifteen years ago I came here with Lily," he thought. "We sat somewhere over there by a lake and I begged her to marry me all through the hot afternoon. How the dragonfly kept circling round us: how clearly I see the dragonfly and her shoe with the square silver buckle at the toe. All the time I spoke I saw her shoe and when it moved impatiently I knew without looking up what she was going to say: the whole of her seemed to be in her shoe. And my love, my desire, were in the dragonfly; for some reason I thought that if it settled there, on that leaf, the broad one with the red flower in the middle of it, if the dragonfly settled on the leaf she would say 'Yes' at once. But the dragonfly went round and round: it never settled anywhere—of course not, happily not, or I shouldn't be walking here with Eleanor and the children. Tell me, Eleanor. D'you ever think of the past?"

"Why do you ask, Simon?"

"Because I've been thinking of the past. I've been thinking of Lily, the woman I might have married. . . . Well, why are you silent? Do you mind my thinking of the past?"

"Why should I mind, Simon? Doesn't one always think of the past, in a garden with men and women lying under the trees? Aren't they one's past, all that remains of it, those men and women, those ghosts lying under the trees, . . . one's happiness, one's reality?"

"For me, a square silver shoe buckle and a dragonfly—"

"For me, a kiss. Imagine six little girls sitting before their easels twenty years ago, down by the side of a lake, painting the water-lilies, the first red water-lilies I'd ever seen. And suddenly a kiss, there on the back of my neck. And my hand shook all the afternoon so that I couldn't paint. I took out my watch and marked the hour when I would allow myself to think of the kiss for five minutes only—it was so precious—the kiss of an old grey-haired woman with a wart on her nose, the mother of all my kisses all my life. Come, Caroline, come, Hubert."

They walked on past the flower-bed, now walking four

abreast, and soon diminished in size among the trees and looked half transparent as the sunlight and shade swam over their backs in large trembling irregular patches.

In the oval flower-bed the snail, whose shell had been stained red, blue and yellow for the space of two minutes or so, now appeared to be moving very slightly in its shell, and next began to labour over the crumbs of loose earth which broke away and rolled down as it passed over them. It appeared to have a definite goal in front of it, differing in this respect from the singular high stepping angular green insect who attempted to cross in front of it, and waited for a second with its antennae trembling as if in deliberation, and then stepped off as rapidly and strangely in the opposite direction. Brown cliffs with deep green lakes in the hollows, flat, blade-like trees that waved from root to tip, round boulders of grey stone, vast crumpled surfaces of a thin crackling texture—all these objects lay across the snail's progress between one stalk and another to his goal. Before he had decided whether to circumvent the arched tent of a dead leaf or to breast it there came past the bed the feet of other human beings.

This time they were both men. The younger of the two wore an expression of perhaps unnatural calm; he raised his eyes and fixed them very steadily in front of him while his companion spoke, and directly his companion had done speaking he looked on the ground again and sometimes opened his lips only after a long pause and sometimes did not open them at all. The elder man had a curiously uneven and shaky method of walking, jerking his hand forward and throwing up his head abruptly, rather in the manner of an impatient carriage horse tired of waiting outside a house; but in the man these gestures were irresolute and pointless. He talked almost incessantly; he smiled to himself and again began to talk, as if the smile had been an answer. He was talking about spirits—the spirits of the dead, who, according to him, were even now telling him all sorts of odd things about their experiences in Heaven.

"Heaven was known to the ancients as Thessaly, William, and now, with this war, the spirit matter is rolling between the hills like thunder." He paused, seemed to listen, smiled, jerked his head and continued:

"You have a small electric battery and a piece of rubber to insulate the wire—isolate?—insulate?—well, we'll skip the details, no good going into details that wouldn't be understood—and in short the little machine stands in any convenient position by the head of the bed, we will say, on a neat mahogany stand. All arrangements being properly fixed by workmen under my direction, the widow applies her ear and summons the spirit by sign as agreed. Women! Widows! Women in black—"

Here he seemed to have caught sight of a woman's dress in the distance, which in the shade looked a purple black. He took off his hat, placed his hand upon his heart, and hurried towards her muttering and gesticulating feverishly. But William caught him by the sleeve and touched a flower with the tip of his walking-stick in order to divert the old man's attention. After looking at it for a moment in some confusion the old man bent his ear to it and seemed to answer a voice speaking from it, for he began talking about the forests of Uruguay which he had visited hundreds of years ago in company with the most beautiful young woman in Europe. He could be heard murmuring about forests of Uruguay blanketed with the wax petals of tropical roses, nightingales, sea beaches, mermaids, and women drowned at sea, as he suffered himself to be moved on by William, upon whose face the look of stoical patience grew slowly deeper and deeper.

Following his steps so closely as to be slightly puzzled by his gestures came two elderly women of the lower middle class, one stout and ponderous, the other rosy cheeked and nimble. Like most people of their station they were frankly fascinated by any signs of eccentricity betokening a disordered brain, especially in the well-to-do; but they were too far off to be certain whether the gestures were merely eccentric or genuinely mad. After they had scrutinized the old man's back in silence for a moment and given each other a queer, sly look, they went on energetically piecing together their very complicated dialogue:

"Nell, Bert, Lot, Cess, Phil, Pa, he says, I says, she says, I says, I says—"

"My Bert, Sis, Bill, Grandad, the old man, sugar,
            Sugar, flour, kippers, greens,
            Sugar, sugar, sugar."

The ponderous woman looked through the pattern of falling words at the flowers standing cool, firm, and upright in the earth, with a curious expression. She saw them as a sleeper waking from a heavy sleep sees a brass candlestick reflecting the light in an unfamiliar way, and closes his eyes and opens them, and seeing the brass candlestick again, finally starts broad awake and stares at the candlestick with all his powers. So the heavy woman came to a standstill opposite the oval-shaped flower-bed, and ceased even to pretend to listen to what the other woman was saying. She stood there letting the words fall over her, swaying the top part of her body slowly backwards and forwards, looking at the flowers. Then she suggested that they should find a seat and have their tea.

The snail had now considered every possible method of reaching his goal without going round the dead leaf or climbing over it. Let alone the effort needed for climbing a leaf, he was doubtful whether the thin texture which vibrated with such an alarming crackle when touched even by the tips of his horns would bear his weight; and this determined him finally to creep beneath it, for there was a point where the leaf curved high enough from the ground to admit him. He had just inserted his head in the opening and was taking stock of the high brown roof and was getting used to the cool brown light when two other people came past outside on the turf. This time they were both young, a young man and a young woman. They were both in the prime of youth, or even in that season which precedes the prime of youth, the season before the smooth pink folds of the flower have burst their gummy case, when the wings of the butterfly, though fully grown, are motionless in the sun.

"Lucky it isn't Friday," he observed.

"Why? D'you believe in luck?"

"They make you pay sixpence on Friday."

"What's sixpence anyway? Isn't it worth sixpence?"

"What's 'it'—what do you mean by 'it'?"

"O, anything—I mean—you know what I mean."

Long pauses came between each of these remarks; they were uttered in toneless and monotonous voices. The couple stood still on the edge of the flower-bed, and together pressed the end of her parasol deep down into the soft earth. The action and the fact that his hand rested on the top of hers expressed their feelings in a strange way, as these short insignificant words also expressed something, words with short wings for their heavy body of meaning, inadequate to carry them far and thus alighting awkwardly upon the very common objects that surrounded them, and were to their inexperienced touch so massive; but who knows (so they thought as they pressed the parasol into the earth) what precipices aren't concealed in them, or what slopes of ice don't shine in the sun on the other side? Who knows? Who has ever seen this before? Even when she wondered what sort of tea they gave you at Kew, he felt that something loomed up behind her words, and stood vast and solid behind them; and the mist very slowly rose and uncovered—O, Heavens, what were those shapes?—little white tables, and waitresses who looked first at her and then at him; and there was a bill that he would pay with a real two shilling piece, and it was real, all real, he assured himself, fingering the coin in his pocket, real to everyone except to him and to her; even to him it began to seem real; and then—but it was too exciting to stand and think any longer, and he pulled the parasol out of the earth with a jerk and was impatient to find the place where one had tea with other people, like other people.

"Come along, Trissie; it's time we had our tea."

"Wherever *does* one have one's tea?" she asked with the oddest thrill of excitement in her voice, looking vaguely round and letting herself be drawn on down the grass path, trailing her parasol; turning her head this way and that way forgetting her tea, wishing to go down there and then down there, remembering orchids and cranes among wild flowers, a Chinese pagoda and a crimson crested bird; but he bore her on.

Thus one couple after another with much the same irregular

and aimless movement passed the flower-bed and were enveloped in layer after layer of green-blue vapour, in which at first their bodies had substance and a dash of colour, but later both substance and colour dissolved in the green-blue atmosphere. How hot it was! So hot that even the thrush chose to hop, like a mechanical bird, in the shadow of the flowers, with long pauses between one movement and the next; instead of rambling vaguely the white butterflies danced one above another, making with their white shifting flakes the outline of a shattered marble column above the tallest flowers; the glass roofs of the palm house shone as if a whole market full of shiny green umbrellas had opened in the sun; and in the drone of the aeroplane the voice of the summer sky murmured its fierce soul. Yellow and black, pink and snow white, shapes of all these colours, men, women, and children were spotted for a second upon the horizon, and then, seeing the breadth of yellow that lay upon the grass, they wavered and sought shade beneath the trees, dissolving like drops of water in the yellow and green atmosphere, staining it faintly with red and blue. It seemed as if all gross and heavy bodies had sunk down in the heat motionless and lay huddled upon the ground, but their voices went wavering from them as if they were flames lolling from the thick waxen bodies of candles. Voices. Yes, voices. Wordless voices, breaking the silence suddenly with such depth of contentment, such passion of desire, or, in the voices of children, such freshness of surprise; breaking the silence? But there was no silence; all the time the motor omnibuses were turning their wheels and changing their gear; like a vast nest of Chinese boxes all of wrought steel turning ceaselessly one within another the city murmured; on the top of which the voices cried aloud and the petals of myriads of flowers flashed their colours into the air.

F R O M

A Room of
One's Own

A Room of One's Own *is based on two papers read at Newnham and Girton, Cambridge, called "Women and Fiction."
Today it stands alone as the classic essay on feminism. Published in 1929, it is best characterized by its diamond-hard
reason, aristocratic understatement, and imaginative sweep. The
matter of equal rights for both sexes was, from childhood, a
sensitive spot for Virginia Woolf. Born and raised "the uneducated daughter" (as she sometimes referred to herself) of the
Victorian patriarch Sir Leslie Stephen, she could not fail to
notice that the expensive educations given her two brothers
afforded them powers and privileges that she herself was denied.
To drive her point home, she bids us in this essay observe her
on a fictitious tour of Oxbridge (Oxford and Cambridge).*

*In that venerable university, where male power has its
sovereignty, we are shown corruptions in the social arrangement and the destructive effects of sexual polarization. All of this
is the result of male economic dominance. It is the male population that, over the centuries, has bestowed its great wealth
upon already wealthy universities. And that wealth has done
everything to keep women outside the sturdy walls of learning.
It has kept women over kitchen fires or in confinement with end-*

less pregnancies. Over the centuries, women have been kept mute and maternal. And in poverty.

But what has all this to do with women and fiction? Simply this. The writer of fiction must be free of the hatred and bitterness that originate in the human injustice of sexual politics— free to express a larger, more comprehensive sympathy, which embraces the feelings of both women and men; a sympathy that encourages sexual unity. The militant feminist is as incapable of producing worthwhile fiction as the male chauvinist, precisely because her artistic powers are forever inflamed with ill feeling. Great artists, asserted Virginia Woolf, are androgynous. Their minds are unimpeded and their imaginations incandescent. But androgyny can flourish only when one has intellectual freedom, and that freedom depends upon certain material comforts, the most fundamental of which are five hundred pounds a year and a room of one's own.

BUT, YOU MAY SAY, WE ASKED YOU TO SPEAK ABOUT women and fiction—what has that got to do with a room of one's own? I will try to explain. When you asked me to speak about women and fiction I sat down on the banks of a river and began to wonder what the words meant. They might mean simply a few remarks about Fanny Burney; a few more about Jane Austen; a tribute to the Brontës and a sketch of Haworth Parsonage under snow; some witticisms if possible about Miss Mitford; a respectful allusion to George Eliot; a reference to Mrs. Gaskell and one would have done. But at second sight the words seemed not so simple. The title women and fiction might mean, and you may have meant it to mean, women and what they are like; or it might mean women and the fiction that they write; or it might mean women and the fiction that is written about them; or it might mean that somehow all three are inextricably mixed together and you want me to consider them in that light. But when

I began to consider the subject in this last way, which seemed the most interesting, I soon saw that it had one fatal drawback. I should never be able to come to a conclusion. I should never be able to fulfil what is, I understand, the first duty of a lecturer—to hand you after an hour's discourse a nugget of pure truth to wrap up between the pages of your notebooks and keep on the mantelpiece for ever. All I could do was to offer you an opinion upon one minor point—a woman must have money and a room of her own if she is to write fiction; and that, as you will see, leaves the great problem of the true nature of woman and the true nature of fiction unsolved. I have shirked the duty of coming to a conclusion upon these two questions—women and fiction remain, so far as I am concerned, unsolved problems. But in order to make some amends I am going to do what I can to show you how I arrived at this opinion about the room and the money. I am going to develop in your presence as fully and freely as I can the train of thought which led me to think this. Perhaps if I lay bare the ideas, the prejudices, that lie behind this statement you will find that they have some bearing upon women and some upon fiction. At any rate, when a subject is highly controversial—and any question about sex is that—one cannot hope to tell the truth. One can only show how one came to hold whatever opinion one does hold. One can only give one's audience the chance of drawing their own conclusions as they observe the limitations, the prejudices, the idiosyncrasies of the speaker. Fiction here is likely to contain more truth than fact. Therefore I propose, making use of all the liberties and licences of a novelist, to tell you the story of the two days that preceded my coming here— how, bowed down by the weight of the subject which you have laid upon my shoulders, I pondered it, and made it work in and out of my daily life. I need not say that what I am about to describe has no existence; Oxbridge is an invention; so is Fernham; "I" is only a convenient term for somebody who has no real being. Lies will flow from my lips, but there may perhaps be some truth mixed up with them; it is for you to seek out this truth and to decide whether any part of it is worth keeping. If not, you will of course throw the whole of it into the wastepaper basket and forget all about it.

Here then was I (call me Mary Beton, Mary Seton, Mary Carmichael or by any name you please—it is not a matter of any importance) sitting on the banks of a river a week or two ago in fine October weather, lost in thought. That collar I have spoken of, women and fiction, the need of coming to some conclusion on a subject that raises all sorts of prejudices and passions, bowed my head to the ground. To the right and left bushes of some sort, golden and crimson, glowed with the colour, even it seemed burnt with the heat, of fire. On the further bank the willows wept in perpetual lamentation, their hair about their shoulders. The river reflected whatever it chose of sky and bridge and burning tree, and when the undergraduate had oared his boat through the reflections they closed again, completely, as if he had never been. There one might have sat the clock round lost in thought. Thought—to call it by a prouder name than it deserved—had let its line down into the stream. It swayed, minute after minute, hither and thither among the reflections and the weeds, letting the water lift it and sink it, until—you know the little tug—the sudden conglomeration of an idea at the end of one's line: and then the cautious hauling of it in, and the careful laying of it out? Alas, laid on the grass how small, how insignificant this thought of mine looked; the sort of fish that a good fisherman puts back into the water so that it may grow fatter and be one day worth cooking and eating. I will not trouble you with that thought now, though if you look carefully you may find it for yourselves in the course of what I am going to say.

But however small it was, it had, nevertheless, the mysterious property of its kind—put back into the mind, it became at once very exciting, and important; and as it darted and sank, and flashed hither and thither, set up such a wash and tumult of ideas that it was impossible to sit still. It was thus that I found myself walking with extreme rapidity across a grass plot. Instantly a man's figure rose to intercept me. Nor did I at first understand that the gesticulations of a curious-looking object, in a cut-away coat and evening shirt, were aimed at me. His face expressed horror and indignation. Instinct rather than reason came to my help; he was a Beadle; I was a woman. This was the turf; there was the path. Only the Fellows and Scholars are allowed here; the gravel is the place for me. Such thoughts were the work of a moment. As I regained the path the arms of the Beadle sank, his face assumed its usual repose, and though turf is better walking than gravel, no very great harm was done. The only charge I could bring against the Fellows and Scholars of whatever the college might happen to be was that in protection of their turf, which has been rolled for 300 years in succession, they had sent my little fish into hiding.

What idea it had been that had sent me so audaciously trespassing I could not now remember. The spirit of peace descended like a cloud from heaven, for if the spirit of peace dwells anywhere, it is in the courts and quadrangles of Oxbridge on a fine October morning. Strolling through those colleges past those ancient halls the roughness of the present seemed smoothed away; the body seemed contained in a miraculous glass cabinet through which no sound could penetrate, and the mind, freed from any contact with facts (unless one trespassed on the turf again), was at liberty to settle down upon whatever meditation was in harmony with the moment. As chance would have it, some stray memory of some old essay about revisiting Oxbridge in the long vacation brought Charles Lamb to mind—Saint Charles, said Thackeray, putting a letter of Lamb's to his forehead. Indeed, among all the dead (I give you my thoughts as they came to me), Lamb is one of the most congenial; one to whom one would have liked to say, Tell me then how you wrote your essays? For his essays are superior even to Max Beerbohm's, I thought, with all their perfection, because of that wild flash of imagination, that lightning crack of genius in the middle of them which leaves them flawed and imperfect, but starred with poetry. Lamb then came to Oxbridge perhaps a hundred years ago. Certainly he wrote an essay—the name escapes me—about the manuscript of one of Milton's poems which he saw here. It was *Lycidas* perhaps, and Lamb wrote how it shocked him to think it possible that any word in *Lycidas* could have been different from what it is. To think of Milton changing the words in that poem seemed to him a sort of sacrilege. This led me to remember what I could of *Lycidas* and to amuse myself with guessing which word it could have been that Milton had altered, and why. It then occurred to me that the very manuscript itself which Lamb had looked at was only a few hundred yards away, so that one could follow Lamb's footsteps across the quadrangle to that famous library where the treasure is kept. Moreover, I recollected, as I put this plan into execution, it is in this famous library that the manuscript of Thackeray's *Esmond* is also preserved. The critics often say that *Esmond* is Thackeray's most perfect novel. But the affectation of the style, with its imitation of the eighteenth century, hampers one, so far as I remember; unless indeed the eighteenth-century style was natural to Thackeray—a fact that one might prove by looking at the manuscript and seeing whether the alterations were for the benefit of the style or of the sense. But then one would have to decide what is style and what is meaning, a question which—but here I was actually at the door which leads into the library itself. I must have opened it, for instantly there issued, like a guardian angel barring the way with a flutter of black gown instead of white wings, a deprecating, silvery, kindly gentleman, who regretted in a low voice as he waved me back that ladies are only admitted to the library if accompanied by a Fellow of the College or furnished with a letter of introduction.

That a famous library has been cursed by a woman is a matter of complete indifference to a famous library. Venerable and calm, with all its treasures safe locked within its breast, it sleeps complacently and will, so far as I am concerned, so sleep for ever. Never will I wake those echoes, never will I ask for that hospitality again, I vowed as I descended the steps in anger. Still an hour remained before luncheon, and what was one to do? Stroll on the meadows? sit by the river? Certainly it was a lovely autumn morning; the leaves were fluttering red to the ground;

there was no great hardship in doing either. But the sound of music reached my ear. Some service or celebration was going forward. The organ complained magnificently as I passed the chapel door. Even the sorrow of Christianity sounded in that serene air more like the recollection of sorrow than sorrow itself; even the groanings of the ancient organ seemed lapped in peace. I had no wish to enter had I the right, and this time the verger might have stopped me, demanding perhaps my baptismal certificate, or a letter of introduction from the Dean. But the outside of these magnificent buildings is often as beautiful as the inside. Moreover, it was amusing enough to watch the congregation assembling, coming in and going out again, busying themselves at the door of the chapel like bees at the mouth of a hive. Many were in cap and gown; some had tufts of fur on their shoulders; others were wheeled in bath-chairs; others, though not past middle age, seemed creased and crushed into shapes so singular that one was reminded of those giant crabs and crayfish who heave with difficulty across the sand of an aquarium. As I leant against the wall the University indeed seemed a sanctuary in which are preserved rare types which would soon be obsolete if left to fight for existence on the pavement of the Strand. Old stories of old deans and old dons came back to mind, but before I had summoned up courage to whistle—it used to be said that at the sound of a whistle old Professor ——— instantly broke into a gallop—the venerable congregation had gone inside. The outside of the chapel remained. As you know, its high domes and pinnacles can be seen, like a sailing-ship always voyaging never arriving, lit up at night and visible for miles, far away across the hills. Once, presumably, this quadrangle with its smooth lawns, its massive buildings, and the chapel itself was marsh too, where the grasses waved and the swine rootled. Teams of horses and oxen, I thought, must have hauled the stone in wagons from far countries, and then with infinite labour the grey blocks in whose shade I was now standing were poised in order one on top of another, and then the painters brought their glass for the windows, and the masons were busy for centuries up on that roof

with putty and cement, spade and trowel. Every Saturday somebody must have poured gold and silver out of a leathern purse
into their ancient fists, for they had their beer and skittles
presumably of an evening. An unending stream of gold and silver, I thought, must have flowed into this court perpetually to
keep the stones coming and the masons working; to level, to
ditch, to dig and to drain. But it was then the age of faith, and
money was poured liberally to set these stones on a deep foundation, and when the stones were raised, still more money was
poured in from the coffers of kings and queens and great nobles
to ensure that hymns should be sung here and scholars taught.
Lands were granted; tithes were paid. And when the age of
faith was over and the age of reason had come, still the same
flow of gold and silver went on; fellowships were founded; lectureships endowed; only the gold and silver flowed now, not
from the coffers of the king, but from the chests of merchants
and manufacturers, from the purses of men who had made, say,
a fortune from industry, and returned, in their wills, a bounteous
share of it to endow more chairs, more lectureships, more fellowships in the university where they had learnt their craft.
Hence the libraries and laboratories; the observatories; the
splendid equipment of costly and delicate instruments which now
stands on glass shelves, where centuries ago the grasses waved
and the swine rootled. Certainly, as I strolled round the court,
the foundation of gold and silver seemed deep enough; the
pavement laid solidly over the wild grasses. Men with trays on
their heads went busily from staircase to staircase. Gaudy blossoms flowered in window-boxes. The strains of the gramophone
blared out from the rooms within. It was impossible not to reflect
—the reflection whatever it may have been was cut short. The
clock struck. It was time to find one's way to luncheon.

It is a curious fact that novelists have a way of making us
believe that luncheon parties are invariably memorable for something very witty that was said, or for something very wise that
was done. But they seldom spare a word for what was eaten. It is
part of the novelist's convention not to mention soup and salmon

and ducklings, as if soup and salmon and ducklings were of no importance whatsoever, as if nobody ever smoked a cigar or drank a glass of wine. Here, however, I shall take the liberty to defy that convention and to tell you that the lunch on this occasion began with soles, sunk in a deep dish, over which the college cook had spread a counterpane of the whitest cream, save that it was branded here and there with brown spots like the spots on the flanks of a doe. After that came the partridges, but if this suggests a couple of bald, brown birds on a plate you are mistaken. The partridges, many and various, came with all their retinue of sauces and salads, the sharp and the sweet, each in its order; their potatoes, thin as coins but not so hard; their sprouts, foliated as rosebuds but more succulent. And no sooner had the roast and its retinue been done with than the silent serving-man, the Beadle himself perhaps in a milder manifestation, set before us, wreathed in napkins, a confection which rose all sugar from the waves. To call it pudding and so relate it to rice and tapioca would be an insult. Meanwhile the wineglasses had flushed yellow and flushed crimson; had been emptied; had been filled. And thus by degrees was lit, halfway down the spine, which is the seat of the soul, not that hard little electric light which we call brilliance, as it pops in and out upon our lips, but the more profound, subtle and subterranean glow, which is the rich yellow flame of rational intercourse. No need to hurry. No need to sparkle. No need to be anybody but oneself. We are all going to heaven and Vandyck is of the company—in other words, how good life seemed, how sweet its rewards, how trivial this grudge or that grievance, how admirable friendship and the society of one's kind, as, lighting a good cigarette, one sunk among the cushions in the window-seat.

If by good luck there had been an ash-tray handy, if one had not knocked the ash out of the window in default, if things had been a little different from what they were, one would not have seen, presumably, a cat without a tail. The sight of that abrupt and truncated animal padding softly across the quadrangle changed by some fluke of the subconscious intelligence the emotional light for me. It was as if some one had let fall a shade. Perhaps the excellent hock was relinquishing its hold. Certainly, as I watched the Manx cat pause in the middle of the lawn as if it too questioned the universe, something seemed lacking, something seemed different. But what was lacking, what was different, I asked myself, listening to the talk. And to answer that question I had to think myself out of the room, back into the past, before the war indeed, and to set before my eyes the model of another luncheon party held in rooms not very far distant from these, but different. Everything was different. Meanwhile the talk went on among the guests, who were many and young, some of this sex, some of that; it went on swimmingly, it went on agreeably, freely, amusingly. And as it went on I set it against the background of that other talk, and as I matched the two together I had no doubt that one was the descendant, the legitimate heir of the other. Nothing was changed; nothing was different save only —here I listened with all my ears not entirely to what was being said, but to the murmur or current behind it. Yes, that was it—the change was there. Before the war at a luncheon party like this people would have said precisely the same things but they would have sounded different, because in those days they were accompanied by a sort of humming noise, not articulate, but musical, exciting, which changed the value of the words themselves. Could one set that humming noise to words? Perhaps with the help of the poets one could. A book lay beside me and, opening it, I turned casually enough to Tennyson. And here I found Tennyson was singing:

> There has fallen a splendid tear
>   From the passion-flower at the gate.
> She is coming, my dove, my dear;
>   She is coming, my life, my fate;
> The red rose cries, "She is near, she is near";
>   And the white rose weeps, "She is late";
> The larkspur listens, "I hear, I hear";
>   And the lily whispers, "I wait."

Was that what men hummed at luncheon parties before the war?
And the women?

> My heart is like a singing bird
>   Whose nest is in a water'd shoot;
> My heart is like an apple tree
>   Whose boughs are bent with thick-set fruit;
> My heart is like a rainbow shell
>   That paddles in a halcyon sea;
> My heart is gladder than all these
>   Because my love is come to me.

Was that what women hummed at luncheon parties before the
war?

There was something so ludicrous in thinking of people humming such things even under their breath at luncheon parties
before the war that I burst out laughing, and had to explain my
laughter by pointing at the Manx cat, who did look a little absurd, poor beast, without a tail, in the middle of the lawn. Was
he really born so, or had he lost his tail in an accident? The
tailless cat, though some are said to exist in the Isle of Man, is
rarer than one thinks. It is a queer animal, quaint rather than
beautiful. It is strange what a difference a tail makes—you know
the sort of things one says as a lunch party breaks up and people
are finding their coats and hats.

This one, thanks to the hospitality of the host, had lasted far
into the afternoon. The beautiful October day was fading and the
leaves were falling from the trees in the avenue as I walked
through it. Gate after gate seemed to close with gentle finality
behind me. Innumerable beadles were fitting innumerable keys
into well-oiled locks; the treasure-house was being made secure
for another night. After the avenue one comes out upon a road—
I forget its name—which leads you, if you take the right turning,
along to Fernham. But there was plenty of time. Dinner was not
till half-past seven. One could almost do without dinner after
such a luncheon. It is strange how a scrap of poetry works in the
mind and makes the legs move in time to it along the road.
Those words—

> There has fallen a splendid tear
> From the passion-flower at the gate.
> She is coming, my dove, my dear—

sang in my blood as I stepped quickly along towards Headingley.
And then, switching off into the other measure, I sang, where the
waters are churned up by the weir:

> My heart is like a singing bird
> Whose nest is in a water'd shoot;
> My heart is like an apple tree . . .

What poets, I cried aloud, as one does in the dusk, what poets
they were!

In a sort of jealousy, I suppose, for our own age, silly and
absurd though these comparisons are, I went on to wonder if
honestly one could name two living poets now as great as Tennyson and Christina Rossetti were then. Obviously it is impossible,
I thought, looking into those foaming waters, to compare them.
The very reason why the poetry excites one to such abandon-
ment, such rapture, is that it celebrates some feeling that one
used to have (at luncheon parties before the war perhaps), so
that one responds easily, familiarly, without troubling to check
the feeling, or to compare it with any that one has now. But the
living poets express a feeling that is actually being made and torn
out of us at the moment. One does not recognize it in the first
place; often for some reason one fears it; one watches it with
keenness and compares it jealously and suspiciously with the old
feeling that one knew. Hence the difficulty of modern poetry; and
it is because of this difficulty that one cannot remember more
than two consecutive lines of any good modern poet. For this
reason—that my memory failed me—the argument flagged for
want of material. But why, I continued, moving on towards
Headingley, have we stopped humming under our breath at
luncheon parties? Why has Alfred ceased to sing

> She is coming, my dove, my dear?

Why has Christina ceased to respond

My heart is gladder than all these
Because my love is come to me?

Shall we lay the blame on the war? When the guns fired in
August 1914, did the faces of men and women show so plain in
each other's eyes that romance was killed? Certainly it was a
shock (to women in particular with their illusions about education, and so on) to see the faces of our rulers in the light of the
shell-fire. So ugly they looked—German, English, French—so
stupid. But lay the blame where one will, on whom one will, the
illusion which inspired Tennyson and Christina Rossetti to sing
so passionately about the coming of their loves is far rarer now
than then. One has only to read, to look, to listen, to remember.
But why say "blame"? Why, if it was an illusion, not praise the
catastrophe, whatever it was, that destroyed illusion and put
truth in its place? For truth . . . those dots mark the spot where,
in search of truth, I missed the turning up to Fernham. Yes
indeed, which was truth and which was illusion, I asked myself.
What was the truth about these houses, for example, dim and
festive now with their red windows in the dusk, but raw and red
and squalid, with their sweets and their boot-laces, at nine
o'clock in the morning? And the willows and the river and the
gardens that run down to the river, vague now with the mist
stealing over them, but gold and red in the sunlight—which was
the truth, which was the illusion about them? I spare you the
twists and turns of my cogitations, for no conclusion was found
on the road to Headingley, and I ask you to suppose that I soon
found out my mistake about the turning and retraced my steps to
Fernham.

As I have said already that it was an October day, I dare not
forfeit your respect and imperil the fair name of fiction by changing the season and describing lilacs hanging over garden walls,
crocuses, tulips and other flowers of spring. Fiction must stick
to facts, and the truer the facts the better the fiction—so we are
told. Therefore it was still autumn and the leaves were still yellow and falling, if anything, a little faster than before, because it

was now evening (seven twenty-three to be precise) and a breeze (from the southwest to be exact) had risen. But for all that there was something odd at work:

> My heart is like a singing bird
>   Whose nest is in a water'd shoot;
> My heart is like an apple tree
>   Whose boughs are bent with thick-set fruit—

perhaps the words of Christina Rossetti were partly responsible for the folly of the fancy—it was nothing of course but a fancy—that the lilac was shaking its flowers over the garden walls, and the brimstone butterflies were scudding hither and thither, and the dust of the pollen was in the air. A wind blew, from what quarter I know not, but it lifted the half-grown leaves so that there was a flash of silver grey in the air. It was the time between the lights when colours undergo their intensification and purples and golds burn in window panes like the beat of an excitable heart; when for some reason the beauty of the world revealed and yet soon to perish (here I pushed into the garden, for, unwisely, the door was left open and no beadles seemed about), the beauty of the world which is so soon to perish, has two edges, one of laughter, one of anguish, cutting the heart asunder. The gardens of Fernham lay before me in the spring twilight, wild and open, and in the long grass, sprinkled and carelessly flung, were daffodils and bluebells, not orderly perhaps at the best of times, and now wind-blown and waving as they tugged at their roots. The windows of the building, curved like ships' windows among generous waves of red brick, changed from lemon to silver under the flight of the quick spring clouds. Somebody was in a hammock, somebody, but in this light they were phantoms only, half guessed, half seen, raced across the grass—would no one stop her?—and then on the terrace, as if popping out to breathe the air, to glance at the garden, came a bent figure, formidable yet humble, with her great forehead and her shabby dress—could it be the famous scholar, could it be J——

H—— herself? All was dim, yet intense too, as if the scarf which the dusk had flung over the garden were torn asunder by star or sword—the flash of some terrible reality leaping, as its way is, out of the heart of the spring. For youth——

Here was my soup. Dinner was being served in the great dining-hall. Far from being spring it was in fact an evening in October. Everybody was assembled in the big dining-room. Dinner was ready. Here was the soup. It was a plain gravy soup. There was nothing to stir the fancy in that. One could have seen through the transparent liquid any pattern that there might have been on the plate itself. But there was no pattern. The plate was plain. Next came beef with its attendant greens and potatoes—a homely trinity, suggesting the rumps of cattle in a muddy market, and sprouts curled and yellowed at the edge, and bargaining and cheapening, and women with string bags on Monday morning. There was no reason to complain of human nature's daily food, seeing that the supply was sufficient and coal-miners doubtless were sitting down to less. Prunes and custard followed. And if any one complains that prunes, even when mitigated by custard, are an uncharitable vegetable (fruit they are not), stringy as a miser's heart and exuding a fluid such as might run in misers' veins who have denied themselves wine and warmth for eighty years and yet not given to the poor, he should reflect that there are people whose charity embraces even the prune. Biscuits and cheese came next, and here the water-jug was liberally passed round, for it is the nature of biscuits to be dry, and these were biscuits to the core. That was all. The meal was over. Everybody scraped their chairs back; the swing-doors swung violently to and fro; soon the hall was emptied of every sign of food and made ready no doubt for breakfast next morning. Down corridors and up staircases the youth of England went banging and singing. And was it for a guest, a stranger (for I had no more right here in Fernham than in Trinity or Somerville or Girton or Newnham or Christchurch), to say, "The dinner was not good," or to say (we were now, Mary Seton and I, in her sitting-room), "Could we not have dined up here alone?" for if I had said anything of the kind I should have been prying and searching into the secret economies of a house which to the stranger wears so fine a front of gaiety and courage. No, one could say nothing of the sort. Indeed, conversation for a moment flagged. The human frame being what it is, heart, body and brain all mixed together, and not contained in separate compartments as they will be no doubt in another million years, a good dinner is of great importance to good talk. One cannot think well, love well, sleep well, if one has not dined well. The lamp in the spine does not light on beef and prunes. We are all *probably* going to heaven, and Vandyck is, we *hope*, to meet us round the next corner—that is the dubious and qualifying state of mind that beef and prunes at the end of the day's work breed between them. Happily my friend, who taught science, had a cupboard where there was a squat bottle and little glasses—(but there should have been sole and partridge to begin with)—so that we were able to draw up to the fire and repair some of the damages of the day's living. In a minute or so we were slipping freely in and out among all those objects of curiosity and interest which form in the mind in the absence of a particular person, and are naturally to be discussed on coming together again—how somebody has married, another has not; one thinks this, another that; one has improved out of all knowledge, the other most amazingly gone to the bad—with all those speculations upon human nature and the character of the amazing world we live in which spring naturally from such beginnings. While these things were being said, however, I became shamefacedly aware of a current setting in of its own accord and carrying everything forward to an end of its own. One might be talking of Spain or Portugal, of book or racehorse, but the real interest of whatever was said was none of those things, but a scene of masons on a high roof some five centuries ago. Kings and nobles brought treasure in huge sacks and poured it under the earth. This scene was for ever coming alive in my mind and placing itself by another of lean cows and a muddy market and withered greens and the stringy hearts of old men—these two pictures, disjointed and disconnected and nonsensical as they were, were for ever coming together and combating each other and had me entirely at their mercy. The best course, unless the whole talk was to be distorted, was to expose what was in my mind to the air, when with good luck it would fade and crumble like the head of the dead king when they opened the coffin at Windsor. Briefly, then, I told Miss Seton about the masons who had been all those years on the roof of the chapel, and about the kings and queens and nobles bearing sacks of gold and silver on their shoulders, which they shovelled into the earth; and then how the great financial magnates of our own time came and laid cheques and bonds, I suppose, where the others had laid ingots and rough lumps of gold. All that lies beneath the colleges down there, I said; but this college, where we are now sitting, what lies beneath its gallant red brick and the wild unkempt grasses of the garden? What force is behind the plain china off which we dined, and (here it popped out of my mouth before I could stop it) the beef, the custard and the prunes?

Well, said Mary Seton, about the year 1860—Oh, but you know the story, she said, bored, I suppose, by the recital. And she told me—rooms were hired. Committees met. Envelopes were addressed. Circulars were drawn up. Meetings were held; letters were read out; so-and-so has promised so much; on the contrary, Mr. —— won't give a penny. The *Saturday Review* has been very rude. How can we raise a fund to pay for offices? Shall we hold a bazaar? Can't we find a pretty girl to sit in the front row? Let us look up what John Stuart Mill said on the subject. Can any one persuade the editor of the —— to print a letter? Can we get Lady —— to sign it? Lady —— is out of town. That was the way it was done, presumably, sixty years ago, and it was a prodigious effort, and a great deal of time was spent on it. And it was only after a long struggle and with the utmost difficulty that they got thirty thousand pounds together.[1] So obviously we cannot have wine and partridges and servants carrying tin dishes on their heads, she said. We cannot have sofas and separate rooms. "The amenities," she said, quoting from some book or other, "will have to wait."[2]

At the thought of all those women working year after year and finding it hard to get two thousand pounds together, and as much as they could do to get thirty thousand pounds, we burst out in scorn at the reprehensible poverty of our sex. What had our mothers been doing then that they had no wealth to leave us? Powdering their noses? Looking in at shop windows? Flaunting in the sun at Monte Carlo? There were some photographs on the mantel-piece. Mary's mother—if that was her picture—may have been a wastrel in her spare time (she had thirteen children by a minister of the church), but if so her gay and dissipated life had left too few traces of its pleasures on her face. She was a homely body; an old lady in a plaid shawl which was fastened by a large cameo; and she sat in a basket-chair, encouraging a spaniel to look at the camera, with the amused, yet strained expression of one who is sure that the dog will move directly the bulb is pressed. Now if she had gone into business; had become a manufacturer of artificial silk or a magnate on the Stock Exchange; if she had left two or three hundred thousand pounds to Fernham, we could have been sitting at our ease tonight and the subject of our talk might have been archaeology, botany, anthropology, physics, the nature of the atom, mathematics, astronomy, relativity, geography. If only Mrs. Seton and her mother and her mother before her had learnt the great art of making money and had left their money, like their fathers and their grandfathers before them, to found fellowships and lectureships and prizes and scholarships appropriated to the use of their own sex, we might have dined very tolerably up here alone off a bird and a bottle of wine; we might have looked forward without undue confidence to a pleasant and honourable lifetime spent in the shelter of one of the liberally endowed professions. We might have been exploring or writing; mooning about the venerable places of the earth; sitting contemplative on the steps of the Parthenon, or going at ten to an office and coming home comfortably at half-past four to write a little poetry. Only, if Mrs. Seton and her like had gone into business at the age of fifteen, there would have been—that was the snag in the argument—no

Mary. What, I asked, did Mary think of that? There between the curtains was the October night, calm and lovely, with a star or two caught in the yellowing trees. Was she ready to resign her share of it and her memories (for they had been a happy family, though a large one) of games and quarrels up in Scotland, which she is never tired of praising for the fineness of its air and the quality of its cakes, in order that Fernham might have been endowed with fifty thousand pounds or so by a stroke of the pen? For, to endow a college would necessitate the suppression of families altogether. Making a fortune and bearing thirteen children—no human being could stand it. Consider the facts, we said. First there are nine months before the baby is born. Then the baby is born. Then there are three or four months spent in feeding the baby. After the baby is fed there are certainly five years spent in playing with the baby. You cannot, it seems, let children run about the streets. People who have seen them running wild in Russia say that the sight is not a pleasant one. People say, too, that human nature takes its shape in the years between one and five. If Mrs. Seton, I said, had been making money, what sort of memories would you have had of games and quarrels? What would you have known of Scotland, and its fine air and cakes and all the rest of it? But it is useless to ask these questions, because you would never have come into existence at all. Moreover, it is equally useless to ask what might have happened if Mrs. Seton and her mother and her mother before her had amassed great wealth and laid it under the foundations of college and library, because, in the first place, to earn money was impossible for them, and in the second, had it been possible, the law denied them the right to possess what money they earned. It is only for the last forty-eight years that Mrs. Seton has had a penny of her own. For all the centuries before that it would have been her husband's property—a thought which, perhaps, may have had its share in keeping Mrs. Seton and her mothers off the Stock Exchange. Every penny I earn, they may have said, will be taken from me and disposed of according to my husband's wisdom—perhaps to found a scholarship or to endow a fellowship in Balliol or Kings, so that to earn money, even if I could earn money, is not a matter that interests me very greatly. I had better leave it to my husband.

At any rate, whether or not the blame rested on the old lady who was looking at the spaniel, there could be no doubt that for some reason or other our mothers had mismanaged their affairs very gravely. Not a penny could be spared for "amenities"; for partridges and wine, beadles and turf, books and cigars, libraries and leisure. To raise bare walls out of the bare earth was the utmost they could do.

So we talked standing at the window and looking, as so many thousands look every night, down on the domes and towers of the famous city beneath us. It was very beautiful, very mysterious in the autumn moonlight. The old stone looked very white and venerable. One thought of all the books that were assembled down there; of the pictures of old prelates and worthies hanging in the panelled rooms; of the painted windows that would be throwing strange globes and crescents on the pavement; of the tablets and memorials and inscriptions; of the fountains and the grass; of the quiet rooms looking across the quiet quadrangles. And (pardon me the thought) I thought, too, of the admirable smoke and drink and the deep armchairs and the pleasant carpets: of the urbanity, the geniality, the dignity which are the offspring of luxury and privacy and space. Certainly our mothers had not provided us with anything comparable to all this—our mothers who found it difficult to scrape together thirty thousand pounds, our mothers who bore thirteen children to ministers of religion at St. Andrews.

So I went back to my inn, and as I walked through the dark streets I pondered this and that, as one does at the end of the day's work. I pondered why it was that Mrs. Seton had no money to leave us; and what effect poverty has on the mind; and what effect wealth has on the mind; and I thought of the queer old gentlemen I had seen that morning with tufts of fur upon their shoulders; and I remembered how if one whistled one of them ran; and I thought of the organ booming in the chapel and of the shut doors of the library; and I thought how unpleasant it is to be locked out; and I thought how it is worse perhaps to be locked in; and, thinking of the safety and prosperity of the one sex and of the poverty and insecurity of the other and of the effect of tradition and of the lack of tradition upon the mind of a writer. I thought at last that it was time to roll up the crumpled skin of the day, with its arguments and its impressions and its anger and its laughter, and cast it into the hedge. A thousand stars were flashing across the blue wastes of the sky. One seemed alone with an inscrutable society. All human beings were laid asleep—prone, horizontal, dumb. Nobody seemed stirring in the streets of Oxbridge. Even the door of the hotel sprang open at the touch of an invisible hand—not a boots was sitting up to light me to bed, it was so late.

N O T E S

1. "We are told that we ought to ask for £30,000 at least. . . . It is not a large sum, considering that there is to be but one college of this sort for Great Britain, Ireland and the Colonies, and considering how easy it is to raise immense sums for boys' schools. But considering how few people really wish women to be educated, it is a good deal."—Lady Stephen, *Life of Miss Emily Davies.*
2. Every penny which could be scraped together was set aside for building, and the amenities had to be postponed.—R. Strachey, *The Cause.*

Essays

The essays gathered here combine some that are famous with some that are not so well known. All of them, however, represent essay writing of the highest order—quick perceptions joined to authentic knowledge, sound judgment, and elegant phrasing. One of the curious and most engaging features of these essays is that Virginia Woolf never spoke from a podium. Always her voice is modulated to that of one friend talking to another about literature and life. And what she says is filled with easy discrimination and imaginative energy. Part of the secret of Virginia Woolf's success as an essayist was that she never explained abstract concepts with further abstractions. She had that rare gift of translating ideas into concrete, recognizable images. Few essayists have surpassed her in that difficult and felicitous union of sense and sensibility.

Mr. Bennett and
Mrs. Brown

The first version of the now famous Mr. Bennett and Mrs. Brown *was written in December 1923 as a reply to an article by Arnold Bennett in which he said: "The foundation of good fiction is character-creating and nothing else." He went on to say that Virginia Woolf's characters—he was commenting specifically on her recently published* Jacob's Room—*"do not vitally survive in the mind because the author has been obsessed by details of originality and cleverness." The original essay, enlarged and revised, was read to the Society of Heretics in Cambridge in May 1924 under the title "Character in Fiction." It was again revised, and published finally as* Mr. Bennett and Mrs. Brown *by the Hogarth Press in October 1924.*

The essay has become a kind of literary manifesto, which repudiates the novels of the earlier generation—notably those of Wells, Galsworthy, and Bennett—because they invented all kinds of trivia with which to fill their pages; and, in so doing, deprived their readers of a single insight into human character. The earlier novelists, Virginia Woolf asserted, have never bothered to look at Mrs. Brown in her corner—at life, at human nature.

IT SEEMS TO ME POSSIBLE, PERHAPS DESIRABLE, that I may be the only person in this room who has committed the folly of writing, trying to write, or failing to write, a novel. And when I asked myself, as your invitation to speak to you about modern fiction made me ask myself, what demon whispered in my ear and urged me to my doom, a little figure rose before me—the figure of a man, or of a woman, who said, "My name is Brown. Catch me if you can."

Most novelists have the same experience. Some Brown, Smith, or Jones comes before them and says in the most seductive and charming way in the world, "Come and catch me if you can." And so, led on by this will-o'-the-wisp, they flounder through volume after volume, spending the best years of their lives in the pursuit, and receiving for the most part very little cash in exchange. Few catch the phantom; most have to be content with a scrap of her dress or a wisp of her hair.

My belief that men and women write novels because they are lured on to create some character which has thus imposed itself upon them has the sanction of Mr. Arnold Bennett. In an article from which I will quote he says, "The foundation of good fiction is character-creating and nothing else. . . . Style counts; plot counts; originality of outlook counts. But none of these counts anything like so much as the convincingness of the characters. If the characters are real the novel will have a chance; if they are not, oblivion will be its portion. . . ." And he goes on to draw the conclusion that we have no young novelists of first-rate importance at the present moment, because they are unable to create characters that are real, true, and convincing.

These are the questions that I want with greater boldness than discretion to discuss tonight. I want to make out what we mean when we talk about "character" in fiction; to say something about the question of reality which Mr. Bennett raises; and to suggest some reasons why the younger novelists fail to create characters, if, as Mr. Bennett asserts, it is true that fail they do. This will lead me, I am well aware, to make some very sweeping and some very vague assertions. For the question is an extremely difficult one. Think how little we know about character—think how little we know about art. But, to make a clearance before I begin, I will suggest that we range Edwardians and Georgians into two camps; Mr. Wells, Mr. Bennett, and Mr. Galsworthy I will call the Edwardians; Mr. Forster, Mr. Lawrence, Mr. Strachey, Mr. Joyce, and Mr. Eliot I will call the Georgians. And if I speak in the first person, with intolerable egotism, I will ask you to excuse me. I do not want to attribute to the world at large the opinions of one solitary, ill-informed, and misguided individual.

My first assertion is one that I think you will grant—that every one in this room is a judge of character. Indeed it would be impossible to live for a year without disaster unless one practised character-reading and had some skill in the art. Our marriages, our friendships depend on it; our business largely depends on it; every day questions arise which can only be solved by its help. And now I will hazard a second assertion, which is more disputable perhaps, to the effect that on or about December, 1910, human character changed.

I am not saying that one went out, as one might into a garden, and there saw that a rose had flowered, or that a hen had laid an egg. The change was not sudden and definite like that. But a change there was, nevertheless; and, since one must be arbitrary, let us date it about the year 1910. The first signs of it are recorded in the books of Samuel Butler, in *The Way of All Flesh* in particular; the plays of Bernard Shaw continue to record it. In life one can see the change, if I may use a homely illustration, in the character of one's cook. The Victorian cook lived like a leviathan in the lower depths, formidable, silent, obscure, inscrutable; the Georgian cook is a creature of sunshine and fresh air; in and out of the drawing-room, now to borrow the *Daily Herald*, now to ask advice about a hat. Do you ask for more solemn instances of the power of the human race to change? Read the *Agamemnon*, and see whether, in process of time, your sympathies are not almost entirely with Clytemnestra. Or consider the married life of the Carlyles and bewail the waste, the futility, for him and for her, of the horrible domestic tradition which made it seemly for a woman of genius to spend her time chasing beetles, scouring saucepans, instead of writing books. All human relations have shifted—those between masters and servants, husbands and wives, parents and children. And when human relations change there is at the same time a change in religion, conduct, politics, and literature. Let us agree to place one of these changes about the year 1910.

I have said that people have to acquire a good deal of skill in character-reading if they are to live a single year of life without disaster. But it is the art of the young. In middle age and in old age the art is practised mostly for its uses, and friendships and other adventures and experiments in the art of reading character are seldom made. But novelists differ from the rest of the world because they do not cease to be interested in character when they have learnt enough about it for practical purposes. They go a step further, they feel that there is something permanently interesting in character in itself. When all the practical business of life has been discharged, there is something about people which continues to seem to them of overwhelming importance, in spite of the fact that it has no bearing whatever upon their happiness, comfort, or income. The study of character becomes to them an absorbing pursuit; to impart character an obsession. And this I find it very difficult to explain: what novelists mean when they talk about character, what the impulse is that urges them so powerfully every now and then to embody their view in writing.

So, if you will allow me, instead of analysing and abstracting, I will tell you a simple story which, however pointless, has the merit of being true, of a journey from Richmond to Waterloo, in the hope that I may show you what I mean by character in itself; that you may realize the different aspects it can wear; and the hideous perils that beset you directly you try to describe it in words.

One night some weeks ago, then, I was late for the train and jumped into the first carriage I came to. As I sat down I had the strange and uncomfortable feeling that I was interrupting a conversation between two people who were already sitting there. Not that they were young or happy. Far from it. They were both elderly, the woman over sixty, the man well over forty. They were sitting opposite each other, and the man, who had been leaning over and talking emphatically to judge by his attitude and the flush on his face, sat back and became silent. I had disturbed him, and he was annoyed. The elderly lady, however, whom I will call Mrs. Brown, seemed rather relieved. She was one of those clean, threadbare old ladies whose extreme tidiness —everything buttoned, fastened, tied together, mended and brushed up—suggests more extreme poverty than rags and dirt. There was something pinched about her—a look of suffering, of apprehension, and, in addition, she was extremely small. Her feet, in their clean little boots, scarcely touched the floor. I felt that she had nobody to support her; that she had to make up her mind for herself; that, having been deserted, or left a widow, years ago, she had led an anxious, harried life, bringing up an only son, perhaps, who, as likely as not, was by this time beginning to go to the bad. All this shot through my mind as I sat down, being uncomfortable, like most people, at travelling with fellow passengers unless I have somehow or other accounted for them. Then I looked at the man. He was no relation of Mrs. Brown's I felt sure; he was of a bigger, burlier, less refined type. He was a man of business I imagined, very likely a respectable corn-chandler from the North, dressed in good blue serge with a pocket-knife and a silk handkerchief, and a stout leather bag. Obviously, however, he had an unpleasant business to settle with Mrs. Brown; a secret, perhaps sinister business, which they did not intend to discuss in my presence.

"Yes, the Crofts have had very bad luck with their servants," Mr. Smith (as I will call him) said in a considering way, going back to some earlier topic, with a view to keeping up appearances.

"Ah, poor people," said Mrs. Brown, a trifle condescendingly. "My grandmother had a maid who came when she was fifteen and stayed till she was eighty" (this was said with a kind of hurt and aggressive pride to impress us both perhaps).

"One doesn't often come across that sort of thing nowadays," said Mr. Smith in conciliatory tones.

Then they were silent.

"It's odd they don't start a golf club there—I should have thought one of the young fellows would," said Mr. Smith, for the silence obviously made him uneasy.

Mrs. Brown hardly took the trouble to answer.

"What changes they're making in this part of the world," said Mr. Smith, looking out of the window, and looking furtively at me as he did so.

It was plain, from Mrs. Brown's silence, from the uneasy affability with which Mr. Smith spoke, that he had some power over her which he was exerting disagreeably. It might have been her son's downfall, or some painful episode in her past life, or her daughter's. Perhaps she was going to London to sign some document to make over some property. Obviously against her will she was in Mr. Smith's hands. I was beginning to feel a great deal of pity for her, when she said, suddenly and inconsequently:

"Can you tell me if an oak-tree dies when the leaves have been eaten for two years in succession by caterpillars?"

She spoke quite brightly, and rather precisely, in a cultivated, inquisitive voice.

Mr. Smith was startled, but relieved to have a safe topic of conversation given him. He told her a great deal very quickly about plagues of insects. He told her that he had a brother who kept a fruit farm in Kent. He told her what fruit farmers do every year in Kent, and so on, and so on. While he talked a very odd thing happened. Mrs. Brown took out her little white handkerchief and began to dab her eyes. She was crying. But she went on listening quite composedly to what he was saying, and he went on talking, a little louder, a little angrily, as if he had seen her cry often before; as if it were a painful habit. At last it got on his nerves. He stopped abruptly, looked out of the window, then leant towards her as he had been doing when I got in, and said in a bullying, menacing way, as if he would not stand any more nonsense:

"So about that matter we were discussing. It'll be all right? George will be there on Tuesday?"

"We shan't be late," said Mrs. Brown, gathering herself together with superb dignity.

Mr. Smith said nothing. He got up, buttoned his coat, reached his bag down, and jumped out of the train before it had stopped at Clapham Junction. He had got what he wanted, but he was ashamed of himself; he was glad to get out of the old lady's sight.

Mrs. Brown and I were left alone together. She sat in her corner opposite, very clean, very small, rather queer, and suffering intensely. The impression she made was overwhelming. It came pouring out like a draught, like a smell of burning. What was it composed of—that overwhelming and peculiar impression? Myriads of irrelevant and incongruous ideas crowd into one's head on such occasions; one sees the person, one sees Mrs. Brown, in the centre of all sorts of different scenes. I thought of her in a seaside house, among queer ornaments: sea-urchins, models of ships in glass cases. Her husband's medals were on the mantelpiece. She popped in and out of the room, perching on the edges of chairs, picking meals out of saucers, indulging in long, silent stares. The caterpillars and the oak-trees seemed to imply all that. And then, into this fantastic and secluded life, in broke Mr. Smith. I saw him blowing in, so to speak, on a windy day. He banged, he slammed. His dripping umbrella made a pool in the hall. They sat closeted together.

And then Mrs. Brown faced the dreadful revelation. She took her heroic decision. Early, before dawn, she packed her bag and carried it herself to the station. She would not let Smith touch it. She was wounded in her pride, unmoored from her anchorage; she came of gentlefolks who kept servants—but details could wait. The important thing was to realize her character, to steep oneself in her atmosphere. I had no time to explain why I felt it somewhat tragic, heroic, yet with a dash of the flighty and fantastic, before the train stopped, and I watched her disappear, carrying her bag, into the vast blazing station. She looked very small, very tenacious; at once very frail and very heroic. And I have never seen her again, and I shall never know what became of her.

The story ends without any point to it. But I have not told you this anecdote to illustrate either my own ingenuity or the pleasure of travelling from Richmond to Waterloo. What I want you to see in it is this. Here is a character imposing itself upon another person. Here is Mrs. Brown making someone begin almost automatically to write a novel about her. I believe that all novels begin with an old lady in the corner opposite. I believe that all novels, that is to say, deal with character, and that it is to express character—not to preach doctrines, sing songs, or celebrate the glories of the British Empire, that the form of the novels, so clumsy, verbose, and undramatic, so rich, elastic, and alive, has been evolved. To express character, I have said; but you will at once reflect that the very widest interpretation can be put upon those words. For example, old Mrs. Brown's character will strike you very differently according to the age and country in which you happen to be born. It would be easy enough to write three different versions of that incident in the train, an English, a French, and a Russian. The English writer would make the old lady into a "character"; he would bring out her oddities and mannerisms; her buttons and wrinkles; her ribbons and warts. Her personality would dominate the book. A French writer would rub out all that; he would sacrifice the individual Mrs. Brown to give a more general view of human nature; to make a more abstract, proportioned, and harmonious whole. The Russian would pierce through the flesh; would reveal the soul— the soul alone, wandering out into the Waterloo Road, asking of life some tremendous question which would sound on and on in our ears after the book was finished. And then besides age and country there is the writer's temperament to be considered. You see one thing in character, and I another. You say it means this, and I that. And when it comes to writing each makes a further selection on principles of his own. Thus Mrs. Brown can be treated in an infinite variety of ways, according to the age, country, and temperament of the writer.

But now I must recall what Mr. Arnold Bennett says. He says that it is only if the characters are real that the novel has any chance of surviving. Otherwise, die it must. But, I ask myself, what is reality? And who are the judges of reality? A character may be real to Mr. Bennett and quite unreal to me. For instance, in this article he says that Dr. Watson in *Sherlock Holmes* is real to him: to me Dr. Watson is a sack stuffed with straw, a dummy, a figure of fun. And so it is with character after character—in book after book. There is nothing that people differ about more than the reality of characters, especially in contemporary books. But if you take a larger view I think that Mr. Bennett is perfectly right. If, that is, you think of the novels which seem to you great novels—*War and Peace, Vanity Fair, Tristram Shandy, Madame Bovary, Pride and Prejudice, The Mayor of Casterbridge, Villette*—if you think of these books, you do at once think of some character who has seemed to you so real (I do not by that mean so lifelike) that it has the power to make you think not merely of it itself, but of all sorts of things through its eyes—of religion, of love, of war, of peace, of family life, of balls in country towns, of sunsets, moonrises, the immortality of the soul. There is hardly any subject of human experience that is left out of *War and Peace* it seems to me. And in all these novels all these great novelists have brought us to see whatever they wish us to see through some character. Otherwise, they would not be novelists; but poets, historians, or pamphleteers.

But now let us examine what Mr. Bennett went on to say—he said that there was no great novelist among the Georgian writers because they cannot create characters who are real, true, and convincing. And there I cannot agree. There are reasons, excuses, possibilities which I think put a different colour upon the case. It seems so to me at least, but I am well aware that this is a matter about which I am likely to be prejudiced, sanguine, and near-sighted. I will put my view before you in the hope that you will make it impartial, judicial, and broad-minded. Why, then, is it so hard for novelists at present to create characters which seem real, not only to Mr. Bennett, but to the world at large? Why, when October comes round, do the publishers always fail to supply us with a masterpiece?

Surely one reason is that the men and women who began writing novels in 1910 or thereabouts had this great difficulty to face—that there was no English novelist living from whom they could learn their business. Mr. Conrad is a Pole; which sets him apart, and makes him, however admirable, not very helpful. Mr. Hardy has written no novel since 1895. The most prominent and successful novelists in the year 1910 were, I suppose, Mr. Wells, Mr. Bennett, and Mr. Galsworthy. Now it seems to me that to go to these men and ask them to teach you how to write a novel— how to create characters that are real—is precisely like going to a boot maker and asking him to teach you how to make a watch. Do not let me give you the impression that I do not admire and enjoy their books. They seem to me of great value, and indeed of great necessity. There are seasons when it is more important to have boots than to have watches. To drop metaphor, I think that after the creative activity of the Victorian age it was quite necessary, not only for literature but for life, that someone should write the books that Mr. Wells, Mr. Bennett, and Mr. Galsworthy have written. Yet what odd books they are! Sometimes I wonder if we are right to call them books at all. For they leave one with so strange a feeling of incompleteness and dissatisfaction. In order to complete them it seems necessary to do something—to join a society, or, more desperately, to write a cheque. That done, the restlessness is laid, the book finished; it can be put upon the shelf, and need never be read again. But with the work of other novelists it is different. *Tristram Shandy* or *Pride and Prejudice* is complete in itself; it is self-contained; it leaves one with no desire to do anything, except indeed to read the book again, and to understand it better. The difference perhaps is that both Sterne and Jane Austen were interested in things in themselves; in character, in itself; in the book in itself. Therefore everything was inside the book, nothing outside. But the Edwardians were never interested in character in itself; or in the book in itself. They were interested in something outside. Their books, then, were incomplete as books, and required that the reader should finish them, actively and practically, for himself.

Perhaps we can make this clearer if we take the liberty of imagining a little party in the railway carriage—Mr. Wells, Mr. Galsworthy, Mr. Bennett are travelling to Waterloo with Mrs. Brown. Mrs. Brown, I have said, was poorly dressed and very small. She had an anxious, harassed look. I doubt whether she was what you call an educated woman. Seizing upon all these symptoms of the unsatisfactory condition of our primary schools with a rapidity to which I can do no justice, Mr. Wells would instantly project upon the window-pane a vision of a better, breezier, jollier, happier, more adventurous and gallant world, where these musty railway carriages and fusty old women do not exist; where miraculous barges bring tropical fruit to Camberwell by eight o'clock in the morning; where there are public nurseries, fountains, and libraries, dining-rooms, drawing-rooms, and marriages; where every citizen is generous and candid, manly and magnificent, and rather like Mr. Wells himself. But nobody is in the least like Mrs. Brown. There are no Mrs. Browns in Utopia. Indeed I do not think that Mr. Wells, in his passion to make her what she ought to be, would waste a thought upon her as she is. And what would Mr. Galsworthy see? Can we doubt that the walls of Doulton's factory would take his fancy? There are women in that factory who make twenty-five dozen earthenware pots every day. There are mothers in the Mile End Road who depend upon the farthings which those women earn. But there are employers in Surrey who are even now smoking rich cigars while the nightingale sings. Burning with indignation, stuffed with information, arraigning civilization, Mr. Galsworthy would only see in Mrs. Brown a pot broken on the wheel and thrown into the corner.

Mr. Bennett, alone of the Edwardians, would keep his eyes in the carriage. He, indeed, would observe every detail with im-

mense care. He would notice the advertisements; the pictures of
Swanage and Portsmouth; the way in which the cushion bulged
between the buttons; how Mrs. Brown wore a brooch which had
cost three-and-ten-three at Whitworth's bazaar; and had mended
both gloves—indeed the thumb of the left-hand glove had been
replaced. And he would observe, at length, how this was the non-
stop train from Windsor which calls at Richmond for the convenience of middle-class residents, who can afford to go to the
theatre but have not reached the social rank which can afford
motor-cars, though it is true, there are occasions (he would tell
us what), when they hire them from a company (he would tell us
which). And so he would gradually sidle sedately towards Mrs.
Brown, and would remark how she had been left a little copyhold, not freehold, property at Datchet, which, however, was
mortgaged to Mr. Bungay the solicitor—but why should I pre-
sume to invent Mr. Bennett? Does not Mr. Bennett write novels
himself? I will open the first book that chance puts in my way—
Hilda Lessways. Let us see how he makes us feel that Hilda is
real, true, and convincing, as a novelist should. She shut the door
in a soft, controlled way, which showed the constraint of her
relations with her mother. She was fond of reading *Maud*; she
was endowed with the power to feel intensely. So far, so good; in
his leisurely, surefooted way Mr. Bennett is trying in these first
pages, where every touch is important, to show us the kind of girl
she was.

But then he begins to describe, not Hilda Lessways, but the
view from her bedroom window, the excuse being that Mr.
Skellorn, the man who collects rents, is coming along that way.
Mr. Bennett proceeds:

"The bailiwick of Turnhill lay behind her; and all the murky
district of the Five Towns, of which Turnhill is the northern
outpost, lay to the south. At the foot of Chatterley Wood the
canal wound in large curves on its way towards the undefiled
plains of Cheshire and the sea. On the canal-side, exactly opposite to Hilda's window, was a flour-mill, that sometimes made
nearly as much smoke as the kilns and the chimneys closing the

prospect on either hand. From the flour-mill a bricked path, which separated a considerable row of new cottages from their appurtenant gardens, led straight into Lessways Street, in front of Mrs. Lessways' house. By this path Mr. Skellorn should have arrived, for he inhabited the farthest of the cottages."

One line of insight would have done more than all those lines of description; but let them pass as the necessary drudgery of the novelist. And now—where is Hilda? Alas. Hilda is still looking out of the window. Passionate and dissatisfied as she was, she was a girl with an eye for houses. She often compared this old Mr. Skellorn with the villas she saw from her bedroom window. Therefore the villas must be described. Mr. Bennett proceeds:

"The row was called Freehold Villas: a consciously proud name in a district where much of the land was copyhold and could only change owners subject to the payment of 'fines,' and to the feudal consent of a 'court' presided over by the agent of a lord of the manor. Most of the dwellings were owned by their occupiers, who, each an absolute monarch of the soil, niggled in his sooty garden of an evening amid the flutter of drying shirts and towels. Freehold Villas symbolized the final triumph of Victorian economics, the apotheosis of the prudent and industrious artisan. It corresponded with a Building Society Secretary's dream of paradise. And indeed it was a very real achievement. Nevertheless, Hilda's irrational contempt would not admit this."

Heaven be praised, we cry! At last we are coming to Hilda herself. But not so fast. Hilda may have been this, that, and the other; but Hilda not only looked at houses, and thought of houses; Hilda lived in a house. And what sort of a house did Hilda live in? Mr. Bennett proceeds:

"It was one of the two middle houses of a detached terrace of four houses built by her grandfather Lessways, the teapot manufacturer; it was the chief of the four, obviously the habitation of the proprietor of the terrace. One of the corner houses comprised a grocer's shop, and this house had been robbed of its just proportion of garden so that the seigneurial garden-plot might be triflingly larger than the other. The terrace was not a terrace of cottages, but of houses rated at from twenty-six to thirty-six pounds a year; beyond the means of artisans and petty insurance agents and rent-collectors. And further, it was well-built, generously built; and its architecture, though debased, showed some faint traces of Georgian amenity. It was admittedly the best row of houses in that newly-settled quarter of the town. In coming to it out of Freehold Villas Mr. Skellorn obviously came to something superior, wider, more liberal. Suddenly Hilda heard her mother's voice. . . ."

But we cannot hear her mother's voice, or Hilda's voice; we can only hear Mr. Bennett's voice telling us facts about rents and freeholds and copyholds and fines. What can Mr. Bennett be about? I have formed my own opinion of what Mr. Bennett is about—he is trying to make us imagine for him; he is trying to hypnotize us into the belief that, because he has made a house, there must be a person living there. With all his powers of observation, which are marvellous, with all his sympathy and humanity, which are great, Mr. Bennett has never once looked at Mrs. Brown in her corner. There she sits in the corner of the carriage—that carriage which is travelling, not from Richmond to Waterloo, but from one age of English literature to the next, for Mrs. Brown is eternal, Mrs. Brown is human nature, Mrs. Brown changes only on the surface, it is the novelists who get in and out—there she sits and not one of the Edwardian writers has so much as looked at her. They have looked very powerfully, searchingly, and sympathetically out of the window; at factories, at Utopias, even at the decoration and upholstery of the carriage; but never at her, never at life, never at human nature. And so they have developed a technique of novel-writing which suits their purpose; they have made tools and established conventions which do their business. But those tools are not our tools, and that business is not our business. For us those conventions are ruin, those tools are death.

You may well complain of the vagueness of my language. What is a convention, a tool, you may ask, and what do you mean by saying that Mr. Bennett's and Mr. Wells's and Mr.

Galsworthy's conventions are the wrong conventions for the Georgian's? The question is difficult: I will attempt a short cut. A convention in writing is not much different from a convention in manners. Both in life and in literature it is necessary to have some means of bridging the gulf between the hostess and her unknown guest on the one hand, the writer and his unknown reader on the other. The hostess bethinks her of the weather, for generations of hostesses have established the fact that this is a subject of universal interest in which we all believe. She begins by saying that we are having a wretched May, and, having thus got into touch with her unknown guest, proceeds to matters of greater interest. So it is in literature. The writer must get into touch with his reader by putting before him something which he recognizes, which therefore stimulates his imagination, and makes him willing to co-operate in the far more difficult business of intimacy. And it is of the highest importance that this common meeting-place should be reached easily, almost instinctively, in the dark, with one's eyes shut. Here is Mr. Bennett making use of this common ground in the passage which I have quoted. The problem before him was to make us believe in the reality of Hilda Lessways. So he began, being an Edwardian, by describing accurately and minutely the sort of house Hilda lived in, and the sort of house she saw from the window. House property was the common ground from which the Edwardians found it easy to proceed to intimacy. Indirect as it seems to us, the convention worked admirably, and thousands of Hilda Lessways were launched upon the world by this means. For that age and generation, the convention was a good one.

But now, if you will allow me to pull my own anecdote to pieces, you will see how keenly I felt the lack of a convention, and how serious a matter it is when the tools of one generation are useless for the next. The incident had made a great impression on me. But how was I to transmit it to you? All I could do was to report as accurately as I could what was said, to describe in detail what was worn, to say, despairingly, that all sorts of scenes rushed into my mind, to proceed to tumble them out pell-mell, and to describe this vivid, this overmastering impression by likening it to a draught or a smell of burning. To tell you the truth, I was also strongly tempted to manufacture a three-volume novel about the old lady's son, and his adventures crossing the Atlantic, and her daughter, and how she kept a milliner's shop in Westminster, the past life of Smith himself, and his house at Sheffield, though such stories seem to me the most dreary, irrelevant, and humbugging affairs in the world.

But if I had done that I should have escaped the appalling effort of saying what I meant. And to have got at what I meant I should have had to go back and back and back; to experiment with one thing and another; to try this sentence and that, referring each word to my vision, matching it as exactly as possible, and knowing that somehow I had to find a common ground between us, a convention which would not seem to you too odd, unreal, and far-fetched to believe in. I admit that I shirked that arduous undertaking. I let my Mrs. Brown slip through my fingers. I have told you nothing whatever about her. But that is partly the great Edwardians' fault. I asked them—they are my elders and betters—How shall I begin to describe this woman's character? And they said: "Begin by saying that her father kept a shop in Harrogate. Ascertain the rent. Ascertain the wages of shop assistants in the year 1878 Discover what her mother died of. Describe cancer. Describe calico. Describe—" But I cried: "Stop! Stop!" And I regret to say that I threw that ugly, that clumsy, that incongruous tool out of the window, for I knew that if I began describing the cancer and the calico, my Mrs. Brown, that vision to which I cling though I know no way of imparting it to you, would have been dulled and tarnished and vanished for ever.

That is what I mean by saying that the Edwardian tools are the wrong ones for us to use. They have laid an enormous stress upon the fabric of things. They have given us a house in the hope that we may be able to deduce the human beings who live there. To give them their due, they have made that house much better worth living in. But if you hold that novels are in the first place about people, and only in the second about the houses they live in, that is the wrong way to set about it. Therefore, you see, the Georgian writer had to begin by throwing away the method that was in use at the moment. He was left alone there facing Mrs. Brown without any method of conveying her to the reader. But that is inaccurate. A writer is never alone. There is always the public with him—if not on the same seat, at least in the compartment next door. Now the public is a strange travelling companion. In England it is a very suggestible and docile creature, which, once you get it to attend, will believe implicitly what it is told for a certain number of years. If you say to the public with sufficient conviction: "All women have tails, and all men humps," it will actually learn to see women with tails and men with humps, and will think it very revolutionary and probably improper if you say: "Nonsense. Monkeys have tails and camels humps. But men and women have brains, and they have hearts; they think and they feel,"—that will seem to it a bad joke, and an improper one into the bargain.

But to return. Here is the British public sitting by the writer's side and saying in its vast and unanimous way: "Old women have houses. They have fathers. They have incomes. They have servants. They have hot-water bottles. That is how we know that they are old women. Mr. Wells and Mr. Bennett and Mr. Galsworthy have always taught us that this is the way to recognize them. But now with your Mrs. Brown—how are we to believe in her? We do not even know whether her villa was called Albert or Balmoral; what she paid for her gloves; or whether her mother died of cancer or of consumption. How can she be alive? No; she is a mere figment of your imagination."

And old women of course ought to be made of freehold villas and copyhold estates, not of imagination.

The Georgian novelist, therefore, was in an awkward predicament. There was Mrs. Brown protesting that she was different, quite different, from what people made out, and luring the novelist to her rescue by the most fascinating if fleeting glimpse of her charms; there were the Edwardians handing out tools appropriate to house building and house breaking; and there was the British public asseverating that they must see the hot-water bottle first. Meanwhile the train was rushing to that station where we must all get out.

Such, I think, was the predicament in which the young Georgians found themselves about the year 1910. Many of them —I am thinking of Mr. Forster and Mr. Lawrence in particular —spoilt their early work because, instead of throwing away those tools, they tried to use them. They tried to compromise. They tried to combine their own direct sense of the oddity and significance of some character with Mr. Galsworthy's knowledge of the Factory Acts, and Mr. Bennett's knowledge of the Five Towns. They tried it, but they had too keen, too overpowering a sense of Mrs. Brown and her peculiarities to go on trying it much longer. Something had to be done. At whatever cost of life, limb, and damage to valuable property Mrs. Brown must be rescued, expressed, and set in her high relations to the world before the train stopped and she disappeared for ever. And so the smashing and the crashing began. Thus it is that we hear all round us, in poems and novels and biographies, even in newspaper articles and essays, the sound of breaking and falling, crashing and destruction. It is the prevailing sound of the Georgian age —rather a melancholy one if you think what melodious days there have been in the past, if you think of Shakespeare and Milton and Keats or even of Jane Austen and Thackeray and Dickens; if you think of the language, and the heights to which it can soar when free, and see the same eagle captive, bald, and croaking.

In view of these facts— with these sounds in my ears and these fancies in my brain—I am not going to deny that Mr. Bennett has some reason when he complains that our Georgian writers are unable to make us believe that our characters are real. I am forced to agree that they do not pour out three immortal masterpieces with Victorian regularity every autumn. But, instead of being gloomy, I am sanguine. For this state of things is, I think, inevitable whenever from hoar old age or callow youth the convention ceases to be a means of communication between writer and reader, and becomes instead an obstacle and an impediment. At the present moment we are suffering, not from decay, but from having no code of manners which writers and readers accept as a prelude to the more exciting intercourse of friendship. The literary convention of the time is so artificial—you have to talk about the weather and nothing but the weather throughout the entire visit—that, naturally, the feeble are tempted to outrage, and the strong are led to destroy the very foundations and rules of literary society. Signs of this are everywhere apparent. Grammar is violated; syntax disintegrated; as a boy staying with an aunt for the week-end rolls in the geranium bed out of sheer desperation as the solemnities of the sabbath wear on. The more adult writers do not, of course, indulge in such wanton exhibitions of spleen. Their sincerity is desperate, and their courage tremendous; it is only that they do not know which to use, a fork or their fingers. Thus, if you read Mr. Joyce and Mr. Eliot you will be struck by the indecency of the one, and the obscurity of the other. Mr. Joyce's indecency in *Ulysses* seems to me the conscious and calculated indecency of a desperate man who feels that in order to breathe he must break the windows. At moments, when the window is broken, he is magnificent. But what a waste of energy! And, after all, how dull indecency is, when it is not the overflowing of a superabundant energy or savagery, but the determined and public-spirited act of a man who needs fresh air! Again, with the obscurity of Mr. Eliot. I think that Mr. Eliot has written some of the loveliest single lines in modern poetry. But how intolerant he is of the old usages and politenesses of society—respect for the weak, consideration for the dull! As I sun myself upon the intense and ravishing beauty of one of his lines, and reflect that I must make a dizzy and dangerous leap to the next, and so on from line to line, like an acrobat flying precariously from bar to bar, I cry out, I confess, for the old decorums, and envy the indolence of my ancestors who, instead of spinning madly through mid-air, dreamt quietly in the shade with a book. Again, in Mr. Strachey's books, *Eminent Victorians* and *Queen Victoria*, the effort and strain of writing against the grain and current of the times is visible too. It is much less visible, of course, for not only is he dealing with facts, which are stubborn things, but he has fabricated, chiefly from eighteenth-century material, a very discreet code of manners of his own, which allows him to sit at table with the highest in the land and to say a great many things under cover of that exquisite apparel which, had they gone naked, would have been chased by the men-servants from the room. Still, if you compare *Eminent Victorians* with some of Lord Macaulay's essays, though you will feel that Lord Macaulay is always wrong, and Mr. Strachey always right, you will also feel a body, a sweep, a richness in Lord Macaulay's essays which show that his age was behind him; all his strength went straight into his work; none was used for purposes of concealment or of conversion. But Mr. Strachey has had to open our eyes before he made us see; he has had to search out and sew together a very artful manner of speech; and the effort, beautifully though it is concealed, has robbed his work of some of the force that should have gone into it, and limited his scope.

For these reasons, then, we must reconcile ourselves to a season of failures and fragments. We must reflect that where so much strength is spent on finding a way of telling the truth, the truth itself is bound to reach us in rather an exhausted and chaotic condition. Ulysses, Queen Victoria, Mr. Prufrock—to give Mrs. Brown some of the names she has made famous lately —is a little pale and dishevelled by the time her rescuers reach her. And it is the sound of their axes that we hear—a vigorous and stimulating sound in my ears—unless of course you wish to sleep, when, in the bounty of his concern, Providence has provided a host of writers anxious and able to satisfy your needs.

Thus I have tried, at tedious length, I fear, to answer some of the questions which I began by asking. I have given an account of some of the difficulties which in my view beset the Georgian writer in all his forms. I have sought to excuse him. May I end by venturing to remind you of the duties and responsibilities that are yours as partners in this business of writing books, as companions in the railway carriage, as fellow travellers with Mrs. Brown? For she is just as visible to you who remain silent as to us who tell stories about her. In the course of your daily life this past week you have had far stranger and more interesting experiences than the one I have tried to describe. You have overheard scraps of talk that filled you with amazement. You have gone to bed at night bewildered by the complexity of your feelings. In one day thousands of ideas have coursed through your brains; thousands of emotions have met, collided, and disappeared in astonishing disorder. Nevertheless, you allow the writers to palm off upon you a version of all this, an image of Mrs. Brown, which has no likeness to that surprising apparition whatsoever. In your modesty you seem to consider that writers are different blood and bone from yourselves; that they know more of Mrs. Brown than you do. Never was there a more fatal mistake. It is this division between reader and writer, this humility on your part, these professional airs and graces on ours, that corrupt and emasculate the books which should be the healthy offspring of a close and equal alliance between us. Hence spring those sleek, smooth novels, those portentous and ridiculous biographies, that milk and watery criticism, those poems melodiously celebrating the innocence of roses and sheep which pass so plausibly for literature at the present time.

Your part is to insist that writers shall come down off their plinths and pedestals, and describe beautifully if possible, truthfully at any rate, our Mrs. Brown. You should insist that she is an old lady of unlimited capacity and infinite variety; capable of appearing in any place; wearing any dress; saying anything and doing heaven knows what. But the things she says and the things she does and her eyes and her nose and her speech and her silence have an overwhelming fascination, for she is, of course, the spirit we live by, life itself.

But do not expect just at present a complete and satisfactory presentment of her. Tolerate the spasmodic, the obscure, the fragmentary, the failure. Your help is invoked in a good cause. For I will make one final and surpassingly rash prediction—we are trembling on the verge of one of the great ages of English literature. But it can only be reached if we are determined never, never to desert Mrs. Brown.

Life Itself

"Life Itself," reprinted in The Captain's Death Bed and Other Essays, *was written in 1927 and published that year in* The New Republic. *A revision appeared in 1932 in* The Common Reader: Second Series *under the title "James Woodforde," half of an essay called "Two Parsons." It is one of Virginia Woolf's "lives of the obscure"—a miniature biography, based on one James Woodforde's sixty-eight small volumes of diary, written almost daily over forty-three years. The date of his birth, the year of his death, the peaks of his life—the very basic materials of all biography—none of these are to be found here. In fact, there is only one date given: April 27, 1780, on which afternoon the Parson's niece, Nancy, "expressed a wish to read Aristotle's philosophy. . . ." In this strange new kind of biography, Virginia Woolf keeps us in the valleys of the Parson's life, immersed in the small daily preoccupations and affections of unhurried living. With one minor detail after another, the mist starts to lift, and a personality begins to emerge. The good Parson begins to breathe and move before us as a mild-tempered man any one of us might once have known.*

ONE COULD WISH THAT THE PSYCHO-ANALYSTS WOULD
go into the question of diary keeping. For often it is the one
mysterious fact in a life otherwise as clear as the sky and as
candid as the dawn. Parson Woodforde is a case in point—his
diary is the only mystery about him. For forty-three years he sat
down almost daily to record what he did on Monday and what
he had for dinner on Tuesday; but for whom he wrote or why he
wrote it is impossible to say. He does not unburden his soul in
his diary; yet it is no mere record of engagements and expenses.
As for literary fame, there is no sign that he ever thought of it,
and finally, though the man himself is peaceable above all things,
there are little indiscretions and criticisms which would have got
him into trouble and hurt the feelings of his friends had they read
them. What purpose, then, did the sixty-eight little books fulfil?
Perhaps it was the desire for intimacy. When James Woodforde
opened one of his neat manuscript books, he entered into conversation with a second James Woodforde, who was not quite
the same as the reverend gentleman who visited the poor and
preached in the church. These two friends said much that all the
world might hear; but they had a few secrets which they shared
with each other only. It was a great comfort, for example, that
Christmas when Nancy, Betsy, and Mr. Walker seemed to be in
conspiracy against him, to exclaim in the diary: "The treatment
I meet with for my Civility this Christmas is to me abominable."
The second James Woodforde sympathized and agreed. Again,
when a stranger abused his hospitality it was a relief to inform
the other self who lived in the little book that he had put him to
sleep in the attic story "and I treated him as one that would be
too free if treated kindly." It is easy to understand why in the
quiet life of a country parish these two bachelor friends became
in time inseparable. An essential part of him would have died
had he been forbidden to keep his diary. And as we read—if
reading is the word for it—we seem to be listening to someone
who is murmuring over the events of the day to himself in the
quiet space which precedes sleep. It is not writing, and to speak

the truth it is not reading. It is slipping through half a dozen pages and strolling to the window and looking out. It is going on thinking about the Woodfordes while we watch the people in the street below. It is taking a walk and making up the life and character of James Woodforde as we make up our friends' characters, turning over something they have said, pondering the meaning of something they have done, remembering how they looked one day when they thought themselves unobserved. It is not reading; it is ruminating.

James Woodforde, then, was one of those smooth-cheeked, steady-eyed men, demure to look at, whom we can never imagine except in the prime of life. He was of an equable temper, with only such acerbities and touchinesses as are generally to be found in those who have had a love affair in their youth and remained, as they fancy, unwed because of it. The Parson's love affair, however, was nothing very tremendous. Once when he was a young man in Somerset he liked to walk over to Shepton and to visit a certain "sweet-tempered" Betsy White who lived there. He had a great mind "to make a bold stroke" and ask her to marry him. He went so far, indeed, as to propose marriage "when opportunity served" and Betsy was willing. But he delayed; time passed; four years passed, indeed, and Betsy went to Devonshire, met a Mr. Webster who had five hundred pounds a year, and married him. When James Woodforde met them in the turnpike road, he could say little, "being shy," but to his diary he remarked—and this no doubt was his private version of the affair ever after—"she has proved herself to me a mere jilt."

But he was a young man then, and as time went on we cannot help suspecting that he was glad to consider the question of marriage shelved once and for all, so that he might settle down with his niece Nancy at Weston Longueville and give himself simply and solely, every day and all day, to the great business of living. What else to call it we do not know. It seems to be life itself.

For James Woodforde was nothing in particular. Life had it all her own way with him. He had no special gift; he had no oddity or infirmity. It is idle to pretend that he was a zealous priest. God in Heaven was much the same to him as King George upon the throne—a kindly monarch, that is to say, whose festivals one kept by preaching a sermon on Sunday much as one kept the royal birthday by firing a blunderbuss and drinking a toast at dinner. Should anything untoward happen, like the death of a boy who was dragged and killed by a horse, he would instantly, but rather perfunctorily, exclaim: "I hope to God the Poor Boy is happy," and add: "We all came home singing"; just as when Justice Creed's peacock spread its tail—"and most noble it is"—he would exclaim: "How wonderful are Thy Works O God in every Being." But there was no fanaticism, no enthusiasm, no lyric impulse about James Woodforde. In all these pages, indeed, each so neatly divided into compartments, and each of those again filled, as the days themselves were, so quietly and fully in a hand like the pacing of a well-tempered nag, one can only call to mind a single poetic phrase about the transit of Venus, how "It appeared as a black patch upon a fair Lady's face." The words themselves are mild enough, but they hang over the undulating expanse of the Parson's prose with the resplendence of the star itself. So in the fen country a barn or a tree appears twice its natural size against the surrounding flats. But what led him to this palpable excess that summer's night we do not know. It cannot have been that he was drunk. He spoke out too roundly against such failings in his brother Jack to have been guilty himself. Jack was the wild one of the family. Jack drank at the "Catherine Wheel." Jack came home and had the impudence to defend suicide to his old father. James himself drank his pint of port, but he was a man who liked his meat. When we think of the Woodfordes, uncle and niece, we think of them as often as not waiting with some impatience for their dinner. They gravely watch the joint set upon the table; they swiftly get their knives and forks to work upon the succulent leg or loin, and without much comment, unless a word is passed about the gravy or the stuffing, go on eating. They munch, day after day, year after year, until they have devoured herds of sheep and oxen, flocks of poultry, an odd dozen or so of swans and cygnets, bushels of apples and plums, while the pastries and the jellies crumble and squash beneath their spoons in mountains, in pyramids, in pagodas. Never was there a book so stuffed with food as this one is. To read the bill of fare respectfully and punctually set forth gives one a sense of repletion. It is as if one had lunched at Simpsons daily for a week. Trout and chicken, mutton and peas, pork and apple sauce—so the joints succeed each other at dinner; and there is supper with more joints still to come, all, no doubt, home grown, and of the juiciest and sweetest; all cooked, often by the mistress herself, in the plainest English way, save when the dinner was at Weston Hall and Mrs. Custance surprised them with a London dainty—a pyramid of jelly, that is to say, with a "landscape appearing through it." Then Mrs. Custance, for whom James Woodforde had a chivalrous devotion, would play the "Sticcardi Pastorale" and make "very soft music indeed"; or would get out her work-box and show them how neatly contrived it was, unless indeed Mrs. Custance were giving birth to another child upstairs, whom the Parson would baptize and very frequently bury. The Parson had a deep respect for the Custances. They were all that country gentry should be—a little given to the habit of keeping mistresses, perhaps, but that peccadillo could be forgiven them in view of their generosity to the poor, the kindness they showed to Nancy, and their condescension in asking the Parson to dinner when they had great people staying with them. Yet great people were not much to James's liking. Deeply though he respected the nobility, "one must confess," he said, "that being with our equals is much more agreeable."

He was too fond of his ease and too shrewd a judge of the values of things to be much troubled with snobbery; he much preferred the quiet of his own fireside to adventuring after dissipation abroad. If an old man brought a Madagascar monkey to the door, or a Polish dwarf or a balloon was being shown at Norwich, the Parson would go and have a look at them, and be free with his shillings, but he was a quiet man, a man without ambition, and it is more than likely that his niece found him a little dull. It is the niece Nancy, to speak plainly, who makes us uneasy. There are the seeds of domestic disaster in her character, unless we mistake. It is true that on the afternoon of April 27th, 1780, she expressed a wish to read Aristotle's philosophy, which Miss Millard had got of a married woman, but she is a stolid girl; she eats too much, she grumbles too much, and she takes too much to heart the loss of her red box. No doubt she was sensible enough; we will not blame her for being pert and saucy, or for losing her temper at cards, or even for hiding the parcel that came by post when her uncle longed to know what was in it, and had never done such a thing by her. But when we compare her with Betsy Davy, we realize that one human being has only to come into the room to raise our spirits, and another sets us on edge merely by the way she blows her nose. Betsy, the daughter of that frivolous wanton Mrs. Davy (who fell down-stairs the day Miss Donne swallowed the barleycorn with its stalk), Betsy the shy little girl, Betsy livening up and playing with the Parson's wig, Betsy falling in love with Mr. Walker, Betsy receiving the present of a fox's brush from him, Betsy compromising her reputation with a scamp, Betsy bereaved of him—for Mr. Walker died at the age of twenty-three and was buried in a plain coffin—Betsy left, it is to be feared, in a very scandalous condition—Betsy always charms; we forgive Betsy anything. The trouble with Nancy is that she is beginning to find Weston dull. No suitor has yet appeared. It is but too likely that the ten years of Parson Woodforde's life that still remain will often have to record how Nancy teased him with her grumbling.

The ten years that remain—one knows, of course, that it must come to an end. Already the Custances have gone to Bath; the Parson has had a touch of gout; far away, with a sound like distant thunder, we hear the guns of the French Revolution. But it is comforting to observe that the imprisonment of the French king and queen, and the anarchy and confusion in Paris, are only mentioned after it has been recorded that Thomas Ram has lost his cow and that Parson Woodforde has "brewed another Barrell of Table Beer today." We have a notion, indeed—and here it must be confessed that we have given up reading Parson Woodforde altogether, and merely tell over the story on a stroll through fields where the hares are scampering and the rooks rising above the elm trees—we have a notion that Parson Woodforde does not die. Parson Woodforde goes on. It is we who change and perish. It is the kings and queens who lie in prison. It is the great towns that are ravaged with anarchy and confusion. But the river Wensum still flows; Mrs. Custance is brought to bed of yet another baby; there is the first swallow of the year. The spring comes, and summer with its hay and its strawberries; then autumn, when the walnuts are exceptionally fine, though the pears are poor; so we lapse into winter, which is indeed boisterous, but the house, thank God, withstands the storm; and then again there is the first swallow, and Parson Woodforde takes his greyhounds out a-coursing.

Jane Austen

This essay appeared in The Common Reader *in 1925. It is distinguished by its economy of phrase as well as by its biographical compactness and critical insight. In a few pages, we are given a snapshot of young Jane Austen, her family, her relatives, her home—the small world she knew so intimately and satirized so exquisitely. At the age of fifteen, "she had few illusions about other people and none about herself." And whatever she wrote, Virginia Woolf goes on, was "finished and turned and set in its relation, not to the parsonage, but to the universe." Yet she laughed at the world she knew: at its fools and its follies. Mrs. Bennett and Mr. Collins and Lady Bertram to this day excite our laughter, and, as often, our derision. But even as we delight in their frivolity and their spite, something far below the surface foam of words begins to quicken in us. From the small accumulation of day-to-day existence, from triviality and commonplace, a deep knot of feeling begins to shape itself into that concentration of experience which Virginia Woolf called a "moment of being."*

It is surely not by accident of phrasing that Katherine Mansfield, who of all contemporary writers best understood Virginia Woolf's artistic method, compared her to Jane Austen. In exactly what way they were alike, Mansfield did not say. But in this very essay, perhaps without realizing it, Virginia Woolf herself makes Mansfield's comparison explicit: "Jane Austen," she said, "is . . . a mistress of much deeper emotion than appears upon the surface. She stimulates us to supply what is not there. What she offers is, apparently, a trifle, yet is composed of something that expands in the reader's mind. . . ."

IT IS PROBABLE THAT IF MISS CASSANDRA AUSTEN had had her way, we should have had nothing of Jane Austen's except her novels. To her elder sister alone did she write freely; to her alone she confided her hopes and, if rumour is true, the one great disappointment of her life; but when Miss Cassandra Austen grew old, and the growth of her sister's fame made her suspect that a time might come when strangers would pry and scholars speculate, she burnt, at great cost to herself, every letter that could gratify their curiosity, and spared only what she judged too trivial to be of interest.

Hence our knowledge of Jane Austen is derived from a little gossip, a few letters, and her books. As for the gossip, gossip which has survived its day is never despicable; with a little re arrangement it suits our purpose admirably. For example, Jane "is not at all pretty and very prim, unlike a girl of twelve . . . Jane is whimsical and affected," says little Philadelphia Austen of her cousin. Then we have Mrs. Mitford, who knew the Austens as girls and thought Jane "the prettiest, silliest, most affected, husband-hunting butterfly she ever remembers." Next, there is Miss Mitford's anonymous friend "who visits her now [and] says that she has stiffened into the most perpendicular, precise, taciturn piece of 'single blessedness' that ever existed, and that, until *Pride and Prejudice* showed what a precious gem was hidden in that unbending case, she was no more regarded in society than a poker or firescreen. . . . The case is very different now," the good lady goes on; "she is still a poker—but a poker of whom everybody is afraid. . . . A wit, a delineator of character, who does not talk is terrific indeed!" On the other side, of course, there are the Austens, a race little given to panegyric of themselves, but nevertheless, they say, her brothers "were very fond and very proud of her. They were attached to her by her talents, her virtues, and her engaging manners, and each loved afterwards to fancy a resemblance in some niece or daughter of his own to the dear sister Jane, whose perfect equal they yet never expected to see." Charming but perpendicular, loved at home but feared by strangers, biting of tongue but tender of heart—these contrasts are by no means incompatible, and when we turn to the novels we shall find ourselves stumbling there too over the same complexities in the writer.

To begin with, that prim little girl whom Philadelphia found so unlike a child of twelve, whimsical and affected, was soon to be the authoress of an astonishing and unchildish story, *Love and Freindship* [*sic*], which, incredible though it appears, was written at the age of fifteen. It was written, apparently, to amuse the schoolroom; one of the stories in the same book is dedicated with mock solemnity to her brother; another is neatly illustrated with water-colour heads by her sister. There are jokes which, one feels, were family property; thrusts of satire, which went home because all little Austens made mock in common of fine ladies who "sighed and fainted on the sofa."

Brothers and sisters must have laughed when Jane read out loud her last hit at the vices which they all abhorred. "I die a martyr to my grief for the loss of Augustius. One fatal swoon has cost me my life. Beware of Swoons, Dear Laura. . . . Run mad as often as you chuse, but do not faint. . . ." And on she rushed, as fast as she could write and quicker than she could spell, to tell the incredible adventures of Laura and Sophia, of Philander and Gustavus, of the gentleman who drove a coach between Edinburgh and Stirling every other day, of the theft of the fortune that was kept in the table drawer, of the starving mothers and the sons who acted Macbeth. Undoubtedly, the story must have roused the schoolroom to uproarious laughter. And yet, nothing is more obvious than that this girl of fifteen, sitting in her private corner of the common parlour, was writing not to draw a laugh from brothers and sisters, and not for home consumption. She was writing for everybody, for nobody; for our age, for her own; in other words, even at that early age Jane Austen was writing. One hears it in the rhythm and shapeliness and severity of the sentences. "She was nothing more than a mere good tempered, civil, and obliging young woman; as such we could scarcely dislike her—she was only an object of contempt." Such a sentence is meant to outlast the Christmas holidays. Spirited, easy, full of fun, verging with freedom upon sheer nonsense,—*Love and Freindship* is all that, but what is this note which never merges in the rest, which sounds distinctly and penetratingly all through the volume? It is the sound of laughter. The girl of fifteen is laughing, in her corner, at the world.

Girls of fifteen are always laughing. They laugh when Mr. Binney helps himself to salt instead of sugar. They almost die of laughing when old Mrs. Tomkins sits down upon the cat. But they are crying the moment after. They have no fixed abode from which they see that there is something eternally laughable in human nature, some quality in men and women that for ever excites our satire. They do not know that Lady Greville who snubs, and poor Maria who is snubbed, are permanent features of every ballroom. But Jane Austen knew it from her birth upwards. One of those fairies who perch upon cradles must have taken her a flight through the world directly she was born. When she was laid in the cradle again she knew not only what the world looked like, but had already chosen her kingdom. She had agreed that if she might rule over that territory, she would covet no other. Thus at fifteen she had few illusions about other people and none about herself. Whatever she writes is finished and turned and set in its relation, not to the parsonage, but to the universe. She is impersonal; she is inscrutable. When the writer, Jane Austen, wrote down in the most remarkable sketch in the book a little of Lady Greville's conversation, there is no trace of anger at the snub which the clergyman's daughter, Jane Austen, once received. Her gaze passes straight to the mark, and we know precisely where, upon the map of human nature, that mark is. We know because Jane Austen kept to her compact; she never trespassed beyond her boundaries. Never, even at the emotional age of fifteen, did she round upon herself in shame, obliterate a sarcasm in a spasm of compassion, or blur an outline in a mist of rhapsody. Spasms and rhapsodies, she seems to have said, pointing with her stick, end *there*; and the boundary line is perfectly distinct. But she does not deny that moons and mountains and castles exist—on the other side. She has even one romance of her own. It is for the Queen of Scots. She really admired her very much. "One of the first characters in the world," she called her, "a bewitching Princess whose only friend was then the Duke of Norfolk, and whose only ones now Mr. Whitaker, Mrs. Lefroy, Mrs. Knight and myself." With these words her passion is neatly circumscribed, and rounded with a laugh. It is amusing to remember in what terms the young Brontës wrote, not very much later, in their northern parsonage, about the Duke of Wellington.

The prim little girl grew up. She became "the prettiest, silliest, most affected, husband-hunting butterfly" Mrs. Mitford ever remembered, and, incidentally, the authoress of a novel called *Pride and Prejudice*, which, written stealthily under cover of a creaking door, lay for many years unpublished. A little later, it is thought, she began another story, *The Watsons*, and being for some reason dissatisfied with it, left it unfinished. Unfinished and unsuccessful, it may throw more light upon its writer's genius than the polished masterpiece blazing in universal fame. Her difficulties are more apparent in it, and the method she took to overcome them less artfully concealed. To begin with, the stiffness and the bareness of the first chapters prove that she was one of those writers who lay their facts out rather baldly in the first version and then go back and back and back and cover them with flesh and atmosphere. How it would have been done we cannot say—by what suppressions and insertions and artful devices. But the miracle would have been accomplished; the dull history of fourteen years of family life would have been converted into another of those exquisite and apparently effortless introductions; and we should never have guessed what pages of preliminary drudgery Jane Austen forced her pen to go through. Here we perceive that she was no conjuror after all. Like other writers, she had to create the atmosphere in which her own peculiar genius could bear fruit. Here she fumbles; here she keeps us waiting. Suddenly, she has done it; now things can happen as she likes things to happen. The Edwards' are going to the ball. The Tomlinsons' carriage is passing; she can tell us that Charles is "being provided with his gloves and told to keep them on"; Tom Musgrove retreats to a remote corner with a barrel of oysters and is famously snug. Her genius is freed and active. At once our senses quicken; we are possessed with the peculiar intensity which she alone can impart. But of what is it all composed? Of a ball in a country town; a few couples meeting and taking hands in an assembly room; a little eating and drinking; and for catastrophe, a boy being snubbed by one young lady and kindly treated by another. There is no tragedy and no heroism. Yet for some reason the little scene is moving out of all proportion to its surface solemnity. We have been made to see that if Emma acted so in the ball-room, how considerate, how tender, inspired by what sincerity of feeling she would have shown herself in those graver crises of life which, as we watch her, come inevitably before our eyes. Jane Austen is thus a mistress of much deeper emotion than appears upon the surface. She stimulates us to supply what is not there. What she offers is, apparently, a trifle, yet is composed of something that expands in the reader's mind and endows with the most enduring form of life scenes which are outwardly trivial. Always the stress is laid upon character. How, we are made to wonder, will Emma behave when Lord Osborne and Tom Musgrove make their call at five minutes before three, just as Mary is bringing in the tray and the knife-case? It is an extremely awkward situation. The young men are accustomed to much greater refinement. Emma may prove herself ill-bred, vulgar, a nonentity. The turns and twists of the dialogue keep us on the tenterhooks of suspense. Our attention is half upon the present moment, half upon the future. And when, in the end, Emma behaves in such a way as to vindicate our highest hopes of her, we are moved as if we had been made witnesses of a matter of the highest importance. Here, indeed, in this unfinished and in the main inferior story are all the elements of Jane Austen's greatness. It has the permanent quality of literature. Think away the surface animation, the likeness to life, and there remains to provide a deeper pleasure, an exquisite discrimination of human values. Dismiss this too from the mind and one can dwell with extreme satisfaction upon the more abstract art which, in the ball-room scene, so varies the emotions and proportions the parts that it is possible to enjoy it, as one enjoys poetry, for itself, and not as a link which carries the story this way and that.

But the gossip says of Jane Austen that she was perpendicular, precise, and taciturn—"a poker of whom everybody is afraid." Of this too there are traces; she could be merciless enough; she is one of the most consistent satirists in the whole of literature. Those first angular chapters of *The Watsons* prove that hers was not a prolific genius; she had not, like Emily Brontë, merely to open the door to make herself felt. Humbly and gaily she collected the twigs and straws out of which the nest was to be made and placed them neatly together. The twigs and straws were a little dry and a little dusty in themselves. There was the big house and the little house; a tea party, a dinner party, and an occasional picnic; life was hedged in by valuable connections and adequate incomes; by muddy roads, wet feet, and a tendency on the part of the ladies to get tired; a little money supported it, a little consequence, and the education commonly enjoyed by upper middle-class families living in the country. Vice, adventure, passion were left outside. But of all this prosiness, of all this littleness, she evades nothing, and nothing is slurred over. Patiently and precisely she tells us how they "made no stop anywhere till they reached Newbury, where a comfortable meal, uniting dinner and supper, wound up the enjoyments and fatigues of the day." Nor does she pay to conventions merely the tribute of lip homage; she believes in them besides accepting them. When she is describing a clergyman, like Edmund Bertram, or a sailor, in particular, she appears debarred by the sanctity of his office from the free use of her chief tool, the comic genius, and is apt therefore to lapse into decorous panegyric or matter-of-fact description. But these are exceptions; for the most part her attitude recalls the anonymous ladies' ejaculation—"A wit, a delineator of character, who does not talk is terrific indeed!" She wishes neither to reform nor to annihilate; she is silent; and that is terrific indeed. One after another she creates her fools, her prigs, her worldlings, her Mr. Collins', her Sir Walter Elliotts, her Mrs. Bennetts. She encircles them with the lash of a whip-like phrase which, as it runs round them, cuts out their silhouettes for ever. But there they remain; no excuse is found for them and no mercy shown them. Nothing remains of Julia and Maria Bertram when she has done with them; Lady Bertram is left "sitting and calling to Pug and trying to keep him from the flower beds" eternally. A divine justice is meted out; Dr. Grant, who begins by liking his goose tender, ends by bringing on "apoplexy and death, by three great institutionary dinners in one week." Sometimes it seems as if her creatures were born merely to give Jane Austen the supreme delight of slicing their heads off. She is satisfied; she is content; she would not alter a hair on anybody's head, or move one brick or one blade of grass in a world which provides her with such exquisite delight.

Nor, indeed, would we. For even if the pangs of outraged vanity, or the heat of moral wrath, urged us to improve away a world so full of spite, pettiness, and folly, the task is beyond our powers. People are like that—the girl of fifteen knew it; the mature woman proves it. At this very moment some Lady Bertram finds it almost too trying to keep Pug from the flower beds; she sends Chapman to help Miss Fanny, a little late. The discrimination is so perfect, the satire so just that, consistent though it is, it almost escapes our notice. No touch of pettiness, no hint of spite, rouses us from our contemplation. Delight strangely mingles with our amusement. Beauty illumines these fools.

That elusive quality is indeed often made up of very different parts, which it needs a peculiar genius to bring together. The wit of Jane Austen has for partner the perfection of her taste. Her fool is a fool, her snob is a snob, because he departs from the model of sanity and sense which she has in mind, and conveys to us unmistakably even while she makes us laugh. Never did any novelist make more use of an impeccable sense of human values. It is against the disc of an unerring heart, an unfailing good taste, an almost stern morality, that she shows up those deviations from kindness, truth, and sincerity which are among the most delightful things in English literature. She depicts a Mary Crawford in her mixture of good and bad entirely by this means. She lets her rattle on against the clergy, or in favour of a baronetage and ten thousand a year with all the ease and spirit possible; but now and again she strikes one note of her own, very quietly, but in perfect tune, and at once all Mary Crawford's chatter, though it continues to amuse, rings flat. Hence the depth, the beauty, the complexity of her scenes. From such contrasts there comes a beauty, a solemnity even which are not only as remarkable as her wit, but an inseparable part of it. In *The Watsons* she gives us a foretaste of this power; she makes us wonder why an ordinary act of kindness, as she describes it, becomes so full of meaning. In her masterpieces, the same gift is brought to perfection. Here is nothing out of the way; it is midday in Northamptonshire; a dull young man is talking to rather a weakly young woman on the stairs as they go up to dress for dinner, with housemaids passing. But, from triviality, from commonplace, their words become suddenly full of meaning, and the moment for both one of the most memorable in their lives. It fills itself; it shines; it glows; it hangs before us, deep, trembling, serene for a second; next, the housemaid passes, and this drop in which all the happiness of life has collected gently subsides again to become part of the ebb and flow of ordinary existence.

What more natural then, with this insight into their profundity, than that Jane Austen should have chosen to write of the

trivialities of day to day existence, of parties, picnics, and country dances? No "suggestions to alter her style of writing" from
the Prince Regent or Mr. Clarke could tempt her; no romance,
no adventure, no politics or intrigue could hold a candle to life
on a country-house staircase as she saw it. Indeed, the Prince
Regent and his librarian had run their heads against a very
formidable obstacle; they were trying to tamper with an incor-
ruptible conscience, to disturb an infallible discretion. The child
who formed her sentences so finely when she was fifteen never
ceased to form them, and never wrote for the Prince Regent or his
librarian, but for the world at large. She knew exactly what her
powers were, and what material they were fitted to deal with as
material should be dealt with by a writer, whose standard of
finality was high. There were impressions that lay outside her
province; emotions that by no stretch or artifice could be properly coated and covered by her own resources. For example, she
could not make a girl talk enthusiastically of banners and cha-
pels. She could not throw herself wholeheartedly into a romantic
moment. She had all sorts of devices for evading scenes of passion. Nature and its beauties she approached in a sidelong way
of her own. She describes a beautiful night without once men-
tioning the moon. Nevertheless, as we read the few formal
phrases about "the brilliancy of an unclouded night and the
contrast of the deep shade of the woods" the night is at once as
"solemn, and soothing, and lovely" as she tells us, quite simply,
that it was.

The balance of her gifts was singularly perfect. Among her
finished novels there are no failures, and among her many chapters few that sink markedly below the level of the others. But,
after all, she died at the age of forty-two. She died at the height
of her powers. She was still subject to those changes which often
make the final period of a writer's career the most interesting of
all. Vivacious, irrepressible, gifted with an invention of great
vitality, there can be no doubt that she would have written more,
had she lived, and it is tempting to consider whether she would
not have written differently. The boundaries were marked;

moons, mountains, and castles lay on the other side. But was she not sometimes tempted to trespass for a minute? Was she not beginning, in her own gay and brilliant manner, to contemplate a little voyage of discovery?

Let us take *Persuasion*, the last completed novel, and look by its light at the books she might have written had she lived. There is a peculiar beauty and a peculiar dullness in *Persuasion*. The dullness is that which so often marks the transition stage between two different periods. The writer is a little bored. She has grown too familiar with the ways of her world; she no longer notes them freshly. There is an asperity in her comedy which suggests that she has almost ceased to be amused by the vanities of a Sir Walter or the snobbery of a Miss Elliott. The satire is harsh, and the comedy crude. She is no longer so freshly aware of the amusements of daily life. Her mind is not altogether on her object. But, while we feel that Jane Austen has done this before, and done it better, we also feel that she is trying to do something which she has never yet attempted. There is a new element in *Persuasion*, the quality, perhaps, that made Dr. Whewell fire up and insist that it was "the most beautiful of her works." She is beginning to discover that the world is larger, more mysterious, and more romantic than she had supposed. We feel it to be true of herself when she says of Anne: "She had been forced into prudence in her youth, she learned romance as she grew older— the natural sequel of an unnatural beginning." She dwells frequently upon the beauty and the melancholy of nature, upon the autumn where she had been wont to dwell upon the spring. She talks of the "influence so sweet and so sad of autumnal months in the country." She marks "the tawny leaves and withered hedges." "One does not love a place the less because one has suffered in it," she observes. But it is not only in a new sensibility to nature that we detect the change. Her attitude to life itself is altered. She is seeing it, for the greater part of the book, through the eyes of a woman who, unhappy herself, has a special sympathy for the happiness and unhappiness of others, which, until the very end, she is forced to comment upon in silence.

Therefore the observation is less of facts and more of feelings than is usual. There is an expressed emotion in the scene at the concert and in the famous talk about woman's constancy which proves not merely the biographical fact that Jane Austen had loved, but the aesthetic fact that she was no longer afraid to say so. Experience, when it was of a serious kind, had to sink very deep, and to be thoroughly disinfected by the passage of time, before she allowed herself to deal with it in fiction. But now, in 1817, she was ready. Outwardly, too, in her circumstances, a change was imminent. Her fame had grown very slowly. "I doubt," wrote Mr. Austen Leigh, "whether it would be possible to mention any other author of note whose personal obscurity was so complete." Had she lived a few more years only, all that would have been altered. She would have stayed in London, dined out, lunched out, met famous people, made new friends, read, travelled, and carried back to the quiet country cottage a hoard of observations to feast upon at leisure.

And what effect would all this have had upon the six novels that Jane Austen did not write? She would not have written of crime, of passion, or of adventure. She would not have been rushed by the importunity of publishers or the flattery of friends into slovenliness or insincerity. But she would have known more. Her sense of security would have been shaken. Her comedy would have suffered. She would have trusted less (this is already perceptible in *Persuasion*) to dialogue and more to reflection to give us a knowledge of her characters. Those marvellous little speeches which sum up, in a few minutes' chatter, all that we need in order to know an Admiral Croft or a Mrs. Musgrove for ever, that shorthand, hit-or-miss method which contains chapters of analysis and psychology, would have become too crude to hold all that she now perceived of the complexity of human nature. She would have devised a method, clear and composed as ever, but deeper and more suggestive, for conveying not only what people say, but what they leave unsaid; not only what they are, but what life is. She would have stood farther away from her characters, and seen them more as a group, less as individuals.

Her satire, while it played less incessantly, would have been more stringent and severe. She would have been the forerunner of Henry James and of Proust—but enough. Vain are these speculations: the most perfect artist among women, the writer whose books are immortal, died "just as she was beginning to feel confidence in her own success."

How Should One Read a Book?

On January 30, 1926, Virginia Woolf gave a lecture at a girls' school at Hayes Court in Kent. A revision of the lecture entitled "How Should One Read a Book?" was published in the Yale Review in October of that year. It was reprinted in 1932 in The Common Reader: Second Series.

Her advice, as good today as it was then, was "to take no advice, to follow your own instincts, to use your own reason, to come to your own conclusions." Like so many other of her ideas that have put her in the cultural vanguard of our century, those expressed in this essay rest upon the assumption that the act of reading is a highly personal matter; and that no critic, no authority, "however heavily furred and gowned," should be allowed to dictate "how to read, what to read, what value to place upon what we read." For to do so would be to destroy the very spirit of freedom that underlies the uniqueness and pleasure of the literary experience itself.

IN THE FIRST PLACE, I WANT TO EMPHASISE THE note of interrogation at the end of my title. Even if I could answer the question for myself, the answer would apply only to me and not to you. The only advice, indeed, that one person can give another about reading is to take no advice, to follow your own instincts, to use your own reason, to come to your own conclusions. If this is agreed between us, then I feel at liberty to put forward a few ideas and suggestions because you will not allow them to fetter that independence which is the most important quality that a reader can possess. After all, what laws can be laid down about books? The battle of Waterloo was certainly fought on a certain day; but is *Hamlet* a better play than *Lear*? Nobody can say. Each must decide that question for himself. To admit authorities, however heavily furred and gowned, into our libraries and let them tell us how to read, what to read, what value to place upon what we read, is to destroy the spirit of freedom which is the breath of those sanctuaries. Everywhere else we may be bound by laws and conventions—there we have none.

But to enjoy freedom, if the platitude is pardonable, we have of course to control ourselves. We must not squander our powers, helplessly and ignorantly, squirting half the house in order to water a single rose-bush; we must train them, exactly and powerfully, here on the very spot. This, it may be, is one of the first difficulties that faces us in a library. What is "the very spot"? There may well seem to be nothing but a conglomeration and huddle of confusion. Poems and novels, histories and memoirs, dictionaries and blue-books; books written in all languages by men and women of all tempers, races, and ages jostle each other on the shelf. And outside the donkey brays, the women gossip at the pump, the colts gallop across the fields. Where are we to begin? How are we to bring order into this multitudinous chaos and so get the deepest and widest pleasure from what we read?

It is simple enough to say that since books have classes—fiction, biography, poetry—we should separate them and take from each what it is right that each should give us. Yet few people ask from books what books can give us. Most commonly we come to books with blurred and divided minds, asking of fiction that it shall be true, of poetry that it shall be false, of biography that it shall be flattering, of history that it shall enforce our own prejudices. If we could banish all such preconceptions when we read, that would be an admirable beginning. Do not dictate to your author; try to become him. Be his fellowworker and accomplice. If you hang back, and reserve and criticise at first, you are preventing yourself from getting the fullest possible value from what you read. But if you open your mind as widely as possible, then signs and hints of almost imperceptible fineness, from the twist and turn of the first sentences, will bring you into the presence of a human being unlike any other. Steep yourself in this, acquaint yourself with this, and soon you will find that your author is giving you, or attempting to give you, something far more definite. The thirty-two chapters of a novel —if we consider how to read a novel first—are an attempt to make something as formed and controlled as a building: but words are more impalpable than bricks; reading is a longer and more complicated process than seeing. Perhaps the quickest way to understand the elements of what a novelist is doing is not to read, but to write; to make your own experiment with the dangers and difficulties of words. Recall, then, some event that has left a distinct impression on you—how at the corner of the street, perhaps, you passed two people talking. A tree shook; an electric light danced; the tone of the talk was comic, but also tragic; a whole vision, an entire conception, seemed contained in that moment.

But when you attempt to reconstruct it in words, you will find that it breaks into a thousand conflicting impressions. Some must be subdued; others emphasised; in the process you will lose, probably, all grasp upon the emotion itself. Then turn from your blurred and littered pages to the opening pages of some great novelist—Defoe, Jane Austen, Hardy. Now you will be better able to appreciate their mastery. It is not merely that we are in the presence of a different person—Defoe, Jane Austen, or Thomas Hardy—but that we are living in a different world. Here, in *Robinson Crusoe*, we are trudging a plain highroad; one thing happens after another; the fact and the order of the fact is enough. But if the open air and adventure mean everything to Defoe they mean nothing to Jane Austen. Hers is the drawing-room, and people talking, and by the many mirrors of their talk revealing their characters. And if, when we have accustomed ourselves to the drawing-room and its reflections, we turn to Hardy, we are once more spun round. The moors are round us and the stars are above our heads. The other side of the mind is now exposed—the dark side that comes uppermost in solitude, not the light side that shows in company. Our relations are not towards people, but towards Nature and destiny. Yet different as these worlds are, each is consistent with itself. The maker of each is careful to observe the laws of his own perspective, and however great a strain they may put upon us they will never confuse us, as lesser writers so frequently do, by introducing two different kinds of reality into the same book. Thus to go from one great novelist to another—from Jane Austen to Hardy, from Peacock to Trollope, from Scott to Meredith—is to be wrenched and uprooted; to be thrown this way and then that. To read a novel is a difficult and complex art. You must be capable not only of great fineness of perception, but of great boldness of imagination if you are going to make use of all that the novelist —the great artist—gives you.

But a glance at the heterogeneous company on the shelf will show you that writers are very seldom "great artists"; far more often a book makes no claim to be a work of art at all. These biographies and autobiographies, for example, lives of great men, of men long dead and forgotten, that stand cheek by jowl with the novels and poems, are we to refuse to read them because they are not "art"? Or shall we read them, but read them in a different way, with a different aim? Shall we read them in the first place to satisfy that curiosity which possesses us sometimes when in the evening we linger in front of a house where the lights are lit and the blinds not yet drawn, and each floor of the house shows us a different section of human life in being? Then we are consumed with curiosity about the lives of these people—the servants gossiping, the gentlemen dining, the girl dressing for a party, the old woman at the window with her knitting. Who are they, what are they, what are their names, their occupations, their thoughts, and adventures?

Biographies and memoirs answer such questions, light up innumerable such houses; they show us people going about their daily affairs, toiling, failing, succeeding, eating, hating, loving, until they die. And sometimes as we watch, the house fades and the iron railings vanish and we are out at sea; we are hunting, sailing, fighting; we are among savages and soldiers; we are taking part in great campaigns. Or if we like to stay here in England, in London, still the scene changes; the street narrows; the house becomes small, cramped, diamond-paned, and malodorous. We see a poet, Donne, driven from such a house because the walls were so thin that when the children cried their voices cut through them. We can follow him, through the paths that lie in the pages of books, to Twickenham; to Lady Bedford's Park, a famous meeting-ground for nobles and poets; and then turn our steps to Wilton, the great house under the downs, and hear Sidney read the *Arcadia* to his sister; and ramble among the very marshes and see the very herons that figure in that famous romance; and then again travel north with that other Lady Pembroke, Anne Clifford, to her wild moors, or plunge into the city and control our merriment at the sight of Gabriel Harvey in his black velvet suit arguing about poetry with Spenser. Nothing is more fascinating than to grope and stumble in the alternate darkness and splendour of Elizabethan London. But there is no staying there. The Temples and the Swifts, the Harleys and the St. Johns beckon us on; hour upon hour can be spent disentangling their quarrels and deciphering their characters; and when we tire of them we can stroll on, past a lady in black wearing diamonds, to Samuel Johnson and Goldsmith and Garrick; or cross the channel, if we like, and meet Voltaire and Diderot, Madame du Deffand; and so back to England and Twickenham—how certain places repeat themselves and certain names!—where Lady Bedford had her Park once and Pope lived later, to Walpole's home at Strawberry Hill. But Walpole introduces us to such a swarm of new acquaintances, there are so many houses to visit and bells to ring that we may well hesitate for a moment, on the Miss Berrys' doorstep, for example, when behold, up comes Thackeray; he is the friend of the woman whom Walpole loved; so that merely by going from friend to friend, from garden to garden, from house to house, we have passed from one end of English literature to another and wake to find ourselves here again in the present, if we can so differentiate this moment from all that have gone before. This, then, is one of the ways in which we can read these lives and letters; we can make them light up the many windows of the past; we can watch the famous dead in their familiar habits and fancy sometimes that we are very close and can surprise their secrets, and sometimes we may pull out a play or a poem that they have written and see whether it reads differently in the presence of the author. But this again rouses other questions. How far, we must ask ourselves, is a book influenced by its writer's life—how far is it safe to let the man interpret the writer? How far shall we resist or give way to the sympathies and antipathies that the man himself rouses in us—so sensitive are words, so receptive of the character of the author? These are questions that press upon us when we read lives and letters, and we must answer them for ourselves, for nothing can be more fatal than to be guided by the preferences of others in a matter so personal.

But also we can read such books with another aim, not to throw light on literature, not to become familiar with famous people, but to refresh and exercise our own creative powers. Is there not an open window on the right hand of the bookcase? How delightful to stop reading and look out! How stimulating the scene is, in its unconsciousness, its irrelevance, its perpetual movement—the colts galloping round the field, the woman filling her pail at the well, the donkey throwing back his head and emitting his long, acrid moan. The greater part of any library is nothing but the record of such fleeting moments in the lives of men, women, and donkeys. Every literature, as it grows old, has its rubbish-heap, its record of vanished moments and forgotten lives told in faltering and feeble accents that have perished. But if you give yourself up to the delight of rubbish-reading you will be surprised, indeed you will be overcome, by the relics of human life that have been cast out to moulder. It may be one letter—but what a vision it gives! It may be a few sentences—but what vistas they suggest! Sometimes a whole story will come together with such beautiful humour and pathos and completeness that it seems as if a great novelist had been at work, yet it is only an old actor, Tate Wilkinson, remembering the strange story of Captain Jones; it is only a young subaltern serving under Arthur Wellesley and falling in love with a pretty girl at Lisbon; it is only Maria Allen letting fall her sewing in the empty drawing-room and sighing how she wishes she had taken Dr. Burney's good advice and had never eloped with her Rishy. None of this has any value; it is negligible in the extreme; yet how absorbing it is now and again to go through the rubbish-heaps and find rings and scissors and broken noses buried in the huge past and try to piece them together while the colt gallops round the field, the woman fills her pail at the well, and the donkey brays.

But we tire of rubbish-reading in the long run. We tire of searching for what is needed to complete the half-truth which is all that the Wilkinsons, the Bunburys, and the Maria Allens are able to offer us. They had not the artist's power of mastering and eliminating; they could not tell the whole truth even about their own lives; they have disfigured the story that might have been so shapely. Facts are all that they can offer us, and facts are a very inferior form of fiction. Thus the desire grows upon us to have done with half-statements and approximations; to cease from searching out the minute shades of human character, to enjoy the greater abstractness, the purer truth of fiction. Thus we create the mood, intense and generalised, unaware of detail, but stressed by some regular, recurrent beat, whose natural expression is poetry; and that is the time to read poetry when we are almost able to write it.

> Western wind, when wilt thou blow?
> The small rain down can rain.

> Christ, if my love were in my arms,
> And I in my bed again!

The impact of poetry is so hard and direct that for the moment there is no other sensation except that of the poem itself. What profound depths we visit then—how sudden and complete is our immersion! There is nothing here to catch hold of; nothing to stay us in our flight. The illusion of fiction is gradual; its effects are prepared; but who when they read these four lines stops to ask who wrote them, or conjures up the thought of Donne's house or Sidney's secretary; or enmeshes them in the intricacy of the past and the succession of generations? The poet is always our contemporary. Our being for the moment is centred and constricted, as in any violent shock of personal emotion. Afterwards, it is true, the sensation begins to spread in wider rings through our minds; remoter senses are reached; these begin to sound and to comment and we are aware of echoes and reflections. The intensity of poetry covers an immense range of emotion. We have only to compare the force and directness of

> I shall fall like a tree, and find my grave,
> Only remembering that I grieve,

with the wavering modulation of

> Minutes are numbered by the fall of sands,
> As by an hour glass; the span of time
> Doth waste us to our graves, and we look on it;
> An age of pleasure, revelled out, comes home
> At last, and ends in sorrow; but the life,
> Weary of riot, numbers every sand,
> Wailing in sighs, until the last drop down,
> So to conclude calamity in rest,

or place the meditative calm of

> whether we be young or old,
> Our destiny, our being's heart and home,
> Is with infinitude, and only there;

> With hope it is, hope that can never die,
> Effort, and expectation, and desire,
> And something evermore about to be,

beside the complete and inexhaustible loveliness of

> The moving Moon went up the sky,
> And no where did abide:
> Softly she was going up,
> And a star or two beside—

or the splendid fantasy of

> And the woodland haunter
> Shall not cease to saunter
>   When, far down some glade,
> Of the great world's burning,
> One soft flame upturning
> Seems, to his discerning,
>   Crocus in the shade.

to bethink us of the varied art of the poet; his power to make us at once actors and spectators; his power to run his hand into character as if it were a glove, and be Falstaff or Lear; his power to condense, to widen, to state, once and for ever.

"We have only to compare"—with those words the cat is out of the bag, and the true complexity of reading is admitted. The first process, to receive impressions with the utmost understanding, is only half the process of reading; it must be completed, if we are to get the whole pleasure from a book, by another. We must pass judgment upon these multitudinous impressions; we must make of these fleeting shapes one that is hard and lasting. But not directly. Wait for the dust of reading to settle; for the conflict and the questioning to die down; walk, talk, pull the dead petals from a rose, or fall asleep. Then suddenly without our willing it, for it is thus that Nature undertakes these transitions, the book will return, but differently. It will float to the top of the mind as a whole. And the book as a whole is different from the book received currently in separate phrases. Details now fit themselves into their places. We see the shape from start to finish; it is a barn, a pig-sty, or a cathedral. Now then we can compare book with book as we compare building with building. But this act of comparison means that our attitude has changed; we are no longer the friends of the writer, but his judges; and just as we cannot be too sympathetic as friends, so as judges we cannot be too severe. Are they not criminals, books that have wasted our time and sympathy; are they not the most insidious enemies of society, corrupters, defilers, the writers of false books, faked books, books that fill the air with decay and disease? Let us then be severe in our judgments; let us compare each book with the greatest of its kind. There they hang in the mind the shapes of the books we have read solidified by the judgments we have passed on them—*Robinson Crusoe, Emma, The Return of the Native.* Compare the novels with these—even the latest and least of novels has a right to be judged with the best. And so with poetry—when the intoxication of rhythm has died down and the splendour of words has faded a visionary shape will return to us and this must be compared with *Lear,* with *Phèdre,* with *The Prelude;* or if not with these, with whatever is the best or seems to us to be the best in its own kind. And we may be sure that the newness of new poetry and fiction is its most superficial quality and that we have only to alter slightly, not to recast, the standards by which we have judged the old.

It would be foolish, then, to pretend that the second part of reading, to judge, to compare, is as simple as the first—to open the mind wide to the fast flocking of innumerable impressions. To continue reading without the book before you, to hold one shadow-shape against another, to have read widely enough and with enough understanding to make such comparisons alive and illuminating—that is difficult; it is still more difficult to press further and to say, "Not only is the book of this sort, but it is of this value; here it fails; here it succeeds; this is bad; that is good." To carry out this part of a reader's duty needs such imagination, insight, and learning that it is hard to conceive any one mind sufficiently endowed; impossible for the most self-confident to find more than the seeds of such powers in himself. Would it not be wiser, then, to remit this part of reading and to allow the critics, the gowned and furred authorities of the library, to decide the question of the book's absolute value for us? Yet how impossible! We may stress the value of sympathy; we may try to sink our own identity as we read. But we know that we cannot sympathise wholly or immerse ourselves wholly; there is always a demon in us who whispers, "I hate, I love," and we cannot silence him. Indeed, it is precisely because we hate and we love that our relation with the poets and novelists is so intimate that we find the presence of another person intolerable. And even if the results are abhorrent and our judgments are wrong, still our taste, the nerve of sensation that sends shocks through us, is our chief illuminant; we learn through feeling; we cannot suppress our own idiosyncrasy without impoverishing it. But as time goes on perhaps we can train our taste; perhaps we can make it submit to some control. When it has fed greedily and lavishly upon books of all sorts—poetry, fiction, history, biography—and has stopped reading and looked for long spaces upon the variety, the incongruity of the living world, we shall find that it is changing a little; it is not so greedy, it is more reflective. It will begin to bring us not merely judgments on particular books, but it will tell us that there is a quality common to certain books. Listen, it will say, what shall we call *this*? And it will read us perhaps *Lear* and then perhaps the *Agamemnon* in order to bring out that common quality. Thus, with our taste to guide us, we shall venture beyond the particular book in search of qualities that group books together; we shall give them names and thus frame a rule that brings order into our perceptions. We shall gain a further and a rarer pleasure from that discrimination. But as a rule only lives when it is perpetually broken by contact with the books themselves—nothing is easier and more stultifying than to make rules which exist out of touch with facts, in a vacuum—now at last, in order to steady ourselves in this difficult attempt, it may be well to turn to the very rare writers who are able to enlighten us upon literature as an art. Coleridge and Dryden and Johnson, in their considered criticism, the poets and novelists themselves in their unconsidered sayings, are often surprisingly relevant; they light up and solidify the vague ideas that have been tumbling in the misty depths of our minds. But they are only able to help us if we come to them laden with questions and suggestions won honestly in the course of our own reading. They can do nothing for us if we herd ourselves under their authority and lie down like sheep in the shade of a hedge. We can only understand their ruling when it comes in conflict with our own and vanquishes it.

If this is so, if to read a book as it should be read calls for the rarest qualities of imagination, insight, and judgment, you may perhaps conclude that literature is a very complex art and that it is unlikely that we shall be able, even after a lifetime of reading, to make any valuable contribution to its criticism. We must remain readers; we shall not put on the further glory that belongs to those rare beings who are also critics. But still we have our responsibilities as readers and even our importance. The standards we raise and the judgments we pass steal into the air and become part of the atmosphere which writers breathe as they work. An influence is created which tells upon them even if it never finds its way into print. And that influence, if it were well instructed, vigorous and individual and sincere, might be of great value now when criticism is necessarily in abeyance; when books pass in review like the procession of animals in a shooting-gallery, and the critic has only one second in which to load and aim and shoot and may well be pardoned if he mistakes rabbits for tigers, eagles for barndoor fowls, or misses altogether and wastes his shot upon some peaceful cow grazing in a further field. If behind the erratic gunfire of the press the author felt that there was another kind of criticism, the opinion of people reading for the love of reading, slowly and unprofessionally, and judging with great sympathy and yet with great severity, might this not improve the quality of his work? And if by our means books were to become stronger, richer, and more varied, that would be an end worth reaching.

Yet who reads to bring about an end however desirable? Are there not some pursuits that we practise because they are good in themselves, and some pleasures that are final? And is not this among them? I have sometimes dreamt, at least, that when the Day of Judgment dawns and the great conquerors and lawyers and statesmen come to receive their rewards—their crowns, their laurels, their names carved indelibly upon imperishable marble —the Almighty will turn to Peter and will say, not without a certain envy when He sees us coming with our books under our arms, "Look, these need no reward. We have nothing to give them here. They have loved reading."

Street Haunting

A LONDON ADVENTURE

"Street Haunting" appeared originally in the Yale Review *in October 1927 and was published in a limited and signed edition by the Westgate Press, San Francisco, in May 1930. It is a superb example of Virginia Woolf's method of creating distinct moments of vibrancy out of the myriad impressions which strike one, in this case, during an early winter evening's ramble through the streets of London—or of any other large city, for that matter.*

The whole expedition seems unplanned, entirely random. Each moment, however, is filled to the brim with human emotion of the most unexpected sort, for Virginia Woolf has pointed us in a particular direction and urged us to look upon these commonplaces of daily life in a way that we may never before have looked at them.

———————————

NO ONE PERHAPS HAS EVER FELT PASSIONATELY TO-wards a lead pencil. But there are circumstances in which it can become supremely desirable to possess one; moments when we are set upon having an object, an excuse for walking half across

London between tea and dinner. As the foxhunter hunts in order to preserve the breed of foxes, and the golfer plays in order that open spaces may be preserved from the builders, so when the desire comes upon us to go street rambling a pencil does for a pretext, and getting up we say: "Really I must buy a pencil," as if under cover of this excuse we could indulge safely in the greatest pleasure of town life in winter—rambling the streets of London.

The hour should be the evening and the season winter, for in winter the champagne brightness of the air and the sociability of the streets are grateful. We are not then taunted as in the summer by the longing for shade and solitude and sweet airs from the hayfields. The evening hour, too, gives us the irresponsibility which darkness and lamplight bestow. We are no longer quite ourselves. As we step out of the house on a fine evening between four and six, we shed the self our friends know us by and become part of that vast republican army of anonymous trampers, whose society is so agreeable after the solitude of one's own room. For there we sit surrounded by objects which perpetually express the oddity of our own temperaments and enforce the memories of our own experience. That bowl on the mantelpiece, for instance, was bought at Mantua on a windy day. We were leaving the shop when the sinister old woman plucked at our skirts and said she would find herself starving one of these days, but, "Take it!" she cried, and thrust the blue and white china bowl into our hands as if she never wanted to be reminded of her quixotic generosity. So, guiltily, but suspecting nevertheless how badly we had been fleeced, we carried it back to the little hotel where, in the middle of the night, the innkeeper quarrelled so violently with his wife that we all leant out into the courtyard to look, and saw the vines laced about among the pillars and the stars white in the sky. The moment was stabilized, stamped like a coin indelibly among a million that slipped by imperceptibly. There, too, was the melancholy Englishman, who rose among the coffee cups and the little iron tables and revealed the secrets of his soul—as travellers do. All this—Italy, the windy morning, the vines laced about the pillars, the Englishman and the secrets of his soul—rise up in a cloud from the china bowl on the mantelpiece. And there, as our eyes fall to the floor, is that brown stain on the carpet. Mr. Lloyd George made that. "The man's a devil!" said Mr. Cummings, putting the kettle down with which he was about to fill the teapot so that it burnt a brown ring on the carpet.

But when the door shuts on us, all that vanishes. The shell-like covering which our souls have excreted to house themselves, to make for themselves a shape distinct from others, is broken, and there is left of all these wrinkles and roughnesses a central oyster of perceptiveness, an enormous eye. How beautiful a street is in winter! It is at once revealed and obscured. Here vaguely one can trace symmetrical straight avenues of doors and windows; here under the lamps are floating islands of pale light through which pass quickly bright men and women, who, for all their poverty and shabbiness, wear a certain look of unreality, an air of triumph, as if they had given life the slip, so that life, deceived of her prey, blunders on without them. But, after all, we are only gliding smoothly on the surface. The eye is not a miner, not a diver, not a seeker after buried treasure. It floats us smoothly down a stream; resting, pausing, the brain sleeps perhaps as it looks.

How beautiful a London street is then, with its islands of light, and its long groves of darkness, and on one side of it perhaps some tree-sprinkled, grass-grown space where night is folding herself to sleep naturally and, as one passes the iron railing, one hears those little cracklings and stirrings of leaf and twig which seem to suppose the silence of fields all round them, an owl hooting, and far away the rattle of a train in the valley. But this is London, we are reminded; high among the bare trees are hung oblong frames of reddish yellow light—windows; there are points of brilliance burning steadily like low stars—lamps; this empty ground, which holds the country in it and its peace, is only a London square, set about by offices and houses where at this hour fierce lights burn over maps, over documents, over desks where clerks sit turning with wetted forefinger the files of endless correspondences; or more suffusedly the firelight wavers and the lamplight falls upon the privacy of some drawing-room, its easy chairs, its papers, its china, its inlaid table, and the figure of a woman, accurately measuring out the precise number of spoons of tea which— She looks at the door as if she heard a ring downstairs and somebody asking, is she in?

But here we must stop peremptorily. We are in danger of digging deeper than the eye approves; we are impeding our passage down the smooth stream by catching at some branch or root. At any moment, the sleeping army may stir itself and wake in us a thousand violins and trumpets in response; the army of human beings may rouse itself and assert all its oddities and sufferings and sordidities. Let us dally a little longer, be content still with surfaces only—the glossy brilliance of the motor omnibuses; the carnal splendour of the butchers' shops with their yellow flanks and purple steaks; the blue and red bunches of flowers burning so bravely through the plate glass of the florists' windows.

For the eye has this strange property: it rests only on beauty; like a butterfly it seeks colour and basks in warmth. On a winter's night like this, when nature has been at pains to polish and preen herself, it brings back the prettiest trophies, breaks off little lumps of emerald and coral as if the whole earth were made of precious stone. The thing it cannot do (one is speaking of the average unprofessional eye) is to compose these trophies in such a way as to bring out the more obscure angles and relationships. Hence after a prolonged diet of this simple, sugary fare, of beauty pure and uncomposed, we become conscious of satiety. We halt at the door of the boot shop and make some little excuse, which has nothing to do with the real reason, for folding up the bright paraphernalia of the streets and withdrawing to some duskier chamber of the being where we may ask, as we raise our left foot obediently upon the stand: "What, then, is it like to be a dwarf?"

She came in escorted by two women who, being of normal size, looked like benevolent giants beside her. Smiling at the shop girls, they seemed to be disclaiming any lot in her deformity and assuring her of their protection. She wore the peevish yet apologetic expression usual on the faces of the deformed. She needed their kindness, yet she resented it. But when the shop girl had been summoned and the giantesses, smiling indulgently, had asked for shoes for "this lady" and the girl had pushed the little stand in front of her, the dwarf stuck her foot out with an impetuosity which seemed to claim all our attention. Look at that! Look at that! she seemed to demand of us all, as she thrust her foot out, for behold it was the shapely, perfectly proportioned foot of a well-grown woman. It was arched; it was aristocratic. Her whole manner changed as she looked at it resting on the stand. She looked soothed and satisfied. Her manner became full of self-confidence. She sent for shoe after shoe; she tried on pair after pair. She got up and pirouetted before a glass which reflected the foot only in yellow shoes, in fawn shoes, in shoes of lizard skin. She raised her little skirts and displayed her little legs. She was thinking that, after all, feet are the most important part of the whole person; women, she said to herself, have been loved for their feet alone. Seeing nothing but her feet, she imagined perhaps that the rest of her body was of a piece with those beautiful feet. She was shabbily dressed, but she was ready to lavish any money upon her shoes. And as this was the only occasion upon which she was not afraid of being looked at but positively craved attention, she was ready to use any device to prolong the choosing and fitting. Look at my feet, she seemed to be saying, as she took a step this way and then a step that way. The shop girl good-humouredly must have said something flattering, for suddenly her face lit up in ecstasy. But, after all, the giantesses, benevolent though they were, had their own affairs to see to; she must make up her mind; she must decide which to choose. At length, the pair was chosen and, as she walked out between her guardians, with the parcel swinging from her finger, the ecstasy faded, knowledge returned, the old peevishness, the old apology came back, and by the time she had reached the street again she had become a dwarf only.

But she had changed the mood; she had called into being an atmosphere which, as we followed her out into the street, seemed actually to create the humped, the twisted, the deformed. Two bearded men, brothers, apparently, stone-blind, supporting themselves by resting a hand on the head of a small boy between them, marched down the street. On they came with the unyielding yet tremulous tread of the blind, which seems to lend to their approach something of the terror and inevitability of the fate that has overtaken them. As they passed, holding straight on, the little convoy seemed to cleave asunder the passers-by with the momentum of its silence, its directness, its disaster. Indeed, the dwarf had started a hobbling grotesque dance to which everybody in the street now conformed: the stout lady tightly swathed in shiny sealskin; the feeble-minded boy sucking the silver knob of his stick; the old man squatted on a doorstep as if, suddenly overcome by the absurdity of the human spectacle, he had sat down to look at it—all joined in the hobble and tap of the dwarf's dance.

In what crevices and crannies, one might ask, did they lodge, this maimed company of the halt and the blind? Here, perhaps, in the top rooms of these narrow old houses between Holborn and Soho, where people have such queer names, and pursue so many curious trades, are gold beaters, accordion pleaters, cover buttons, or support life, with even great fantasticality, upon a traffic in cups without saucers, china umbrella handles, and highly-coloured pictures of martyred saints. There they lodge, and it seems as if the lady in the sealskin jacket must find life tolerable, passing the time of day with the accordion pleater, or the man who covers buttons; life which is so fantastic cannot be altogether tragic. They do not grudge us, we are musing, our prosperity; when, suddenly, turning the corner, we come upon a bearded Jew, wild, hunger-bitten, glaring out of his misery; or pass the humped body of an old woman flung abandoned on the step of a public building with a cloak over her like the hasty covering thrown over a dead horse or donkey. At such sights the nerves of the spine seem to stand erect; a sudden flare is brandished in our eyes; a question is asked which is never answered. Often enough these derelicts choose to lie not a stone's throw from theatres, within hearing of barrel organs, almost, as night draws on, within touch of the sequined cloaks and bright legs of diners and dancers. They lie close to those shop windows where commerce offers to a world of old women laid on doorsteps, of blind men, of hobbling dwarfs, sofas which are supported by the gilt necks of proud swans; tables inlaid with baskets of many coloured fruit; sideboards paved with green marble the better to support the weight of boars' heads; and carpets so softened with age that their carnations have almost vanished in a pale green sea.

Passing, glimpsing, everything seems accidentally but miraculously sprinkled with beauty, as if the tide of trade which deposits its burden so punctually and prosaically upon the shores of Oxford Street had this night cast up nothing but treasure. With no thought of buying, the eye is sportive and generous; it creates; it adorns; it enhances. Standing out in the street, one may build up all the chambers of an imaginary house and furnish them at one's will with sofa, table, carpet. That rug will do for the hall. That alabaster bowl shall stand on a carved table in the window. Our merrymaking shall be reflected in that thick round mirror. But, having built and furnished the house, one is happily under no obligation to possess it; one can dismantle it in the twinkling of an eye, and build and furnish another house with other chairs and other glasses. Or let us indulge ourselves at the antique jewellers, among the trays of rings and the hanging necklaces. Let us choose those pearls, for example, and then imagine how, if we put them on, life would be changed. It becomes instantly between two and three in the morning; the lamps are burning very white in the deserted streets of Mayfair. Only motor-cars are abroad at this hour, and one has a sense of emptiness, of airiness, of secluded gaiety. Wearing pearls, wearing silk, one steps out on to a balcony which overlooks the gardens of sleeping Mayfair. There are a few lights in the bedrooms of great peers returned from Court, of silk-stockinged footmen, of dowagers who have pressed the hands of statesmen. A cat creeps

along the garden wall. Love-making is going on sibilantly, se-
ductively in the darker places of the room behind thick green
curtains. Strolling sedately as if he were promenading a terrace
beneath which the shires and counties of England lie sun-bathed,
the aged Prime Minister recounts to Lady So-and-So with the
curls and the emeralds the true history of some great crisis in the
affairs of the land. We seem to be riding on the top of the highest
mast of the tallest ship; and yet at the same time we know that
nothing of this sort matters; love is not proved thus, nor great
achievements completed thus; so that we sport with the moment
and preen our feathers in it lightly, as we stand on the balcony
watching the moonlit cat creep along Princess Mary's garden
wall.

But what could be more absurd? It is, in fact, on the stroke of
six; it is a winter's evening; we are walking to the Strand to buy a
pencil. How, then, are we also on a balcony, wearing pearls in
June? What could be more absurd? Yet it is nature's folly, not
ours. When she set about her chief masterpiece, the making of
man, she should have thought of one thing only. Instead, turning
her head, looking over her shoulder, into each one of us she let
creep instincts and desires which are utterly at variance with his
main being, so that we are streaked, variegated, all of a mixture;
the colours have run. Is the true self this which stands on the
pavement in January, or that which bends over the balcony in
June? Am I here, or am I there? Or is the true self neither this
nor that, neither here nor there, but something so varied and
wandering that it is only when we give the rein to its wishes and
let it take its way unimpeded that we are indeed ourselves? Circumstances compel unity; for convenience' sake a man must be a
whole. The good citizen when he opens his door in the evening
must be banker, golfer, husband, father; not a nomad wandering
the desert, a mystic staring at the sky, a debauchee in the slums
of San Francisco, a soldier heading a revolution, a pariah
howling with scepticism and solitude. When he opens his door,
he must run his fingers through his hair and put his umbrella in
the stand like the rest.

But here, none too soon, are the second-hand bookshops.

Here we find anchorage in these thwarting currents of being; here we balance ourselves after the splendours and miseries of the streets. The very sight of the bookseller's wife with her foot on the fender, sitting beside a good coal fire, screened from the door, is sobering and cheerful. She is never reading, or only the newspaper; her talk, when it leaves bookselling, which it does so gladly, is about hats; she likes a hat to be practical, she says, as well as pretty. O no, they don't live at the shop; they live in Brixton; she must have a bit of green to look at. In summer a jar of flowers grown in her own garden is stood on the top of some dusty pile to enliven the shop. Books are everywhere; and always the same sense of adventure fills us. Second-hand books are wild books, homeless books; they have come together in vast flocks of variegated feather, and have a charm which the domesticated volumes of the library lack. Besides, in this random miscellaneous company we may rub against some complete stranger who will, with luck, turn into the best friend we have in the world. There is always a hope, as we reach down some greyish-white book from an upper shelf, directed by its air of shabbiness and desertion, of meeting here with a man who set out on horseback over a hundred years ago to explore the woollen market in the Midlands and Wales; an unknown traveller, who stayed at inns, drank his pint, noted pretty girls and serious customs, wrote it all down stiffly, laboriously for sheer love of it (the book was published at his own expense); was infinitely prosy, busy, and matter-of-fact, and so let flow in without his knowing it the very scent of hollyhocks and the hay together with such a portrait of himself as gives him forever a seat in the warm corner of the mind's inglenook. One may buy him for eighteen pence now. He is marked three and sixpence, but the bookseller's wife, seeing how shabby the covers are and how long the book has stood there since it was bought at some sale of a gentleman's library in Suffolk, will let it go at that.

Thus, glancing round the bookshop, we make other such sudden capricious friendships with the unknown and the vanished whose only record is, for example, this little book of poems, so fairly printed, so finely engraved, too, with a portrait of the author. For he was a poet and drowned untimely, and his verse, mild as it is and formal and sententious, sends forth still a frail fluty sound like that of a piano organ played in some back street resignedly by an old Italian organ-grinder in a corduroy jacket. There are travellers, too, row upon row of them, still testifying, indomitable spinsters that they were, to the discomforts that they endured and the sunsets they admired in Greece when Queen Victoria was a girl. A tour in Cornwall with a visit to the tin mines was thought worthy of voluminous record. People went slowly up the Rhine and did portraits of each other in Indian ink, sitting reading on deck beside a coil of rope; they measured the pyramids; were lost to civilization for years; converted Negroes in pestilential swamps. This packing up and going off, exploring deserts and catching fevers, settling in India for a lifetime, pene-trating even to China and then returning to lead a parochial life at Edmonton, tumbles and tosses upon the dusty floor like an un-easy sea, so restless the English are, with the waves at their very door. The waters of travel and adventure seem to break upon little islands of serious effort and lifelong industry stood in jagged column upon the floor. In these piles of puce-bound volumes with gilt monograms on the back, thoughtful clergymen expound the gospels; scholars are to be heard with their hammers and their chisels chipping clear the ancient texts of Euripides and Aeschy-lus. Thinking, annotating, expounding goes on at a prodigious rate all around us and over everything, like a punctual, everlast-ing tide, washes the ancient sea of fiction. Innumerable volumes tell how Arthur loved Laura and they were separated and they were unhappy and then they met and they were happy ever after, as was the way when Victoria ruled these islands.

The number of books in the world is infinite, and one is forced to glimpse and nod and move on after a moment of talk, a flash of understanding, as, in the street outside, one catches a word in passing and from a chance phrase fabricates a lifetime. It is about a woman called Kate that they are talking, how "I said to her quite straight last night . . . if you don't think I'm worth a penny stamp, I said . . ." But who Kate is, and to what crisis in their friendship that penny stamp refers, we shall never know; for Kate sinks under the warmth of their volubility; and here, at the street corner, another page of the volume of life is laid open by the sight of two men consulting under the lamp-post. They are spelling out the latest wire from Newmarket in the stop press news. Do they think, then, that fortune will ever convert their rags into fur and broadcloth, sling them with watch-chains, and plant diamond pins where there is now a ragged open shirt? But the main stream of walkers at this hour sweeps too fast to let us ask such questions. They are wrapt, in this short passage from work to home, in some narcotic dream, now that they are free from the desk, and have the fresh air on their cheeks. They put on those bright clothes which they must hang up and lock the key upon all the rest of the day, and are great cricketers, famous actresses, soldiers who have saved their country at the hour of need. Dreaming, gesticulating, often muttering a few words aloud, they sweep over the Strand and across Waterloo Bridge whence they will be slung in long rattling trains, to some prim little villa in Barnes or Surbiton where the sight of the clock in the hall and the smell of the supper in the basement puncture the dream.

But we are come to the Strand now, and as we hesitate on the curb, a little rod about the length of one's finger begins to lay its bar across the velocity and abundance of life. "Really I must— really I must"—that is it. Without investigating the demand, the mind cringes to the accustomed tyrant. One must, one always must, do something or other; it is not allowed one simply to enjoy oneself. Was it not for this reason that, some time ago, we fabricated the excuse, and invented the necessity of buying something? But what was it? Ah, we remember, it was a pencil. Let us go then and buy this pencil. But just as we are turning to obey the command, another self disputes the right of the tyrant to insist. The usual conflict comes about. Spread out behind the rod of duty we see the whole breadth of the river Thames—wide, mournful, peaceful. And we see it through the eyes of somebody who is leaning over the Embankment on a summer evening, without a care in the world. Let us put off buying the pencil; let us go in search of this person—and soon it becomes apparent that this person is ourselves. For if we could stand there where we stood six months ago, should we not be again as we were then—calm, aloof, content? Let us try then. But the river is rougher and greyer than we remembered. The tide is running out to sea. It brings down with it a tug and two barges, whose load of straw is tightly bound down beneath tarpaulin covers. There is, too, close by us, a couple leaning over the balustrade with the curious lack of self-consciousness lovers have, as if the importance of the affair they are engaged on claims without question the indulgence of the human race. The sights we see and the sounds we hear now have none of the quality of the past; nor have we any share in the serenity of the person who, six months ago, stood precisely where we stand now. His is the happiness of death; ours the insecurity of life. He has no future; the future is even now invading our peace. It is only when we look at the past and take from it the element of uncertainty that we can enjoy perfect peace. As it is, we must turn, we must cross the Strand again, we must find a shop where, even at this hour, they will be ready to sell us a pencil.

It is always an adventure to enter a new room; for the lives and characters of its owners have distilled their atmosphere into it, and directly we enter it we breast some new wave of emotion. Here, without a doubt, in the stationer's shop people had been quarrelling. Their anger shot through the air. They both stopped; the old woman—they were husband and wife evidently—retired to a back room; the old man whose rounded forehead and globular eyes would have looked well on the frontispiece of some Elizabethan folio, stayed to serve us. "A pencil, a pencil," he repeated, "certainly, certainly." He spoke with the distraction yet effusiveness of one whose emotions have been roused and checked in full flood. He began opening box after box and shutting them again. He said that it was very difficult to find things when they kept so many different articles. He launched into a story about some legal gentleman who had got into deep waters owing to the conduct of his wife. He had known him for years; he had been connected with the Temple for half a century, he said, as if he wished his wife in the back room to overhear him. He upset a box of rubber bands. At last, exasperated by his incompetence, he pushed the swing door open and called out roughly: "Where d'you keep the pencils?" as if his wife had hidden them. The old lady came in. Looking at nobody, she put her hand with a fine air of righteous severity upon the right box. There were pencils. How then could he do without her? Was she not indispensable to him? In order to keep them there, standing side by side in forced neutrality, one had to be particular in one's choice of pencils; this was too soft, that too hard. They stood silently looking on. The longer they stood there, the calmer they grew; their heat was going down, their anger disappearing. Now, without a word said on either side, the quarrel was made up. The old man, who would not have disgraced Ben Jonson's title-page, reached the box back to its proper place, bowed profoundly his good-night to us, and they disappeared. She would get out her sewing; he would read his newspaper; the canary would scatter them impartially with seed. The quarrel was over.

In these minutes in which a ghost has been sought for, a quarrel composed, and a pencil bought, the streets had become completely empty. Life had withdrawn to the top floor, and lamps were lit. The pavement was dry and hard; the road was of hammered silver. Walking home through the desolation one could tell oneself the story of the dwarf, of the blind men, of the party in the Mayfair mansion, of the quarrel in the stationer's shop. Into each of these lives one could penetrate a little way, far enough to give oneself the illusion that one is not tethered to a single mind, but can put on briefly for a few minutes the bodies and minds of others. One could become a washerwoman, a publican, a street singer. And what greater delight and wonder can there be than to leave the straight lines of personality and deviate into those footpaths that lead beneath brambles and thick tree trunks into the heart of the forest where live those wild beasts, our fellow men?

That is true: to escape is the greatest of pleasures; street haunting in winter the greatest of adventures. Still as we approach our own doorstep again, it is comforting to feel the old possessions, the old prejudices, fold us round; and the self, which has been blown about at so many street corners, which has battered like a moth at the flame of so many inaccessible lanterns, sheltered and enclosed. Here again is the usual door; here the chair turned as we left it and the china bowl and the brown ring on the carpet. And here—let us examine it tenderly, let us touch it with reverence—is the only spoil we have retrieved from all the treasures of the city, a lead pencil.

A Letter to
a Young Poet

In a letter to Virginia Woolf, praising The Waves, John Lehmann said that the time had come for her to define her views
on modern poetry. In her reply of September 17, 1931, she said:
"I think your idea of a Letter most brilliant—To a Young
Poet? because I'm seething with immature and ill considered
and wild and annoying ideas about prose and poetry." A Letter
to a Young Poet, addressed to John Lehmann, was first published in the Yale Review in June 1932 and again on July 7 as
one of the Hogarth Letters series.

Although sustaining the illusion of playful informality
throughout, Virginia Woolf succeeds in making her argument
clear: the young poet believes that in order to get at the truth,
he must resort to the actual and the colloquial—which he seeks
to find in himself only. The result is that he stresses more the
differences which separate him from his kind than the deeper
similarities that all human beings have in common. Young
poets must open their eyes once more to other people. "How
can you learn to write if you write only about one single person?" The question is as valid today as it was when it was first
asked, more than a half century ago.

MY DEAR JOHN,

Did you ever meet, or was he before your day, that old gentleman—I forget his name—who used to enliven conversation,
especially at breakfast when the post came in, by saying that the
art of letter-writing is dead? The penny post, the old gentleman
used to say, has killed the art of letter-writing. Nobody, he continued, examining an envelope through his eye-glasses, has the
time even to cross their t's. We rush, he went on, spreading his
toast with marmalade, to the telephone. We commit our half-
formed thoughts in ungrammatical phrases to the post card.
Gray is dead, he continued; Horace Walpole is dead; Madame de
Sévigné—she is dead too, I suppose he was about to add, but a
fit of choking cut him short, and he had to leave the room before
he had time to condemn all the arts, as his pleasure was, to the
cemetery. But when the post came in this morning and I opened
your letter stuffed with little blue sheets written all over in a
cramped but not illegible hand—I regret to say, however, that
several t's were uncrossed and the grammar of one sentence
seems to me dubious—I replied after all these years to that
elderly necrophilist—Nonsense. The art of letter-writing has only
just come into existence. It is the child of the penny post. And
there is some truth in that remark, I think. Naturally when a
letter cost half a crown to send, it had to prove itself a document
of some importance; it was read aloud; it was tied up with green
silk; after a certain number of years it was published for the
infinite delectation of posterity. But your letter, on the contrary,
will have to be burnt. It only cost three-halfpence to send. Therefore you could afford to be intimate, irreticent, indiscreet in the
extreme. What you tell me about poor dear C. and his adventure
on the Channel boat is deadly private; your ribald jests at the
expense of M. would certainly ruin your friendship if they got
about; I doubt, too, that posterity, unless it is much quicker in
the wit than I expect, could follow the line of your thought from
the roof which leaks ("splash, splash, splash into the soap
dish") past Mrs. Gape, the charwoman, whose retort to the

greengrocer gives me the keenest pleasure, via Miss Curtis and her odd confidence on the steps of the omnibus; to Siamese cats ("Wrap their noses in an old stocking my Aunt says if they howl"); so to the value of criticism to a writer; so to Donne; so to Gerard Hopkins; so to tombstones; so to gold-fish; and so with a sudden alarming swoop to "Do write and tell me where poetry's going, or if it's dead?" No, your letter, because it is a true letter—one that can neither be read aloud now, nor printed in time to come—will have to be burnt. Posterity must live upon Walpole and Madame de Sévigné. The great age of letter-writing, which is, of course, the present, will leave no letters behind it. And in making my reply there is only one question that I can answer or attempt to answer in public; about poetry and its death.

But before I begin, I must own up to those defects, both natural and acquired, which, as you will find, distort and invalidate all that I have to say about poetry. The lack of a sound university training has always made it impossible for me to distinguish between an iambic and a dactyl, and if this were not enough to condemn one for ever, the practice of prose has bred in me, as in most prose writers, a foolish jealousy, a righteous indignation—anyhow, an emotion which the critic should be without. For how, we despised prose writers ask when we get together, could one say what one meant and observe the rules of poetry? Conceive dragging in "blade" because one had mentioned "maid"; and pairing "sorrow" with "borrow"? Rhyme is not only childish, but dishonest, we prose writers say. Then we go on to say, And look at their rules! How easy to be a poet! How strait the path is for them, and how strict! This you must do; this you must not. I would rather be a child and walk in a crocodile down a suburban path than write poetry, I have heard prose writers say. It must be like taking the veil and entering a religious order—observing the rites and rigours of metre. That explains why they repeat the same thing over and over again. Whereas we prose writers (I am only telling you the sort of nonsense prose writers talk when they are alone) are masters of language, not its slaves; nobody can teach us; nobody can coerce us; we say what we mean; we have the whole of life for our province. We are the creators, we are the explorers. . . . So we run on—nonsensically enough, I must admit.

Now that I have made a clean breast of these deficiencies, let us proceed. From certain phrases in your letter I gather that you think that poetry is in a parlous way, and that your case as a poet in this particular autumn of 1931 is a great deal harder than Shakespeare's, Dryden's, Pope's, or Tennyson's. In fact it is the hardest case that has ever been known. Here you give me an opening, which I am prompt to seize, for a little lecture. Never think yourself singular, never think your own case much harder than other people's. I admit that the age we live in makes this difficult. For the first time in history there are readers—a large body of people, occupied in business, in sport, in nursing their grandfathers, in tying up parcels behind counters—they all read now; and they want to be told how to read and what to read; and their teachers—the reviewers, the lecturers, the broadcasters— must in all humanity make reading easy for them; assure them that literature is violent and exciting, full of heroes and villains; of hostile forces perpetually in conflict; of fields strewn with bones; of solitary victors riding off on white horses wrapped in black cloaks to meet their death at the turn of the road. A pistol shot rings out. "The age of romance was over. The age of realism had begun"—you know the sort of thing. Now of course writers themselves know very well that there is not a word of truth in all this—there are no battles, and no murders and no defeats and no victories. But as it is of the utmost importance that readers should be amused, writers acquiesce. They dress themselves up. They act their parts. One leads; the other follows. One is romantic, the other realist. One is advanced, the other out of date. There is no harm in it, so long as you take it as a joke, but once you believe in it, once you begin to take yourself seriously as a leader or as a follower, as a modern or as a conservative, then you become a self-conscious, biting, and scratching little animal whose work is not of the slightest value or importance to anybody. Think of yourself rather as something much humbler and less spectacular, but to my mind far more interesting—a poet in whom live all the poets of the past, from whom all poets in time to come will spring. You have a touch of Chaucer in you, and something of Shakespeare; Dryden, Pope, Tennyson—to mention only the respectable among your ancestors—stir in your blood and sometimes move your pen a little to the right or to the left. In short you are an immensely ancient, complex, and continuous character, for which reason please treat yourself with respect and think twice before you dress up as Guy Fawkes and spring out upon timid old ladies at street corners, threatening death and demanding twopence-halfpenny.

However, as you say that you are in a fix ("it has never been so hard to write poetry as it is today") and that poetry may be, you think, at its last gasp in England ("the novelists are doing all the interesting things now"), let me while away the time before the post goes in imagining your state and in hazarding one or two guesses which, since this is a letter, need not be taken too seriously or pressed too far. Let me try to put myself in your place; let me try to imagine, with your letter to help me, what it feels like to be a young poet in the autumn of 1931. (And taking my own advice, I shall treat you not as one poet in particular, but as several poets in one.) On the floor of your mind, then—is it not this that makes you a poet?—rhythm keeps up its perpetual beat. Sometimes it seems to die down to nothing; it lets you eat, sleep, talk like other people. Then again it swells and rises and attempts to sweep all the contents of your mind into one dominant dance. Tonight is such an occasion. Although you are alone, and have taken one boot off and are about to undo the other, you cannot go on with the process of undressing, but must instantly write at the bidding of the dance. You snatch pen and paper; you hardly trouble to hold the one or to straighten the other. And while you write, while the first stanzas of the dance are being fastened down, I will withdraw a little and look out of the window. A woman passes, then a man; a car glides to a stop and then—but there is no need to say what I see out of the window, nor indeed is there time, for I am suddenly recalled from my observations by a cry of rage or despair. Your page is crumpled in a ball; your pen sticks upright by the nib in the carpet. If there were a cat to swing or a wife to murder now would be the time. So at least I infer from the ferocity of your expression. You are rasped, jarred, thoroughly out of temper. And if I am to guess the reason, it is, I should say, that the rhythm which was opening and shutting with a force that sent shocks of excitement from your head to your heels has encountered some hard and hostile object upon which it has smashed itself to pieces. Something has worked in which cannot be made into poetry; some foreign body, angular, sharp-edged, gritty, has refused to join in the dance. Obviously, suspicion attaches to Mrs. Gape; she has asked you to make a poem of her; then to Miss Curtis and her confidences on the omnibus; then to C., who has infected you with a wish to tell his story—and a very amusing one it was—in verse. But for some reason you cannot do their bidding. Chaucer could; Shakespeare could; so could Crabbe, Byron, and perhaps Robert Browning. But it is October 1931, and for a long time now poetry has shirked contact with—what shall we call it?— Shall we shortly and no doubt inaccurately call it life? And will you come to my help by guessing what I mean? Well then, it has left all that to the novelist. Here you see how easy it would be for me to write two or three volumes in honour of prose and in mockery of verse; to say how wide and ample is the domain of the one, how starved and stunted the little grove of the other. But it would be simpler and perhaps fairer to check these theories by opening one of the thin books of modern verse that lie on your table. I open and I find myself instantly confuted. Here are the common objects of daily prose—the bicycle and the omnibus. Obviously the poet is making his muse face facts. Listen:

> Which of you waking early and watching daybreak
> Will not hasten in heart, handsome, aware of wonder
> At light unleashed, advancing, a leader of movement,
> Breaking like surf on turf on road and roof,

Or chasing shadow on downs like whippet racing,
The stilled stone, halting at eyelash barrier,
Enforcing in face a profile, marks of misuse,
Beating impatient and importunate on boudoir shutters
Where the old life is not up yet, with rays
Exploring through rotting floor a dismantled mill—
The old life never to be born again?

Yes, but how will he get through with it? I read on and find:

Whistling as he shuts
His door behind him, traveling to work by tube
Or walking to the park to it to *ease the bowels*,

and read on and find again:

As a boy lately come up from country to town
Returns for the day to his village in *expensive shoes—*

and so on again to:

Seeking a heaven on earth he chases his shadow,
Loses his capital and his nerve in pursuing
What yachtsmen, explorers, climbers and *buggers are after.*

These lines and the words I have emphasized are enough to
confirm me in part of my guess at least. The poet is trying to
include Mrs. Gape. He is honestly of opinion that she can be
brought into poetry and will do very well there. Poetry, he feels,
will be improved by the actual, the colloquial. But though I
honour him for the attempt, I doubt that it is wholly successful. I
feel a jar. I feel a shock. I feel as if I had stubbed my toe on the
corner of the wardrobe. Am I then, I go on to ask, shocked,
prudishly and conventionally, by the words themselves? I think
not. The shock is literally a shock. The poet as I guess has
strained himself to include an emotion that is not domesticated
and acclimatized to poetry; the effort has thrown him off his
balance; he rights himself, as I am sure I shall find if I turn the
page, by a violent recourse to the poetical—he invokes the moon

or the nightingale. Anyhow, the transition is sharp. The poem is cracked in the middle. Look, it comes apart in my hands: here is reality on one side, here is beauty on the other; and instead of acquiring a whole object rounded and entire, I am left with broken parts in my hands which, since my reason has been roused and my imagination has not been allowed to take entire possession of me, I contemplate coldly, critically, and with distaste.

Such at least is the hasty analysis I make of my own sensations as a reader; but again I am interrupted. I see that you have overcome your difficulty, whatever it was; the pen is once more in action, and having torn up the first poem you are at work upon another. Now then if I want to understand your state of mind I must invent another explanation to account for this return of fluency. You have dismissed, as I suppose, all sorts of things that would come naturally to your pen if you had been writing prose—the charwoman, the omnibus, the incident on the Channel boat. Your range is restricted—I judge from your expression—concentrated and intensified. I hazard a guess that you are thinking now, not about things in general, but about yourself in particular. There is a fixity, a gloom, yet an inner glow that seem to hint that you are looking within and not without. But in order to consolidate these flimsy guesses about the meaning of an expression on a face, let me open another of the books on your table and check it by what I find there. Again I open at random and read this:

> To penetrate that room is my desire,
> The extreme attic of the mind, that lies
> Just beyond the last bend in the corridor.
> Writing I do it. Phrases, poems are keys.
> Loving's another way (but not so sure).
> A fire's in there, I think, there's truth at last
> Deep in a lumber chest. Sometimes I'm near,
> But draughts puff out the matches, and I'm lost.
> Sometimes I'm lucky, find a key to turn,

> Open an inch or two—but always then
> A bell rings, someone calls, or cries of "fire"
> Arrest my hand when nothing's known or seen,
> And running down the stairs again I mourn.

and then this:

> There is a dark room,
> The locked and shuttered womb,
> Where negative's made positive.
> Another dark room,
> The blind and bolted tomb,
> Where positives change to negative.
> We may not undo that or escape this, who
> Have birth and death coiled in our bones,
> Nothing we can do
> Will sweeten the real rue,
> That we begin, and end, with groans.

And then this:

> Never being, but always at the edge of Being
> My head, like Death mask, is brought into the Sun.
> The shadow pointing finger across cheek,
> I move lips for tasting, I move hands for touching,
> But never am nearer than touching,
> Though the spirit leans outward for seeing.
> Observing rose, gold, eyes, an admired landscape,
> My senses record the act of wishing
> Wishing to be
> Rose, gold, landscape or another—
> Claiming fulfilment in the act of loving.

Since these quotations are chosen at random and I have yet found three different poets writing about nothing, if not about the poet himself, I hold that the chances are that you too are engaged in the same occupation. I conclude that self offers no impediment; self joins in the dance; self lends itself to the rhythm; it is apparently easier to write a poem about oneself than about any other subject. But what does one mean by "oneself"? Not the self that Wordsworth, Keats, and Shelley have described—not the self that loves a woman, or that hates a tyrant, or that broods over the mystery of the world. No, the self that you are engaged in describing is shut out from all that. It is a self that sits alone in the room at night with the blinds drawn. In others words the poet is much less interested in what we have in common than in what he has apart. Hence I suppose the extreme difficulty of these poems—and I have to confess that it would floor me completely to say from one reading or even from two or three what these poems mean. The poet is trying honestly and exactly to describe a world that has perhaps no existence except for one particular person at one particular moment. And the more sincere he is in keeping to the precise outline of the roses and cabbages of his private universe, the more he puzzles us who have agreed in a lazy spirit of compromise to see roses and cabbages as they are seen, more or less, by the twenty-six passengers on the outside of an omnibus. He strains to describe; we strain to see; he flickers his torch; we catch a flying gleam. It is exciting; it is stimulating; but is that a tree, we ask, or is it perhaps an old woman tying up her shoe in the gutter?

Well, then, if there is any truth in what I am saying—if that is you cannot write about the actual, the colloquial, Mrs. Gape or the Channel boat or Miss Curtis on the omnibus, without straining the machine of poetry, if, therefore, you are driven to contemplate landscapes and emotions within and must render visible to the world at large what you alone can see, then indeed yours is a hard case, and poetry, though still breathing—witness these little books—is drawing her breath in short, sharp gasps. Still, consider the symptoms. They are not the symptoms of death in the least. Death in literature, and I need not tell you how often literature has died in this country or in that, comes gracefully, smoothly, quietly. Lines slip easily down the accustomed grooves. The old designs are copied so glibly that we are half inclined to think them original, save for that very glibness. But here the very opposite is happening: here in my first quotation the poet breaks his machine because he will clog it with raw fact. In my second, he is unintelligible because of his desperate determination to tell the truth about himself. Thus I cannot help thinking that though you may be right in talking of the difficulty of the time, you are wrong to despair.

Is there not, alas, good reason to hope? I say "alas" because then I must give my reasons, which are bound to be foolish and certain also to cause pain to the large and highly respectable society of necrophiles—Mr. Peabody, and his like—who much prefer death to life and are even now intoning the sacred and comfortable words, Keats is dead, Shelley is dead, Byron is dead. But it is late: necrophily induces slumber; the old gentlemen have fallen asleep over their classics, and if what I am about to say takes a sanguine tone—and for my part I do not believe in poets dying; Keats, Shelley, Byron are alive here in this room in you and you and you—I can take comfort from the thought that my hoping will not disturb their snoring. So to continue—why should not poetry, now that it has so honestly scraped itself free from certain falsities, the wreckage of the great Victorian age, now that it has so sincerely gone down into the mind of the poet and verified its outlines—a work of renovation that has to be done from time to time and was certainly needed, for bad poetry is almost always the result of forgetting oneself—all becomes distorted and impure if you lose sight of that central reality— now, I say, that poetry has done all this, why should it not once more open its eyes, look out of the window and write about other people? Two or three hundred years ago you were always writing about other people. Your pages were crammed with characters of the most opposite and various kinds—Hamlet, Cleopatra, Falstaff. Not only did we go to you for drama, and for the subtleties of human character, but we also went to you, incredible though this now seems, for laughter. You made us roar with laughter. Then later, not more than a hundred years ago, you were lashing our follies, trouncing our hypocrisies, and dashing off the most brilliant of satires. You were Byron, remember; you wrote *Don Juan.* You were Crabbe also; you took the most sordid details of the lives of peasants for your theme. Clearly therefore you have it in you to deal with a vast variety of subjects; it is only a temporary necessity that has shut you up in one room, alone, by yourself.

But how are you going to get out, into the world of other people? That is your problem now, if I may hazard a guess—to find the right relationship, now that you know yourself, between the self that you know and the world outside. It is a difficult problem. No living poet has, I think, altogether solved it. And there are a thousand voices prophesying despair. Science, they say, has made poetry impossible; there is no poetry in motor cars and wireless. And we have no religion. All is tumultuous and transitional. Therefore, so people say, there can be no relation between the poet and the present age. But surely that is nonsense. These accidents are superficial; they do not go nearly deep enough to destroy the most profound and primitive of instincts, the instinct of rhythm. All you need now is to stand at the window and let your rhythmical sense open and shut, open and shut, boldly and freely, until one thing melts in another, until the taxis are dancing with the daffodils, until a whole has been made from all these separate fragments. I am talking nonsense, I know. What I mean is, summon all your courage, exert all your vigilance, invoke all the gifts that Nature has been induced to bestow. Then let your rhythmical sense wind itself in and out among men and women, omnibuses, sparrows—whatever come along the street—until it has strung them together in one harmonious whole. That perhaps is your task—to find the relation between things that seem incompatible yet have a mysterious affinity, to absorb every experience that comes your way fearlessly and saturate it completely so that your poem is a whole, not a fragment; to re-think human life into poetry and so give us tragedy again and comedy by means of characters not spun out at length in the novelist's way, but condensed and synthesised in the poet's way—that is what we look to you to do now. But as I do not know what I mean by rhythm nor what I mean by life, and as most certainly I cannot tell you which objects can properly be combined together in a poem—that is entirely your affair —and as I cannot tell a dactyl from an iambic, and am therefore unable to say how you must modify and expand the rites and ceremonies of your ancient and mysterious art—I will move on to safer ground and turn again to these little books themselves.

When, then, I return to them I am, as I have admitted, filled, not with forebodings of death, but with hopes for the future. But one does not always want to be thinking of the future, if, as sometimes happens, one is living in the present. When I read these poems, now, at the present moment, I find myself— reading, you know, is rather like opening the door to a horde of rebels who swarm out attacking one in twenty places at once— hit, roused, scraped, bared, swung through the air, so that life seems to flash by; then again blinded, knocked on the head—all of which are agreeable sensations for a reader (since nothing is more dismal than to open the door and get no response), and all I believe certain proof that this poet is alive and kicking. And yet mingling with these cries of delight, of jubilation, I record also, as I read, the repetition in the bass of one word intoned over and over again by some malcontent. At last then, silencing the others, I say to this malcontent, "Well, and what do *you* want?" Whereupon he bursts out, rather to my discomfort, "Beauty." Let me repeat, I take no responsibility for what my senses say when I read; I merely record the fact that there is a malcontent in me who complains that it seems to him odd, considering that English is a mixed language, a rich language; a language unmatched for its sound and colour, for its power of imagery and suggestion—it seems to him odd that these modern poets should write as if they had neither ears nor eyes, neither soles to their feet nor palms to their hands, but only honest enterprising book-fed brains, unisexual bodies and—but here I interrupted him. For when it comes to saying that a poet should be bi-sexual, and that I think is what he was about to say, even I, who have had no scientific training whatsoever, draw the line and tell that voice to be silent.

But how far, if we discount these obvious absurdities, do you think there is truth in this complaint? For my own part now that I have stopped reading, and can see the poems more or less as a whole, I think it is true that the eye and ear are starved of their rights. There is no sense of riches held in reserve behind the admirable exactitude of the lines I have quoted, as there is, for example, behind the exactitude of Mr. Yeats. The poet clings to his one word, his only word, as a drowning man to a spar. And if this is so, I am ready to hazard a reason for it all the more readily because I think it bears out what I have just been saying. The art of writing, and that is perhaps what my malcontent means by "beauty," the art of having at one's beck and call every word in the language, of knowing their weights, colours, sounds, associations, and thus making them, as is so necessary in English, suggest more than they can state, can be learnt of course to some extent by reading—it is impossible to read too much; but much more drastically and effectively by imagining that one is not oneself but somebody different. How can you learn to write if you write only about one single person? To take the obvious example. Can you doubt that the reason why Shakespeare knew every sound and syllable in the language and could do precisely what he liked with grammar and syntax, was that Hamlet, Falstaff and Cleopatra rushed him into this knowledge; that the lords, officers, dependants, murderers and common soldiers of the plays insisted that he should say exactly what they felt in the words expressing their feelings? It was they who taught him to write, not the begetter of the Sonnets. So that if you want to satisfy all those senses that rise in a swarm whenever we drop a poem among them—the reason, the imagination, the eyes, the ears, the palms of the hands and the soles of the feet, not to mention a million more that the psychologists have yet to name, you will do well to embark upon a long poem in which people as unlike yourself as possible talk at the tops of their voices. And for heaven's sake, publish nothing before you are thirty.

That, I am sure, is of very great importance. Most of the faults in the poems I have been reading can be explained, I think, by the fact that they have been exposed to the fierce light of publicity while they were still too young to stand the strain. It has shrivelled them into a skeleton austerity, both emotional and verbal, which should not be characteristic of youth. The poet writes very well; he writes for the eye of a severe and intelligent public; but how much better he would have written if for ten years he had written for no eye but his own! After all, the years from twenty to thirty are years (let me refer to your letter again) of emotional excitement. The rain dripping, a wing flashing, someone passing—the commonest sounds and sights have power to fling one, as I seem to remember, from the heights of rapture to the depths of despair. And if the actual life is thus extreme, the visionary life should be free to follow. Write then, now that you are young, nonsense by the ream. Be silly, be sentimental, imitate Shelley, imitate Samuel Smiles; give the rein to every impulse; commit every fault of style, grammar, taste, and syntax; pour out; tumble over; loose anger, love, satire, in whatever words you can catch, coerce or create, in whatever metre, prose, poetry, or gibberish that comes to hand. Thus you will learn to write. But if you publish, your freedom will be checked; you will be thinking what people will say; you will write for others when you ought only to be writing for yourself. And what point can there be in curbing the wild torrent of spontaneous nonsense which is now, for a few years only, your divine gift in order to publish prim little books of experimental verses? To make money? That, we both know, is out of the question. To get criticism? But your friends will pepper your manuscripts with far more serious and searching criticism than any you will get from the reviewers. As for fame, look I implore you at famous people; see how the waters of dullness spread around them as they enter; observe their pomposity, their prophetic airs; reflect that the greatest poets were anonymous; think how Shakespeare cared nothing for fame; how Donne tossed his poems into the waste-paper basket; write an essay giving a single instance of any modern English writer who has survived the disciples and the admirers, the autograph hunters and the interviewers, the dinners and the luncheons, the celebrations and the commemorations with which English society so effectively stops the mouths of its singers and silences their songs.

But enough. I, at any rate, refuse to be necrophilous. So long as you and you and you, venerable and ancient representatives of Sappho, Shakespeare, and Shelley, are aged precisely twenty-three and propose—O enviable lot!—to spend the next fifty years of your lives in writing poetry, I refuse to think that the art is dead. And if ever the temptation to necrophilize comes over you, be warned by the fate of that old gentleman whose name I forget, but I think that it was Peabody. In the very act of consigning all the arts to the grave he choked over a large piece of hot buttered toast and the consolation then offered him that he was about to join the elder Pliny in the shades gave him, I am told, no sort of satisfaction whatsoever.

And now for the intimate, the indiscreet, and indeed, the only really interesting parts of this letter. . . .

Professions
for Women

"Professions for Women" is an abbreviated version of the speech Virginia Woolf delivered before a branch of the National Society for Women's Service on January 21, 1931; it was published posthumously in The Death of the Moth and Other Essays. *On the day before the speech, she wrote in her diary: "I have this moment, while having my bath, conceived an entire new book—a sequel to a* Room of Ones Own—*about the sexual life of women: to be called Professions for Women perhaps—Lord how exciting!" More than a year and a half later, on October 11, 1932, Virginia Woolf began to write her new book:* "THE PARGITERS: *An Essay based upon a paper read to the London/National Society for women's service." "The Pargiters" evolved into* The Years *and was published in 1937. The book that eventually did become the sequel to* A Room of One's Own *was* Three Guineas (1938), *and its first working title was "Professions for Women."*

The essay printed here concentrates on that Victorian phantom known as the Angel in the House (borrowed from Coventry Patmore's poem celebrating domestic bliss)—that selfless, sacrificial woman in the nineteenth century whose sole purpose in life was to soothe, to flatter, and to comfort the male half of the world's population. "Killing the Angel in the House," wrote

Virginia Woolf, "was part of the occupation of a woman writer." That has proved to be a prophetic statement, for today, not only in the domain of letters, but in the entire professional world, women are still engaged in that deadly contest in their struggle for social and economic equality.

WHEN YOUR SECRETARY INVITED ME TO COME HERE, she told me that your Society is concerned with the employment of women and she suggested that I might tell you something about my own professional experiences. It is true I am a woman; it is true I am employed; but what professional experiences have I had? It is difficult to say. My profession is literature; and in that profession there are fewer experiences for women than in any other, with the exception of the stage—fewer, I mean, that are peculiar to women. For the road was cut many years ago— by Fanny Burney, by Aphra Behn, by Harriet Martineau, by Jane Austen, by George Eliot—many famous women, and many more unknown and forgotten, have been before me, making the path smooth, and regulating my steps. Thus, when I came to write, there were very few material obstacles in my way. Writing was a reputable and harmless occupation. The family peace was not broken by the scratching of a pen. No demand was made upon the family purse. For ten and sixpence one can buy paper enough to write all the plays of Shakespeare—if one has a mind that way. Pianos and models, Paris, Vienna and Berlin, masters and mistresses, are not needed by a writer. The cheapness of writing paper is, of course, the reason why women have succeeded as writers before they have succeeded in the other professions.

But to tell you my story—it is a simple one. You have only got to figure to yourselves a girl in a bedroom with a pen in her hand. She had only to move that pen from left to right—from ten o'clock to one. Then it occurred to her to do what is simple and cheap enough after all—to slip a few of those pages into an envelope, fix a penny stamp in the corner, and drop the envelope into the red box at the corner. It was thus that I became a journalist; and my effort was rewarded on the first day of the following month—a very glorious day it was for me—by a letter from an editor containing a cheque for one pound ten shillings and sixpence. But to show you how little I deserve to be called a professional woman, how little I know of the struggles and difficulties of such lives, I have to admit that instead of spending that sum upon bread and butter, rent, shoes and stockings, or butcher's bills, I went out and bought a cat—a beautiful cat, a Persian cat, which very soon involved me in bitter disputes with my neighbours.

What could be easier than to write articles and to buy Persian cats with the profits? But wait a moment. Articles have to be about something. Mine, I seem to remember, was about a novel by a famous man. And while I was writing this review, I discovered that if I were going to review books I should need to do battle with a certain phantom. And the phantom was a woman, and when I came to know her better I called her after the heroine of a famous poem, The Angel in the House. It was she who used to come between me and my paper when I was writing reviews. It was she who bothered me and wasted my time and so tormented me that at last I killed her. You who come of a younger and happier generation may not have heard of her—you may not know what I mean by the Angel in the House. I will describe her as shortly as I can. She was intensely sympathetic. She was immensely charming. She was utterly unselfish. She excelled in the difficult arts of family life. She sacrificed herself daily. If there was chicken, she took the leg; if there was a draught she sat in it—in short she was so constituted that she never had a mind or a wish of her own, but preferred to sympathize always with the minds and wishes of others. Above all—I need not say it— she was pure. Her purity was supposed to be her chief beauty— her blushes, her great grace. In those days—the last of Queen Victoria—every house had its Angel. And when I came to write

I encountered her with the very first words. The shadow of her wings fell on my page; I heard the rustling of her skirts in the room. Directly, that is to say, I took my pen in hand to review that novel by a famous man, she slipped behind me and whispered: "My dear, you are a young woman. You are writing about a book that has been written by a man. Be sympathetic; be tender; flatter; deceive; use all the arts and wiles of our sex. Never let anybody guess that you have a mind of your own. Above all, be pure." And she made as if to guide my pen. I now record the one act for which I take some credit to myself, though the credit rightly belongs to some excellent ancestors of mine who left me a certain sum of money—shall we say five hundred pounds a year?—so that it was not necessary for me to depend solely on charm for my living. I turned upon her and caught her by the throat. I did my best to kill her. My excuse, if I were to be had up in a court of law, would be that I acted in self-defence. Had I not killed her she would have killed me. She would have plucked the heart out of my writing. For, as I found, directly I put pen to paper, you cannot review even a novel without having a mind of your own, without expressing what you think to be the truth about human relations, morality, sex. And all these questions, according to the Angel in the House, cannot be dealt with freely and openly by women; they must charm, they must conciliate, they must—to put it bluntly—tell lies if they are to succeed. Thus, whenever I felt the shadow of her wing or the radiance of her halo upon my page, I took up the inkpot and flung it at her. She died hard. Her fictitious nature was of great assistance to her. It is far harder to kill a phantom than a reality. She was always creeping back when I thought I had despatched her. Though I flatter myself that I killed her in the end, the struggle was severe; it took much time that had better have been spent upon learning Greek grammar; or in roaming the world in search of adventures. But it was a real experience; it was an experience that was bound to befall all women writers at that time. Killing the Angel in the House was part of the occupation of a woman writer.

But to continue my story. The Angel was dead; what then remained? You may say that what remained was a simple and common object—a young woman in a bedroom with an inkpot. In other words, now that she had rid herself of falsehood, that young woman had only to be herself. Ah, but what is "herself"? I mean, what is a woman? I assure you, I do not know. I do not believe that you know. I do not believe that anybody can know until she has expressed herself in all the arts and professions open to human skill. That indeed is one of the reasons why I have come here—out of respect for you, who are in process of showing us by your experiments what a woman is, who are in process of providing us, by your failures and successes, with that extremely important piece of information.

But to continue the story of my professional experiences. I made one pound ten and six by my first review; and I bought a Persian cat with the proceeds. Then I grew ambitious. A Persian cat is all very well, I said; but a Persian cat is not enough. I must have a motor car. And it was thus that I became a novelist—for it is a very strange thing that people will give you a motor car if you will tell them a story. It is a still stranger thing that there is nothing so delightful in the world as telling stories. It is far pleasanter than writing reviews of famous novels. And yet, if I am to obey your secretary and tell you my professional experiences as a novelist, I must tell you about a very strange experience that befell me as a novelist. And to understand it you must try first to imagine a novelist's state of mind. I hope I am not giving away professional secrets if I say that a novelist's chief desire is to be as unconscious as possible. He has to induce in himself a state of perpetual lethargy. He wants life to proceed with the utmost quiet and regularity. He wants to see the same faces, to read the same books, to do the same things day after day, month after month, while he is writing, so that nothing may break the illusion in which he is living—so that nothing may disturb or disquiet the mysterious nosings about, feelings round, darts, dashes and sudden discoveries of that very shy and illusive spirit, the imagination. I suspect that this state is the same both for men and women. Be that as it may, I want you to imagine me writing a novel in a state of trance. I want you to figure to yourselves a girl sitting with a pen in her hand, which for minutes, and indeed for hours, she never dips into the inkpot. The image that comes to my mind when I think of this girl is the image of a fisherman lying sunk in dreams on the verge of a deep lake with a rod held out over the water. She was letting her imagination sweep unchecked round every rock and cranny of the world that lies submerged in the depths of our unconscious being. Now came the experience, the experience that I believe to be far commoner with women writers than with men. The line raced through the girl's fingers. Her imagination had rushed away. It had sought the pools, and depths, the dark places where the largest fish slumber. And then there was a smash. There was an explosion. There was foam and confusion. The imagination had dashed itself against something hard. The girl was roused from her dream. She was indeed in a state of the most acute and difficult distress. To speak without figure she had thought of something, something about the body, about the passions which it was unfitting for her as a woman to say. Men, her reason told her, would be shocked. The consciousness of what men will say of a woman who speaks the truth about her passions had roused her from her artist's state of unconsciousness. She could write no more. The trance was over. Her imagination could work no longer. This I believe to be a very common experience with women writers—they are impeded by the extreme conventionality of the other sex. For though men sensibly allow themselves great freedom in these respects, I doubt that they realize or can control the extreme severity with which they condemn such freedom in women.

These then were two very genuine experiences of my own. These were two of the adventures of my professional life. The first—killing the Angel in the House—I think I solved. She died. But the second, telling the truth about my own experiences as a body, I do not think I solved. I doubt that any woman has solved it yet. The obstacles against her are still immensely powerful— and yet they are very difficult to define. Outwardly, what is simpler than to write books? Outwardly, what obstacles are there for a woman rather than for a man? Inwardly, I think, the case is very different; she has still many ghosts to fight, many prejudices to overcome. Indeed it will be a long time still, I think, before a woman can sit down to write a book without finding a phantom to be slain, a rock to be dashed against. And if this is so in literature, the freest of all professions for women, how is it in the new professions which you are now for the first time entering?

Those are the questions that I should like, had I time, to ask you. And indeed, if I have laid stress upon these professional experiences of mine, it is because I believe that they are, though in different forms, yours also. Even when the path is nominally open—when there is nothing to prevent a woman from being a doctor, a lawyer, a civil servant—there are many phantoms and obstacles, as I believe, looming in her way. To discuss and define them is I think of great value and importance; for thus only can the labour be shared, the difficulties be solved. But besides this, it is necessary also to discuss the ends and the aims for which we are fighting, for which we are doing battle with these formidable obstacles. Those aims cannot be taken for granted; they must be perpetually questioned and examined. The whole position, as I see it—here in this hall surrounded by women practising for the first time in history I know not how many different professions— is one of extraordinary interest and importance. You have won rooms of your own in the house hitherto exclusively owned by men. You are able, though not without great labour and effort, to pay the rent. You are earning your five hundred pounds a year. But this freedom is only a beginning; the room is your own, but it is still bare. It has to be furnished; it has to be decorated; it has to be shared. How are you going to furnish it, how are you going to decorate it? With whom are you going to share it, and upon what terms? These, I think are questions of the utmost impor- tance and interest. For the first time in history you are able to ask them; for the first time you are able to decide for yourselves what the answers should be. Willingly would I stay and discuss those questions and answers—but not tonight. My time is up; and I must cease.

Modern Fiction

"Modern Fiction" is perhaps the best known of all Virginia Woolf's essays. It is a revision of an article under the title "Modern Novels," printed in the Times Literary Supplement in April 1919. The edited version here was published in 1925 in The Common Reader.

Virginia Woolf's argument in this essay is built on the materialistic preoccupations of novelists who see only the body and nothing of the mind. The novel of the future, so her assertion goes, must leave the external and move to the mysterious interior of human character. It must look inside the human mind on an ordinary day, and make those mental contents its subject. "Life is not a series of gig lamps symmetrically arranged; but a luminous halo, a semi-transparent envelope surrounding us from the beginning of consciousness to the end. Is it not the task of the novelist to convey this varying, this unknown and uncircumscribed spirit, whatever aberration or complexity it may display, with as little mixture of the alien and external as possible?" No passage in the critical canon has been more frequently quoted than this one, and we need only read Jacob's Room, Mrs. Dalloway, and To the Lighthouse to realize how thoroughly Virginia Woolf honored her own principle of modern fiction.

IN MAKING ANY SURVEY, EVEN THE FREEST AND loosest, of modern fiction it is difficult not to take it for granted that the modern practice of the art is somehow an improvement upon the old. With their simple tools and primitive materials, it might be said, Fielding did well and Jane Austen even better, but compare their opportunities with ours! Their masterpieces certainly have a strange air of simplicity. And yet the analogy between literature and the process, to choose an example, of making motor cars scarcely holds good beyond the first glance. It is doubtful whether in the course of the centuries, though we have learnt much about making machines, we have learnt anything about making literature. We do not come to write better; all that we can be said to do is to keep moving, now a little in this direction, now in that, but with a circular tendency should the whole course of the track be viewed from a sufficiently lofty pinnacle. It need scarcely be said that we make no claim to stand, even momentarily, upon that vantage ground. On the flat, in the crowd, half blind with dust, we look back with envy to those happier warriors, whose battle is won and whose achievements wear so serene an air of accomplishment that we can scarcely refrain from whispering that the fight was not so fierce for them as for us. It is for the historian of literature to decide; for him to say if we are now beginning or ending or standing in the middle of a great period of prose fiction, for down in the plain little is visible. We only know that certain gratitudes and hostilities inspire us; that certain paths seem to lead to fertile land, others to the dust and the desert; and of this perhaps it may be worth while to attempt some account.

Our quarrel, then, is not with the classics, and if we speak of quarrelling with Mr. Wells, Mr. Bennett, and Mr. Galsworthy it is partly that by the mere fact of their existence in the flesh their work has a living, breathing, every-day imperfection which bids us take what liberties with it we choose. But it is also true that, while we thank them for a thousand gifts, we reserve our unconditional gratitude for Mr. Hardy, for Mr. Conrad, and in a much lesser degree for the Mr. Hudson of *The Purple Land, Green Mansions,* and *Far Away and Long Ago.* Mr. Wells, Mr. Bennett, and Mr. Galsworthy have excited so many hopes and disappointed them so persistently that our gratitude largely takes the form of thanking them for having shown us what they might have done but have not done; what we certainly could not do, but as certainly, perhaps, do not wish to do. No single phrase will sum up the charge or grievance which we have to bring against a mass of work so large in its volume and embodying so many qualities, both admirable and the reverse. If we tried to formulate our meaning in one word we should say that these three writers are materialists. It is because they are concerned not with the spirit but with the body that they have disappointed us, and left us with the feeling that the sooner English fiction turns its back upon them, as politely as may be, and marches, if only into the desert, the better for its soul. Naturally, no single word reaches the centre of three separate targets. In the case of Mr. Wells it falls notably wide of the mark. And yet even with him it indicates to our thinking the fatal alloy in his genius, the great clod of clay that has got itself mixed up with the purity of his inspiration. But Mr. Bennett is perhaps the worst culprit of the three, inasmuch as he is by far the best workman. He can make a book so well constructed and solid in its craftsmanship that it is difficult for the most exacting of critics to see through what chink or crevice decay can creep in. There is not so much as a draught between the frames of the windows, or a crack in the boards. And yet—if life should refuse to live there? That is a risk which the creator of *The Old Wives' Tale,* George Cannon, Edwin Clayhanger, and hosts of other figures, may well claim to have surmounted. His characters live abundantly, even unexpectedly, but it remains to ask how do they live, and what do they live for? More and more they seem to us, deserting even the well-built villa in the Five Towns, to spend their time in some softly padded first-class railway carriage, pressing bells and buttons innumerable; and the destiny to which they travel so luxuriously becomes more and more unquestionably an eternity of bliss spent in the very best hotel in Brighton. It can scarcely be said of Mr. Wells that he is a materialist in the sense that he takes too much delight in the solidity of his fabric. His mind is too generous in its sympathies to allow him to spend much time in making things shipshape and substantial. He is a materialist from sheer goodness of heart, taking upon his shoulders the work that ought to have been discharged by Government officials, and in the plethora of his ideas and facts scarcely having leisure to realise, or forgetting to think important, the crudity and coarseness of his human beings. Yet what more damaging criticism can there be both of his earth and of his Heaven than that they are to be inhabited here and hereafter by his Joans and his Peters? Does not the inferiority of their natures tarnish whatever institutions and ideals may be provided for them by the generosity of their creator? Nor, profoundly though we respect the integrity and humanity of Mr. Galsworthy, shall we find what we seek in his pages.

If we fasten, then, one label on all these books, on which is one word, materialists, we mean by it that they write of unimportant things; that they spend immense skill and immense industry making the trivial and the transitory appear the true and the enduring.

We have to admit that we are exacting, and, further, that we find it difficult to justify our discontent by explaining what it is that we exact. We frame our question differently at different times. But it reappears most persistently as we drop the finished novel on the crest of a sigh— Is it worth while? What is the point of it all? Can it be that owing to one of those little deviations which the human spirit seems to make from time to time Mr. Bennett has come down with his magnificent apparatus for catching life just an inch or two on the wrong side? Life escapes; and perhaps without life nothing else is worth while. It is a confession of vagueness to have to make use of such a figure as this, but we scarcely better the matter by speaking, as critics are prone to do, of reality. Admitting the vagueness which afflicts all criticism of novels, let us hazard the opinion that for us at this moment the form of fiction most in vogue more often misses than secures the thing we seek. Whether we call it life or spirit, truth or reality, this, the essential thing, has moved off, or on, and refuses to be contained any longer in such ill-fitting vestments as we provide. Nevertheless, we go on perseveringly, conscientiously, constructing our two and thirty chapters after a design which more and more ceases to resemble the vision in our minds. So much of the enormous labour of proving the solidity, the likeness to life, of the story is not merely labour thrown away but labour misplaced to the extent of obscuring and blotting out the light of the conception. The writer seems constrained, not by his own free will but by some powerful and unscrupulous tyrant who has him in thrall to provide a plot, to provide comedy, tragedy, love, interest, and an air of probability embalming the whole so impeccable that if all his figures were to come to life they would find themselves dressed down to the last button of their coats in the fashion of the hour. The tyrant is obeyed; the novel is done to a turn. But sometimes, more and more often as time goes by, we suspect a momentary doubt, a spasm of rebellion, as the pages fill themselves in the customary way. Is life like this? Must novels be like this?

Look within and life, it seems, is very far from being "like this." Examine for a moment an ordinary mind on an ordinary day. The mind receives a myriad impressions—trivial, fantastic, evanescent, or engraved with the sharpness of steel. From all sides they come, an incessant shower of innumerable atoms; and as they fall, as they shape themselves into the life of Monday or Tuesday, the accent falls differently from of old; the moment of importance came not here but there; so that if a writer were a free man and not a slave, if he could write what he chose, not what he must, if he could base his work upon his own feeling and not upon convention, there would be no plot, no comedy, no tragedy, no love interest or catastrophe in the accepted style, and perhaps not a single button sewn on as the Bond Street tailors would have it. Life is not a series of gig lamps symmetrically arranged; but a luminous halo, a semi-transparent envelope surrounding us from the beginning of consciousness to the end. Is it not the task of the novelist to convey this varying, this unknown and uncircumscribed spirit, whatever aberration or complexity it may display, with as little mixture of the alien and external as possible? We are not pleading merely for courage and sincerity; we are suggesting that the proper stuff of fiction is a little other than custom would have us believe it.

It is, at any rate, in some such fashion as this that we seek to define the quality which distinguishes the work of several young writers, among whom Mr. James Joyce is the most notable, from that of their predecessors. They attempt to come closer to life, and to preserve more sincerely and exactly what interests and moves them, even if to do so they must discard most of the conventions which are commonly observed by the novelist. Let us record the atoms as they fall upon the mind in the order in which they fall, let us trace the pattern, however disconnected and incoherent in appearance, which each sight or incident scores upon the consciousness. Let us not take it for granted that life exists more fully in what is commonly thought big than in what is commonly thought small. Any one who has read *The Portrait of the Artist as a Young Man* or, what promises to be a far more interesting work, *Ulysses*, now appearing in the *Little Review*, will have hazarded some theory of this nature as to Mr. Joyce's intention. On our part, with such a fragment before us, it is hazarded rather than affirmed; but whatever the intention of the whole there can be no question but that it is of the utmost sincerity and that the result, difficult or unpleasant as we may judge it, is undeniably important. In contrast with those whom we have called materialists Mr. Joyce is spiritual; he is concerned at all costs to reveal the flickerings of that innermost flame which flashes its messages through the brain, and in order to preserve it he disregards with complete courage whatever seems to him adventitious, whether it be probability, or coherence or any other of these signposts which for generations have served to support the imagination of a reader when called upon to imagine what he can neither touch nor see. The scene in the cemetery, for instance, with its brilliancy, its sordidity, its incoherence, its sudden lightning flashes of significance, does undoubtedly come so close to the quick of the mind that, on a first reading at any rate, it is difficult not to acclaim a masterpiece. If we want life itself here, surely we have it. Indeed, we find ourselves fumbling rather awkwardly if we try to say what else we wish, and for what reason a work of such originality yet fails to compare, for we must take high examples, with *Youth* or *The Mayor of Casterbridge*. It fails because of the comparative poverty of the writer's mind, we might say simply and have done with it. But it is possible to press a little further and wonder whether we may not refer our sense of being in a bright yet narrow room, confined and shut in, rather than enlarged and set free, to some limitation imposed by the method as well as by the mind. Is it the method that inhibits the creative power? Is it due to the method that we feel neither jovial nor magnanimous, but centred in a self which, in spite of its tremor of susceptibility, never embraces or creates what is outside itself and beyond? Does the emphasis laid, perhaps didactically, upon indecency, contribute to the effect of something angular and isolated? Or is it merely that in any effort of such originality it is much easier, for contemporaries especially, to feel what it lacks than to name what it gives? In any case it is a mistake to stand outside examining "methods." Any method is right, every method is right, that expresses what we wish to express, if we are writers; that brings us closer to the novelist's intention if we are readers. This method has the merit of bringing us closer to what we were prepared to call life itself; did not the reading of *Ulysses* suggest how much of life is excluded or ignored, and did it not come with a shock to open *Tristram Shandy* or even *Pendennis* and be by them convinced that there are not only other aspects of life, but more important ones into the bargain.

However this may be, the problem before the novelist at present, as we suppose it to have been in the past, is to contrive means of being free to set down what he chooses. He has to have the courage to say that what interests him is no longer "this" but "that": out of "that" alone must he construct his work. For the moderns "that," the point of interest, lies very likely in the dark places of psychology. At once, therefore, the accent falls a little differently; the emphasis is upon something hitherto ignored; at once a different outline of form becomes necessary, difficult for us to grasp, incomprehensible to our predecessors. No one but a modern, perhaps no one but a Russian, would have felt the interest of the situation which Tchekov has made into the short story which he calls "Gusev." Some Russian soldiers lie ill on board a ship which is taking them back to Russia. We are given a few scraps of their talk and some of their thoughts; then one of them dies and is carried away; the talk goes on among the others for a time, until Gusev himself dies, and looking "like a carrot or a radish" is thrown overboard. The emphasis is laid upon such unexpected places that at first it seems as if there were no emphasis at all; and then, as the eyes accustom themselves to twilight and discern the shapes of things in a room we see how complete the story is, how profound, and how truly in obedience to his vision Tchekov has chosen this, that, and the other, and placed them together to compose something new. But it is impossible to say "this is comic," or "that is tragic," nor are we certain, since short stories, we have been taught, should be brief and conclusive, whether this, which is vague and inconclusive, should be called a short story at all.

The most elementary remarks upon modern English fiction can hardly avoid some mention of the Russian influence, and if the Russians are mentioned one runs the risk of feeling that to write of any fiction save theirs is waste of time. If we want understanding of the soul and heart where else shall we find it of comparable profundity? If we are sick of our own materialism the least considerable of their novelists has by right of birth a natural reverence for the human spirit. "Learn to make yourself akin to people. . . . But let this sympathy be not with the mind—for it is easy with the mind—but with the heart, with love towards them." In every great Russian writer we seem to discern the features of a saint, if sympathy for the sufferings of others, love towards them, endeavour to reach some goal worthy of the most exacting demands of the spirit constitute saintliness. It is the saint in them which confounds us with a feeling of our own irreligious triviality, and turns so many of our famous novels to tinsel and trickery. The conclusions of the Russian mind, thus comprehensive and compassionate, are inevitably, perhaps, of the utmost sadness. More accurately indeed we might speak of the inconclusiveness of the Russian mind. It is the sense that there is no answer, that if honestly examined life presents question after question which must be left to sound on and on after the story is over in hopeless interrogation that fills us with a deep, and finally it may be with a resentful, despair. They are right perhaps; unquestionably they see further than we do and without our gross impediments of vision. But perhaps we see something that escapes them, or why should this voice of protest mix itself with our gloom? The voice of protest is the voice of another and an ancient civilisation which seems to have bred in us the instinct to enjoy and fight rather than to suffer and understand. English fiction from Sterne to Meredith bears witness to our natural delight in humour and comedy, in the beauty of earth, in the activities of the intellect, and in the splendour of the body. But any deductions that we may draw from the comparison of two fictions so immeasurably far apart are futile save indeed as they flood us with a view of the infinite possibilities of the art and remind us that there is no limit to the horizon, and that nothing—no "method," no experiment, even of the wildest —is forbidden, but only falsity and pretence. "The proper stuff of fiction" does not exist; everything is the proper stuff of fiction, every feeling, every thought; every quality of brain and spirit is drawn upon; no perception comes amiss. And if we can imagine the art of fiction come alive and standing in our midst, she would undoubtedly bid us break her and bully her, as well as honour and love her, for so her youth is renewed and her sovereignty assured.

FROM

The
Diary of
Virginia
Woolf

Virginia Woolf's diary was the most private of her writing and was never meant for anyone's eyes but her own. She turned to its blank pages whenever she had a few spare minutes before lunch or after tea. The diary offered her a place to work off her nervous fidgets; sometimes it provided her with an empty page where she might unburden herself of some worry. At other times, it became a kind of exercise book in which she could practice certain stylistic turns of phrase or experiment with new subtleties of expression. Because she wrote in her diary with some regularity, its entries present collectively an intimate sense of the continuity and variety of her daily life—whether in London or in Rodmell—a series of engrossing reconstructions executed with unself-conscious originality and imaginative ease. That is to say, these dialogues with herself are entirely lacking in artistic strain, in the wish to perform, or in the need for applause. This absence is their singular distinction. She wrote at a "rapid haphazard gallop" that more often than not swept up the hidden "diamonds of the dustheap." More than once, Virginia Woolf considered the art of the daily chronicle: "I got out this diary, & read as one always does read one's own writing, with a kind of guilty intensity. I confess that the rough & random style of it, often so ungrammatical, & crying for a word altered, afflicted me somewhat. . . . I can write very much better; & take no time over this. . . . And now I may add my little compliment to the effect that it has a slapdash & vigour, & sometimes hits an unexpected bulls eye."

What strikes the reader almost at once in all of these entries is their verbal economy. Katherine Mansfield, T. S. Eliot, E. M. Forster spring to life and to utterance in a few seemingly random words. The same holds true in conveying an emotion: intensity results not from elaborate verbal adornment, but from its complete absence. The last words of The Waves have just been written "& I have been sitting these 15 minutes in a state of glory, & calm, & some tears, thinking of Thoby. . . ." There is a parting kiss for a friend on his deathbed, "But I must not cry, I thought, & so went." In a mood of melancholy, life seems "a little strip of pavement over an abyss." But these little frag-

ments serve to remind us that the diary was a secret, interior book. Across its pages, exhilaration and despair alternate. In every scene and in every season, however, we never forget that we are in the company of a powerful writer and an extraordinary woman.

Monday 25 January 1915

My birthday—& let me count up all the things I had. L[eonard]. had sworn he would give me nothing, & like a good wife, I believed him. But he crept into my bed, with a little parcel, which was a beautiful green purse. And he brought up breakfast, with a paper which announced a naval victory (we have sunk a German battle ship[1]) & a square brown parcel, with The Abbot in it—a lovely first edition—[2] So I had a very merry & pleasing morning—which indeed was only surpassed by the afternoon. I was then taken up to town, free of charge, & given a treat, first at a Picture Palace, & then at Buszards.[3] I don't think I've had a birthday treat for 10 years; & it felt like one too—being a fine frosty day, everything brisk & cheerful, as it should be, but never is. The Picture Palace was a little disappointing—as we never got to the War pictures, after waiting 1 hour & a half. But to make up, we exactly caught a non-stop train, & I have been very happy reading father on Pope, which is very witty & bright—without a single dead sentence in it.[4] In fact I dont know when I have enjoyed a birthday so much—not since I was a child anyhow. Sitting at tea we decided three things: in the first place to take Hogarth, if we can get it; in the second, to buy a Printing press; in the third to buy a Bull dog, probably called John. I am very much excited at the idea of all three—particularly the press. I was also given a packet of sweets to bring home.

Sunday 31 January 1915

O dear! We quarrelled almost all the morning! & it was a lovely morning, & now gone to Hades for ever, branded with the marks of our ill humour. Which began it? Which carried it on? God knows. This I will say: I explode: & L. smoulders. However, quite suddenly we made it up, (but the morning was wasted) & we walked after lunch in the Park, & came home by way of Hogarth, & tried to say that we shan't be much disappointed if we don't get it. Anyhow, it hasn't got the Green in front of it. After tea, as no one came (we've hardly seen anyone this week) I started reading The Wise Virgins, & I read it straight on till bedtime, when I finished it.[5] My opinion is that its a remarkable book; very bad in parts; first rate in others. A writer's book, I think, because only a writer perhaps can see why the good parts are so very good, & why the very bad parts aren't very bad. It seems to me to have the stuff of 20 Duke Jones' in it, although there are howlers which wd. make Miss Sidgwick turn grey.[6] I was made very happy by reading this: I like the poetic side of L. & it gets a little smothered in Blue-books, & organisations.

Wednesday 7 August 1918

Asheham diary drains off my meticulous observations of flowers, clouds, beetles & the price of eggs; &, being alone, there is no other event to record.[7] Our tragedy has been the squashing of a caterpillar; our excitement the return of the servants from Lewes last night, laden with all L.'s war books & the English review for me, with Brailsford upon a League of Nations, & Katherine Mansfield on Bliss. I threw down Bliss with the exclamation, "She's done for!" Indeed I dont see how much faith in her as woman or writer can survive that sort of story. I shall have to accept the fact, I'm afraid, that her mind is a very thin soil, laid an inch or two deep upon very barren rock. For Bliss is long enough to give her a chance of going deeper. Instead she is content with superficial smartness; & the whole conception is poor, cheap, not the vision, however imperfect, of an interesting mind. She writes badly too. And the effect was as I say, to give me an impression of her callousness & hardness as a human being. I shall read it again; but I dont suppose I shall change. She'll go on doing this sort of thing, perfectly to her & [John

Middleton] Murry's satisfaction.[8] I'm relieved now that they didn't come. Or is it absurd to read all this criticism of her personally into a story?

Friday 15 November 1918

I was interrupted somewhere on this page by the arrival of Mr [T. S.] Eliot. Mr Eliot is well expressed by his name—a polished, cultivated, elaborate young American, talking so slow, that each word seems to have special finish allotted it. But beneath the surface, it is fairly evident that he is very intellectual, intolerant, with strong views of his own, & a poetic creed. I'm sorry to say that this sets up Ezra Pound & Wyndham Lewis as great poets, or in the current phrase "very interesting" writers. He admires Mr Joyce immensely.[9] He produced 3 or 4 poems for us to look at—the fruit of two years, since he works all day in a Bank, & in his reasonable way thinks regular work good for people of nervous constitutions. I became more or less conscious of a very intricate & highly organised framework of poetic belief; owing to his caution, & his excessive care in the use of language we did not discover much about it. I think he believes in "living phrases" & their difference from dead ones; in writing with extreme care, in observing all syntax & grammar; & so making this new poetry flower on the stem of the oldest.

As an illustration of Eliot's views I may add what Desmond [MacCarthy] has just (Thursday 21st Nov.) told me; D. asked him how on earth he came to add that remark at the end of a poem on his Aunt & the Boston Evening Transcript that phrase about an infinitely long street, & "I like La Rochefoucauld saying good bye" (or words to that effect). Eliot replied that they were a recollection of Dante's Purgatorio![10]

Sunday (Easter) 20 April 1919

In the idleness which succeeds any long article, & Defoe is the 2nd leader this month, I got out this diary, & read as one always does read one's own writing, with a kind of guilty intensity. I confess that the rough & random style of it, often so ungrammatical, & crying for a word altered, afflicted me somewhat. I am trying to tell whichever self it is that reads this hereafter that I can write very much better; & take no time over this; & forbid her to let the eye of man behold it. And now I may add my little compliment to the effect that it has a slapdash & vigour, & sometimes hits an unexpected bulls eye. But what is more to the point is my belief that the habit of writing thus for my own eye only is good practise. It loosens the ligaments. Never mind the misses & the stumbles. Going at such a pace as I do I must make the most direct & instant shots at my object, & thus have to lay hands on words, choose them, & shoot them with no more pause than is needed to put my pen in the ink. I believe that during the past year I can trace some increase of ease in my professional writing which I attribute to my casual half hours after tea. Moreover there looms ahead of me the shadow of some kind of form which a diary might attain to. I might in the course of time learn what it is that one can make of this loose, drifting material of life; finding another use for it than the use I put it to, so much more consciously & scrupulously, in fiction. What sort of diary should I like mine to be? Something loose knit, & yet not slovenly, so elastic that it will embrace any thing, solemn, slight or beautiful that comes into my mind. I should like it to resemble some deep old desk, or capacious hold-all, in which one flings a mass of odds & ends without looking them through. I should like to come back, after a year or two, & find that the collection had sorted itself & refined itself & coalesced, as such deposits so mysteriously do, into a mould, transparent enough to reflect the light of our life, & yet steady, tranquil composed with the aloofness of a work of art. The main requisite, I think on re-reading my old volumes, is not to play the part of censor, but to write as the mood comes or of anything whatever; since I was curious to find how I went for things put in haphazard, & found the significance to lie where I never saw it at the time. But looseness quickly becomes slovenly. A little effort is needed to face a character or an incident which needs to be recorded.

Thursday 3 July 1919

. . . We own Monks House (this is almost the first time I've written a name which I hope to write many thousands of times before I've done with it) for ever. It happened thus. As we walked up the steep road from the station last Thursday on our way to inspect the Round House, we both read out a placard stuck on the auctioneers wall. Lot 1. Monks House, Rodmell. An old fashioned house standing in three quarters of an acre of land to be sold with possession. The sale we noted was on Tuesday; to take place at the White Hart.[11] "That would have suited us exactly" L. said as we passed, & I, loyal to the Round House, murmured something about the drawbacks of Rodmell, but suggested anyhow a visit to the place; & so we went on. I think a slight shade of anti-climax had succeeded my rather excessive optimism; at any rate the Round House no longer seemed so radiant & unattainable when we examined it as owners. I thought L. a little disappointed, though just & polite even to its merits. The day lacked sun. The bedrooms were very small. The garden not a country garden. Anyhow it seemed well to plan a visit to Rodmell on the following day. I bicycled over against a strong cold wind. This time I flatter myself that I kept my optimism in check. "These rooms are small, I said to myself; you must discount the value of that old chimney piece & the niches for holy water. Monks are nothing out of the way. The kitchen is distinctly bad. Theres an oil stove, & no grate. Nor is there hot water, nor a bath, & as for the E.C. I was never shown it." These prudent objections kept excitement at bay; yet even they were forced to yield place to a profound pleasure at the size & shape & fertility & wildness of the garden. There seemed an infinity of fruitbearing trees; the plums crow[d]ed so as to weigh the tip of the branch down; unexpected flowers sprouted among cabbages. There were well kept rows of peas, artichokes, potatoes; raspberry bushes had pale little pyramids of fruit; & I could fancy a very pleasant walk in the orchard under the apple trees, with the grey extinguisher of the church steeple pointing my boundary. On the other hand there is little view—O but I've forgotten the lawn smoothly rolled, & rising in a bank, sheltered from winds too, a refuge in cold & storm; & a large earthen pot holds sway where the path strikes off, crowned with a tuft of purple samphire. *One* pot; not two. There is little ceremony or precision at Monks House. It is an unpretending house, long & low, a house of many doors; on one side fronting the street of Rodmell, & wood boarded on that side, though the street of Rodmell is at our end little more than a cart track running out on to the flat of the water meadows. There are, if memory serves me, no less than three large outhouses of different kinds, & a stable; & a hen house—& the machinery of a granary, & one shed full of beams of ancient oak; & another stored with pea props; but our fruit & vegetables are said to flow over each summer into these receptacles, & to need selling; though so obliging in its prolific way as to flourish under the care of a single old man whose heart is of gold, & who, for 40 years I think, has spent his spare time in tending these trees for the late Mr Jacob Verrall[12]— All this made a happy kind of jumble in my brain, together with the store of old fashioned chairs & tables, glass & furniture with which every inch of room space is crowded; I came back & told my story as quietly as I could, & next day L. & I went together & made a thorough inspection. He was pleased beyond his expectation. The truth is he has the making of a fanatical lover of that garden. It suits me very well, too, to ramble off among the Telscombe downs, when fine; or tread out my paces up the path & across the lawn when dark or wind blown. In short, we decided walking home to buy if we could, & sell Round House, as we conjecture we can. Eight hundred we made our limit, which, according to Wycherley, gave us a good chance of possession. The sale was on Tuesday. I don't suppose many spaces of five minutes in the course of my life have been so close packed with sensation. Was I somehow waiting to hear the result, while I watched the process, of an operation? The room at the White Hart was crowded. I looked at every face, & in particular at every coat & skirt, for signs of opulence, & was cheered to discover none. But then, I thought, getting L. into line, does *he* look as if he had £800 in his pocket? Some of the substantial farmers might well have their rolls of notes stuffed inside their stockings. Bidding began. Someone offered £300. "Not an offer", said the auctioneer, who was immediately opposed to us as a smiling courteous antagonist, "a beginning." The next bid was £400. Then they rose by fifties. Wycherley standing by us, silent & unmoved, added his advance. Six hundred was reached too quick for me. Little hesitations interposed themselves, but went down rather dismally fast. The auctioneer egged us on. I daresay there were six voices speaking, though after £600, 4 of them dropped out, & left only a Mr Tattersall competing with Mr Wycherley. We were allowed to bid in twenties; then tens; then fives; & still short of £700, so that our eventual victory seemed certain. Seven hundred reached, there was a pause; the auctioneer raised his hammer, very slowly; held it up a considerable time; urged & exhorted all the while it slowly sank towards the table. "Now Mr Tattershall, another bid from you—no more bidding once I've struck the table—ten pounds? five pounds?—no more? for the last time then—*dump!*" & down it came on the table, to our thanksgiving—I purple in the cheeks, & L. trembling like a reed —"sold to Mr Wycherley." We stayed no longer.

Monday 31 May 1920

I had my interview with K[atherine]. M[ansfield]. on Friday. A steady discomposing formality & coldness at first. Enquiries about house & so on. No pleasure or excitement at seeing me. It struck me that she is of the cat kind: alien, composed, always solitary & observant. And then we talked about solitude, & I found her expressing my feelings, as I never heard them expressed. Whereupon we fell into step, & as usual, talked as easily as though 8 months were minutes—till Murry came in. . . . But Murry going at length, K. & I once more got upon literature. Question of her stories. This last one, Man without a T., is her first in the new manner. She says she's mastered something—is beginning to do what she wants. Prelude a coloured post card. Her reviews mere scribbling without a serious thought in them.

And Sullivan's praise in the A[*thenaeum*]. detestable to her.[13]
A queer effect she produces of someone apart, entirely self-
centred; altogether concentrated upon her 'art': almost fierce
to me about it, I pretending I couldn't write. "What else is there
to do? We have got to do it. Life——" then how she tells herself
stories at night about all the lives in a town. "Its a spring night. I
go down to the docks—I hear the travellers say—" acting it in
her usual way, & improvising. Then asked me to write stories for
the A. "But I don't know that I can write stories" I said, honestly enough, thinking that in her view, after her review of me,
anyhow, those were her secret sentiments. Whereupon she turned
on me, & said no one else could write stories except me—Kew
[Gardens] the right 'gesture'; a turning point— Well but Night &
Day? I said, though I hadn't meant to speak of it.

'An amazing achievement' she said. Why, we've not had such
a thing since I don't know when—,

But I thought you didn't like it?[14]

Then she said she could pass an examination in it. Would I
come & talk about it—lunch—so I'm going to lunch; but what
does her reviewing mean then?—or is she emotional with me?
Anyhow, once more as keenly as ever I feel a common certain
understanding between us—a queer sense of being 'like'—not
only about literature—& I think it's independent of gratified
vanity. I can talk straight out to her.

Monday 25 October (first day of winter time) 1920

Why is life so tragic; so like a little strip of pavement over an
abyss. I look down; I feel giddy; I wonder how I am ever to walk
to the end. But why do I feel this? Now that I say it I don't feel
it. The fire burns; we are going to hear the Beggars Opera.[15]
Only it lies about me; I can't keep my eyes shut. It's a feeling of
impotence: of cutting no ice. Here I sit at Richmond, & like a
lantern stood in the middle of a field my light goes up in darkness. Melancholy diminishes as I write. Why then don't I write it
down oftener? Well, one's vanity forbids. I want to appear a
success even to myself. Yet I dont get to the bottom of it. Its

having no children, living away from friends, failing to write well, spending too much on food, growing old— I think too much of whys & wherefores: too much of myself. I dont like time to flap round me. Well then, work. Yes, but I so soon tire of work—can't read more than a little, an hour's writing is enough for me. Out here no one comes in to waste time pleasantly. If they do, I'm cross. The labour of going to London is too great. Nessa's children grow up, & I cant have them in to tea, or go to the Zoo. Pocket money doesn't allow of much. Yet I'm persuaded that these are trivial things: its life itself, I think sometimes, for us in our generation so tragic—no newspaper placard without its shriek of agony from some one.

Monday 12 September 1921

I have finished the Wings of the Dove, & make this comment. His [Henry James's] manipulations become so elaborate towards the end that instead of feeling the artist you merely feel the man who is posing the subject. And then I think he loses the power to feel the crisis. He becomes merely excessively ingenious. This, you seem to hear him saying, is the way to do it. Now just when you expect a crisis, the true artist evades it. Never do the thing, & it will be all the more impressive. Finally, after all this juggling & arranging of silk pocket handkerchiefs, one ceases to have any feeling for the figure behind. Milly thus manipulated, disappears. He overreaches himself. And then one can never read it again. The mental grasp & stret[c]h are magnificent. Not a flabby or slack sentence, but much emasculated by this timidity or consciousness or whatever it is. Very highly American, I conjecture, in the determination to be highly bred, & the slight obtuseness as to what high breeding is.

Wednesday 16 August 1922

I should be reading Ulysses, & fabricating my case for & against. I have read 200 pages so far—not a third; & have been amused, stimulated, charmed interested by the first 2 or 3 chapters—to the end of the Cemetery scene; & then puzzled, bored, irritated, & disillusioned as by a queasy undergraduate scratching his pimples. And Tom [T. S. Eliot], great Tom, thinks this on a par with War & Peace! An illiterate, underbred book it seems to me: the book of a self taught working man, & we all know how distressing they are, how egotistic, insistent, raw, striking, & ultimately nauseating. When one can have the cooked flesh, why have the raw? But I think if you are anaemic, as Tom is, there is a glory in blood. Being fairly normal myself I am soon ready for the classics again. I may revise this later. I do not compromise my critical sagacity. I plant a stick in the ground to mark page 200.

Wednesday 6 September 1922

I finished Ulysses, & think it a mis-fire. Genius it has I think; but of the inferior water. The book is diffuse. It is brackish. It is pretentious. It is underbred, not only in the obvious sense, but in the literary sense. A first rate writer, I mean, respects writing too much to be tricky; startling; doing stunts. I'm reminded all the time of some callow board school boy, say like Henry Lamb, full of wits & powers, but so self-conscious & egotistical that he loses his head, becomes extravagant, mannered, uproarious, ill at ease, makes kindly people feel sorry for him, & stern ones merely annoyed; & one hopes he'll grow out of it; but as Joyce is 40 this scarcely seems likely. I have not read it carefully; & only once; & it is very obscure; so no doubt I have scamped the virtue of it more than is fair. I feel that myriads of tiny bullets pepper one & spatter one; but one does not get one deadly wound straight in the face—as from Tolstoy, for instance; but it is entirely absurd to compare him with Tolstoy.

Thursday 7 September 1922

Having written this, L. put into my hands a very intelligent review of Ulysses, in the American Nation;[16] which, for the first time, analyses the meaning; & certainly makes it very much more impressive than I judged. Still I think there is virtue & some lasting truth in first impressions; so I don't cancell mine. I must read some of the chapters again. Probably the final beauty of writing is never felt by contemporaries; but they ought, I think, to be bowled over; & this I was not. Then again, I had my back up on purpose; then again I was over stimulated by Tom's praises.

Tuesday 16 January 1923

Katherine has been dead a week, & how far am I obeying her "do not quite forget Katherine" which I read in one of her old letters?[17] Am I already forgetting her? It is strange to trace the progress of one's feelings. Nelly said in her sensational way at breakfast on Friday "Mrs Murry's dead! It says so in the paper!" At that one feels—what? A shock of relief?—a rival the less? Then confusion at feeling so little—then, gradually, blankness & disappointment; then a depression which I could not rouse myself from all that day. When I began to write, it seemed to me there was no point in writing. Katherine wont read it. Katherine's my rival no longer. More generously I felt, But though I can do this better than she could, where is she, who could do what I can't! Then, as usual with me, visual impressions kept coming & coming before me—always of Katherine putting on a white wreath, & leaving us, called away; made dignified, chosen. And then one pitied her. And one felt her reluctant to wear that wreath, which was an ice cold one. And she was only 33. And I could see her before me so exactly, & the room at Portland Villas. I go up. She gets up, very slowly, from her writing table. A glass of milk & a medicine bottle stood there. There were also piles of novels. Everything was very tidy, bright, & somehow like a dolls house. At once, or almost, we got out of shyness. She (it was summer) half lay on the sofa by the window. She had her look of a Japanese doll, with the fringe combed quite straight across her forehead. Sometimes we looked very steadfastly at each other, as though we had reached some durable relationship, independent of the changes of the body, through the eyes. Hers were beautiful eyes—rather doglike, brown, very wide apart, with a steady slow rather faithful & sad expression. Her nose was sharp, & a little vulgar. Her lips thin & hard. She wore short

skirts & liked "to have a line round her" she said. She looked
very ill—very drawn, & moved languidly, drawing herself across
the room, like some suffering animal. I suppose I have written
down some of the things we said. Most days I think we reached
that kind of certainty, in talk about books, or rather about our
writings, which I thought had something durable about it. And
then she was inscrutable. Did she care for me? Sometimes she
would say so—would kiss me—would look at me as if (is this
sentiment?) her eyes would like always to be faithful. She would
promise never never to forget. That was what we said at the end
of our last talk. She said she would send me her diary to read, &
would write always. For our friendship was a real thing we said,
looking at each other quite straight. It would always go on whatever happened. What happened was, I suppose, faultfindings &
perhaps gossip. She never answered my letter.[18] Yet I still feel,
somehow that friendship persists. Still there are things about
writing I think of & want to tell Katherine. If I had been in Paris
& gone to her, she would have got up & in three minutes, we
should have been talking again. Only I could not take the step.
The surroundings—Murry & so on—& the small lies & treach-
eries, the perpetual playing & teasing, or whatever it was, cut
away much of the substance of friendship. One was too uncertain. And so one let it all go. Yet I certainly expected that we
should meet again next summer, & start fresh. And I was jealous
of her writing—the only writing I have ever been jealous of. This
made it harder to write to her; & I saw in it, perhaps from
jealousy, all the qualities I disliked in her.

Wednesday 9 January 1924

At this very moment, or fifteen minutes ago, to be precise, I
bought the ten years lease of 52 Tavistock Sqre London W.C.1
—I like writing Tavistock. Subject of course to the lease, & to
Providence, & to the unforeseen vagaries on the part of old Mrs
Simons, the house is ours: & the basement, & the billiard room,
with the rock garden on top, & the view of the square in front &
the desolated buildings behind, & Southampton Row, & the

whole of London—London thou art a jewel of jewels, & jasper of jocunditie[19]—music, talk, friendship, city views, books, publishing, something central & inexplicable, all this is now within my reach, as it hasn't been since August 1913, when we left Cliffords Inn, for a series of catastrophes which very nearly ended my life, & would, I'm vain enough to think, have ruined Leonard's.[20] So I ought to be grateful to Richmond & Hogarth, & indeed, whether its my invincible optimism or not, I am grateful. Nothing could have suited better all through those years when I was creeping about, like a rat struck on the head, & the aeroplanes were over London at night, & the streets dark, & no penny buns in the window. Moreover, nowhere else could we have started the Hogarth Press, whose very awkward beginning had rise in this very room, on this very green carpet. Here that strange offspring grew & throve; it ousted us from the dining room, which is now a dusty coffin; & crept all over the house.

Monday 5 May 1924

This is the 29th anniversary of mothers death. I think it happened early on a Sunday morning, & I looked out of the nursery window & saw old Dr Seton walking away with his hands behind his back, as if to say It is finished, & then the doves descending, to peck in the road, I suppose, with a fall & descent of infinite peace. I was 13, & could fill a whole page & more with my impressions of that day, many of them ill received by me, & hidden from the grown ups, but very memorable on that account: how I laughed, for instance, behind the hand which was meant to hide my tears; & through the fingers saw the nurses sobbing.[21]

Saturday 5 July 1924

Just back, not from the 1917 Club; but from Knole, where indeed I was invited to lunch alone with his Lordship.[22] His lordship lives in the kernel of a vast nut. You perambulate miles of galleries; skip endless treasures—chairs that Shakespeare

might have sat on—tapestries, pictures, floors made of the halves
of oaks; & penetrate at length to a round shiny table with a cover
laid for one. A dozen glasses form a circle each with a red rose
in it. What can one human being do to decorate itself in such a
setting? One feels that one ought to be an elephant able to con-
sume flocks & be hung about with whole blossoming trees—
whereas one solitary peer sits lunching by himself in the centre,
with his napkin folded into the shape of a lotus flower. Obviously, I did not keep my human values & my aesthetic values
distinct. Knole is a conglomeration of buildings half as big as
Cambridge I daresay; if you stuck Trinity Clare & King's together you might approximate. But the extremities & indeed the
inward parts are gone dead. Ropes fence off half the rooms; the
chairs & the pictures look preserved; life has left them. Not for a
hundred years have the retainers sat down to dinner in the great
hall. Then there is Mary Stuart's altar, where she prayed before
execution. "An ancestor of ours took her the death warrant" said
Vita.[23]

Monday 15 September 1924

Here I am waiting for L. to come back from London, & at this
hour, having been wounded last year when he was late, I always
feel the old wound twingeing. He has been seeing Nancy Cunard,
so I expect a fair gossip. Vita was here for Sunday, gliding down
the village in her large new blue Austin car, which she manages
consummately. She was dressed in ringed yellow jersey, & large
hat, & had a dressing case all full of silver & night gowns wrapped
in tissue. Nelly said "If only she weren't an honourable!" &
couldn't take her hot water. But I like her being honourable,
& she is it; a perfect lady, with all the dash & courage of the
aristocracy, & less of its childishness than I expected. She left
with us a story which really interests me rather.[24] I see my own
face in it, its true. But she has shed the old verbiage, & come to
terms with some sort of glimmer of art; so I think; & indeed, I
rather marvel at her skill, & sensibility; for is she not mother,
wife, great lady, hostess, as well as scribbling? How little I do of

all that: my brain would never let me milk it to the tune of 20,000 words in a fortnight, & so I must lack some central vigour, I imagine. Here I am, peering across Vita at my blessed Mrs Dalloway; & can't stop, of a night, thinking of the next scene, & how I'm to wind up. Vita, to attempt a return, is like an over ripe grape in features, moustached, pouting, will be a little heavy; meanwhile, she strides on fine legs, in a well cut skirt, & though embarrassing at breakfast, has a manly good sense & simplicity about her which both L. & I find satisfactory. Oh yes, I like her; could tack her on to my equipage for all time; & suppose if life allowed, this might be a friendship of a sort.

Friday 17 October 1924

It is disgraceful. I did run up stairs thinking I'd make time to enter that astounding fact—the last words of the last page of Mrs Dalloway; but was interrupted. Anyhow I did them a week ago yesterday. "For there she was." & I felt glad to be quit of it, for it has been a strain the last weeks, yet fresher in the head; with less I mean of the usual feeling that I've shaved through, & just kept my feet on the tight rope. I feel indeed rather more fully relieved of my meaning than usual—whether this will stand when I re-read is doubtful. But in some ways this book is a feat; finished without break from illness, wh. is an exception; & written really, in one year. . . .

The thought of Katherine Mansfield comes to me—as usual rather reprehensibly—first wishing she could see Southampton Row, thinking of the dulness of her death, lying there at Fontainebleau—an end where there was no end, & then thinking yes, if she'd lived, she'd have written on, & people would have seen that I was the more gifted—that wd. only have become more & more apparent. Indeed, so I suppose it would. I think of her in this way off & on—that strange ghost, with the eyes far apart, & the drawn mouth, dragging herself across her room. And Murry married again to a woman who spends an hour in the W.C. & so the Anreps have turned them out.[25] Murry whines publicly for a flat in the Adelphi. That's a sordid page of my life by the way,

Murry. But I stick to it; K. & I had our relationship; & never again shall I have one like it.

Wednesday 8 April 1925

Since I wrote, which is these last months, Jacques Raverat has died; after longing to die; & he sent me a letter about Mrs Dalloway which gave me one of the happiest days of my life.[26] I wonder if this time I have achieved something? . . . Jacques died, as I say; & at once the siege of emotions began. I got the news with a party here. . . . Nevertheless, I do not any longer feel inclined to doff the cap to death. I like to go out of the room talking, with an unfinished casual sentence on my lips. That is the effect it had on me—no leavetakings, no submission—but someone stepping out into the darkness. For her [Gwen Raverat] though the nightmare was terrific. All I can do now is to keep natural with her, which is I believe a matter of considerable importance. More & more do I repeat my own version of Montaigne "Its life that matters".[27]

Thursday 14 May 1925

. . . I'm now all on the strain with desire to stop journalism & get on to *To the Lighthouse*. This is going to be fairly short: to have father's character done complete in it; & mothers; & St Ives; & childhood; & all the usual things I try to put in—life, death &c. But the centre is father's character, sitting in a boat, reciting We perished, each alone, while he crushes a dying mackerel—However, I must refrain.[28] I must write a few little stories first, & let the Lighthouse simmer, adding to it between tea & dinner till it is complete for writing out.

Monday 20 July 1925

I should consider my work list now. I think a little story, perhaps a review, this fortnight; having a superstitious wish to begin To the Lighthouse the first day at Monks House. I now think I shall finish it in the two months there. The word 'sentimental' sticks in my gizzard (I'll write it out of me in a story—

Ann Watkins of New York is coming on Wednesday to enquire about my stories).[29] But this theme may be sentimental; father & mother & child in the garden: the death; the sail to the lighthouse. I think, though, that when I begin it I shall enrich it in all sorts of ways; thicken it; give it branches & roots which I do not perceive now. It might contain all characters boiled down; & childhood; & then this impersonal thing, which I'm dared to do by my friends, the flight of time, & the consequent break of unity in my design. That passage (I conceive the book in 3 parts: 1. at the drawing room window; 2. seven years passed; 3. the voyage:) interests me very much. A new problem like that breaks fresh ground in ones mind; prevents the regular ruts.

What shall I read at Rodmell? I have so many books at the back of my mind. I want to read voraciously & gather material for the Lives of the Obscure—which is to tell the whole history of England in one obscure life after another. Proust I should like to finish. Stendhal, & then to skirmish about hither & thither. These 8 weeks at Rodmell always seem capable of holding an infinite amount.

Monday 21 December 1925

But no Vita! But Vita for 3 days at Long Barn, from which L. & I returned yesterday.[30] These Sapphists *love* women; friendship is never untinged with amorosity. In short, my fears & refrainings, my 'impertinence' my usual self-consciousness in intercourse with people who mayn't want me & so on—were all, as L. said, sheer fudge; &, partly thanks to him (he made me write) I wound up this wounded & stricken year in great style. I like her & being with her, & the splendour—she shines in the grocers shop in Sevenoaks with a candle lit radiance, stalking on legs like beech trees, pink glowing, grape clustered, pearl hung. That is the secret of her glamour, I suppose. Anyhow she found me incredibly dowdy, no woman cared less for personal appearance—no one put on things in the way I did. Yet so beautiful, &c. What is the effect of all this on me? Very mixed. There is her maturity & full breastedness: her being so much in full sail on the high tides, where I am coasting down backwaters; her capacity I mean to take the floor in any company, to represent her country, to visit Chatsworth, to control silver, servants, chow dogs; her motherhood (but she is a little cold & offhand with her boys[31]) her being in short (what I have never been) a real woman. Then there is some voluptuousness about her; the grapes are ripe; & not reflective. No. In brain & insight she is not as highly organised as I am. But then she is aware of this, & so lavishes on me the maternal protection which, for some reason, is what I have always most wished from everyone. What L. gives me, & Nessa gives me, & Vita, in her more clumsy external way, tries to give me. For of course, mingled with all this glamour, grape clusters & pearl necklaces, there is something loose fitting. How much, for example, shall I really miss her when she is motoring across the desert? I will make a note on that next year. Anyhow, I am very glad that she is coming to tea today, & I shall ask her, whether she minds my dressing so badly? I think she does. I read her poem; which is more compact, better seen & felt than anything yet of hers.[32]

Saturday 20 *March* 1926

But what is to become of all these diaries, I asked myself yesterday. If I died, what would Leo make of them? He would be disinclined to burn them; he could not publish them. Well, he should make up a book from them, I think; & then burn the body. I daresay there is a little book in them: if the scraps & scratches were straightened out a little. God knows.

This is dictated by a slight melancholia, which comes upon me sometimes now, & makes me think I am old: I am ugly. I am repeating things. Yet, as far as I know, as a writer I am only now writing out my mind.

Sunday 18 *April* 1926

Yesterday I finished the first part of To the Lighthouse, & today began the second. I cannot make it out—here is the most difficult abstract piece of writing—I have to give an empty house, no people's characters, the passage of time, all eyeless & featureless with nothing to cling to: well, I rush at it, & at once scatter out two pages. Is it nonsense, is it brilliance? Why am I so flown with words, & apparently free to do exactly what I like? When I read a bit it seems spirited too; needs compressing, but not much else. Compare this dashing fluency with the excruciating hard wrung battles I had with Mrs Dalloway (save the end). This is not made up: it is the literal fact. Yes, & I am rather famous.

Tuesday 23 November 1926

. . . Fame grows. Chances of meeting this person, doing that thing, accumulate. Life is as I've said since I was 10, awfully interesting—if anything, quicker, keener at 44 than 24—more desperate I suppose, as the river shoots to Niagara—my new vision of death; active, positive, like all the rest, exciting; & of great importance—as an experience.

'The one experience I shall never describe' I said to Vita yesterday. She was sitting on the floor in her velvet jacket & red striped silk shirt, I knotting her pearls into heaps of great lustrous eggs. She had come up to see me—so we go on—a spirited, creditable affair, I think, innocent (spiritually) & all gain, I think; rather a bore for Leonard, but not enough to worry him. The truth is one has room for a good many relationships.

Wednesday 10 August 1927

. . . Various little improvements in the house keep me on the thrill with hope & despair. Shall I lavish £5 that will be mine on a new spare bed?—alas, I fear I must; then the great & distasteful operations of furnishing will be over, & next year I shall add ornament & comfort. Perhaps if I make an extra sum we might build a bed sitting room for me in the attic, enlarge L.'s study, & so have a desirable, roomy, light house. For if we had £300 every year to spend, it is difficult to think of anything, except this, travel, & pocket money, to spend it on. Here at the age of 45 are Nessa & I growing little wings again after our lean years.

She may rake in another £500; perhaps more.[33] Already she has bought a roll of linoleum & a cupboard. But my state is precarious. With The Lighthouse I may just have climbed to the top of my hill; or again we may wobble back; my journalism may pall on the Americans: no rich father in law will endow me; but Heavens knows, I have not much anxiety. We are flexible, adventurous still I hope.

Wednesday 5 October 1927

If my pen allowed, I should now try to make out a work table, having done my last article for the Tribune, & now being free again. And instantly the usual exciting devices enter my mind: a biography beginning in the year 1500 & continuing to the present day, called Orlando: Vita; only with a change about from one sex to another. I think, for a treat, I shall let myself dash this in for a week. . . .

Saturday 22 October 1927

"I shall let myself dash this in for a week"—I have done nothing, nothing, nothing else for a fortnight; & am launched somewhat furtively but with all the more passion upon Orlando: A Biography. It is to be a small book, & written by Christmas. I thought I could combine it with *Fiction,* but once the mind gets hot it cant stop; I walk making up phrases; sit, contriving scenes; am in short in the thick of the greatest rapture known to me; from which I have kept myself since last February, or earlier. Talk of planning a book, or waiting for an idea! . . . I had very little idea what the story was to be about. But the relief of turning my mind that way about was such that I felt happier than for months; as if put in the sun, or laid on cushions; & after two days entirely gave up my time chart & abandoned myself to the pure delight of this farce: which I enjoy as much as I've ever enjoyed anything; & have written myself into half a headache & had to come to a halt, like a tired horse, & take a little sleeping draught last night: which made our breakfast fiery. I did not finish my egg. I am writing Orlando half in a mock style very clear & plain, so that people will understand every word. But the balance between truth & fantasy must be careful. It is based on Vita, Violet Trefusis, Lord Lascelles, Knole &c.[34]

Tuesday 20 December 1927

This flashed to my mind at Nessa's children's party last night. The little creatures acting moved my infinitely sentimental throat. Angelica so mature, & composed; all grey & silver; such an epitome of all womanliness; & such an unopened bud of sense & sensibility; wearing a grey wig & a sea coloured dress. And yet oddly enough I scarcely want children of my own now. This insatiable desire to write something before I die, this ravaging sense of the shortness & feverishness of life, make me cling, like a man on a rock, to my one anchor. I don't like the physicalness of having children of one's own. This occurred to me at Rodmell; but I never wrote it down. I can dramatise myself as parent, it is true. And perhaps I have killed the feeling instinctively; as perhaps nature does.

Friday 4 May 1928

The prize was an affair of dull stupid horror: a function; not alarming; stupefying. Hugh Walpole saying how much he disliked my books; rather, how much he feared for his own. Little Miss Robins, like a red breast, creeping out.[35] I remember your mother—the most beautiful Madonna & at the same time the most complete woman of the world. Used to come & see me in my flat (I see this as a summer visit on a hot day). She never confided. She would suddenly say something so unexpected, from that Madonna face, one thought it *vicious*. This I enjoyed: nothing else made much impression. Afterwards there was the horror of having looked ugly in cheap black clothes. I cannot control this complex. I wake at dawn with a start. Also the 'fame' is becoming vulgar & a nuisance. It means nothing; & yet takes one's time.

Friday 31 August 1928

Morgan [E. M. Forster] was here for the week end; timid, touchy, infinitely charming. One night we got drunk, & talked of sodomy, & sapphism, with emotion—so much so that next day he said he had been drunk. This was started by Radclyffe Hall & her meritorious dull book. They wrote articles for Hubert all day, & got up petitions; & then Morgan saw her & she screamed like a herring gull, mad with egotism & vanity. Unless they say her book is good, she wont let them complain of the laws. Morgan said that Dr Head can convert the sodomites.[36] "Would you like to be converted?" Leonard asked. "No" said Morgan, quite definitely. He said he thought Sapphism disgusting: partly from convention, partly because he disliked that women should be independent of men.

Wednesday 28 November 1928

1928

Father's birthday. He would have been $\frac{1832\ \ 96}{96}$, yes, today;

& could have been 96, like other people one has known; but mercifully was not. His life would have entirely ended mine. What would have happened? No writing, no books;—inconceivable. I used to think of him & mother daily; but writing The Lighthouse, laid them in my mind. And now he comes back sometimes, but differently. (I believe this to be true—that I was obsessed by them both, unhealthily; & writing of them was a necessary act.) He comes back now more as a contemporary. I must read him some day. I wonder if I can feel again, I hear his voice, I know this by heart?

Tuesday 18 December 1928

L. has just been in to consult about a 3rd edition of Orlando. This has been ordered; we have sold over 6000 copies; & sales are still amazingly brisk—150 today for instance; most days between 50 & 60; always to my surprise. Will they stop or go on? Anyhow my room is secure. For the first time since I married

1912—1928—16 years—I have been spending money. The spending muscle does not work naturally yet. I feel guilty; put off buying, when I know that I should buy; & yet have an agreeable luxurious sense of coins in my pocket beyond my weekly 13/- which was always running out, or being encroached upon. Yesterday I spent 15/- on a steel brooch. I spent £3 on a mother of pearl necklace—& I haven't bought a jewel for 20 years perhaps! I have carpeted the dining room—& so on. I think one's soul is the better for this lubrication; & I am going to spend freely, & then write, & so keep my brain on the boil. All this money making originated in a spasm of black despair one night at Rodmell 2 years ago. I was tossing up & down on those awful waves: when I said that I could find a way out. (For part of my misery was the perpetual limitation of everything; no chairs, or beds, no comfort, no beauty; & no freedom to move: all of which I determined there & then to win). And so came, with some argument, even tears one night (& how seldom I have ever cried!) to an agreement with Leonard about sharing money after a certain sum; & then opened a bank account; & now, at the lowest shall have £200 to put there on Jan. 1st. The important thing is to spend freely, without fuss or anxiety; & to trust to one's power of making more— Indeed, I cannot at this moment very seriously doubt that I shall earn more, this next 5 years, than ever before.

Wednesday 25 September 1929

But what interests me is of course my oil stove.[37] We found it here last night on coming back from Worthing. At this moment it is cooking my dinner in the glass dishes perfectly I hope, without smell, waste, or confusion: one turns handles, there is a thermometer. And so I see myself freer, more independent—& all one's life is a struggle for freedom—able to come down here with a chop in a bag & live on my own. I go over the dishes I shall cook—the rich stews, the sauces. The adventurous strange dishes with dashes of wine in them. Of course Leonard puts a drag on, & I must be very cautious, like a child, not to make too much noise playing. Nelly goes on Friday & so I shall [have] a whole week to experiment in—to become free in.

Friday 11 October 1929

And I snatch at the idea of writing here in order not to write Waves or Moths or whatever it is to be called. One thinks one has learnt to write quickly; & one hasn't. And what is odd, I'm not writing with gusto or pleasure: because of the concentration. I am not reeling it off; but sticking it down. Also, never, in my life, did I attack such a vague yet elaborate design; whenever I make a mark I have to think of its relation to a dozen others. And though I could go on ahead easily enough, I am always stopping to consider the whole effect. In particular is there some radical fault in my scheme? I am not quite satisfied with this method of picking out things in the room & being reminded by them of other things. Yet I cant at the moment devise anything which keeps so close to the original design & admits of movement.

Hence, perhaps, these October days are to me a little strained & surrounded with silence. What I mean by this last word I dont quite know, since I have never stopped 'seeing' people. . . . No; its not physical silence; its some inner loneliness—interesting to analyse if one could. To give an example—I was walking up Bedford Place is it—the straight street with all the boarding houses this afternoon, & I said to myself spontaneously, something like this. How I suffer, & no one knows how I suffer, walking up this street, engaged with my anguish, as I was after Thoby died—alone; fighting something alone. But then I had the devil to fight, & now nothing. And when I come indoors, it is all so silent—I am not carrying a great rush of wheels in my head— Yet I am writing—oh & we are very successful— & there is— what I most love—change ahead. Yes, that last evening at Rodmell when Leonard came down against his will to fetch me, the Keynes's came over. And Maynard is giving up the Nation, & so is Hubert, & so no doubt shall we.[38] And it is autumn; & the lights are going up; & Nessa is in Fitzroy Street—in a great misty room, with flaring gas & unsorted plates & glasses on the floor,—& the Press is booming—& this celebrity business is quite chronic—& I am richer than I have ever been—& bought a pair of earrings today—& for all this, there is vacancy & silence somewhere in the machine. On the whole, I do not much mind; because, what I like is to flash & dash from side to side, goaded on by what I call reality. If I never felt these extraordinarily pervasive strains—of unrest, or rest, or happiness, or discomfort —I should float down into acquiescence. Here is something to fight: & when I wake early I say to myself, Fight, fight. If I could catch the feeling, I would: the feeling of the singing of the real world, as one is driven by loneliness & silence from the habitable world; the sense that comes to me of being bound on an adventure; of being strangely free now, with money & so on, to do anything.

Saturday 7 February 1931

Here in the few minutes that remain, I must record, heaven be praised, the end of The Waves. I wrote the words O Death fifteen minutes ago, having reeled across the last ten pages with some moments of such intensity & intoxication that I seemed only to stumble after my own voice, or almost, after some sort of speaker (as when I was mad). I was almost afraid, remembering the voices that used to fly ahead. Anyhow it is done; & I have been sitting these 15 minutes in a state of glory, & calm, & some tears, thinking of Thoby & if I could write Julian Thoby Stephen, 1881–1906 on the first page. I suppose not. How physical the sense of triumph & relief is! Whether good or bad, its done; & as I certainly felt at the end, not merely finished, but rounded off, completed, the thing stated—how hastily, how fragmentarily I know; but I mean that I have netted that fin in the waste of waters which appeared to me over the marshes out of my window at Rodmell when I was coming to an end of To the Lighthouse.[39]

Friday 14 February 1931

Janet Case yesterday, shrivelled, narrowed, dimmed, aged, & very poverty struck. I noted her cheap shoes & dirty old velvet hat. I suppose over 70 now; & yet I always think of her as 45. She clings to youth. "But we never see any young people" & so reads Tom Eliot &c: has her wits about her: but oh dear, the pathos when our teachers become our learners. She has had I suppose a far harder life than I knew—illness, poverty, & all the narrowness of living; alone with Emphie; without any luxury, & the thought—I dont know about this—of leaving E. or being left. She was staying with an old man of 91. A curious clutching anxious sense such old age gives one: her face has become pointed, whitened; shrunk; her eyes remain. How I used to wait for her lesson: & then the arguments, the excitements. I was 17 she said when she came. She felt unsuccessful.[40]

Monday 5 October 1931

A note, to say I am all trembling with pleasure—cant go on with my Letter [to a Young Poet]—because Harold Nicolson has rung up to say The Waves is a masterpiece. Ah hah—so it wasn't all wasted then. I mean this vision I had here has some force upon other minds. Now for a cigarette, & then a return to sober composition.

Sunday 17 October 1931

. . . The unknown provincial reviewers say with almost one accord, here is Mrs. Woolf doing her best work; it cant be popular; but we respect her for so doing; & find The Waves positively exciting. I am in danger, indeed, of becoming our leading novelist, & not with the highbrows only.

Friday 22 January 1932

Much better was much weaker. Lytton[41] died yesterday morning.

I see him coming along the street, muffled up with his beard resting on his tie: how we should stop: his eyes glow. Now I am too numb with all the emotion yesterday to do more than think thoughts like this. Well, as I know, the pain will soon begin. One toys about with this & that. How queer it was last night at the party, the tightness round everyone's lips—ours I mean. Duncan Nessa[42] & I sobbing together in the studio—the man looking out of the mews window—a sensē of something spent, gone: that is to me so intolerable: the impoverishment: then the sudden vividness.

Sunday 31 January 1932

. . . I want to use these pages for dialogue for a time. Let me race down the subdued & dulled interview with my mother in law.[43] Oh the heat in that rose pink bed sitting room, with 3 fierce lights on, the tables crowded with flowers; & with cakes, a fire blazing. Mrs W. sitting upright with her feet on a stool on a high straight backed chair: more pink silk cushions behind her: pearl necklaces swinging. I came in late; she was talking about— I forget: had been talking about the girl whom Cecil might have loved: the daughter of a solicitor at Colchester: Oh yes: she had had influenza & gone to a house kept up by funds left by Mr Andrews. And she was reluctant at first—a home you know. But when she got there what was her amazement? All gentlewomen: flowers everywhere; a cupboard with tonics & sweets to take after them; & Georgian silver on the dinner table; & a garden; & a saloon car to take them out; & grounds; & hot milk at eleven, or chocolate; & the wireless, & a page boy coming for orders; & gardeners. Everything you could wish & not a penny to pay for it! Thats so rare—charity that is really thoughtful; charity for educated women with nice feelings who have fallen on bad times. Well Virginia—& whats your news? Oh & there's Captain Steel: every Christmas he has a card from the Duke of Gloucester: & he now sells Hoovers for £2.10 a week. But what can one do, in these days? One must do what one can. And what is your news, Virginia? Exodus? Dont you know Exodus? I sometimes scold myself that I haven't read the Bible lately. Deuteronomy? Oh yes—thats about the building of the Temple. I dont say its all true; but what stories to tell children! I shall never forget telling Bella. Of course a first child is always a wonder child. She used to have her dinner with me when she was 2. And she said what a pity it was summer when Eve stole the apple. If it had been winter, there wouldn't have been an apple. And she said too: I know where gold comes from—that's in the ground: but where do picture frames come from? We had large gilt picture frames with family portraits in the dining room. (V.) Well why dont you write about your children? Oh no: I couldn't say all I think about them. And you're going so soon? But you haven't hardly come. And you'll dine with me next week? She came down to the hall, & was I think going into the lounge to talk to some flushed women playing cards.

Monday 29 February 1932

And this morning I opened a letter; & it was from 'yours very sincerely J. J. Thompson'—the Master of Trinity; & it was to say that the council have decided to ask me to deliver the <Ford> Clark Lectures next year. Six of them.[44] This, I suppose, is the first time a woman has been asked; & so it is a great honour—think of me, the uneducated child reading books in my room at 22 H.P.G.—now advanced to this glory. But I shall refuse: because how. could I write 6 lectures, to be delivered in full term, without giving up a year to criticism; without becoming a functionary; without sealing my lips when it comes to tilting at Universities; without putting off my Knock at the Door; without perhaps shelving another novel. But I am rather inclined to smile as I lunch with Miss Dodge today, & she gives me a book with Donne's autograph; as I buy a pair of shoes at Babers;[45] as I sit down dutifully to correct an article for the Common Reader. Yes; all that reading, I say, has borne this odd fruit. And I am pleased; & still more pleased that I wont do it; & like to think that father would have blushed with pleasure could I have told him 30 years ago, that his daughter—my poor little Ginny—was to be asked to succeed him: the sort of compliment he would have liked.

Wednesday 2 November 1932

. . . And I have entirely remodelled my 'Essay'. Its to be an Essay-Novel, called the Pargiters—& its to take in everything, sex, education, life &c; & come, with the most powerful & agile leaps, like a chamois across precipices from 1880 to here & now—Thats the notion anyhow, & I have been in such a haze & dream & intoxication, declaiming phrases, seeing scenes, as I walk up Southampton Row that I can hardly say I have been alive at all, since the 10th Oct. Everything is running of its own accord into the stream, as with Orlando. What has happened of course is that after abstaining from the novel of fact all these years—since 1919—& N[ight]. & D[ay]. indeed, I find myself infinitely delighting in facts for a change, & in possession of quantities beyond counting: though I feel now & then the tug to vision, but resist it. This is the true line, I am sure, after The Waves—The Pargiters—this is what leads naturally on to the next stage—the essay-novel.

Saturday 2 September 1933

I am reading with extreme greed a book by Vera Britain, called The Testament of Youth.[46] Not that I much like her. A stringy metallic mind, with I suppose, the sort of taste I should dislike in real life. But her story, told in detail, without reserve, of the war, & how she lost lover & brother, & dabbled her hands in entrails, & was forever seeing the dead, & eating scraps, & sitting five on one WC, runs rapidly, vividly across my eyes. A very good book of its sort. The new sort, the hard anguished sort, that the young write; that I could never write. Nor has anyone written that kind of book before. Why now? What urgency is there on them to stand bare in public? She feels that these facts must be made known, in order to help—what? herself partly I suppose. And she has the social conscience. I have still to read how she married the infinitely dreary Catlin & found beauty & triumph in poor, gaping Holtby. But I give her credit for having lit up a long passage to me at least.

Wednesday 12 September 1934

Roger died on Sunday.[47] I was walking with Clive on the terrace when Nessa came out. We sat on the seat there for a time. On Monday we went up with Nessa. Ha came. Nessa saw Helen [Anrep]. Tomorrow we go up, following some instinct, to the funeral. I feel dazed: very wooden. Women cry, L. says: but I dont know why I cry—mostly with Nessa. And I'm too stupid to write anything. My head all stiff. I think the poverty of life now is what comes to me. a thin blackish veil over everything. Hot weather. A wind blowing. The substance gone out of everything. I dont think this is exaggerated. It'll come back I suppose. Indeed I feel a great wish, now & then, to live more all over the place, to see people, to create, only for the time one cant make the effort.

Thursday 11 October 1934

Well: do I think I shall be among the English novelists after my death? I hardly ever think about it. Why then do I shrink from reading W[yndham]. L[ewis].? Why am I sensitive? I think vanity. I dislike the thought of being laughed at. of the glow of satisfaction that A B & C will get from hearing V.W. demolished: also it will strengthen further attacks. Perhaps I feel uncertain of my own gifts: but then, I know more about them than W.L.: & anyhow I intend to go on writing. What I shall do is craftily to gather the nature of the indictment from talk & reviews: &, in a year perhaps, when my book is out, I shall read it. Already I am feeling the calm that always comes to me with abuse: my back is against the wall: I am writing for the sake of writing: &c. & then there is the queer disreputable pleasure in being abused—in being a figure, in being a martyr. & so on.

Monday 11 March 1935

. . . My friendship with Vita is over. Not with a quarrel, not with a bang, but as ripe fruit falls. No I shant be coming to London before I go to Greece, she said. And then I got into the car. But her voice saying "Virginia?" outside the tower room was as enchanting as ever. Only then nothing happened. And she has grown very fat, very much the indolent county lady, run to seed, incurious now about books; has written no poetry; only kindles about dogs, flowers, & new buildings. S[issinghurs]t is to have a new wing; a new garden; a new wall. Well, its like cutting off a picture: there she hangs, in the fishmongers at Sevenoaks, all pink jersey & pearls; & thats an end of it.[48] And there is no bitterness, & no disillusion, only a certain emptiness.

Tuesday 9 April 1935

I met Morgan in the London Library yesterday & flew into a passion.

"Virginia, my dear" he said. I was pleased by that little affectionate familiar tag.

"Being a good boy & getting books on Bloomsbury?" I said.

"Yes. You listen. Is my book down?" he asked Mr Mannering.

"We were just posting it" said Mr M.

"And Virginia, you know I'm on the Co[mmi]ttee here" said Morgan. "And we've been discussing whether to allow ladies—

It came over me that they were going to put me on: & I was then to refuse: Oh but they do—I said. There was Mrs Green . . .

"Yes yes—there was Mrs Green. And Sir Leslie Stephen said, never again. She was so troublesome. And I said, havent ladies improved? But they were all quite determined. No no no, ladies are quite impossible. They wouldnt hear of it."[49]

See how my hand trembles. I was so angry (also very tired) standing. And I saw the whole slate smeared. I thought how perhaps M. had mentioned my name, & they had said no no no: ladies are impossible. And so I quieted down & said nothing & this morning in my bath I made up a phrase in my book on Being Despised which is to run—a friend of mine, who was offered. . . . . one of those prizes—for her sake the great exception was to be made—who was in short to be given an honour— I forget what— . . She said, And they actually thought I would take it. They were, on my honour, surprised, even at my very modified & humble rejection. You didnt tell them what you thought of them for daring to suggest that you should rub your nose in that pail of offal? I remarked. Not for a hundred years, she observed. And I will bring in M. Pattison:[50] & I will say sympathy uses the same force required to lay 700 bricks. And I will show how you cant sit on Ctees if you also pour out tea— that by the way Sir L.S. spent his evenings with widow Green; yes, these flares up are very good for my book: for they simmer & become transparent: & I see how I can transmute them into beautiful clear reasonable ironical prose. God damn Morgan for thinking I'd have taken that . . .

Saturday 20 *February* 1937

I turn my eyes away from the Press as I go upstairs, because there are all the Review Copies of The Years packed & packing. They go out next week: this is my last week end of comparative peace. What do I anticipate with such clammy coldness? I think chiefly that my friends wont mention it, will turn the conversation rather awkwardly. I think I anticipate considerable luke-warmness among the friendly reviewers—I suppose what I expect is that they'll say now Mrs W. has written a long book all about nothing—respectful tepidity; & a whoop of red Indian delight from the Grigs, who will joyfully & loudly announce that this is the long drawn twaddle of a prim prudist bourgeois mind, & say that now no one can take Mrs W. seriously again. But violence I shant so much mind. What I think I shall mind most is the awkwardness when I go, say to Tilton or Charleston, & they dont know what to say. And since we shant get away till June I must expect a very full exposure to this damp firework atmosphere. They will say its a tired book; a last effort . . . Well, now that I've written that down I feel that even so I can exist in that shadow. That is if I keep hard at work. And there's no lack of that. . . . L. wants if possible to have 3 Gs. for the autumn: & I have my Gibbon, my broadcast, & a possible leader on Biography to fill in chinks.[51] I plan to keep out of literary circles till the mild boom is over. And this, waiting, under consideration is after all the worst. This time next month I shall feel more at ease. And its only now & then I mind now . .

Friday 2 April 1937

How I interest myself! Quite set up & perky today with a mind brimming, *because* I was so damnably depressed & smacked on the cheek by Edwin Muir in The Listener & by Scott James in the Life & Letters on Friday. They both gave me a smart snubbing: EM says The Years is dead & disappointing—so in effect did S. James. All the lights sank; my reed bent to the ground. Dead & disappointing—so I'm found out & that odious rice pudding of a book is what I thought it—a dank failure. No life in it. Much inferior to the bitter truth & intense originality of Miss Compton Burnett.[52] Now this pain woke me at 4 am. & I suffered acutely. All day driving to Janet & back I was under the cloud. But about 7 it lifted. There was a good review, of 4 lines, in The Empire review [*not traced*]. The best of my books: did that help? I dont think very much. But the delight of being exploded is quite real. One feels braced for some reason; amused; roused; combative; more than by praise. Of course I was pleased when L. said none of our friends read The Listener. Anyhow, my spirits rose, calm & steady; & I feel once more immune, set on my own feet, a fighter.

Friday 6 August 1937

Well but one must make a beginning. Its odd that I can hardly bring myself, with all my verbosity—the expression mania which is inborn in me—to say anything about Julian's death—I mean about that last 10 days in London. But one must get into the current again. That was a complete break; almost a blank; like a blow on the head: a shrivelling up. Going round to 8 [Fitzroy Street, Vanessa's studio] that night; & then all the other times, & sitting there. When Roger died I noticed; & blamed myself; yet it was a great relief I think. Here there was no relief. An incredible suffering—to watch it—an accident, & someone bleeding. Then I thought the death of a child is childbirth again; sitting there listening.

No no, I will not go back to those days. The only thing was a kind of comfort in being there with Nessa Duncan, Quentin & Angelica, & losing completely the isolation, the spectator's attitude in being wanted; & spontaneous. Then we came down here last Thursday; & the pressure being removed, one lived; but without much of a future. Thats one of the specific qualities of this death—how it brings close the immense vacancy, & our short little run into inanity. Now this is what I intend to combat. How? how make good what I protest, that I will not yield an inch or a fraction of an inch to nothingness, so long as something remains? Work of course. I plunged on Monday into Congreve, & have about done him this morning. And undoubtedly that sets the wheels running. Directly I am not working, or see the end in sight, then nothingness begins. I have to go over though every other day to Charleston. We sit in the studio door. It is very hot, happily. A hot bank holiday—a child killed at the top; aeroplanes droning. The thought of Julian changing so queerly, no so usually; now distant, now close; now of him there, in the flesh; now some physical encounter—kissing him surreptitiously; & so on. And then I had some relief when Tom rejected his essays, for I felt then I had not been merely spiteful, merely jealous.[53] But how it curtails the future: how it reduces ones vision to ones own life—save for Q. & Angelica. A curiously physical sense; as if one had been living in another body, which is removed, & all that living is ended. As usual, the remedy is to enter other lives, I suppose; & the old friction of the brain. . . .

Sunday 29 January 1939

Yes, Barcelona has fallen: Hitler speaks tomorrow; the next dress rehearsal begins: I have seen Marie Stopes, Princesse de Polignac, Philip & Pippin, & Dr Freud in the last 3 days. also had Tom to dinner & to the Stephens' party.[54]

Dr Freud gave me a narcissus. Was sitting in a great library with little statues at a large scrupulously tidy shiny table. We like patients on chairs. A screwed up shrunk very old man: with a monkeys light eyes, paralysed spasmodic movements, inarticulate: but alert. On Hitler. Generations before the poison will be worked out. About his books. Fame? I was infamous rather than famous. didnt make £50 by his first book. Difficult talk. An interview. Daughter & Martin helped. Immense potential, I mean an old fire now flickering. When we left he took up the stand What are *you* going to do? The English—war.

Wednesday 15 May 1940

An appeal last night for home defence—against parachutists. L. says he'll join.[55] An acid conversation. Our nerves are harassed—mine at least: L. evidently relieved by the chance of doing something. Gun & uniform to me slightly ridiculous. Behind that the strain: this morning we discussed suicide if Hitler lands. Jews beaten up. What point in waiting? Better shut the garage doors. This a sensible, rather matter of fact talk. . . . A thunderous hot day. Dutch laid down arms last night. The great battle now raging. Ten days, we say, will settle it. I guess we hold: then dig in; about Novr. the USA comes in as arbitrator. On the other hand—

Mabel just come. She says theyre building wooden bridges beside the others on the Thames. Pop-pop-pop, as we play bowls. Probably a raider over Eastbourne way. Now thunder rain sets in. . . . No, I dont want the garage to see the end of me. I've a wish for 10 years more, & to write my book wh. as usual darts into my brain. L. finished his yesterday.[56] So we've cleared up our book accounts—tho' its doubtful if we shall publish this June. Why am I optimistic? Or rather not either way? because its all bombast, this war. One old lady pinning on her cap has more reality. So if one dies, it'll be a common sense, dull end—not comparable to a days walk, & then an evening reading over the fire. Hospital trains go by. A hot day to be wounded. Anyhow, it cant last, this intensity—so we think—more than 10 days. A fateful book this. Still some blank pages—& what shall I write on the next 10?

This idea struck me: the army is the body: I am the brain. Thinking is my fighting.

Friday 16 August 1940

They came very close. We lay down under the tree. The sound was like someone sawing in the air just above us. We lay flat on our faces, hands behind head. Dont close yr teeth said L. They seemed to be sawing at something stationary. Bombs shook the windows of my lodge. Will it drop I asked? If so, we shall be broken together. I thought, I think, of nothingness— flatness, my mood being flat. Some fear I suppose. Shd we take Mabel to garage. Too risky to cross the garden L. said. Then another came from Newhaven. Hum & saw & buzz all round us. A horse neighed on the marsh. Very sultry. Is it thunder? I said. No guns, said L. from Ringmer, from Charleston way. Then slowly the sound lessened. Mabel in kitchen said the windows shook. Air raid still on, distant planes. Leslie playing bowls I well beaten.

My books only gave me pain, Ch Brontë said. Today I agree. Very heavy dull & damp. This must at once be cured. The all clear. 5 to 7. 144 down last night.[57]

Saturday 31 August 1940

Now we are in the war. England is being attacked. I got this feeling for the first time completely yesterday. The feeling of pressure, danger horror. Vita rang up at 6 to say she cdn't come. She was sitting at S[issinghurs]t. the bombs were falling round the house. Theyd been fighting all day. I'm too jaded to give the feeling—of talking to someone who might be killed any moment. Can you hear that? she said. No, I cdnt. Thats another. That's another. She repeated the same thing—about staying in order to drive the ambulance—time after time, like a person who cant think. She'd heard that Christopher Hobhouse was killed by a bomb: that Cynthia North—so lovely like a young colt she was killed by a bomb she trod on.[58] It was very difficult talking. She said it was a comfort to talk. She broke off—Oh how I do mind this, & put the telephone down. I went & played bowls. A perfect quiet hot evening. Later the planes began zooming. Explosions. . . . A great raid on London last night. Today quiet here. When I rang up St. after dinner, someone cut in with a call to Maldon. "Restricted service. Things very bad there just now." The feeling is that a battle is going on—a fierce battle. May last 4 weeks. Am I afraid? Intermittently. The worst of it ones mind wont work with a spring next morning. Of course this may be the beginning of invasion. A sense of pressure. Endless local stories. No—its no good trying to capture the feeling of England being in a battle.

Saturday 8 March 1941

Just back from L.'s speech at Brighton.[59] Like a foreign town: the first spring day. Women sitting on seats. A pretty hat in a teashop—how fashion revives the eye! And the shell en-crusted old women, rouged, decked, cad[a]verous at the tea shop. The waitress in checked cotton.

No: I intend no introspection. I mark Henry James's sen-tence: Observe perpetually. Observe the oncome of age. Observe greed. Observe my own despondency. By that means it becomes serviceable. Or so I hope.[60] I insist upon spending this time to the best advantage. I will go down with my colours flying. This I see verges on introspection; but doesn't quite fall in. Suppose, I bought a ticket at the Museum; biked in daily & read history. Suppose I selected one dominant figure in every age & wrote round & about. Occupation is essential. And now with some pleasure I find that its seven; & must cook dinner. Haddock & sausage meat. I think it is true that one gains a certain hold on sausage & haddock by writing them down.

NOTES

1. The German armoured cruiser *Blücher* was sunk, and their battle cruiser *Seydlitz* seriously damaged, at the Battle of the Dogger Bank on 14 January 1915; the British flagship *Lion* was damaged.
2. Sir Walter Scott's novel, published in three volumes in Edinburgh in 1820; inscribed 'V.W. from L.W. 25th Jan. 1915'.
3. Buszard's Tea Rooms, 197–201 Oxford Street.

4. Leslie Stephen wrote a biography of Pope (1880) for the 'English Men of Letters' series; and an essay, 'Pope as a Moralist' was included in his *Hours in a Library* (new edition, 1892).

5. LW's second novel, *The Wise Virgins, A Story of Words, Opinions, and a Few Emotions*. Completed in 1913, the book was not published until October 1914 owing to objections to certain passages by his publisher Edward Arnold. The book contains generally unsympathetic portraits based on LW himself, VW, and their families and friends; it was perhaps for this reason together with the state of her health that VW had not hitherto read the book.

6. Ethel Sidgwick, author of *Duke Jones, A Sequel to A Lady of Leisure*, 1914.

7. There are daily entries in the Asheham Diary from 31 July to 6 October inclusive, with the exception of four days, 9–12 September. They are written in the laconic style of those of the previous summer and deal of the matters VW here mentions.

8. The August number of the literary monthly *English Review* (edited by Austin Harrison) contained the first publication of Katherine Mansfield's *Bliss*, and the League of Nations' Prize Essay *Foundations of Internationalism* by H. N. Brailsford. Katherine Mansfield married John Middleton Murry, literary critic, editor, and author, in 1918.

9. Ezra Loomis Pound (1885–1972), the American-born but Europe-based poet, a supporter, both critically and materially, of the *avant-garde*, which included at this period Eliot himself, James Joyce, and Percy Wyndham Lewis (1882–1957), the writer and artist. Lewis's first novel *Tarr* had been published in July by The Egoist, Ltd., the firm started by Miss Harriet Weaver as an offshoot of her periodical *The Egoist* (of which Eliot was still assistant editor).

10. 'When evening quickens faintly in the street,
     Wakening the appetites of life in some
   And to others bringing the *Boston Evening Transcript*,
     I mount the steps and ring the bell, turning
   Wearily, as one would turn to nod good-bye to Rochefoucauld,
     If the street were time and he at the end of the street,
   And I say, "Cousin Harriet, here is the *Boston Evening Transcript*." '
   From *Prufrock and other Observations*, 1917. Faber, London, Harcourt Brace Jovanovich, New York.

11. The White Hart Hotel in High Street is a large inn facing the Law Courts in the centre of Lewes.

12. For the history of Monks House and its previous owners see LW's *Beginning Again*, Hogarth Press, 1964, pp. 61–64, and LW's *Downhill All the Way*, Hogarth Press, 1967, pp. 12–15.

13. Katherine Mansfield's *Prelude* had been hand-printed by the Woolfs and published in July 1918. Her story 'Je ne parle pas Français' was reviewed in the *Athenaeum* of 2 April 1920 by J. W. N. Sullivan under the heading 'The Story-Writing Genius', and compared to Chekhov and Dostoievsky.

14. Katherine Mansfield had reviewed *Night and Day* in the *Athenaeum* of 26 November 1919 (see *The Diary of Virginia Woolf*, ed. by Anne Olivier Bell, Hogarth Press, V. I, 1977, 28 November 1919). She had written of it to Murry (10 November 1919): 'I don't like it. My private opinion is that it is a lie in the soul.'

15. A musical play by John Gay, first produced in 1728 and revived with great success at the Lyric Theatre, Hammersmith, in 1920 by Giles Playfair.

16. The review by Gilbert Seldes appeared in the New York *Nation* of 30 August 1922. See *James Joyce, 1907–27* in the Critical Heritage Series, edited by Robert H. Deming, Routledge & Kegan Paul, 1970.

17. Katherine Mansfield died quickly on the night of 9 January 1923 following a haemorrhage; Murry was visiting her at the Gurdjieff Institute for the Harmonious Development of Man at Fontainebleau where she had been living since October. Copies of 30 of her letters to VW are in MHP: *Monks House Papers*, University of Sussex Library Catalogue, July 1972; the final sentence, omitted by Murry in his edition of his wife's letters (1928, vol. I, p 75), of one written in July 1917 reads: 'Do let us meet in the nearest future darling Virginia, and don't quite forget.'

18. See *The Letters of Virginia Woolf*, ed. by Nigel Nicolson, Hogarth Press, V. II, 1976, footnote to no. 1156, referring to a letter to Katherine Mansfield dated 13 February 1921 'not yet available for publication'. This would appear to be the letter also referred to by VW in writing to Dorothy Brett on 2 March 1923 (*VW Letters*, V. III, 1977, no. 1365): 'I must have written to her sometime in March 1921. . . . perhaps she never did get my letter. . . . Murry . . . said she was lonely and asked me to write. . . . It hurt me that she never answered.' As VW sat next to Murry at his 'farewell dinner' on 11 February 1921, her letter was probably the one dated 13 February, and she was mistaken in thinking she had written in March.

19.   'London, thou art the flour of cities all.

    Gemme of all joy, jaspre of jocunditie,

    Most myghty carbuncle of vertue and valour;'

In Honour of the City of London by William Dunbar (1465?–1530?)

20. VW refers to her breakdown and madness of the late summer, autumn and winter of 1913 in the course of which, on the evening of 9 September, she had tried to kill herself. See *II QB* [Quentin Bell, *Mrs Woolf*, V. II of *Virginia Woolf. A Biography*, Hogarth Press, 1972], pp 11–19. The Woolfs had taken rooms in Clifford's Inn, off the Strand, shortly after returning to London in October 1912 from their honeymoon.

21. Cf 'A Sketch of the Past' written fifteen years later (see *Moments of Being*, p 84). Dr David Elphinstone Seton (*c.* 1827–1917) MD Edin 1856, of Emperor's Gate, South Kensington, was the Stephens' family doctor until the death of Sir Leslie.

22. Vita Sackville-West (1892–1962) was a novelist and poet, thirteen of

whose books were published by the Hogarth Press. Lionel Edward Sackville-West, 3rd Baron Sackville (1867–1926), Vita's father, lived at Knole, one of the largest and finest baronial houses in England. Begun in 1456, it was greatly extended in the early seventeenth century by Thomas Sackville, 1st Earl of Dorset, to whom it was presented by his kinswoman, Queen Elizabeth. Vita's mother, the volatile half-Spanish Lady Sackville, had left Knole and her husband in 1919.

23. It had fallen to Thomas Sackville to deliver the death-warrant to Mary Queen of Scots on the eve of her execution at Fotheringay in 1586; in recognition of the delicacy with which he performed this painful duty, Mary presented him with a carved wooden triptych of saints and the procession to Calvary, which is still preserved in the chapel at Knole.

24. This was *Seducers in Ecuador* which the Hogarth Press published in November 1924.

25. Murry had been living in rooms in Boris Anrep's house in Pond Street, Hampstead. In the summer of 1924 after his second marriage he bought an old coastguard station in Dorset, but needed a London *pied-à-terre*— which he acquired in Chelsea.

26. Jacques Pierre Raverat (1885–1925), a Frenchman who had studied mathematics at Cambridge and was one of the group of friends called by VW the 'neo-Pagans', another of whom, the wood-engraver Gwendolen Mary Darwin (1885–1957), he married in 1911. They lived at Vence in the Alpes-Maritimes, and he became a painter. He had suffered for some years from a form of disseminated sclerosis, a paralysing disease, and his letters were dictated to his wife. About a month before his death on 7 March 1925, VW had sent him advance proofs of *Mrs Dalloway*, and he responded: 'Almost it's enough to make me want to live a little longer, to continue to receive such letters and such books . . . I am flattered & you know how important an element that is in one's sensations, and proud & pleased . . .' The correspondence between VW and Jacques and Gwen Raverat is preserved in MHP, Sussex.

27. See 'Montaigne' in *The Common Reader*, p 95: 'But enough of death; it is life that matters.' *The Common Reader* was published by the Hogarth Press on 23 April 1925 in an edition of 1250 copies.

28. From the last verse of William Cowper's poem, 'The Castaway':
> 'No voice divine the storm allay'd,
>> No light propitious shone,
> When, snatch'd from all effectual aid,
>> We perish'd, each alone:
> But I beneath a rougher sea,
>> And whelm'd in deeper gulfs than he.'

29. J. F. Holms wrote in the *Calendar of Modern Letters*, July 1925, that 'despite its pure and brilliant impressionism' *Mrs Dalloway* is 'sentimental in conception and texture, and is accordingly aesthetically worthless'. Ann Watkins was a New York literary agent.

30. VW went to stay with V. Sackville-West at Long Barn on 17 December; it was, according to Nigel Nicolson (*III VW Letters*, p 223), 'the be-

ginning of their love affair'. LW joined them on the afternoon of 19 December, and Vita motored them to London next day.

31. Vita's sons were (Lionel) Benedict (1914–1978) and Nigel (b. 1917) Nicolson.

32. V. Sackville-West's journey from Cairo to Persia in March 1926 is described in her *Passenger to Teheran*, published by the Hogarth Press in 1926 (*A Checklist of the Hogarth Press*, compiled by J. Howard Woolmer, 107); the final four days' travel, over high mountain passes and desert plains, was by Trans-Desert Mail car. Her poem was probably 'On the Lake' which appeared in the *Nation & Athenaeum* on 26 December 1925.

33. i.e. as a result of her father-in-law's death.

34. Violet Trefusis, *née* Keppel (1894–1972), with whom Vita, often disguised as a man, had had a passionate and dramatic love affair between 1918–21 (see Nigel Nicolson, *Portrait of a Marriage*, 1973). Henry, Viscount Lascelles (1882–1974), who married the Princess Royal in 1922 and was to succeed his father as 6th Earl of Harewood in 1929, had courted Vita before she engaged herself to Harold Nicolson in 1913. Sasha the Russian Princess and the Archduchess Harriet in *Orlando* were based upon what VW learned of these two from Vita.

35. The Femina-Vie Heureuse Prize (£40) was presented to VW at the Institut Français in South Kensington on 2 May by the popular novelist Hugh (Seymour) Walpole (1884–1941), whom she had once met at luncheon with Lady Colefax (see *VW Diary*, V. II, 1978, 16 November 1923); their picture appeared on the back page of the *Times* on 3 May. Elizabeth Robins (1862–1952), actress, author, and feminist, born in Louisville, Kentucky. In 1888 she had settled in London where, in the 'nineties, she pioneered and acted in productions of Ibsen's plays, financed by a subscription fund of which Gerald Duckworth had been treasurer (her *Ibsen and the Actress* (*HP Checklist* 174) was published in the Hogarth Essays series in October 1928). She gave up acting in 1902, but wrote a play *Votes for Women!* (1907), and was a prolific novelist.

36. *The Well of Loneliness*, a novel of Lesbian love by Radclyffe Hall (1886–1943), had been published in July by Jonathan Cape, who had withdrawn it in the face of outraged objections in the popular press and from the Home Secretary. E. M. Forster and LW were united in their opposition, on principle, to such suppression, and organised protests, which included a joint letter from Forster and VW published in the *N & A*, 8 September 1928. (See also P. N. Furbank, *E. M. Forster: A Life*, V. II (1978), pp 153–5.) Sir Henry Head (1861–1940; knighted 1927), FRS, neurologist. Roger Fry, who had a high opinion of him, had recommended that the Woolfs should consult him when VW was in a suicidal condition in 1913; and they did.

37. Cooking at Monks House had hitherto been done on a solid fuel range.

38. Since April 1923, when Maynard Keynes and his associates had acquired control of it, Hubert Henderson had edited the *N & A*; he was now leaving at the end of the year to take up an appointment as joint secre-

tary to the newly-formed Economic Advisory Council. Keynes, as chairman of the *N & A* board, was seeking an amalgamation with the *New Statesman*—which was eventually effected in 1931.

39. See *VW Diary*, V. III, 1980, 30 September 1926: 'Ones sees a fin passing far out. What image can I reach to convey what I mean? . . . All I mean to make is a note of a curious state of mind. I hazard the guess that it may be the impulse behind another book.'

40. Janet Elizabeth Case (1862–1937), Classical scholar, had taught VW Greek at the beginning of the century. She and her sister Euphemia ('Emphie') now lived in retirement at Minstead in the New Forest.

41. Lytton Strachey (1880–1932) was a critic and biographer, and a good friend of the Woolfs.

42. Duncan Grant and Vanessa Bell (VW's sister), both painters, lived and worked together until Vanessa's death in 1961. Their daughter, Angelica, was born in 1918.

43. The Woolfs went to tea with LW's mother on 30 January; her next-youngest son Cecil (1887–1917), who was killed at the Battle of Cambrai, had been stationed at Colchester early in the war. Bella (1877–1960), now Mrs Thomas Southorn, was the eldest of her eight surviving children.

44. Sir J. J. Thomson (1856–1940), OM, FRS, had been Master of Trinity College, Cambridge, since 1918. VW's father Leslie Stephen gave the first Clark lectures in 1883, taking 18th century literature as his subject.

45. Mary Dodge's present to VW was John Donne's copy, with his signature and notes, of the first edition (1605) of *Regales Disputationes Tres* by Alberico Gentilis; see lot 143 of Sotheby's sale of books, 27 July 1970. Charles H. Baber of Upper Regent Street were specialists in foot fitting.

46. *Testament of Youth* by Vera Brittain (1894–1970) was published in August 1933. In 1925 she married George Catlin (1879–1979), from 1924–35 Professor of Politics at Cornell University; he had been an Exhibitioner at New College, Oxford, and VW possibly met him there when staying with her cousin the Warden, H. A. L. Fisher. Until her marriage Vera Brittain shared a flat with Winifred Holtby, whom she had met on returning to Oxford after war service as a nurse, and about whom she wrote in *Testament of Friendship* (1940).

47. Roger Fry (1866–1934), art critic, painter, and close friend, died of heart failure on Sunday 9 September at the Royal Free Hospital, following a fall two days earlier at his home in Bernard Street.

48. Cf *III VW Diary*, 21 December 1925: '—she shines in the grocers shop in Sevenoaks with a candle lit radiance, stalking on legs like beech trees, pink glowing, grape clustered, pearl hung.'

49. George Ernest Manwaring (1882–1939) was Assistant Librarian at the London Library (and a naval historian). Alice Stopford Green (1847–1929), wife and collaborator of the historian J. R. Green, author of *A Short History of the English People* (1874). Leslie Stephen succeeded Tennyson as President of the London Library in 1892; 'Widow Green' served on the library committee for many years; by 1900, when he

agreed to her request to edit her husband's letters, Leslie Stephen wrote: 'I have come to think better of her.' (*Mausoleum Book*, p. 108).

50. Mark Pattison (1813–1884), Rector of Lincoln College, Oxford: 'For many years he was a member of the committee of the London Library, and regularly attended its meetings. But he was singularly inefficient on a board or committee. . . .' (*DNB*).

51. VW had been asked to give a talk for the B.B.C. in April in a series called "Words Fail Me."

52. Edwin Muir reviewed *The Years* in *The Listener*, 31 March 1937; and R. A. Scott James in the April issue of *The London Mercury* (of which he was editor): "Mrs Woolf has not removed from the picture the sense of dreariness and fatuity, however brightly coloured the strands with which the pattern is woven. . . ." Ivy Compton-Burnett (1892–1969) had recently published her seventh novel, *Daughters and Sons*.

53. Before his departure for Spain, Julian Bell, VW's nephew, had assembled three long polemical essays—including the "Letter to A." rejected by the Woolfs—which, he wrote to his brother, were "meant to cause pain to intellectuals, thought if possible, but pain anyway." and asked his mother, Vanessa, to send them to T. S. Eliot in the hope that his firm, Faber and Faber, would publish them as a book. After his death, Eliot wrote to VW to tell her, and through her Vanessa, that although he himself found them very interesting, they could not do so. In the event they were published by the Hogarth Press in *Julian Bell: Essays, Poems and Letters* in 1938.

54. The writer and sex-educationist Dr Marie Stopes (1880–1958) saw VW on 25 January, probably to secure her support for an appeal to the Royal Literary Fund on behalf of the indigent Lord Alfred Douglas. The Princesse de Polignac had tea with VW on 27 January. Philip Woolf and a daughter lunched on 28 January; that afternoon VW and LW went to visit Freud in Hampstead; and after dinner went with T. S. Eliot to Adrian Stephen's fancy-dress party at York Terrace, Regent's Park.

55. The Local Defence Volunteers—soon to be re-named the "Home Guard." LW did not join, but undertook Fire Watching and Air Raid Precautions duties in the village.

56. LW's book was *The War for Peace*, a short book written for the Labour Book Club and published by Routledge in September 1940.

57. In the Battle of Britain—the prelude to the intended invasion—the Luftwaffe suffered its heaviest reverses in the week ending 17 August, when the RAF claimed 496 German aircraft were brought down. The air assault, particularly on Kent, Sussex, and Greater London, was maintained but, having failed to achieve mastery of the air over England, on 17 September Hitler decided to postpone, and later to call off, his plans to invade in 1940, and to concentrate on the destruction of London and other cities by night bombing.

58. Christopher Hobhouse (1910–1940), barrister and author and a close friend of Harold Nicolson, was killed in a bombing attack on Ports-

mouth on 26 August. Lady Cynthia Williams (1908–1940), daughter of the Earl of Guilford, and her brother Lord North were both killed on 15 August by the explosion of a landmine on the South-East coast.

59. LW lectured to the WEA on "Common Sense in History."

60. Cf "Henry James" in Desmond MacCarthy's *Portraits* (1931), p. 155t "He had been describing to me the spiral of depression which a recent nervous illness had compelled him . . . to descend. . . . 'But it has been good . . . for my genius.' Then he added, 'Never cease to watch whatever happens to you.' "

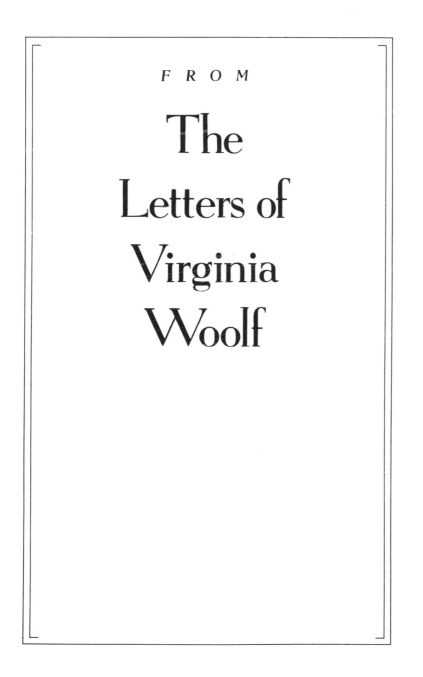

F R O M

The
Letters of
Virginia
Woolf

Virginia Woolf's earliest surviving letter was written when she was six years old, to her godfather, the American poet James Russell Lowell. The last was addressed to her husband, Leonard Woolf, on March 28, 1941, the day she ended her life. She was one of the best letter writers of her day, and the entire collection represents one of the liveliest and often most elegantly written bodies of correspondence of this century. The range of subject and variety of mood are among their most characteristic features. The emotional canvas stretches in every direction: from the comic to the tragic, from the benevolent to the malicious, from the serious to the frivolous. Every letter reflects some facet of this multifaceted and complex personality. In almost every letter, too, we glimpse her uncanny awareness of the person to whom she is writing. This will amuse you, she seems to be saying, or will make you think or whet your curiosity. Or this will make you shout with laughter—or silence you with sympathy. As one of her critics wrote, her letters are "sparkling, spluttering, dangerously explosive. To read them is to listen to her talk."

The fact that almost four thousand letters have been preserved for over a half century is testimony to their significance to each of their recipients. They chronicle an intimacy that survives in memory long after the principal figures themselves have vanished.

To Violet Dickinson[1]   *46 Gordon Square*
Nov. 9th [1905]

I have had such a run of work as is not remembered for I cant say how many years; books from the Times, the Academy, the Guardian—it must be confessed that I write great nonsense, but you will understand that I have to make money to pay my bills. The Quaker wont see it; and talks with deep significance of *serious* work, not *pot boilers*. Really I have almost more review-

343

ing than I feel to be quite moral; but I manage some Greek and good English in between.

Then on Wednesdays I have my English Composition; 10 people: 4 men 6 women.[2] It is I suppose the most useless class in the College; and so Sheepshanks thinks. She sat through the whole lesson last night; and almost stamped with impatience. But what can I do? I have an old Socialist of 50, who thinks he must bring the Parasite (the Aristocrat, that is you and Nelly) into an essay upon Autumn; and a Dutchman who thinks—at the end of the class too—that I have been treaching him Arithmetic; and anaemic shop girls who say they would write more but they only get an hour for their dinner, and there doesn't seem much time for writing.

TO VIOLET DICKINSON   [*The Steps, Playden,*
Sunday [*25 August* 1907]   *Sussex*]

You drive me to write. O melancholy creature why do you see specialists? I wish to god you wouldnt. What you want, probably, is air and food and good society; here you should have a couch beneath an Apple tree, and sometimes I would sing to you, and sometimes I would leap from branch to branch, and sometimes I would recite, my own works, to the Zither.

. . . Now, dirty devil (for your language is hot and strong— comes bubbling from the deep natural spring) amuse me. Well then, we went and had tea with Henry James[3] today, and Mr and Mrs [George] Prothero, at the golf club; and Henry James fixed me with his staring blank eye—it is like a childs marble— and said, "My dear Virginia, they tell me—they tell me—they tell me—that you—as indeed being your fathers daughter nay your grandfathers grandchild—the descendant I may say of a century—of a century—of quill pens and ink—ink—ink pots, yes, yes, yes, they tell me—ahm m m—that you, that you, that you *write* in short." This went on in the public street, while we all waited, as farmers wait for the hen to lay an egg—do they?— nervous, polite, and now on this foot now on that. I felt like a condemned person, who sees the knife drop and stick and drop again. Never did any woman hate 'writing' as much as I do. But when I am old and famous I shall discourse like Henry James. We had to stop periodically to let him shake himself free of the thing; he made phrases over the bread and butter 'rude and rapid' it was, and told us all the scandal of Rye. "Mr Jones has eloped, I regret to say, to Tasmania; leaving 12 little Jones, and a possible 13th to Mrs Jones; most regrettable, most unfortunate, and yet not wholly an action to which one has no private key of ones own so to speak."

TO CLIVE BELL⁴   *Lelant Hotel, Lelant*
26th Dec [1909]   *[Cornwall]*

The life I lead is very nearly perfect. A horrid tone of egoistic joy pervades this sheet I know. What with the silence, and the possibility of walking out, at any moment, over long wonderfully coloured roads to cliffs with the sea beneath, and coming back past lighted windows to one's tea and fire and book—and then one has thoughts and a conception of the world and moments like a dragon fly in air—with all this I am kept very lively in my head. For conversation there are the maid and the landlady, who tell me about the moon and the chickens and the wreck. A ferryman this morning told me about trawling and angling and drowned sailors. I pick up a certain amount of gossip by stretching my head out of the window and listening to the leaning men beneath. Now, suddenly at half past nine, the carols have stopped, and there is only one man walking quickly, and whistling. A strange affair is life! However, one might run on and on, covering sheets, with mysticism, ridiculous in the daylight. My Lady Hester got into the habit of talking so that she could never read, and must dictate letters, and took herself for the Messiah. Suppose I stayed here, and thought myself an early virgin, and danced on May nights, in the British camp!—a scandalous Aunt for Julian, and yet rather pleasant, when he was older, like Norton, and wished for eccentric relations. Can't you imagine how airily he would produce her, on Thursday nights. "I have an Aunt who copulates in a tree, and thinks herself with child by a grasshopper—charming isn't it? She dresses in green, and my mother sends her nuts from the Stores".

TO VIOLET DICKINSON   *Pelham Arms, Lewes*
New Years Day [1911]   *[Sussex]*

Many happy returns of the day. The only present I have got for you is a picture of some cattle, which will interest you when you hear that the same people use them as used them when the Domesday Book was written. So the guide book says. In fact, it is altogether an interesting picture, when you think that your Sp: may be going to take a cottage in the neighborhood. It is a very ugly villa; but underneath the downs, in a charming village [Firle].

We have been spending Christmas here, with an extremely considerate landlady, who is so much struck by my incompetence to face life, that she always offers to lace my boots, and give me my bath. Miss Thomas[5] came down for a night, in an interval between discharging a woman who wished to commit murder, and taking one, who wants to kill herself. Can you imagine living like that?—always watching the knives, and expecting to find bedroom doors locked, or a corpse in the bath? I said I thought it was too great a strain—but, upheld by Christianity, I believe she will do it.

TO LEONARD WOOLF   *Asheham [Rodmell,*
May 1st [1912]   *Sussex]*

To deal with the facts first (my fingers are so cold I can hardly write) I shall be back about 7 tomorrow, so there will be time to discuss—but what does it mean? You can't take the leave, I suppose if you are going to resign certainly at the end of it. Anyhow, it shows what a career you're ruining!

Well then, as to all the rest. It seems to me that I am giving you a great deal of pain—some in the most casual way—and therefore I ought to be as plain with you as I can, because half the time I suspect, you're in a fog which I don't see at all. Of course I can't explain what I feel—these are some of the things that strike me. The obvious advantages of marriage stand in my way. I say to myself. Anyhow, you'll be quite happy with him; and he will give you companionship, children, and a busy life—then I say By God, I will not look upon marriage as a profession. The only people who know of it, all think it suitable; and that makes me scrutinise my own motives all the more. Then, of course, I feel angry sometimes at the strength of your desire. Possibly, your being a Jew comes in also at this point. You seem so foreign. And then I am fearfully unstable. I pass from hot to cold in an instant, without any reason; except that I believe sheer physical effort and exhaustion influence me. All I can say is that in spite of these feelings which go chasing each other all day long when I am with you, there is some feeling which is permanent, and growing. You want to know of course whether it will ever make me marry you. How can I say? I think it will, because there seems no reason why it shouldn't—But I don't know what the future will bring. I'm half afraid of myself. I sometimes feel that no one ever has or ever can share something —Its the thing that makes you call me like a hill, or a rock. Again, I want everything—love, children, adventure, intimacy, work. (Can you make any sense out of this ramble? I am putting down one thing after another). So I go from being half in love with you, and wanting you to be with me always, and know everything about me, to the extreme of wildness and aloofness. I sometimes think that if I married you, I could have everything— and then—is it the sexual side of it that comes between us? As I told you brutally the other day, I feel no physical attraction in you. There are moments—when you kissed me the other day was one—when I feel no more than a rock. And yet your caring for me as you do almost overwhelms me. It is so real, and so strange. Why should you? What am I really except a pleasant attractive creature? But its just because you care so much that I feel I've got to care before I marry you. I feel I must give you everything; and that if I can't, well, marriage would only be second-best for you as well as for me. If you can still go on, as before, letting me find my own way, as that is what would please me best; and then we must both take the risks. But you have made me very happy too. We both of us want a marriage that is a tremendous living thing, always alive, always hot, not dead and easy in parts as most marriages are. We ask a great deal of life, don't we? Perhaps we shall get it; then, how splendid!

One doesn't get much said in a letter does one? I haven't touched upon the enormous variety of things that have been happening here—but they can wait.

D'you like this photograph?—rather too noble, I think. Here's another.[6]

TO JANET CASE[7]   *The Plough Inn, Holford,*
[*17 August 1912*]   *Somerset*

Its really a very good way to be married—very simple and soon done. You stand up and repeat two sentences, and then sign your name. Nothing went wrong, the only disturbance was about Vanessa and Virginia, which the registrar, who was half blind and otherwise deformed, mixed hopelessly and Nessa upset him worse by suddenly deciding to change her son's name from Quentin to Christopher.[8]

TO VIOLET DICKINSON   *Asheham House, Rodmell,*
Friday, April 11th [*1913*]   *Lewes* [*Sussex*]

I was very glad to hear from you but you really must buy some great sheets like this to accommodate your lean long hand, if our intimacy is to live on ink. We come up to London this day, and wish you would ask us to tea, but I suppose you are now settled in at the [Burnham] Wood [Welwyn].

Perhaps you will invite us for 3 hours there.

We shall live here more or less this summer, but spend one out of 3 weeks in London.

We aren't going to have a baby, but we want to have one, and 6 months in the country or so is said to be necessary first.

However, on the whole, in spite of rain, there's nothing so nice as this place. We are wrestling with the garden. It is riddled with weeds, with roots a yard long, and finally we've had to dig a vast ditch, fill it with wood and straw, lay the earth on top, and set fire, in the hope that the nettles will be burnt out. After digging and fetching for 6 hours, until we both rained sweat and were the laughing stock of the yokels, we poured a can of paraffin on top and set alight—when a storm burst, and put the fire out, damped the earth, so that we must now begin again. We're also re-constructing the terrace and fighting moles rabbits and mysterious flower diseases, which attack tulips so that they never unfold. You *must* come here, and give advice. Will you? ...

All the morning we write in two separate rooms. Leonard is in the middle of a new novel [*The Wise Virgins*]; but as the clock strikes twelve, he begins an article upon Labour for some pale sheet, or a review of French literature for the Times, or a history of Co-operation.[9]

TO VIOLET DICKINSON   *Asheham, Rodmell,*
Tuesday [*10 April 1917*]   *Lewes* [*Sussex*]

Nessa and Duncan [Grant][10] came over yesterday, having previously washed themselves; and then went back in a storm late at night to help ducklings out of their eggs, for they were heard quacking inside, and couldn't break through. Nessa seems to have slipped civilization off her back, and splashes about entirely nude, without shame, and enormous spirit. Indeed, Clive now takes up the line that she has ceased to be a presentable lady—I think it all works admirably. The wind rages incessantly, and Leonard spends his day cutting up the fallen trees. We live on the wood, which smells so delicious. I am trying to read Conrad's new book,[11] but owing to endless talk, I haven't got far. Now we are going to Lewes to buy some plants—for the summer. Potatoes there are none. However, the old ewes give birth nightly behind hurdles at the back of the house. And all day the lambs keep up an extraordinary loud noise.

I hope I shall see you again soon—We have bought our Press![12] We don't know how to work it, but now I must find some young novelists or poets. Do you know any?

To Vanessa Bell   *Asheham [Rodmell,*
Tuesday [31 December 1918]   *Sussex]*

Its most disappointing that I shan't see you and Anonyma
[Angelica] before we go, but we've now settled to go tomorrow,
and I'm afraid I shan't be able to come over today. The children
are both perfectly well, and more angelic than words can say.
Lottie however has surpassed herself; she has got into such a
state about her own health that she makes life here impossible
and it seems best to go back where at any rate we are near
doctors and chemists. . . .

However, as I say, the children are perfectly well, and no
trouble at all. They play in the drawing room most of the morning, and we go for a walk after luncheon, and they seem to be full
of their own games and ideas, which fit in extremely well with
mine. They are amazingly interesting as well as attractive. Julian
of course, knows infinitely more about science and history and geography than I do. He and Leonard had an argument yesterday
about what would happen if you put a barometer into deep
water. Leonard was very much impressed by his intelligence, and
is, I see, getting to be very fond of them. Quentin's mind is very
like mine, I expect. I hear him telling himself stories about Lady
Suffolk, and how she will only eat chickens, which she breeds in
enormous numbers, and she's the richest woman in the world
and a Peeress in her own right. How they get hold of all their
language I don't know; it seems to me very superior—in fact
their minds altogether seem much quicker and more intelligent
than ours. Mrs B. must have trained them very well, to do what
they are told. Their great delight is to pretend to be dolphins in
the bath, but they get out the moment I tell them to seriously,
and their table manners are perfect. They seem to have most
economical minds. Quentin told me the first night "I think it is
an unnecessary expense for you to have bolsters in your beds",
and Julian said "You seem to me to be very extragavant [*sic*]
with your coal." Quentin would only put a scraping of strawberry jam on his bread, because he said that it was very precious
in war time. However, their appetites are very good,—They have

just been in to say will I ask you to send them King Solomon's Mines [H. Rider Haggard], and Quentin's black book, as he wants to do some writing. You are not to send Adrian's book as Julian has finished it.

Lord! What a mercy they are to talk to after the servants!

. . . But the thing Julian wants to do *almost* most of all is to learn the Greek alphabet! So I shall teach him that, and they are also very anxious to write essays and stories for me to judge, so we shall be very literary, and I hope to persuade Quentin to be a writer and not a painter when he grows up.

To Vanessa Bell   *Hogarth* [*House,*
Thursday [*27 February 1919*]   *Richmond*]

My dinner with Ottoline [Morrell][13] was a frigid success. The poor woman has broken out into eruptions which she tries to make dramatic by pasting pieces of black plaster on them— but they exude at the edges. It's a terrific business whipping her into life now. One has to bow and scrape and do all sorts of antics, and implore her to tell one the history of her life from the beginning before she will get up steam at all. She fishes for compliments worse than I do—I mean without that airy certainty which is so adorable in me that there is no limit to one's store and one has merely to shake the tree for them to fall thick as apple blossom in May. She shakes the tree—oh yes,— However, I did my best; and when she said that I dressed so beautifully that I made her feel older and uglier than ever, I said, "My dear Ottoline, like the Lombardy poplar you have only to stand up naked to put us all to shame!" She liked that. But still she is fundamentally suspicious of us all, I'm afraid, and goes ravening like a dog about Bloomsbury. She insisted upon walking from the Strand to Gordon Square in a bitter wind merely to see your wretched cockatoo [Clive] and get a little of the strong wine of the male, when she felt me flagging. She now walks exactly as Queen Alexandra is said to do; and her mind vapours off about friendship and love and literature—"I could never love anyone who does not care for literature—that is my cross—my refuge, Virginia—when people are cruel—and they are *so* cruel sometimes—And I suffer so terribly—my back gives me agonies —my feet are swollen with chillblains, and I am *always, always* tired. What would I not give to be able to work as you do—to create—to be an artist—" imagine crossing Holborn with this dribbling out, as painfully as two old witches on crutches.

To Lytton Strachey[14]   *Ponion, Zennor,*
Wednesday [*30*] *March* [*1921*]   *St Ives* [*Cornwall*]

... I met a man yesterday by appointment to discuss literature —"which is my whole life, Mrs Woolf." But I can give you no idea—He lives with a half perished dumb wife on a headland in a cottage with Everyman's Library entire. "I read no moderns. Life is not long enough for anything save the best. Hardy has taught me to look into my heart. I have enjoyed this conversation, Mrs Woolf. It has confirmed me in my own opinions." This stunted animal was a clerk in the post office, became infected with books, and is now like the oldest kernel of a monkey's nut in the Gray's Inn Road. However—why is it that human beings are so terribly pathetic? God knows. Or am I becoming rotten with middle age? I did refrain from asking him to correspond; but left with tears in my eyes—almost. I can't help thinking that we are hopelessly muddled. Then there was the theosophist, Mr Watt in the cottage which I once hired; and he lives on nuts from Selfridges, and a few vegetables, and has visions, and wears boots with soles like slabs of beef and an orange tie; and then his wife crept out of her hole, all blue, with orange hair, and cryptic ornaments, serpents, you know, swallowing their tails in token of eternity, round her neck. The rain, they said, often comes through the walls on a wet day, so I'm glad I didn't settle there. But can you explain the human race at all—I mean these queer fragments of it which are so terribly like ourselves, and so like Chimpanzees at the same time, and so lofty and high minded, with their little shelves of classics and clean china and nice check curtains and purity that I can't see why its all wrong. We tried to imagine you there, snipping their heads off with something very witty.

TO MOLLY MACCARTHY[15]   *Monk's House, Rodmell,*
[*20 June 1921*]   *Lewes [Sussex]*

I am reading the Bride of Lammermoor—by that great man Scott: and Women in Love by D. H. Lawrence, lured on by the portrait of Ottoline which appears from time to time.[16] She has just smashed Lawrence's head open with a ball of lapis lazuli— but then balls are smashed on every other page—cats—cattle— even the fish and the water lilies are at it all day long. There is no suspense or mystery: water is all semen: I get a little bored, and make out the riddles too easily. Only this puzzles me: what does it mean when a woman does eurythmics in front of a herd of Highland cattle? But I must stop.

TO JACQUES RAVERAT[17]   *Monk's House, Rodmell*
Dec. 26th 1924   *[Sussex]*

Who is there next? Well, only a high aristocrat called Vita Sackville-West, daughter of Lord Sackville, daughter of Knole, wife of Harold Nicolson, and novelist, but her real claim to consideration, is, if I may be so coarse, her legs. Oh they are exquisite—running like slender pillars up into her trunk, which is that of a breastless cuirassier (yet she has 2 children) but all about her is virginal, savage, patrician; and why she writes, which she does with complete competency, and a pen of brass, is a puzzle to me. If I were she, I should merely stride, with 11 Elk hounds, behind me, through my ancestral woods. She descends from Dorset, Buckingham, Sir Philip Sidney, and the whole of English history, which she keeps, stretched in coffins, one after another, from 1300 to the present day, under her dining room floor. But you, poor Frog, care nothing for all this.

TO GWEN RAVERAT   *52 Tavistock Square,*
11th March [1925]   *W.C.1*

Your and Jacques' letter came yesterday, and I go about thinking of you both in starts, and almost constantly underneath everything, and I don't know what to say.[18] The thing that comes over and over is the strange wish I have to go on telling Jacques things. This is for Jacques, I say to myself; I want to write to him about happiness, about Rupert [Brooke], and love. It had become to me a sort of private life, and I believe I told him more than anyone, except Leonard; I become mystical as I grow older and feel an alliance with you and Jacques which is eternal, not interrupted, or hurt by never meeting. Then of course, I have now for you—how can I put it?—I mean the feeling that one must reverence?—is that the word—feel shy of, so tremendous an experience; for I cannot conceive what you have suffered. It seems to me that if we met, one would have to chatter about every sort of little trifle, because there is nothing to be said.

And then, being, as you know, so fundamentally an optimist, I want to make you enjoy life. Forgive me, for writing what comes into my head. I think I feel that I would give a great deal to share with you the daily happiness. But you know that if there is anything I could ever give you, I would give it, but perhaps the only thing to give is to be oneself with people. One could say anything to Jacques. And that will always be the same with you and me. But oh, dearest Gwen, to think of you is making me cry—why should you and Jacques have had to go through this? As I told him, it is your love that has forever been love to me—all those years ago, when you used to come to Fitzroy Square, I was so angry and you were so furious, and Jacques wrote me a sensible manly letter, which I answered, sitting at my table in the window. Perhaps I was frightfully jealous of you both, being at war with the whole world at the moment. Still, the vision has become to me a source of wonder—the vision of your face; which if I were painting I should cover with flames, and put you on a hill top. Then, I don't think you would believe how it moves me that you and Jacques should have been reading Mrs Dalloway, and liking it. I'm awfully vain I know; and I was on pins and needles about sending it to Jacques; and now I feel exquisitely relieved; not flattered: but one does want that side of one to be acceptable—I was going to have written to Jacques about his children, and about my having none—I mean, these efforts of mine to communicate with people are partly childlessness, and the horror that sometimes overcomes me.

There is very little use in writing this. One feels so ignorant, so trivial, and like a child, just teasing you. But it is only that one keeps thinking of you, with a sort of reverence, and of that adorable man, whom I loved.

To V. SACKVILLE-WEST   52 *Tavistock Square,*
16th March 1926   *London, W.C.1*

... As for the *mot juste*, you are quite wrong. Style is a very simple matter; it is all rhythm. Once you get that, you can't use the wrong words. But on the other hand here am I sitting after half the morning, crammed with ideas, and visions, and so on, and can't dislodge them, for lack of the right rhythm. Now this is very profound, what rhythm is, and goes far deeper than words. A sight, an emotion, creates this wave in the mind, long before it makes words to fit it; and in writing (such is my present belief) one has to recapture this, and set this working (which has nothing apparently to do with words) and then, as it breaks and tumbles in the mind, it makes words to fit it: But no doubt I shall think differently next year. Then there's my character (you see how egotistic I am, for I answer only questions that are about myself) I agree about the lack of jolly vulgarity. But then think how I was brought up! No school; mooning about alone among my father's books; never any chance to pick up all that goes on in schools —throwing balls; ragging: slang; vulgarity; scenes; jealousies—only rages with my half brothers, and being walked off my legs round the Serpentine by my father. This is an excuse: I am often conscious of the lack of jolly vulgarity but did Proust pass that way? Did you? Can you chaff a table of officers?

To V. SACKVILLE-WEST   *The Hogarth Press,*
                                         52 Tavistock Square,
29th March 1926   *London, W.C.1*

I cannot think what it will interest you to be told of, now you are embedded in Persia. I see you always picking little bright red flowers high up on stony mountains. Raymond [Mortimer][19] (give him my love) will be with you now; and so you will have heard all about London—how Clive is in love, and Lady Cole-fax, and all that. Do you infer from this that Sybil is in love? No, no. She has not been tainted by *that* passion: she has merely stayed with Coolidge, Esme Howard,[20] Doug [Fairbanks] and Mary [Pickford], Charlie Chaplin, been four thousand miles in a motor car; etc. etc. Does it matter what Sybil does? A coal mine, heaven, its all the same. She pants a little harder—that is all. Then there were Lord Ivor S. Churchill; Roger Fry[21] and Vir-ginia Woolf—and all very brilliant at Clives the other night; and Walter Sickert, Therese Lessore, Leigh Ashton,[22] all very silent at Vanessa's the other night; and a ghastly party at Rose Macaulays, where in the whirl of meaningless words I thought Mr O'donovan said Holy Ghost, whereas he said "The Whole Coast" and I asking "Where is the Holy Ghost?" got the reply "Where ever the sea is" "Am I mad, I thought, or is this wit?" "The Holy Ghost?" I repeated. "The Whole Coast" he shouted, and so we went on, in an atmosphere so repellent that it became, like the smell of bad cheese, repulsively fascinating: Robert Lynds, Gerald Goulds,[23] Rose Macaulays, all talking shop; and saying Masefield is as good as Chaucer, and the best novel of the year is Shining Domes by Mildred Peake; until Leonard shook all over, picked up what he took to be Mrs Gould's napkin, discov-ered it to be her sanitary towel and the foundations of this tenth rate literary respectability (all gentlemen in white waistcoats, ladies shingled, unsuccessfully) shook to its foundations. I kept saying "Vita would love this" Now would you?

TO VANESSA BELL　　　　　　　*Hotel de France, Palermo*
9th April 1927　　　　　　　　　*[Sicily]*

　. . . I am sure Rome is the city where I shall come to die—a few months before death however, for obviously the country round it is far the loveliest in the world. I dont myself care so much for the melodramatic mountains here, which go the colour of picture postcards at sunset; but outside Rome it is perfection —smooth, suave, flowing, classical, with the sea on one side, hills on the other, a flock of sheep here, and an olive grove.

There I shall come to die; and I suggest, as an idea you may consider, the foundation of a colony of the aged—Roger, you, Lytton, I: all sunken cheeked, tottering and urbane, supporting each others steps along Roman roads; I dont mind if one does die at the street corner; you with a beautiful handkerchief over your head (how ashamed you made me feel of my poor partridges rump!)[24] and the rest of us with large sticks in our hands. A death colony will certainly become desirable. However we only had time to see the Coliseum and to eat a vast dish of maccaroni. Then we crossed over to Palermo by night and I shared a cabin with an unknown but by no means romantic Swedish lady who complained that there was no lock on the door, whereupon I poked my head out from the curtains and said in my best French "Madame, we have neither of us any cause for fear" which happily she took in good part. Its odd how much the Scandinavians scrape, scent, gurgle and clean at night considering the results next morning: as hard as a board, and as gray as a scullery pail. She suggested nothing but paring potatoes. Much though I love my own sex, my gorge heaves at the travelling female. We had two with us from Toulon to Mentone, arch and elderly, with handbags packed with face powder and complexions that not all the thyme and mint in England could sweeten—elderly virgins from Cheltenham, playing golf in France; but one feels sure they cant hit the ball—they cant do anything—they spend enough to keep you and me a year on their clothes—they have no reason to exist in this world or the next.

To V. Sackville-West   52 *Tavistock Square*
Friday [*13 May 1927*]   [*W.C.*1]

What a generous woman you are! Your letter has just come,[25] and I must answer it, though in a chaos. (Nelly returning: her doctor; her friends; her diet etc) I was honest though in thinking you wouldn't care for The Lighthouse: too psychological; too many personal relationships, I think. . . . The dinner party the best thing I ever wrote: the one thing that I think justifies my faults as a writer: This damned 'method'. Because I dont think one could have reached those particular emotions in any other way. I was doubtful about Time Passes. It was written in the gloom of the Strike: then I re-wrote it: then I thought it impossible as prose —I thought you could have written it as poetry. I don't know if I'm like Mrs Ramsay: as my mother died when I was 13 probably it is a child's view of her: but I have some sentimental delight in thinking that you like her. She has haunted me: but then so did that old wretch my father: Do you think it sentimental? Do you think it irreverent about him? I should like to know. I was more like him than her, I think; and therefore more critical: but he was an adorable man, and somehow, tremendous.

To V. Sackville-West   *Monks House* [*Rodmell,*
Wednesday [*3 August 1927*]   *Sussex*]

Yes, darling creature, your letter was handed me just as we left Auppegard, and caused me, I suppose, to forget my box, so that the exquisite butler had to motor into Dieppe after us. Yes, darling, it was a nice letter. Sauqueville[26] aint a very grand place, all the same. I looked for traces of you. Did your ancestors own a saw mill? Thats what they do now, and not a specially fine leg among them. But I'll tell you all about it when you come.

My God, how you would have laughed yesterday! Off for our first drive in the Singer: the bloody thing wouldn't start. The accelerator died like a duck—starter jammed. All the village came to watch—Leonard almost sobbed with rage. At last we had to bicycle in and fetch a man from Lewes. He said it was the magnetos—would you have known that? Should we have known? Another attempt today, we are bitter and sullen and determined. We think of nothing else. Leonard will shoot himself if it dont start again.

Come down, dearest Creature

To Ethel Smyth[27]   [*52 Tavistock Square,*
Sunday, 22nd June [*1930*]   *W.C.1*]

. . . I did not mean, though I must have said, that Leonard served 7 years for his wife.[28] He saw me it is true; and thought me an odd fish; and went off next day to Ceylon, with a vague romance about us both [Virginia and Vanessa]! And I heard stories of him; how his hand trembled and he had bit his thumb through in a rage; and Lytton said he was like Swift and would murder his wife; and someone else said Woolf had married a black woman. That was my romance—Woolf in a jungle. And then I set up house alone with a brother [Adrian], and Nessa married, and I was rather adventurous, for those days; that is we were sexually very free—Elizabeth owes her emancipation and mathematics partly to us—but I was always sexually cowardly, and never walked over Mountains with Counts as you did, nor plucked all the flowers of life in a bunch as you did. My terror of real life has always kept me in a nunnery. And much of this talking and adventuring in London alone, and sitting up to all hours with young men, and saying whatever came first, was rather petty, as you were not petty: at least narrow; circumscribed; and leading to endless ramifications of intrigue. We had violent rows—oh yes, I used to rush through London in such rages, and stormed Hampstead heights at night in white or purple fury. And then I married, and then my brains went up in a shower of fireworks. As an experience, madness is terrific I can assure you, and not to be sniffed at; and in its lava I still find most of the things I write about. It shoots out of one everything shaped, final, not in mere driblets, as sanity does. And the six months—not three—that I lay in bed taught me a good deal about what is called oneself. Indeed I was almost crippled when I came back to the world, unable to move a foot in terror, after that discipline. Think—not one moment's freedom from doctor discipline—perfectly strange – conventional men; 'you shant read this' and 'you shant write a word' and 'you shall lie still and drink milk'—for six months.

To Ethel Smyth   *52 Tavistock Square*
Thursday, 16th Oct [1930]   [*W.C.1*]
   . . . One of these days I will write out some phases of my writer's life; and expound what I now merely say in short—After being ill and suffering every form and variety of nightmare and extravagant intensity of perception—for I used to make up

poems, stories, profound and to me inspired phrases all day long as I lay in bed, and thus sketched, I think, all that I now, by the light of reason, try to put into prose (I thought of the Lighthouse then, and Kew and others, not in substance, but in idea)—after all this, when I came to, I was so tremblingly afraid of my own insanity that I wrote Night and Day [1919] mainly to prove to my own satisfaction that I could keep entirely off that dangerous ground. I wrote it, lying in bed, allowed to write only for one half hour a day. And I made myself copy from plaster casts, partly to tranquillise, partly to learn anatomy. Bad as the book is, it composed my mind, and I think taught me certain elements of composition which I should not have had the patience to learn had I been in full flush of health always. These little pieces in Monday or (and) Tuesday were written by way of diversion; they were the treats I allowed myself when I had done my exercise in the conventional style. I shall never forget the day I wrote The Mark on the Wall—all in a flash, as if flying, after being kept stone breaking for months. The Unwritten Novel was the great discovery, however. That—again in one second—showed me how I could embody all my deposit of experience in a shape that fitted it—not that I have ever reached that end; but anyhow I saw, branching out of the tunnel I made, when I discovered that method of approach, Jacobs Room [1922], Mrs Dalloway [1925] etc—How I trembled with excitement; and then Leonard came in, and I drank my milk, and concealed my excitement, and wrote I suppose another page of that interminable Night and Day (which some say is my best book). All this I will tell you one day—here I suppress my natural inclination to say, if dear Ethel you have the least wish to hear anymore on a subject that cant be of the least interest to you.

T O V A N E S S A B E L L   *Monks House, Rodmell*
Sunday Nov 2nd [*1930*]   [*Sussex*]

. . . Lytton came to dinner to meet Lady Colefax. I spent 17/6 on a jar of pâté de foie gras; and Rivett really cooked admirably (she is erratic and has failures but on the whole I like her erraticity better than complete humdrum) and Sibyl has transformed herself into a harried, downright woman of business,[29] sticking her fork in the pot; and has lost almost all her glitter and suavity. Even her voice has changed. She is now of the family of Champcommunal[30] and other money makers. She is at her office from 9.30 to 7: has had to give up entertaining, and on the whole is improved, though rather tragic. After all, she is 55, I daresay, and has practised society for 35 years; and now to become a hardhearted shopkeeper,—she is very successful too, decorating houses from top to bottom and standing on ladders and fixing sinks—must be a grind. She too has shrunk and faded. Lytton was smooth as silk and sweet as honey. You were praised. I think probably you do now represent the only island that keeps afloat. Everyone else seems at the moment money grubbing and precarious. And then there is old Ethel, who took me to one of the very smartest of parties in Belgrave Square, and unpeeled herself of sweater, jersey and mothy moleskin before all the flunkeys, knocking her pasteboard hat to right and left and finally producing from a cardboard box fastened at the edge by paper fasteners a pair of black leather shoes, which she put on, because she said "The truth is I'm a damned snob, and like to be smart." She also said, "Isn't this slow movement sublime— natural and heavy and irresistible like the movement of one's own bowels." All the dapper little diplomats blushed.

To VANESSA BELL   *Monks House* [*Rodmell,*
23rd May [*1931*]   *Sussex*]

I've had to retire to bed for 2 days with a headache, but am now practically recovered. This was not due to my Jolly, but to Ethel Smyth, whom I think, seriously, to be deranged in the head. We'd spent the morning trapesing round the Chelsea flower show, a very remarkable sight, banks and banks of flowers, all colours, under a livid awning, for it was perishing cold, and all the county families parading with their noses red against the lilies,—a fascinating but rather exhausting performance, and then Ethel appeared, stamping like a dragoon with a wallet full of documents. For 3 hours she nailed me to my chair while she rehearsed the story of her iniquitous treatment by Adrian Boult.[31] I cant (you'll be glad to hear) go into it all, but she seems to have gone into the green room, after he'd been conducting a Bach Mass for 6 hours, and insisted that he should do the Prison at the BBC; whereafter, according to her, he grossly insulted her, in the presence of the finest artists in Europe, and finally after a screaming and scratching which rung through The Queen's Hall, ordered her out of the room. She then went through, with the minuteness and ingenuity of a maniac, the whole history of her persecution for the past 50 years; brought out old letters and documents and read them aloud, beat on my chair with her fists; made me listen, and answer, and agree at every moment; and finally I had to shout that I had such a headache that unless she stopped talking I should burst into flames and be combusted. One is perfectly powerless. She raves and rants; yet has a demoniac shrewdness, so that there's no escape. "You've got to listen to me—You've got to listen" she kept saying and indeed the whole of 52 rang with her vociferations. And its all fabricated, contorted, twisted with red hot egotism; and she's now launched on a campaign which means bullying every conductor and worrying every publisher, and rich man or woman, as well as unfortunate friends, until she gets that hopeless farrago of birds and last posts played and all HB's[32] rubbish printed again. I dont feel I can even face her unless 2 keepers are present with red hot pokers—at the same time, considering her age, I suppose she's a marvel—I see her merits as a writer—but undoubtedly sex and egotism have brewed some bitter insanity.

TO V. SACKVILLE-WEST   [Monk's House, Rodmell,
Saturday [8 August 1931]   Sussex]

   . . . As for Katherine [Mansfield], I think you've got it very nearly right. We did not ever coalesce; but I was fascinated, and she respectful, only I thought her cheap, and she thought me priggish; and yet we were both compelled to meet simply in order to talk about writing. This we did by the hour. Only then she came out with a swarm of little stories, and I was jealous, no doubt; because they were so praised; but gave up reading them not on that account, but because of their cheap sharp sentimentality, which was all the worse, I thought, because she had, as you say, the zest and the resonance—I mean she could permeate one with her quality; and if one felt this cheap scent in it, it reeked in ones nostrils. But I must read her some day. Also, she was for ever pursued by her dying; and had to press on through stages that should have taken years in ten minutes—so that our relationship became unreal also. And there was [John Middleton] Murry squirming and oozing a sort of thick motor oil in the background—dinners with them were about the most unpleasant exhibitions, humanly speaking, I've ever been to. But the fact remains—I mean, that she had a quality I adored, and needed; I think her sharpness and reality—her having knocked about with prostitutes and so on, whereas I had always been respectable— was the thing I wanted then. I dream of her often—now thats an odd reflection—how one's relation with a person seems to be continued after death in dreams, and with some odd reality too.

To Vanessa Bell   *Delphi* [*Greece*]
Monday, May 2nd [*1932*]

Here we are in Delphi, all well except for Roger's inside falling out and my skin peeling in great sores. The wind and sun, the bitter cold and violent heat, the driving all day along rocky or pitted roads, make one feel like a parboiled cactus. All the same, it is so far a great success—I mean from our point of view. No quarrels, no accidents,—in fact, we live in considerable comfort, and have a car to drive in, instead of pottering about in trains and flies as we used.[33] The Inns are now clean as new pins—not a bug, or even a flea to be seen; no corpses on the wall, and the food about as good as English—too many olives and sardines for me; but Leonard and Roger love them and plunge into octopuses and lizards,—I mean they eat them, fried—oily lengths like old rubber tires cut into squares. There's not an English man or woman to be seen; our only society is our own, and some peasants, but as Roger learnt Greek out of the wrong book, most of our talk gets wrong, and when I correct with pure Classical Greek—as my way is—the only result is that we are supposed to have bought 2 kids. No, I haven't probed Margery: old age brings its sad wisdoms—I see one cant eviscerate the elderly unless one wishes to have decomposing carcases hung round one's neck. There is the less need, however, as she has told us all about her emasculated life, with the old Frys—how her father dismissed her lover, and her mother never let her laugh at any story a man told lest it should be thought fast. The dulness of her youth and the 6 sisters was she says worse than a convent. At the age of 97 Lady Fry, having shut them all up in so many band boxes pouring out tea and watering flowers owned that her policy had been a mistake.[34] But it was then too late—Margery has missed having a child, and has to paint and botanise and watch birds and philanthropise for ever instead. I daresay it would be better if she married Roger as you suggest. They hum and buzz like two boiling pots. I've never heard people, after the age of 6, talk so incessantly. Whats more, there's not a word of it what you and I might call foolish: its all about facts, and information and at the most trying moments when Roger's inside is falling down, and Margery must make water instantly or perish, one has only to mention Themistocles and the battle of Platea for them both to become like youth at its spring. The amount they know about art, history, archaeology, biology, stones, sticks, birds, flowers is in fact a constant reproof to me. Margery caught me smiling the other day at my own thoughts and said no Fry had ever done that. "No" said Roger, "we have no power of dissociation." which is why of course they're such bad painters—they never simmer for a second.

. . . I cant think why we dont live in Greece. Its very cheap. The exchange is now in our favour. There has been a financial crisis and we get I dont know how many shillings for our pound. The people are far the most sympathetic I've ever seen. Nobody jeers, or sneers. Everybody smiles. There are no beggars, practically. The peasants all come up across the fields and talk. We can't understand a word and the conflict between Roger's book and Leonards often makes it impossible for us to get a drop to drink, because they cant agree what is the word for wine.

TO QUENTIN BELL   *Monks House [Rodmell,*
Tuesday [19 September 1933]   *Sussex]*

. . . The reason why Ethel Smyth is so repulsive, tell Nessa, is her table manners. She oozes; she chortles; and she half blew her rather red nose on her table napkin. Then she poured the cream —oh the blackberries were divine—into her beer; and I had rather dine with a dog. But you can tell people they are murderers; you can not tell them that they eat like hogs. That is wisdom. She was however full—after dinner—of vigorous charm; she walked four miles; she sang Brahms; the sheep looked up and were not fed. And we packed her off before midnight.

TO LADY OTTOLINE   *Monks House, Rodmell*
MORRELL   *[Sussex]*
31st Dec. [1933]

You are a wonderful woman—for many reasons; but specially for sending a present—a lovely original wild and yet useful present—which arrived on Christmas day. I love being 'remembered' as they say; and I hung it on a chair, when the Keynes's lunched here, and boasted, how you had given it me. What a snob I am aren't I! But I cant help it. It was a very nice Christmas, as it happened; I had my shawl, and the turkey was large enough and we had cream, and lots of coloured fruits, and sat and gorged—Maynard[35] Lydia Leonard and I.

And Vita came with her sons, one Eton, one Oxford, which explains why she has to spin those sleepwalking servant girl novels. I told her you would like to see her. I remain always very fond of her—this I say because on the surface, she's rather red and black and gaudy, I know: and very slow; and very, compared to us, primitive: but she is incapable of insincerity or pose, and digs and digs, and waters, and walks her dogs, and reads her poets, and falls in love with every pretty woman, just like a man, and is to my mind genuinely aristocratic; but I cant swear that she wont bore you: certainly she'll fall in love with you. But do let her come down from her rose-red tower where she sits with thousands of pigeons cooing over her head.

To BENEDICT NICOLSON   *Monk's House, Rodmell,*
13 Aug. 1940   *Lewes [Sussex]*

Just as I began to read your letter, an air raid warning sounded. I'll put down the reflections that occurred to me, as honestly, if I can, as you put down your reflections on reading my life of Roger Fry while giving air raid alarms at Chatham.[36]

Here the raiders came over head. I went and looked at them. Then I returned to your letter. "I am so struck by the fools paradise in which he and his friends lived. He shut himself out from all disagreeable actualities and allowed the spirit of Nazism to grow without taking any steps to check it. . . ." Lord, I thought to myself, Roger shut himself out from disagreeable actualities did he? Roger who faced insanity, death and every sort of disagreeable——what can Ben mean? Are Ben and I facing actualities because we're listening to bombs dropping on other people? And I went on with Ben Nicolson's biography. After returning from a delightful tour in Italy, for which his expensive education at Eton and Oxford had well fitted him, he got a job as keeper of the King's pictures. Well, I thought, Ben was a good deal luckier than Roger. Roger's people were the very devil; when he was Ben's age he was earning his living by extension lecturing and odd jobs of reviewing. He had to wait till he was over sixty before he got a Slade professorship. And I went on to think of that very delightful party that you gave in Guildford Street two months before the war. . . . Then I looked at your letter . . "This intensely private world which Roger Fry culti-vated could only be communicated to a few people as sensitive and intelligent as himself . . ." Why then did Ben Nicolson give these parties? Why did he take a job under Kenneth Clark at Windsor? Why didn't he chuck it all away and go into politics? After all, war was a great deal closer in 1939 than in 1900.

Here the raiders began emitting long trails of smoke. I wondered if a bomb was going to fall on top of me; I wondered if I
was facing disagreeable actualities; I wondered what I could
have done to stop bombs and disagreeable actualities . . . Then I
dipped into your letter again. "This all sounds as though I wish
to say that the artist, the intellectual, has no place in modern
society. On the contrary, his mission is now more vital than it
has ever been. He will still be shocked by stupidity and untruth
but instead of ignoring it he will set out to fight it; instead of
retreating into his tower to uphold certain ethical standards his
job will be to persuade as many other people as possible to
think and behave in the same way—and on his success and
failure depends the future of the world."

Who on earth, I thought, did that job more incessantly and
successfully than Roger Fry? Didn't he spend half his life, not in
a tower, but travelling about England addressing masses of people, who'd never looked at a picture and making them see what
he saw? And wasn't that the best way of checking Nazism? Then
I opened another letter; as it happened from Sebastian Sprott,[37]
a lecturer at Nottingham; and I read how he'd once been mooning around the S.Kensington Museum ". . . then I saw Roger. All
was changed. In ten minutes he caused me to enjoy what I was
looking at. The objects became vivid and intelligible . . . There
must be many people like me, people with scales on their eyes
and wax in their ears . . . if only someone would come along
and remove the scales and dig out the wax. Roger Fry did it . . ."

Then the raiders passed over. And I thought I cant have given
Ben the least notion of what Roger was like. I suppose it was my
fault. Or is it partly, and naturally, that he must have a scape-
goat? I admit I want one. I loathe sitting here waiting for a bomb
to fall; when I want to be writing. If it doesn't kill me its killing
someone else. Where can I lay the blame? On the Sackvilles. On
the Dufferins? On Eton and Oxford? They did precious little it
seems to me to check Nazism. People like Roger and Goldie
Dickinson[38] did an immense deal it seems to me. Well, we differ
in our choice of scapegoats.

But what I'd like to know is, suppose we both survive this

war, what ought we to do to prevent another? I shall be too old to do anything but write. But will you throw up your job as an art critic and take to politics? And if you stick to art criticism, how will you make it more public and less private than Roger did? ...

I hope this letter doesn't sound unkind. Its only because I liked your being honest so much that I've tried to be. And of course I know you're having a much worse time of it at the moment than I am ... Another siren has just sounded.

TO V. SACKVILLE-WEST   Monk's House, Rodmell,
Friday [30 August 1940]   near Lewes, Sussex

I've just stopped talking to you. It seems so strange. Its perfectly peaceful here—theyre playing bowls—I'd just put flowers in your room. And there you sit with the bombs falling round you.

What can one say—except that I love you and I've got to live through this strange quiet evening thinking of you sitting there alone.

TO JOHN LEHMANN   Monk's House, Rodmell,
[27? March 1941]   Lewes [Sussex]

I'd decided, before your letter came,[39] that I cant publish that novel [Between the Acts] as it stands—its too silly and trivial.

What I will do is to revise it, and see if I can pull it together and so publish it in the autumn. If published as it is, it would certainly mean a financial loss; which we dont want. I am sure I am right about this.

I neednt say how sorry I am to have troubled you. The fact is it was written in the intervals of doing Roger with my brain half asleep. And I didnt realise how bad it was till I read it over.

Please forgive me, and believe I'm only doing what is best.

I'm sending back the MSS [for Folios of New Writing] with my notes.

Again, I apologise profoundly.

TO LEONARD WOOLF   [*Monk's House, Rodmell,*
[*28 March 1941*]   *Sussex*]
Dearest,

I want to tell you that you have given me complete happiness. No one could have done more than you have done. Please believe that.

But I know that I shall never get over this: and I am wasting your life. It is this madness. Nothing anyone says can persuade me. You can work, and you will be much better without me. You see I cant write this even, which shows I am right. All I want to say is that until this disease came on we were perfectly happy. It was all due to you. No one could have been so good as you have been, from the very first day till now. Everyone knows that.

                                                            V.

You will find Roger's letters to the Maurons in the writing table drawer in the Lodge. Will you destroy all my papers.

NOTES

1. Violet Dickinson (1865–1948), for many years VW's most intimate friend, who nursed her through her second period of insanity during the summer of 1904. She disapproved of VW's setting up house in 1911 with her Bloomsbury friends, and from this period their relationship became more formal.

2. For about two years, Virginia taught at Morley College, an evening institute for working people.

3. Henry James lived at Lamb House, Rye, from 1898 until his death in 1915.

4. Clive Bell (1881–1964), art critic, married Vanessa Stephen in 1907 and, as VW's brother-in-law, played an important part in her life, as her literary confidant, and as partner in an intermittent flirtation.

5. Jean Thomas ran a mental nursing home.

6. This letter decided Leonard. He resigned from the Colonial Service, and his resignation was accepted on May 7.

7. Janet Case (1862–1937), classical scholar, who taught Virginia Woolf Greek from 1902 and had become a close friend. She lived with her sister, "Emphie," and was an active supporter of women's, liberal, and pacifist causes.

8. Vanessa ("Nessa") Bell, *née* Stephen (1879–1961), VW's elder sister and, after Leonard Woolf, the most important person in her life. Her

marriage to Clive Bell became, after 1914, a matter of convenience and friendship. Her children were Julian (1908–1937); Quentin (b. 1910); and Angelica (b. 1918), who was the daughter of Duncan Grant.

9. Leonard's interest in the Women's Co-operative Movement was stimulated by his growing friendship with Margaret Llewelyn Davies, and his tour with Virginia of the Northern industrial cities in March. His book, *Co-operation and the Future of Industry*, was published in 1919.

10. Duncan Grant (1885–1978), painter, who lived and worked with Vanessa Bell from about 1914 until her death in 1961; their daughter, Angelica Bell, was born on Christmas Day, 1918.

11. *The Shadow-Line* (1917).

12. Their first hand-press, which they bought at a printer's shop in Farringdon St., Holborn, for their Hogarth Press.

13. Ottoline Morrell (1873–1938), patroness of artists and writers and London hostess, who entertained at 44 Bedford Square, Bloomsbury, and at Garsington Manor, near Oxford.

14. Giles Lytton Strachey (1880–1932), critic and biographer, was a contemporary and friend of both Thoby Stephen and Leonard Woolf at Trinity College, Cambridge. After Thoby's death, he became one of VW's closest friends. He is remembered chiefly for *Eminent Victorians*.

15. Mary ("Molly") MacCarthy (1882–1953), like VW, was a niece by marriage of Lady Anne Thackeray Ritchie. Her husband, Desmond MacCarthy (1877–1952), was a literary journalist and drama critic who had known the Stephen family since before Sir Leslie's death in 1904.

16. Lawrence drew an unpleasant portrait of Ottoline in the character of Hermione Roddice.

17. Jacques Raverat (1885–1925), painter, and one of a group of friends VW called the "neo-Pagans," another of whom, Gwendolen ("Gwen") Darwin (1885–1957), he married in 1911.

18. Jacques Raverat died at Vence, in southern France, on March 7. Before his death he dictated a letter to Virginia about *Mrs. Dalloway*, which she had sent him in proof. He wrote her that it made him "want to live a little longer."

19. Raymond Mortimer (1895–1980), critic and man of letters, whom VW first met in 1923. He was a close friend of Clive Bell.

20. The British Ambassador in Washington.

21. Roger Fry (1866–1934), art critic and painter, who created a scandal by introducing the British public to Post-Impressionist art. After his incurably insane wife was consigned to a mental home in 1910, he fell in love with Vanessa Bell—a love she transmuted into lifelong friendship.

22. Therese Lessore was a painter and the third wife of the painter Walter Sickert. Leigh Ashton was Keeper of the Department of Textiles in the Victoria and Albert Museum, of which he became Director in 1945.

23. Robert Lynd, essayist, was also literary editor of the *Daily News*. Gerald Gould (1885–1936) was a critic, journalist, and poet.

24. Virginia had recently had her hair shingled.

25. Vita had written: "Everything is blurred to a haze by your book . . .

I can only say that I am dazzled and bewitched" (11 May 1927, Berg Collection of The New York Public Library).

26. The village near Auppegard, Normandy, from which the Sackville family came to England in the 11th century.

27. Ethel Smyth (1858–1944), composer, author, and feminist. She was a vigorous campaigner for the cause of women's rights and suffrage. After meeting VW in 1930, she became one of her most devoted and demanding friends.

28. Cf the story of Jacob, Leah and Rachel (*Genesis*, Chapter 29).

29. Sibyl Colefax started an interior decoration business in 1928.

30. Elspeth Champcommunal, a friend of Roger Fry, and the widow of a French painter who was killed in the First World War. She was Editor of *Vogue* from 1916 to 1922.

31. Musical Director of the BBC (1930–42) and founder-conductor of the BBC Symphony Orchestra (1930–49).

32. Henry Brewster with whom Ethel Smyth had once been in love.

33. During Virginia's previous visit to Greece, with Vanessa, in 1906.

34. Lady Fry died in 1930 at the age of 97. Her husband, Sir Edward Fry, a distinguished jurist, died in 1918, aged 91.

35. John Maynard Keynes (1883–1946), economist, best known for his *The Economic Consequences of the Peace, A Treatise on Money*, and *The General Theory of Employment, Interest and Money*. He was a member of "old Bloomsbury" and of its reincarnation, The Memoir Club. He married the Russian ballerina Lydia Lopokova in 1925.

36. Ben Nicolson, son of Vita Sackville-West and Harold Nicolson, was then serving as a lance-bombardier in an anti-aircraft battery at Chatham, Kent.

37. W. J. H. ("Sebastian") Sprott (1897–1971), a friend of Keynes and Strachey, was Lecturer in Psychology at Nottingham University.

38. Ben Nicolson was at both Eton and Oxford. His mother was a Sackville. His father's aunt Hariot married the Viceroy of India, Marquess of Dufferin and Ava. G. Lowes Dickinson was the Cambridge historian.

39. John Lehmann was, first, Manager of the Hogarth Press, and later a partner. The sequence of events was as follows. On March 14, when Virginia, Leonard and Lehmann met in London, it was agreed that Lehmann should read the typescript of *Between the Acts*. He assumed from their conversation that there was no doubt that it would be published shortly, and caused the book to be announced in the Spring books issue of the *New Statesman*. Later he received Virginia's letter of March 20, and wrote to her apologizing for his action. Then he read the book, and praised it enthusiastically in another letter. Virginia's reply is the letter printed here.

Books By Virginia Woolf
Available from Harcourt, Inc.
in Harvest Paperback Editions

Between the Acts
Books and Portraits
The Captain's Death Bed and Other Essays
The Common Reader: First Series Annotated Edition
The Common Reader: Second Series Annotated Edition
The Complete Shorter Fiction of Virginia Woolf
Congenial Spirits: The Selected Letters of Virginia Woolf
Contemporary Writers
The Death of the Moth and Other Essays
The Diary of Virginia Woolf *(five volumes)*
The Essays of Virginia Woolf, Vol. One (1904–1912)
The Essays of Virginia Woolf, Vol. Two (1912–1918)
The Essays of Virginia Woolf, Vol. Three (1919–1924)
Flush: A Biography
Freshwater: A Comedy
Granite and Rainbow
A Haunted House and Other Short Stories
Jacob's Room
The Letters of Virginia Woolf *(six volumes)*
The Moment and Other Essays
A Moment's Liberty: The Shorter Diary of Virginia Woolf
Moments of Being
Mrs. Dalloway
Mrs. Dalloway's Party
Night and Day
Orlando: A Biography
A Passionate Apprentice: The Early Journals, 1897–1909
Roger Fry: A Biography
A Room of One's Own
Three Guineas
To the Lighthouse
The Virginia Woolf Reader
The Voyage Out
The Waves
Women and Writing
A Writer's Diary
The Years